THE BACKSIDE OF HADES

"This here place? Worse than the backside of Hades."
—Hank Varney

First let me say, this here trip to Slagton weren't my idea. This place is chock full of bad company done helped itself to a double dose of bad medicine.

Slagton needs cleanin', accordin' to Miss Clem, and I know the crew to do it. I'm one of 'em. Hank Varney's the name. Miss Clem and me, along with the two Sidewinders from Santa Fe—we'll get the sharp-toothed vermin cleared out.

Now, some people say I'm lucky, but I don't know if'n it'll do me any good, what with the army of trouble me an' the crew are facin'. If'n we don't live through it, well, there goes Deadwood. Maybe even the whole of the Black Hills.

We'll all be down the privy hole then, lookin' up at the Backside of Hades.

Dear Reader,

How long has it been? Well, if memory serves, we released Catawampus Christmas Carol in November of 2020. It's now October 2022. Two years. Criminy! Time is funny. It can fly by in an instant or trudge along, passing in donkey's years (a very long time).

It's an odd thing.

It must be a matter of perspective. Take a sunny, lazy day whisked along by the gentle flicks of a fishing pole. It practically races toward sunset, while the same day oozes along for the guy dreading an upcoming afternoon root canal at the dentist.

But that's not the peculiar part. The peculiar part comes in retrospect. How often have you recalled a day that kicked your ass as "not that bad" or gone so far as to have a chuckle at it?

"Remember when cousin Frank fell in the 'crick' and broke his arm? Ha! That was a good day. I caught three brook trout!"

Everybody has a day or two like that. Sometimes it takes a while to find the laugh, but it's there. Eventually the good memories rise to the surface, like cream on unpasteurized milk, and that's the best damned milk you ever had.

Our conclusion? Time is a duplicitous bitch.

Thank you for sticking around for this book, patiently or not. We did our best to tell a good story full of fast-paced action and suspense, and supernatural fun while we were at it. As a bonus, we have maps to help you "see" where the Undertaker crew are throughout the story.

Here is book four in the Deadwood Undertaker series, *The Backside of Hades*. We hope you enjoy it. Hold onto your hat!

Ann & Sam

THE BACKSIDE OF HADES

Book 4

Ann Charles
Sam Lucky

Illustrations by
C.S.Kunkle

For Fans of the Deadwood Undertaker Series
Thank you for your patience.

Cover Art by C.S. Kunkle
Cover Design by B Biddles & Ann Charles
Editing by Eilis Flynn
Formatting by B Biddles

Library of Congress:
E-book ISBN- 978-1-940364-86-5
Print ISBN-: 978-1-940364-87-2

Acknowledgments

We would like to thank the following folks for their help making *The Backside of Hades* (Deadwood Undertaker Book 4) shine like a brand-new penny:

Our children, Beaker and Chicken Noodle, for keeping us smiling. Now go vacuum and do the dishes.

Our kickass First Draft team: Mary Ida Kunkle, Kristy McCaffrey, Becky Binder, Paul Franklin, Diane Garland, Michelle Davis, Vicki Huskey, Lucinda Nelson, Bob Dickerson, Stephanie Kunkle, and Wendy Gildersleeve. If only we could write as fast as you all read! Thank you for your contributions. You helped make this a better book.

Sister Wendy for keeping us organized.

Our rock-solid editor, Elizabeth Flynn, for having our backs.

Diane Garland, WorldKeeper extraordinaire, for helping keep track of all those never ending details.

Our Beta Team for scouring the pages for any last hiccups.

C.S. Kunkle for using your big ol' imagination. We describe it, you bring it to life.

Our readers for sticking with us while life smacked us around with a flyswatter.

And Hank—We'll figure your age out sooner or later.

Also by Ann Charles

Deadwood Mystery Series (Book #)

Short Stories from the Deadwood Mystery Series

Deadwood Undertaker Series
(co-written with Sam Lucky)

Jackrabbit Junction Mystery Series

Dig Site Mystery Series

AC Silly Circus Mystery Series

Goldwash Mystery Series (a future series)

"The trouble is not in dying for a friend, but in finding a friend worth dying for."

~Mark Twain

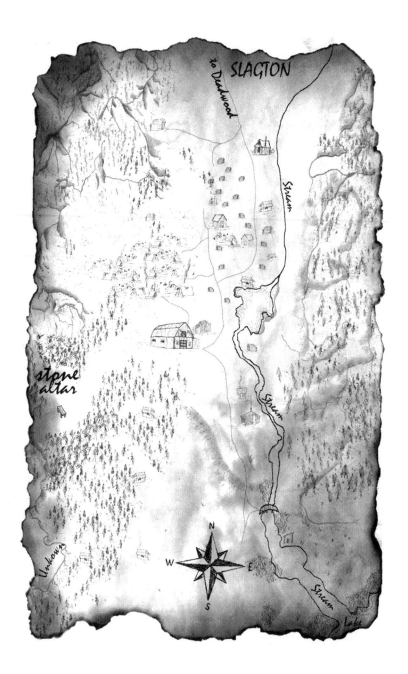

One

Boone McCreery pushed aside a branch of the bush concealing him and his companions to peek at the rickety log cabin, half buried by drifted snow. He squinted against the early morning light. There was no smoke coming from the chimney.

"Definitely somebody in there," he said. "Can't see who or what though."

"It's *Draug*." Clementine Johanssen stood tall next to Boone, almost his height short a couple of inches, with her arms crossed over her thick wool coat. Her expression was as cold and stony as the rocky outcrop behind them. "And it isn't just one, it's a small herd. Eight or ten, I'd guess."

"Of course. We're not even in Slagton yet." Anxiety dropped a pile of stones in his belly at the notion of riding into the small mining town that was supposedly overrun with ... "*Draug*," Boone repeated, sniffing in the cold, dry air. "The diseased, abnormally strong, rotting carcasses of the dearly departed being used as an army by a malevolent usurper who means to take the Black Hills as a prize, killing anything that gets in his way?" He shivered against a frigid gust. "You mean that kind of *Draug*?"

She turned to Boone, lines fanning out from the corners of her gray eyes. "Don't forget shapeshifting."

"What?" He'd heard her, but his sensibilities didn't allow him to believe it.

"Shapeshifting." Clementine shrugged. "Of course, I don't believe

that, or that *Draug* can grow to colossal size. Those are myths." She bit her lower lip. "I think."

"What?" Boone said again. He was listening more intently now, but still having some difficulty comprehending.

"Need help makin' sentences there, Booney?" Jack "Rabbit" Fields piped in, joining them. After a glance through the branches, he grinned big and fluttered his eyelashes at Boone while skinning his pistol and spinning the cylinder. Quick as chain lightning, his expression sobered and his brow furrowed. "I'm good for four, maybe six. You stand behind me, Booney. Don't want you gettin' hurt."

"Shut up, Rabbit." Boone shook his head. After spending the better part of his life with Mr. Quickdraw, who'd become as close to him as a brother before they were even knee-high to a grasshopper, Boone knew Rabbit was just as nervous as he was. He reached for his pistol, too, but changed his mind and instead grabbed the handle of his black-bladed scimitar.

They were holster-deep in a Black Hills bitter cold winter. Boone and his companions, with their mounts alongside, had opted to spend the night out away from Slagton, since none of them carried any intention of approaching the sinister little camp in the dark—not even Clementine, who'd faced off against a town full of *Draug* in her bloodstained past. Boone measured last night in the woods as one of the coldest, most fitful, and frigid he'd ever had the displeasure of spending under the stars, even though Rabbit's heated complaints had helped keep the campsite warm till almost midnight. And his list of expletives was far more colorful than Boone's in spite of the presence of a female. So far, things weren't looking any better in the morning light.

Clementine had been quiet since they'd left Deadwood. She wasn't usually a prattler and on this trip, especially not. Boone could see she was uneasy, apprehensive even. Her normally stoic demeanor was absent, replaced by repeated shifting, twitching, both in and out of her saddle, undoubtedly due to her past experiences with *Draug*. He didn't blame her. The description of the abominations alone nearly curdled his blood.

"Somebody just tell me what I'm shootin' at," Hank Varney spoke up from behind them. Boone turned to see the well-weathered man jerk his new LeMat pistol from its holster. Ice crystals in his finger-length beard added sparkles to his appearance, matching those in his eyes. He was ready to ride to Hades and back, if that was where Clementine was going.

Rabbit daintily fanned his face. "You're so strong and brave, Hank," he said in a high-pitched dainty voice, pretending to swoon.

"Now cut that out, Jack Rabbit. Like to make me blush." Hank lowered his pistol and punched Rabbit on the shoulder.

Clementine peered at the cabin around a branch. "You can't use that pistol, Hank. You'll bring every creature within a half-mile radius down on us. Besides, it's best—"

"Let me guess," Boone cut in.

"Take the heads," Rabbit finished before Boone had the chance.

Clementine nodded, stepping away from the branch. "Leave Fred the Mule and the horses here. We may make camp back here tonight. They can make their way back to Deadwood if necessary." Without a backward glance, she took off for the cabin in long strides.

"There she goes." Boone sprang after her, followed by Rabbit and Hank.

Boone wondered if Clementine knew how predictable she was when it came to dispatching the otherworldly, and often not human, troublemakers that she referred to as *others*. Or in this case, the ambulating remains of several dead humans somehow roaming the forest.

"Dammit, Miss Clementine!" Rabbit said in a loud whisper as he fell into a jog next to Boone.

"No guns," Clementine said over her shoulder.

"Goldurnit, Booney. No guns?" Rabbit holstered his pistol and skinned one of the five throwing knives from his belt sheath.

"You know, well as I do." Boone rushed to keep up with Clementine.

Rabbit sheathed his throwing knife. "This is close-in fighting and I ain't none too fond of it, so's you know. Gonna need my Bowie." He grabbed the gigantic knife from his boot without missing a step.

Hank came along behind, chuffing like a locomotive. "Rather stick an arrow …" He puffed and sucked a breath, "… in 'em myself, Jack Rabbit."

"Wanna trade?" Rabbit pointed his Bowie at Boone's sword.

Boone scoffed. "Not today. But I'll keep an eye on ya, in case you get yourself into a pickle." Boone rested his scimitar on his shoulder as they approached the cabin. "Clementine," he whispered when he caught up with her. "You have a plan?"

"Sure. Kill everything in that cabin." She stopped behind a stand of yearling pines that offered cover and faced the three of them. "You've prepared for this. Remember the cattle-driver terms you used a while back?" When they each nodded, she continued, "Well, I have point. You two are flank," she said to Boone and Rabbit. "And Hank is drag." She started to turn away, but then looked back again. "Oh, and don't let them bite you."

"Yes, ma'am!" Hank puffed. He had secured the LeMat in the holster Rabbit had tooled for him. For Hank, arrows flew swifter and more true than words or bullets and with far deadlier effect.

"Yep. We're with ya, Miss Clementine," Rabbit joined in, pulling a second knife from its sheath.

"No biting." Boone paused mid-nod. "Wait, you didn't say anything about … they bite?" He tried not to allow fear to taint his voice, or let on that his heart was thumping hard in his chest. This was happening too damned fast. His mind was still wrestling with the idea of colossal, shapeshifting corpses.

But Clementine was already heading for the cabin. When Boone and the others caught up with her at the pine pole door, she pulled two thin-bladed swords from within her coat and aimed an intense glare at Boone.

He knew that look. She was bent on destruction, and they were in the thick of it with her.

She cocked her leg and kicked the door, breaking it clean away from the hinges. It flew into the cabin, slamming into two *Draug*, knocking them to the floor.

Stunned, Boone watched as she barreled inside, her swords spinning so fast they looked like wagon wheels on a runaway freight wagon.

He leapt through the doorway to join her. Rabbit pushed in behind him and split left, his Bowie raised and ready to strike.

A wave of humid, fetid air washed over Boone, stinging his eyes and coating his tongue and throat. He doubled over, gagging. His knees wobbled under his weight, and the biscuits he'd had for breakfast worked their way up into his throat.

Rabbit reeled backward, crashing into Boone's side, bending over at the waist. "Somebody stuffed a dead rat in my mouth!" He spit and gagged, wiping at his tongue with his coat sleeve.

Hank pushed in behind them, his knife drawn. "Boonedog! What—

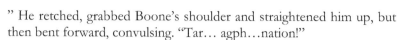

" He retched, grabbed Boone's shoulder and straightened him up, but then bent forward, convulsing. "Tar… agph…nation!"

"Like swimmin' in the guts of a week-dead cow!" Rabbit spit again, coughing in between.

Hank grasped Rabbit's sheepskin collar and stood him up too.

"To *Hel's* kingdom, devils!" Clementine's voice rang out above the din of moaning *Draug*, not to mention Boone's gags, Rabbit's retches, and Hank's curses.

Clementine! Boone wiped the tears from his eyes, raised his sword, and swung around to help her just as the head of the last *Draug* sailed in a graceful arc up and away from its body. It landed with a squishy thump on the chest of one of the many headless *Draug* bodies piled around her feet.

He turned back to Clementine. The dark, cold fury in her eyes and hardened expression on her face chilled him more than a night sleeping under a winter sky.

That's the look of a *Scharfrichter*. A killer.

"Clementine?" He wasn't sure what to expect.

She took a deep breath and then pushed her hair away from her face with the back of her hand. Her face, her entire body, softened somehow. After surveying the carnage around her for a moment, she looked at Boone and scrunched her nose. "I don't remember their odor being this disagreeable. Did I mention they stink? Not this much, I didn't think. Maybe it's because they were penned up in here."

"Sheaat." Rabbit sheathed his knife and evaluated the mess she'd left behind, his expression a mixture of disgust and awe. "Miss Clementine, you didn't give us a chance!"

"You'll get your chance." She pulled a scrap of muslin from her coat pocket and wiped the dark, sticky blood and pieces of rotten flesh from her blades, then tossed the rag on the floor.

Boone flicked a chunk of squishy *Draug* meat from Rabbit's coat with his scimitar and gave Clementine a once-over. "You don't have any *Draug* guts on you. How do you not have any …" he trailed off.

"None at all, even," Hank agreed, inspecting her up and down.

She glanced at herself. "I think I got a little here." She lifted her feet, one at a time, shaking loose the hunks of flesh that clung to her boots.

Boone eyed Rabbit sideways with a "You're-shittin'-me" look. Rabbit was wearing the same expression.

"Miss Clem." Hank patted her back. "We ought to mosey. You shook the tree. No tellin' what might fall out. Vapor in here is like to soak into my disposition if'n we stay." He backed out the doorway, pinching his nose with his finger and thumb. In a nasally voice he added, "Won't never utter complaints about odors in The Pyre ever again."

Rabbit was quick to follow. "I'm with you, Hank. Spurs the mind to bad recollections, like Boone's bedroom when we was growin' up." He disappeared out the doorway.

"Bangtail!" Boone hollered at Rabbit's back.

Clementine chuckled. "Not one to spend time on cleaning your room, huh?" She slid one of her short swords back inside her coat.

"He's full of shit." He shot Clementine a quick frown, not liking the possibility she might get the wrong idea about his cleanliness. Or thinking ill of him in any way, for that matter. "We didn't see the floor of his bedroom for five years after he turned ten. He's just a windbag."

"I heard that, fiddlehead," Rabbit called from outside.

"I hope so. I said it for you, Bunny Rabbit."

"Don't call me 'bunny,' Mr. Tight Britches."

"We should go." Clementine patted his chest, her hand remaining on the lapel of his overcoat for a moment, and then headed out into the morning sun.

Boone fell in behind her, happy to breathe the cold, fresh air again. A glance back at the cabin sparked a realization. "They didn't turn into dirt, or dust, or fire, or whatever it is *others* turn into when you put the squabash on that walking buzzard food in there." Usually, death by Clementine's blade or hand yielded much different results.

"They were human once."

"Ah. Of course." Boone had forgotten to make the distinction between humans and *others*, as in those non–*Homo sapiens* that Clementine had been contracted to eliminate. "Why were the *Draug* crowded into there, do you think?"

"I'm not sure. But did you see the animal carcasses piled in the corner?" She pointed her thumb over her shoulder at the cabin.

"Must've missed that, what with all the body parts flying around."

"It looked to me like someone was keeping them fed." She stopped alongside Hank, scanning the trees and hills around them. "Maybe they were corralling some that escaped. Or they could have been readying them for an attack on a nearby mining camp."

"You see that, Miss Clem? Jack Rabbit?" Hank pointed, his voice low. "Over there, through them trees."

Rabbit used his hat to shield his eyes from a blade of sunlight piercing the trees. "I see it."

"You see, Miss Clem? Thought it was a deer first thing, but it ain't. It's one of your *Draugies*."

Rabbit squinted at it. "He's teeterin' along with a purpose." His voice went high and shrill as he added, " 'Late for supper again, Henry,' his wife'll say."

"Stop it, Rabbit." Boone smirked. The *Draug* lurched along through the snow, barely covered in a tattered and dirty shirt, suspenders, and torn trousers. Its shock of black hair was mussed, sticking up on one side and matted down on the other, as if it had just rolled out of the grave.

Clementine aimed her short sword at it. "Who wants it?"

"I got it." Hank pulled his bow and plucked an arrow from his quiver. "Just gotta get a wee closer." He tiptoed toward the meandering corpse, slinking tree to tree to remain unnoticed.

Clementine drew her other sword, spinning both blades in her palms. "That Sioux bow won't do him any good."

"Are you going to tell him that?" Boone asked, glancing from her to Hank and back.

"No. He can manage one *Draug*. Let's see how he does it."

Boone noticed a twinkle in her eyes to match her grin.

Rabbit smiled, too, but his brow was puckered. Probably from the same concern giving Boone heartburn.

Hank worked his way to a tree within thirty yards of the lone *Draug*. He strung his arrow, drew back, aimed, and the arrow disappeared. *Fwhip.*

Boone watched the *Draug's* head pitch to the side, coming back upright with an arrow protruding from its cheek. "Good aim."

"Nice shot, Hank," Rabbit whispered.

The *Draug* staggered, swatted at the arrow, veered right, and shuffled in Hank's general direction, its legs plowing through the shin-deep snow.

Clementine shook her head. "He needs to—"

"Right," Boone interrupted her.

Rabbit cupped the side of his mouth. "Hank!" he whisper-yelled.

Hank looked back at them and shrugged.

"The head!" Rabbit grabbed his own head and pretended to pop it off and throw it on the ground.

Hank stuck his finger in the air and nodded. He drew his Bowie and began to work his way around the arrow-stuck *Draug*.

Meanwhile, the staggering *Draug* wandered too close to a tree, and the shaft of the arrow tangled in a low branch. It pulled clumsily against the snag, attempting to free itself. Boone would have laughed if the smell of rotting flesh wasn't still clinging to his nostrils ... and except for the fact that what he was looking at was real and not just the result of gulping bad whiskey.

Rabbit did laugh. "Haha! Too beef-headed to free itself."

Hank swung around behind the struggling *Draug* and raised his knife. He paused for a few breaths, then backed up and looked at Clementine, Boone, and Rabbit, and shook his head.

The *Draug* batted feebly at the branch tormenting him.

Boone watched as Hank's shoulders sagged. "He can't do it."

"His heart's too big for his own good." Clementine trotted to Hank's side. She patted his shoulder and in a flash the *Draug* head was sitting half buried in snow, propped upright by the arrow sticking out of its cheek.

"There's another one." Rabbit pointed into the trees to their left.

Boone squinted through the shadowed tree trunks streaked with sunlight. This particular *Draug* had been one hell of a brute judging from the breadth of his shoulders and thick legs. The bull of a man, or what used to be a man, appeared to have spotted them and was headed in their direction, pushing through the snow more quickly than the first, but still clumsily and no faster than a leisurely saunter.

Boone was utterly repulsed by the sight, especially taking into account the smell of these plodding creatures, but they seemed too slow to be very dangerous. Why had Clementine considered them such a threat?

He jabbed Rabbit with his elbow. "You or me?"

Rabbit bowed and with a twirl of his hand said, "Be my guest."

"Watch and learn, whippersnapper." Boone covered the distance quickly. He drew his black-bladed scimitar and sliced cleanly through its thick, rubbery neck skin. He'd already cleaned his blade in the snow before Clementine and Hank returned to Rabbit.

Half an hour and four headless, no-longer-aimlessly-wandering

Draug later, they stood on a rocky bluff overlooking a long valley nearly twice as wide as Deadwood gulch. The cliffs all along each side did not reach as high as those framing Deadwood but were steep and looked impassible, excepting for the slumped landslide directly in front of them that had broken down the cliff to a negotiable grade. Heavy snow covering the thickly grown trees along the tops and sides of the cliffs presented the appearance of white frosting against the pastel tans and browns of the cliff faces. The white snow frosting had oozed over the sides of the cliffs here and there in the form of ice falls reaching down into the valley.

Below, tents and lean-tos were clustered to form the west side of a small town. Not really a town in Boone's eyes, since the shacks were strung out some fair distance, probably indicating each mining claim along the creek that meandered along the eastern side of the valley. The buildings did, however, thicken enough to form the boundaries of a street that looked to Boone a little like the deserted main street of Gayville, a small mining camp outside of Deadwood they'd passed through on their way to deal with a previous menace—*Bahkauv.*

A small stand of trees covered a portion of the valley to the south of the tent village. Many trees had been cut, leaving a bristle of stumps resembling the stubble of a poorly shaved jawline. The valley widened into thick dense forest to the southwest and a small, dark lake to the southeast.

Boone noticed movement in the almost-a-town.

"Look at 'em," Hank whispered. "This what you wanted to know about Slagton, Miss Clem?"

"Movin' slow like *Draug,* near as I can tell," Rabbit said quietly, confirming Boone's thought. "Something else down there, watching. Could be men? Lookouts?"

"They're moving around—can't get a count." Boone cocked his head at Clementine, who stood silent beside him. "Can you make out what else is down there besides *Draug*? It looks like some of them are on four legs."

Clementine squinted. "Humans. I'm not sure what else. There is *caper-sus* symbology on some of the buildings. "

Boone knew the sign of *caper-sus* represented a cult, or rather factions of cults, led by *others,* their ranks composed of humans aspiring to reap the rewards of faithful service. Namely, food and coins in the pocket.

Black Hills gold drew in all sorts of folks, the adventure seekers and the desperate, and everyone in-between. But there were only so many claims in the hills carrying any color. For those that didn't hit it rich, clothes and skin were soon hanging off their bones. Eating didn't come cheap, and the *caper-sus* brand offered a meal ticket few could refuse.

"Look how they're beatin' them *Draugies* with sticks," Hank said, scowling.

"Herding them like they're cows," Rabbit added.

"Looka that one. Fightin' back. Give 'im what for." Hank chuckled deep in his chest, then stopped. "Shouldn't oughta be findin' humor in it."

"They don't like getting hit, looks like." Rabbit scratched at one of his sideburns. "Can't say whose side I'd take, the *Draugies*, or the *caper-sus* sonsabitches."

"They seem to have a mind, but they're slow." Boone smirked. "Like Rabbit."

Rabbit flicked Boone's hat. "Fuck around and see what happens."

"They have a border set up around the town. See?" Clementine used her sword to show them. "There. And there. Those men with the sticks have got to be *caper-sus*. They're blocking all the routes in and out of town. The road. Between buildings."

Boone nodded. "So, they must get free from time to time. The escapees are what we kept finding in the forest."

"Possibly." Clementine rubbed her shoulder, the one that had been stuck with the tip of a *caper-sus* bastard's sword not too many days past.

He tipped his head at her shoulder. "Still sore?"

"A little. The cold makes it ache. Usually wounds like this heal more quickly. This one seems to be taking longer." She carved a larger circle in the air. "They're watching the forest around the town, too."

"The four leggers. Yep." Rabbit nodded. "One … two, three … I count four or six of them. Might be more out under the trees. Don't look like *Bahkauv*, but too far away to tell."

The hair on the back of Boone's neck prickled. *Bahkauv*. "Teeth," he whispered, remembering their fight in the mine.

"I'm with you, Boonedog. Just about every four-legged Black Hills bugger I ever seen come with a mouth full of too many pointy teeth." Hank's whole body shuddered.

Rabbit scratched at Hank. "And claws."

A piercing shriek echoed through the forest. Boone winced and ducked low, along with Rabbit and Hank.

"Lord-a-mighty," Rabbit said as the echoes died, his fingertips still jammed in his ears. "What the fuck was that? Sounded like a wounded puma cat."

"More like a hawk right on my shoulder." Boone's ears were still ringing.

"A woman, mad as a hornet." Hank shook his head. "Got my head t' spinnin'."

"I couldn't tell where that came from." Clementine was still staring down at Slagton, apparently unaffected by the sound. "Look," she said, pointing.

Boone followed her line of sight down to the middle of town.

Slagton was in chaos, as all of the *Draug* seemed to suddenly have purpose, but none could decide where it was or how to achieve it. Lurching and stumbling and bumping into each other. It reminded him of the time the chickens got drunk on the rotted apples that had dropped from the trees back on the ranch in Santa Fe.

"Was it the caterwaul we just heard?" Boone looked at Clementine for the answer.

"Stirred 'em to a tizzy." Hank stood motionless, watching.

A collective moan muffled by distance rose and fell as the *Draug* began to congregate and tear at each other. Wails and cries punctuated the rolling moans.

The comical image of drunken chickens began to fade.

"Jehoshaphat," Hank murmured, his jaw hanging low.

"Booney." Rabbit grabbed Boone's shoulder, holding tight.

Boone glanced his way. "You all right, Rabbit?"

Rabbit slowly shook his head, his brow furrowed. "I don't think so. That ain't right."

Boone's focus returned to the ghoulish scene. He watched as the *Draug* pushed and tore and ripped at each other.

Screams rang out—human screams. He caught site of a *caper-sus* guard who was frantically swinging his stick at the mass of *Draug* but was caught up as more arms wrapped around him or snagged his clothing and pulled him in. He disappeared in the mass of bodies.

They were distant enough from the scene to be spared the grisly details, but it was obvious to Boone what was happening to the man.

More guards attacked, whacking impotently at the milling mass of *Draug*, only to be caught and dragged in as the first had been. Screams continued as more of the guards were swallowed up.

Boone leaned toward Clementine, shoulder bumping her while still keeping his eyes on the scene below. "One wail set all of this off?"

"I'm not sure what that first scream was, but I think you're right. It sent them into a frenzy. They'll attack anything that moves now, including each other."

"Wait just a damned minute." Rabbit shook his finger at Clementine. "When you told us about the time you and your *afi* slaughtered that village full of *Draug*, you never said nothin' about that." He huffed. "Nothin' about them going plumb loco, either."

Clementine grimaced. "I forgot about that part."

"You *forgot?*" Boone pushed the brim of his hat up his forehead. "I don't know if you noticed, but—"

"Wait!" Rabbit grabbed Boone's coat and yanked him into a crouch. He motioned Hank and Clementine to do the same. "There's something else down there."

Boone squinted. "Where?"

"Barn. I think it came out of the barn, or the building beside it," he said in a hushed tone.

"I see it!" Hank whispered loudly. He rummaged in his saddlebag and pulled a monocular out and extended it. It was a long few seconds before he let the monocular drop away from his eye. "Mother Mary."

"What is it?" Boone tried to keep his eyes on it as it flitted from one place to the next, but it moved so fast he kept losing track.

Hank handed the monocular to Clementine.

"It's movin' so fast … hard to keep on it. It's like a shadow," Rabbit said.

Clementine was silent as she watched through the monocular.

"Some sorta … Not like a man … looks like …" Hank was at a loss to even describe it. "Jehoshaphat that thing is fast."

Boone was at a loss too. Its movements weren't anything he was accustomed to seeing. It remained stationary for a moment, then blurred, only to appear somewhere else, almost as if it were disappearing, moving, and then reappearing. He found it, then lost it again in the blur. It was confounding.

"It's herding 'em. Like cattle, just like the bastards with sticks did. It's gettin' the job done though, see?" Rabbit pointed.

He was right. Boone watched as the thing darted this way and that, each time it appeared, the mass of *Draug*, which must have been at least a hundred strong, moved away from it, farther down the street.

"*Un vaquero y su rebaño*," Rabbit said.

"What's that now, Jack Rabbit?" Hank scrunched up his forehead.

" 'A cowboy and his herd,' " Boone translated. "The '*rebaño*' seem to have an aversion to the *vaquero*."

Clementine handed the monocular to Boone but continued to watch the spectacle below.

It was even harder to follow with the magnifier, but the glimpses Boone caught made him feel no better. The thing was generally shaped like a man, only it stood taller. Much taller. It was difficult to determine just how much taller from their vantage point, but the thing was easily half again as tall as the tallest *Draug* or *caper-sus* on the street. It was just too fast and far away to discern more particulars than that.

They all watched as the thing herded the *Draug* farther and farther south, away from their position on top of the cliff. It became apparent to Boone that they were headed for the oversize barn at the southwest end of town.

"They're too far away now." Rabbit reached for the monocular. "Give 'er here. Let me see."

Boone didn't, but began describing the scene before him. "They're filing into the barn. Damn, that's a big barn." It was two stories tall, long enough to fit ten wagons end-to-end, and with the lean-to running along its side, wide enough for five, maybe more, rigs side by side. An unkempt, unpainted exterior and distinct sag sideways reminded him of a drunken, broke miner stumbling along the streets of Deadwood.

"That thing is still herding them. Picking up a stray here and there. Isn't a single one getting away."

"Let me see." Rabbit snatched at the monocular, but Boone swatted his hand away.

"Some of the guys with the sticks are whacking at them, but they're pretty much keeping a distance from the *Draug*. They're keeping away from the *vaquero*, too."

Still, Clementine watched but said nothing.

Boone handed the monocular to Rabbit. "That's the last of them. All inside. The *vaquero* went in too, there or the cabin next to the barn."

Rabbit backhanded Boone's shoulder. "Missed every damn thing, knucklehead."

"Whatcha s'pose they're doing in there?" Hank rose to his feet.

"Suppertime, then to the hoedown?" Rabbit suggested.

"Hoo! Jack Rabbit, stop that. This ain't funny." Hank chuckled anyway.

Clementine's brow lined. "You may be right, Jack."

"Better question." Boone stood. "What happened to those four-legged buggers wandering around in the trees down there? I don't see a one."

"And what the hell was that thing? Nothin' we've seen is that fast. Looks like I'll be savin' Boone's ass again if—"

"Close your trap, Rabbit. Clementine, no ideas on what that thing is? First time?"

Still hunkered low to the ground, Clementine shook her head almost imperceptibly. "I'm not sure. When we get closer maybe I'll have a better idea."

"Closer?" All three men said in unison.

Clementine nodded, firmly this time.

"Sticking to the plan, then?" Boone knew she would.

She nodded again.

"All right, fine by me, but I vote we call that quick sonofagun ..." Rabbit paused, swiping his hand in front of him as if he were reading from a store sign. "*El Vaquero!*"

"What's in that barn?" Boone wondered.

"Yes. Things just got more complicated." Clementine sighed and then pushed to her feet.

"I'd say." It was Boone's estimation that things were likely to get more complicated whenever Clementine was around. "And what screamed to set off the *Draug* in the first place?"

"I don't know." She stood at his side, studying the barn below.

"Them things the same as that German village you was in, Miss

Clem?" Hank asked, moving up next to Clementine.

"The Day of Decay," Boone remembered out loud. His thoughts flitted through Clementine's story about the battle she and her grandfather had fought against a village full of *Draug*. "If I recollect," Boone said, "those *Draug* were made from freshly dead people." He looked around to see all three of them staring at him.

"Booney, c'mon now." Rabbit grimaced. "They ain't beef hangin' on the hook."

Clementine nodded at Boone. "Most of those in Kremplestadt were newly dead, whereas these *Draug* here are well dead."

"Does that make a difference?" Rabbit asked.

"I don't know." She wrinkled her nose. "They smell worse."

"Blah. Think if it was a summer day. Flesh and guts rotting in the hot sun." Rabbit stifled a gag.

"Jack Rabbit! That's a revoltin' thought." Hank shuddered.

"How many were in that German village?" Boone waved an arm at the barn. "That many?"

"Fewer, if I had to guess."

Boone frowned at her. "Then that's too many for just the four of us, right?"

She didn't answer, but instead stared at the valley below, her brow furrowed.

"Seems like too many," Rabbit answered for her.

"Might be we should get us somebody to back our play, Miss Clem?" Hank suggested.

Clementine still didn't answer.

Why was she hesitating? "Let me sum everything up to now," Boone said, leaning over into her line of sight until she made eye contact with him. "We're facing dead-but-walking, half-witted, pestilence-spreading, rotting corpses that may or may not be able to change their appearance at will, and—I can't believe I'm saying this—may or may not be able to make themselves bigger. Oh, and they might or might not be unusually strong."

Clementine pursed her lips. "That's about right."

"And not just one or a couple, but hundreds," Boone added.

"Don't forget the smell." Rabbit buck-snorted at the snow.

"Or that dad-blasted, ghosty devil that'll probably do one or three of us in," Hank tacked on.

"Not to mention," Boone continued, still not finished making his case. "We have no idea what to expect in that barn."

"*And* the four-leggers out in the trees lookin' for some Sidewinder vittles." Hank poked at Rabbit.

"We can expect some *Draug*," Clementine replied with a shrug.

Boone threw up his hands. "Lordy, woman! I'm talking about whatever it was that herded the *Draug* in there."

Rabbit used his deep voice. "*El Vaquero.*"

Boone felt his eye twitch.

"Easy now, Booney." Rabbit patted Boone's shoulder. "We don't *know* that they can grow extra big. Or change the way they look. We don't know they're strong as an ox, neither."

"Well …" Clementine scratched under the side of her fur trapper's hat and scrunched her face. "They are powerful. I once saw one—"

"Miss Clementine," Rabbit interrupted. "You ain't helpin'!"

She pinched her lips together, her gray eyes turning to Boone.

"Right." Boone held her stare, wishing they could climb on their horses and ride out, back to hot coffee and a warm supper. But he knew Clementine too well. "Is there anything else we don't know about *Draug*? Anything else that you might have 'forgotten' to mention?"

"Well, there's one other thing." She picked up her pack. The cold, fierce look was back in her eyes.

Boone grimaced. "What now?"

She leaned closer to him. "They like to eat warm brains."

Hank looked away and coughed into his fist.

Boone gaped at her. "They *what*?"

Rabbit frowned. "No how!"

She grinned. "I made that up." She strung her pack over her shoulder and began picking her way down the embankment toward the town below. "See, it's not as bad as it could be. Now, are you boys ready to go kill some *Draug*?"

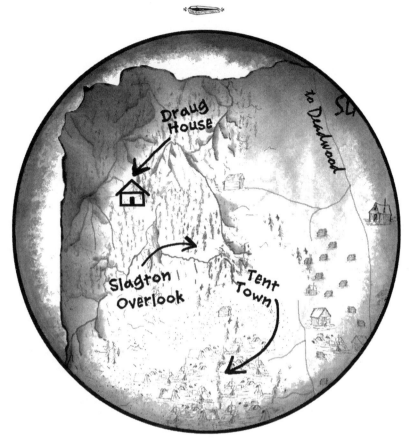

Two

R abbit watched after Clementine. "All that yammerin' about disease and brawn and eatin' brains and off she trots to join in, merry as you please." He didn't feel at all inclined to partake in her notion to hustle down the slope and join the party.

"She said they don't really eat brains." Boone cupped his mouth with both hands and whispered loudly, "Clementine! Get back here!"

She slid to a stop in the shin-deep snow and beaded Boone with a glare.

He motioned her back up the slope. "We need to think this through."

Rabbit nodded dramatically. For once he agreed with Boone. Well, not for once, but he really wasn't inclined to wade into a roiling sea of *Draug*.

"Miss Clem," Hank loud-whispered at her too. "Might be best to put some noggin to it."

Rabbit motioned her back and pointed at the ground in front of him.

She continued to regard them for a few moments, then turned and trudged slowly back up the hill, stopping square in front of Boone. "What?"

"We can't storm into that mess swinging and shooting. You can, but I might end up sticking Rabbit in the gizzard or stabbing Hank in the rump."

Rabbit agreed. "My gizzard's off limits."

"So's my rump," Hank added.

Rabbit knew Boone was making light of it, but he could hear the unease in his voice. He was spooked. "I think you're right, Booney. We need more sharp steel and bullets backin' us."

Clementine shook her head without taking time to think about it.

"Risk more lives? No. In fact, it would be better if the three of you waited here, but I know that isn't going to happen."

"See that look, Rabbit?" Boone tipped his head toward her. "Bloodlust."

"Don't be insulting." She tucked her hands inside her coat. "Bloodlust implies loss of control. I'm in complete control."

"Then how about telling us what your plan is? And don't say 'Kill 'em all.' A lack of strategy makes predicaments out of circumstances."

Rabbit recognized his recently deceased uncle's favorite witticism. "Okay, Uncle Mort."

Although, with his uncle now paying Rabbit visits in his wispy, post-mortem form, he didn't really think of Uncle Mort as "gone" anymore.

Boone grinned. "True, though, isn't it?"

It was true more than Rabbit wanted it to be, since Boone always used it against him like a weapon.

"I'd pace right now but the snow is too deep." Clementine drew in a deep breath.

"Miss Clem. We're in agreement. Them *Draugies* need puttin' down, and you ain't mistakin' with the notion me'n the Sidewinders ain't gonna let you promenade into that town all on your lonesome." Hank pointed down the slope. "So let's fig'r it. Looks like we can slip down to that outcrop of rocks at the bottom of the bank here. Tiptoe over to them bushes, gets us spittin' distance to the tent camp." He glanced at Clementine then at Rabbit and Boone. " 'Course, depends on your intent."

She considered Hank and his idea for a moment, then nodded slightly.

It occurred to Rabbit that for the first time on this venture to Slagton, Clementine was actually contemplating her next move. Good ol' Hank. He'd set Clementine's boil to a simmer with just a few well-chosen words. It reminded Rabbit of the way Boone tended to take the heat out of him, too.

"We'll need to get by those tents down there." Boone pointed at a group of canvas shelters clustered near the trail leading into the mining camp. He pulled a map from his pack and studied it.

"Ludek's?" Rabbit asked. He was happy as a horned toad on an anthill that the pasty white *other* was swinging his sword at the same guys he was. He just wished Ludek had joined in their *Draug*-hunting party instead of sending only a map. They could have used his sword and whatever else he had up his sleeve.

Boone nodded. "Barn there. Cabins. Tents. So we must be right here." He put his finger to the map.

Rabbit peered over Boone's shoulder, then down at the town. "Get to the scrub brush north of the tents, let's see ... around tent town, then quick like a bunny over to the stand of trees behind the barn."

A few *Draug* had actually been overlooked and wandered away past the outlying buildings. So *caper-sus* were pursuing them and whacking them with their sticks to get them turned around and headed back toward the barn. "Dispatch those *caper-sus* bastards and get close to that barn. Get a peek inside. Maybe get a look at the *vaquero* that herded them to the barn dance."

"We might could head along the ridgeline, along here ..." Hank drew a line with his finger on the map paralleling the top of the ridge from where they were standing to a spot adjacent to the barn. "Head down right there."

"I don't think so." Clementine craned her neck to follow the actual ridge. "It's too steep." She waved her hand back and forth at the gentle slope in front of them. "Here, in front of us, there's been a slide."

"You're right," Rabbit said. "Too steep all along there. Right here is the place."

Trees and bushes jutted from the snow at odd angles, some upended with roots reaching for the cold, pale blue sky, others flat on their sides, pointed up the incline as if to say: *That is where I belong.* Rabbit figured it was a surefire indication that the collapse had happened recently and taken the trees and undergrowth with it.

"Overhang let loose, probably," Boone added. "I still think we should send for more weapons, with people attached to them. Maybe that Rogue would be useful."

The Rogue? Rabbit rubbed his jaw. What was the name of Clementine's uppity rival in the Slayer business going by? Prudie? Nah. It was ... Prudence. Rabbit smiled. Maybe she went by Prudie, though. He wouldn't mind sitting back and watching the two Slayers perform the slice and dice duet. Then again, Prudence the Rogue would probably try to stick him between the ribs for staring at her stiletto.

"Bah." Clementine practically spit at the suggestion. "Don't let your thoughts wander, Boone. I'm headed down this hill. Come or not, it's up to you." She took a step, but then stopped and looked back at them.

"My thoughts aren't wandering one bit, Clementine. You don't seem to know when you're holding a bad hand. When to fold or go all in."

She spun to face him. "All in is all there is. There is no 'folding' in my world. If I 'fold,' people die."

Rabbit shot a look at Hank, who squeezed his lips together in silent reply.

Boone waved her off. "Don't be so dramatic. We're going with you, even if it's not such a good idea. If it's your job to eat two frogs, it's best to eat the biggest one first."

"Mark Twain!" Rabbit recognized it and wanted full credit for knowing the quote.

"Samuel Clemens." Boone grinned back. "So are we headed to that barn or are we jawing about it all day?" He stuffed the map into his pack and slung it over his shoulder, stepping up next to Clementine.

Rabbit watched Boone, knowing full well that his *amigo* was giving in against his better judgment. Clementine had some kind of hold on Boone. Something he hadn't seen in, well, ever. But it didn't matter. He'd follow Boone into Hades. "Arr, matey. This buccaneer's ready to skin a cutlass and send these characters to Davey Jones's locker."

Hank patted the bow strung across his chest and nodded, joining in behind Rabbit, Boone, and Clementine.

"Fred and the horses?" Rabbit was tempted to suggest they bring their mounts along. They were good in a fight, as they had proven more than once already.

"All snugged up tight at the edge of the clearing back there, right where we left 'em. Eatin' oats." Hank knew how to tie up the mounts so that they could bolt if they needed. Rabbit didn't even need to ask.

"Might break legs negotiating this slide anyway," Boone added.

They began carefully picking a path down through the debris of the collapsed cliff, Clementine leading the way. Trees and bushes and boulders, partially or wholly obscured by snow, roughened the slope into an unstable and slippery course nearly impossible to navigate. Each carefully chosen step brought the possibility of a behind hitting the ground and a flurry of cussing and arm waving.

Rabbit paused after getting his ass dumped in the snow yet again to watch Clementine dodge and slide and leap her way to the bottom of the hill.

"She moves like those tiptoe dancers in San Francisco, Booney."

Boone stuck out a hand to help Rabbit back to his feet. "Ballerina."

"Right, ballerina." Rabbit regarded Hank, who was close behind, as he grunted over a downed tree trunk and landed on his back in the snow with an "oof." He grinned. "Mr. Nimble back there."

"I don't expect there's a ballerina that could lay out a herd of nasty beasts and kick them into dust the way she does." Boone continued down the hill.

They were all thoroughly discontent by the time they reached the flat at the bottom of the cliff, brushing dirt and snow from their clothes and rubbing whatever was sore. All except Clementine, who had galloped down the rugged hill like a deer bounding across a grassy dell.

"You part mountain goat, Miss Clementine?" Rabbit swung his arm in big loops, attempting to work loose the tweaks and needling pains he'd acquired on the descent. One particularly long slide in the slippery snow had ended with his shoulder smashed against a boulder bigger than his horse.

Boone and Hank animatedly discussed the stumbling journey down the slope while they knocked and brushed off each other's backs.

"You see me bumble down that last part?" Rabbit couldn't keep his voice down. "Thought I was a goner when I went over that last part right there and almost went over the edge over there."

"Hoo hoo!" Hank adjusted his bow and pack. "Did more rump bumpin' and keister skiin' than walkin'."

"We should've taken your way, Hank, since we spent most of the way down on our backsides anyway." Boone brushed at his bottom.

"My hind end is wet as a hen in a soup pot." Rabbit pressed his hands against his rear end. "That's gettin' cold already, goldurn it. Booney, rub my—"

Clementine shushed them. "The noise you three are making is going to shake every living thing around here to action." She had her back to them, watching the group of tents to the south. She turned her head and listened. "I don't see any signs they are occupied, but smoke is coming from three."

Rabbit stilled and listened, too, considering the terrain around them. They were in a wide, relatively shallow and flat valley that fell gently away to the south. Come spring, he'd bet it would fill to waist-deep with lush, tall grass. Shacks of lumber, logs, and stone peppered a rough trail in from the north along a creek and grew thicker at what Rabbit figured was the center of town. Wisps of smoke from a few chimneys rose before dissipating in the air, aided by gusts of wind. The large barn loomed to the south, beyond the clusters of tents.

"Good place to grow a cow or two I'd bet," he whispered. "Good milk."

Hank nodded but kept his lips pressed together, no doubt obediently heeding Clementine's prompt for silence.

Boone quietly stepped up beside Clementine. "A while back, out in the forest, you mentioned that we weren't alone. I mean other than what we saw earlier."

She nodded, still surveying the valley, her gaze lingering on the tents.

"Still feel that way?"

She lifted her nose and took a deep breath. "Even more now."

"You smell somethin', Miss Clem?" Rabbit sniffed. A hint of wood smoke. And dirt, from the backside of his pants most likely. Fresh, clean, cold air, but something else. Something … disagreeable.

"It's difficult to smell anything but the *Draug*," she replied.

"That's it. I think I smell 'em too. Rotten, no-good, malodorous cusses."

"Rabbit, quiet." Boone waved back at him.

Damn Booney. " 'Rabbit quiet.' Always actin' like the boss of me." But he spoke in a hush, only to Hank.

Hank grinned and nodded.

"So you see it too?" Rabbit whispered.

"Yep." Hank jutted his chin at Clementine. "Miss Clem's thinkin' there's an ambush waitin' fer us in those tents, I'm guessin'."

"Oh sheaat!" Rabbit surveyed them for signs of movement. It was the better part of a hundred yards to the closest. He wished he had his Sharps rifle. It wouldn't be useful against large numbers of *Draug*, but taking off a head or two at this distance wouldn't require more effort than skipping a stone on a pond.

"Rabbit." Boone shot a frosty glare at him.

"All right, all right." Rabbit joined Boone with Hank trailing. "Let's go clean those tents out, then lickety-split over to the back of the barn."

"Jack, I think you're right," Clementine said quietly. "We need to make sure there are no surprises there when we go for the barn. Follow me." She darted to a nearby bush in the direction of the tents.

"Wait!" Boone hunched down and took off after her.

They all squeezed together behind a clump of bushes too small to conceal them.

Boone made an arc with his finger indicating out along the base of the cliff. "Why don't we go around those tents. Skirt the bottom of the cliff over to the backside of the barn."

Clementine peeked past the bush. "No time for that." She bolted to the next bush and waved them up behind her, and then held up her hand for silence as they arrived.

"Why are we stopped?" Boone whispered.

"Those two lean-tos are making me nervous." She shot each of them a stern look. "Stay here." And she was off.

Throwing his hands in the air, Boone growled, "There she goes." He chased after her, running, still hunched.

Rabbit had an overwhelming desire to stay right where he was. But he also felt the urge to follow Boone.

Hank, who seemed to be suffering the same dilemma, rose up from a squat, then sank back down, shaking his head. Then he arose only to sink down again.

"You think we should follow 'em Hank?"

"Ding dang it, Jack Rabbit. Let's go. No. I don't know. Miss Clem said we was to stay here."

Clementine and Boone disappeared behind a low line of scrub a few yards short of the closest tents.

You whiptail, Booney! "We should get to covering those two knuckleheads."

"Might be some reasonin' behind Miss Clem tellin' us to stay here."

Hogwash. "Hank, we gotta go." Rabbit scampered out from behind their hiding spot and over to the next bit of scrub brush cover that Clementine and Boone had used.

"Hank, get over here."

Clementine and Boone were still out of sight. Rabbit figured they were already inside the perimeter of the tent village some thirty to forty yards away.

Hank arrived, overshooting his target and bowled straight into Rabbit, nearly knocking him into the snow.

"Jehoshaphat, Hank!"

"Somethin's out there! Somethin' up at the top of the ridge where we just was!" Hank whispered and shrank into the bush, attempting to conceal himself. He pointed at the rim of the canyon, where they had been just minutes before.

"What is that?" Rabbit studied it. It was familiar. Nothing he would expect to see in any forest he'd ever been in. But this wasn't a normal forest. This was the Black Hills.

"White. Big as a grizzly, skinnier though, more muscle to it." Hank's voice was quick and clipped from fear.

Grizzly. Rabbit's mind reeled through his memories. Grizzly. White. "Sheaat!" He shook Hank's shoulder. "The white grizzly. First time we came to Deadwood, me'n Booney fought a white grizzly."

"I remember. Think this'n is that'n?"

Rabbit didn't like the possibility that there was more than one roaming the hills. "I hope so."

They watched the beast paw at the snow, put its nose to the ground, dig, leap to another spot and dig again. Then it loped to the point they had started down the slope and sniffed the air.

"What the hell is it doing?" Rabbit wondered aloud.

"Purgatory if that thing ain't trackin' us. Pardon the language, Jack Rabbit."

Rabbit longed for his Sharps, but it rested, "unusefully," in the scabbard laced to his saddle. On Dime's back. At the top of the hill.

He spent a long moment worrying if the beast had come across their horses up on that plateau. Hank had hidden them away, but this bastard was a tracker, sure enough.

It looked directly at them.

"Fuuuuuck. Does it see us?" He and Hank were far enough away to blur any details of the beast, and they were almost completely concealed by the waist-high scrub brush. If they didn't move …

"Don't think so. Just lookin'."

"Where are Boone and Clementine?" Rabbit rose off his haunches, only a little, to peek at the tent village through a break in the bushes.

A piercing screech cut through the air.

"Now you done it, Jack Rabbit." Hank pointed at the top of the cliff.

The white grizzly stood up on its hind legs, its neck and snout extended out and toward the sky. A long, loud howl echoed through air.

"Howlin' like a wolf, but standin' like a man. Like a man and a wolf and a grizzly put together."

It lowered back onto all fours and leapt over the edge of the cliff and bounded down the slope, dodging trees and rocks without slowing even a little.

"That fucker's gonna be on us in a shake, Hank." Rabbit snatched his pistol from its holster.

"Miss Clem said no guns."

"Miss Clementine ain't here. Best you skin that LeMat and make sure she's not froze up." Rabbit rolled the cylinder of his Colt back and forth. "And don't forget the shotgun under."

"Full up, Jack Rabbit, but Miss Clem said no guns."

Rabbit pointed at the hillside over Hank's shoulder. "Tell me that when it's lickin' your face."

The beast had reached the flat and was heading at them in great long, loping strides, easily soaring over the bushes and rocks in its path.

Rabbit's mind raced. She did say no guns. Sassafras. Knives again? He holstered his pistol and grasped one of the throwing knives sheathed at his waist in his right hand and jerked his oversized Bowie knife from the sheath strapped to his boot with his left. The throwing knife felt entirely inadequate for the situation. *Clementine's gonna get us killed, one way or another.*

Dangnabbit! Fighting close in was for dogs and married folk.

Hank strung an arrow into his bow, his hands trembling enough for Rabbit to see.

"You're a brave man, Mr. Varney." Rabbit's heart warmed at the courage his pal displayed in the path of all those teeth rushing toward them. "I'm right here beside you."

He quickly surveyed the terrain. It wasn't a spot he'd try to defend given a choice. Even an outcropping of rocks would be something to work with. They might be able to use the thick scrub to their advantage. Split to both sides maybe, but he worried about Hank. He hadn't gone against this hunter. But Rabbit had. He'd seen the weapons it was carrying. The extra-long spiky teeth and even longer claws at the ends of powerful legs? Arms?

The white grizzly was close enough Rabbit could hear the snarls and huffing, labored breaths. Snow sprayed from its legs and feet as it pushed through the snow.

"Hank! Back partway around the scrub. Get to a place you can lay in with the string and sticks. If it comes at you, drop the bow. Since you won't jerk the LeMat, skin your Bowie. Wait till it's close and then sidestep. These bastards turn slower than Fred does hitched to a wagon. It'll swipe atcha though, so watch for that."

Hank nocked an arrow and drew back on the bowstring as he backpedaled around the bush.

Rabbit focused on the charging beast. He could see its milky eyes now. It watched Hank for a moment, but then fixed its attention on him.

Thwp! An arrow sank into its neck. Hank was laying in with his bow. It howled and swatted at the shaft, breaking it away.

It was Rabbit's turn. He drew back the throwing knife and heaved, aiming for the beast's head. The grizzly batted the shiny steel away with a massive paw and rushed at Rabbit.

Time was too short for another throw.

Okay, you bastard.

Rabbit raised the Bowie knife, tightened the muscles in his legs and dug his heels into the snow, preparing to spring sideways. If this beast was anything like the first he'd encountered, it would make a leaping attack. That's when Rabbit would make his move.

Thwp! An arrow sank into its shoulder. It growled and broke that shaft away too.

Another long lope and then it coiled up and sprang at Rabbit, opening its mouth wide, baring multiple rows of long teeth. Claws bristled at the ends of thick, white fur–covered arms, filling his vision as it reached for him.

He had been in this predicament before. He knew what to do, and when. Pushing hard against the snow and frozen ground, he launched himself sideways. Then he raised the foot-long Bowie knife in both hands and turned, sinking the knife between its ribs as it flew by, just as he had done the time before.

It crashed into his shoulder and head. He felt his feet swing up over his head … Was he floating?

His back and head smashed into the ground, the crushing pain knocking his vision blurry.

Everything began to spin. He shook his head, and a sharp bolt shot up his neck and filled his skull. He groaned, letting his head drop into the snow. The cold dampened the pain.

I'll sleep a little bit …

A quick string of booming gunshots shocked him back from the churning blackness. It seemed as if the gun had lit up right by his ear.

He opened his eyes and quickly closed them again as warm sticky blood and chunks of flesh rained onto him. "Wha …"

"Get up, Jack Rabbit!" Hank hauled Rabbit to his feet and pointed. " 'Nother's comin'!"

Rabbit wobbled on jelly legs, pulsing blood thrummed in his ears, muffling Hank's voice. He looked down. He was holding Boss, his sawed-off double barrel shotgun, without even realizing he'd yanked it from its holster.

"Followin' up behind the first one. Fifty yards and comin' fast!" Hank picked his bow from the snow, drew an arrow from his quiver and nocked it. "LeMat chain-fired."

So that was the string of gunfire. Rabbit knew nobody could work a pistol that fast.

"Fired four of them nine balls. Didn't fire the shotgun shell though."

Damned LeMat. Rabbit had heard of chain-fires, but being near one was a first. "I got Boss ready. Don't see—"

Hank pointed the tip of his bow northeast. "Thataway."

Rabbit spun and listen-looked in the direction Hank faced, attempting to focus his fuzzy sight on the beast. In the distance, a blurry hulk of white with a black spot in the middle was coming. Fast.

"Hairy beast looks like it grew around a thicket of teeth." Hank drew back on the bowstring. "I'll put this right in the middle of it."

"Use your consarn pistol, Hank!"

"Don't want to."

Rabbit almost laughed. "You just woke up the whole valley with that artillery of yours. I don't think surprise is on our side anymore."

The white grizzly skidded to a stop, howled, and then came on.

"Dirty rotten fucker!" Rabbit was well aware of the shotgun's range. *Maybe try to pepper it with a few .44s before it gets here.* He holstered the shotgun and jerked his Colt.

"I don't like that LeMat. Puts the fear in me, much as that beastie does." Hank pointed his nocked arrow at the bloody, headless white grizzly between them. "Took a good-size chunk off'n that fella, though."

"And sprayed him all over me!" Rabbit wiped at the sticky wetness on his face.

Another howl echoed through the valley.

Hank shot a glance back at Rabbit. "Another'n?"

"And close, too. Get ready Hank. Remember, you're almost nose to nose before you use that shotgun load."

"Right." Hank drew back the bowstring, took aim, and let loose. *Thwp!*

Rabbit couldn't see if the arrow found purchase, the white grizzly was too far away.

It skidded to a stop and batted at something.

"I think you got him! Helluva range you got, Hank!" It lurched into a run again. It was coming quickly, almost within pistol range now.

Where had that other howl come from? The echoes kept Rabbit from pinpointing the direction, but it seemed it came from the south, somewhere near the tent town. *Boone!*

Hank strung another arrow.

Thwp!

That one found its mark too, sinking deep into the shoulder. The beast snarled and snapped the shaft of the arrow and kept coming, but it favored that leg now.

"Slowed him some, anyway." Hank dropped his bow and pulled the LeMat and looked down at it dubiously. "Don't you go catawampus on me now."

Rabbit beaded the beast, waited, breathing slow and steady, until he was sure he had the range. "Just a little bit left ..." he whispered. "Come on ahead. That's it. And right ... there."

Boom! He lit a slug of hot lead at its head. A chuff of black smoke puffed in front of his gun and the crack of the shot echoed through the valley while he waited for the bullet to find its mark. The grizzly crumpled and slid to a stop, pushing a pile of snow in front of it.

"That's two!" Rabbit nodded.

A howl rose from the south again, closer this time.

"Can't see the other'n yet, Jack Rabbit."

"Where the hell are Boone and Clementine?" Rabbit searched for any movement among the tents, tiptoeing to see over the scrub brush. Clusters of pine and spruce saplings blocked much of his view of the tent town, but he was sure the howl came from there. It was exactly the direction Boone and Clementine had gone.

"We should get to Boone and Miss Clementine. They might need help."

"Might be we need theirs." Hank retrieved his bow from the ground and shook it to loosen the snow stuck to its limbs. "I'm on your tail, Jack Rabbit. But we gotta keep an eye for that howler out there."

Rabbit's head and shoulder throbbed. That beast had given him a good wallop. "You wanna reload that LeMat?"

"No sir."

"Think you should?"

Hank shook his head. "Got this." He held up his bow. "And this." He patted the Bowie knife sheathed at his hip.

"Gonna break Boone's heart."

They turned at the sound of scuffling in the snow behind them. The second white grizzly began mewling and rising out of the snow. It was injured but definitely not dead. It squirmed and floundered, wiping at its bloody face with a huge arm—or was it a leg? Rabbit's bullet had smashed through its snout and left eye, and exploded a portion of the back of its head. But the thing was still coming. Thrashing and lurching, writhing with pain or fear or fury.

"Mother make tracks." Hank lowered his bow, his eyes round as saucers. "How's that bugger even managin' to ambulate?"

The injured beast spit blood and a gurgling howl, but still it came. Only feet away from Hank now.

Rabbit raised his pistol, but a rustle from the scrub brush behind him grabbed his attention. Two beasts now! He lit a round at the half-headed grizzly and spun just as the second beast thumped to the ground close enough to share a breath with him.

He raised his pistol, but the bastard was fast. It swiped at his arm, knocking the gun from his hand. Then it lunged at him with sharp teeth aimed directly at his throat.

A flash of shiny steel swept up from below and arced high and out of sight. The white grizzly's head seemed to float toward him for a heartbeat. Rabbit raised his forearm to ward off the blow. It smashed into the side of his face and careened over his shoulder, the teeth raking across his jaw.

A split second later, the beast's massive headless body crashed into him, driving him backward. He landed in the snow, ass first, breathless and near crushed by the weight of the headless grizzly that had landed on top of him.

He shook his head to straighten out his tangled wits and struggled against the soiled white-furred carcass compressing his chest.

"Get outta there. You don't want to be under that thing when it goes." Boone pushed at the hunk of dead meat with his boot and hauled Rabbit to his feet. "It'll stink even worse than it does now."

"Booney!" Rabbit grabbed his friend's shoulders and shook him hard. He was just about the best sight he could think of right now.

"Now we see to you." Rabbit turned to see Clementine raise her blade against the half-faced grizzly. It swiped at her but she easily dodged the long claws and brought her blade down hard on its neck. Sharp steel thunked against bone and sliced through. What was left of its head fell away.

"Watch this. It's disgusting." Boone pointed at the beheaded beast that had seconds ago been lunging for Rabbit's throat.

"What?" Rabbit gingerly poked at the small gashes along his jawline.

"You took one on the jaw, Jack Rabbit." Hank strung his bow over his shoulder and lifted Rabbit's head to get a closer look. "Ain't too awful, lessen these beasties carry poison. Then you're prob'ly dead."

"You don't think—"

"Hoo hoo! Jack Rabbit. Jus' funnin'." He scrunched his face. "These critters ain't carryin' poison." He sobered. "They ain't is they, Miss Clem?"

She laughed. "No, Hank." She turned her attention to the first grizzly. "You two didn't finish this other one either."

Sure enough, the white grizzly that Hank's LeMat had chain-fired on was still struggling to gain a footing.

"Leavin' some of the fun for you is all." Rabbit brushed bits of white grizzly flesh from his coat. "You can go on ahead and dispatch that one too."

"Yeah, you wanna get that off you." Boone grabbed a handful of snow and scrubbed at Rabbit's coat.

"What's so all-fired important about—"

The carcass of the first began to undulate under its thick fur hide, then the second, and third. The hides swelled into large bumps that ripped open and oozed melted flesh and organs over the bodies, covering them in a white gooey mess that bubbled and rippled. The bodies slowly collapsed into pools of slimy white and black liquid that began melting the snow. The rancid odor of decayed flesh wafting up with the smoke had all of them but Clementine covering their noses.

Rabbit looked back and forth between Clementine, Boone, and the puddles of slime.

"There's somethin' I ain't ever seen before." Hank squatted beside one of the pools and stuck his finger toward it.

"Hank! What'er you doin'? Don't touch it!" Rabbit redoubled his efforts at removing any remaining bits of flesh from his coat.

The three pools of white bubbling slime began to turn dark and soak into the ground.

A waft of rancidness found its way straight up Rabbit's nose. "That's gonna take the starch out of my britches." He backed away. So did Boone and Hank.

Clementine wiped her blade in the snow and sheathed it inside her coat.

"Miss Clem, I sure am heartened to see you breathin' still, but I don't believe I'll never not be overly fond of lookin' at the results of your handiwork." Hank faced Boone. "Glad you're breathin' too, Boonedog." He clapped Boone on the shoulder.

"We're heartened to be," Boone said.

It began to dawn on Rabbit that Boone knew more things about the white grizzlies than he would have expected. "You know how these critters die. You and Miss Clem kill one? Did you get to the tents? Were there some in the tents? They don't live in tents, do they?" He reseated Boone's pistol in its holster and adjusted his gun belt.

Boone batted him away. "I can holster my own gun." He leaned in close to get a look at Rabbit's cheek and jaw. "Walloped you good right there, huh? Got your shoulder, too."

"Huh? How'd you …" Rabbit pulled his coat around to take a look. The beast's claws had cut three slashes through the sleeve. He hoped Dmitry wouldn't be angry, since he wasn't sure if the coat was on loan, or if it was really his to keep.

"Nice clean cuts. Sharp claws on those bastards."

"Yeah. Didn't get to skin. Got lucky here, too." Rabbit touched his jaw. The thrum in his temples reminded him his head took some of the blow. "Clobbered my noggin, though."

"Are you dandies done comparing wounds?" Clementine stood with her arms crossed. "We need to clean the tents before we get a look in that barn."

In Rabbit's world, a few hours in the saddle or on the seat of a wagon, facing off against a road agent or barroom thug, and dancing with a girl or two would have filled the day. But this was Clementine's world. Slaughter a few dozen *Bahkauv* before breakfast, have a *Höhlendrache* over for tea, invite a few white grizzlies to supper, then sleeping sound by midnight. Although, that last part wasn't right. She didn't keep to normal hours like any reasonable person would.

Still, his head hurt. And his shoulder. He wasn't against the idea of setting up camp back with the horses and letting his headache subside.

"Miss Clem, you think it's a sound idea to proceed now that Jack Rabbit and I woke up the valley with gunplay?" Hank watched the three dark pools of slime slowly disappearing into the snow.

"I thought I told you two, no guns." Clementine's arms were still folded.

Rabbit patted Boss and his pistol. "I'd buy 'em drinks right about now if they'd take me up on it." He wasn't joking.

"He's not joking," Boone echoed out loud.

Clementine's lips tightened.

He dismissed her chiding and turned to Boone. "You didn't tell me how you know about these things."

"Oh, Clementine here dispatched two that were wandering around near the tents."

"Only two? By herself?" Rabbit smirked at Boone. "You were busy? What? Knittin' again?"

"Happened to be the camp was crawling with *caper-sus*."

One of Clementine's eyebrows lifted.

"There were a lot," Boone replied.

Clementine held up three fingers.

"Three? Practically an army." Rabbit winked at Boone and slapped him on the back. Then he got serious. "Take any injury, either of you?"

Boone shook his head.

"No gunshots. Used your sword?"

Boone nodded.

"Tongue tied in knots, is it? Can't utter a word about it?"

"This is a bad place, Rabbit."

He looked into Boone's eyes and saw fear. No, not fear. Foreboding. Boone didn't really ever show fear. Not Boone. It wouldn't be as simple as fear.

Rabbit nodded slowly, still studying his *amigo*. Something happened, and whatever it was, Boone wasn't ready to spill. He'd need to get him alone to pry it loose. "We'll stick together from now on." He put a reassuring hand on Boone's back and scowled at Clementine. "No more splittin' up."

He was fond of Clementine, but he'd be damned if he was going to let Boone come to harm because of her passion for bloodshed.

Three

*A*re we ready?" Clementine asked, meeting Rabbit's stare, cooling it some, and sending it back to him.

She rarely allowed any nonsense, but rather made things plain and simple. She wouldn't let anything—or anyone—stop her from completing her task, and that usually seemed to be fine for Rabbit. But he was overly protective when it came to Boone. And a little about Hank, too.

"Ready," said the *always* ready Hank. His bow was strung over his shoulder and he was set to march. "Lost some arrows since those beasties snapped 'em off, but still got plenty."

Boone nodded. "Let's see what's in that barn."

"We'll need to be careful." She looked at Rabbit and Hank in particular. "You two rang the bell with that gunfire. I'd be surprised if there was a single creature in this valley that didn't hear it. And there are probably more of your white grizzlies around. Keep a sharp eye." With that, she took off toward the tent camp, and the barn beyond.

After a glance back to make sure the three men fell in behind her, she scurried to a group of saplings, then an uprooted stump of a fallen tree. She worked her way south, using cover where she could. Within a few minutes, they were on the outskirts of the group of tents, huddled near a growth of serviceberry bushes sizable enough to conceal them all.

"We need to figure an escape route in case things go disagreeable." Boone blocked the sun with his hand, probably looking for a direction to retreat.

Apparently, her warning about being careful hadn't fallen on deaf ears.

Rabbit was right. Boone could be counted on to "over-cogitate" a thing. Then again, finding an escape route wasn't a bad idea, it just wasn't first and foremost in Clementine's mind. If her afi were beside her, he would chastise her short-sightedness, but also the delay. Or not. Many times during her training, she had been stalled to inaction, knowing that her afi would reprimand her for any missteps.

She studied the line of the cliff to the west. It meandered generally north to south, like a giant, unmoving snake. It reminded her of the fjords and peninsulas of the coastline where she grew up, but this was more rounded by erosion and time. The tent town occupied the center of a rough semi-circle formed by the cliff that stretched a quarter mile from one end to the other. She was sure her previous conclusion, that it was unclimbable all along this portion of the cliff, was accurate.

Farther south, a large stand of pines obscured any view of the cliff and the plateau at the top and offered no cover below due to a lack of undergrowth. The trunks were clear of branches well high up. There would be no climbing or cover there.

To the south of the tent camp and east of the stand of pines, if she were to push up on tiptoes, she could see the peak of the large barn. Their destination.

Farther south and west, Clementine and Boone had caught glimpses of tall pines that must be part of a larger stand of trees. The undergrowth there was thick enough to hide them if the need arose.

"That forest we saw earlier to the south," she offered as an escape route, though her words were clipped due to the frustration welling inside her. She wasn't in the habit of planning escapes. "Or back the way we came."

Boone shook his finger at the forest. "You know well as I do, that forest is unknown. Ludek said he hadn't explored beyond the clearing with the stone table in the middle."

Ludek had indeed said that when he gave them the map back in Deadwood, along with a warning about the dangers they might run across in and around Slagton. But Clementine hadn't expected so many *Draug*. Or the white grizzlies, as Rabbit and Boone called them. Ludek must not have seen any of the sharp-toothed creatures while scouting here. Certainly he would have spoken of them if he had.

"Get Ludek's map out," she told Boone.

"Who knows what that stone table is used for," Boone said. "If we're not careful, they may string us out one by one on that thing and feed pieces of us to the *Bahkauv*."

"That's *Draug* in that town, Booney, not *Bahkauv*," Rabbit corrected.

Boone stared blankly at him for two moments. "You shittin' me, Rabbit?"

"No." Rabbit pulled away a little.

Clementine scowled. Were these two really going to waste time arguing about the differences between *Draug* and *Bahkauv*?

"What's the difference, Rabbit, when something is eating your guts while you're laid out on a table?"

"Size of its teeth." Rabbit backed up as he said it.

"*Bahkauv*. Them boys is mean," Hank joined in. "Easy enough to put down, tho'. Them *Draugies* don't seem so mean as they do slow in the head. Slow movin'. Like possums in 'Janarary.'"

Clementine tugged at her collar. They really needed to get moving.

"Teeth are teeth." Boone's voice betrayed his exasperation with his companion, or maybe their situation.

"We know they got bad breath. Worse than Tink's after she eats a—"

Boone held up his hand. "Stop right there." He reached inside his jacket and brought out Ludek's map and held it in front of her. "What kind of vermin is hiding in those trees? We don't know."

"Hoo hoo. Wager Tink's breath ain't as bad as the stink comin' offa ol' Elroy's stewpot. Lets it set more'n a week sometimes." Hank scrunched his face and his whole body shook. "Skunk parts in there and who knows what all. He ain't so good at dressin' skunks."

"You should roll the map, Booney." Rabbit snatched it from his hand.

Boone reached for it but Rabbit held it above his head.

"You fold the map, it makes lines across it. Pretty soon, can't see the things on a line. Prob'ly somethin' important along there, but it's all whackered 'cause of the creases." Rabbit rolled it up and handed it back to Boone. "Now put that someplace safe."

Boone snatched it back and pointed it at Rabbit. "I'll put it right up your ..." He tucked it into his inner coat pocket.

Clementine glared up at the sky. *Odin's beard!* She needed to either get moving or kill all three of her companions.

"Never mind, let's go," she said and darted through the bush and scrub, raced the fifty feet to the closest tent, and snuck inside without looking back.

It was near this tent that she had used her swords to bisect the first of the two white grizzlies. If she had to guess, it had been a sentry. Same as the second, which attacked at a precise time and from behind, as if it were taking advantage of the distraction created by the first. In fact, her gut told her they had been working together, hunting in pairs.

She peeked through the tent flaps but saw no one. Her companions apparently hadn't heard her "Let's go" and were continuing their discussion in her absence. She growled under her breath. Their lack of focus was going to get them all killed.

Dropping the tent flap, she pulled her swords from her coat, hunkered down, and waited. Surely they would soon figure out she'd left and follow in her tracks.

So, if the beasts hunted or patrolled in pairs, why had three of them attacked Hank and Jack? Was another close by? It didn't matter much. It was a safe assumption that more white grizzlies—and who knew who else—were lurking or hunting all through this valley. Whoever was moving the *Draug* army into Slagton would assuredly have lookouts.

A shiver wriggled up her back into the base of her skull.

Something was near. Something not human.

Blades ready, she held completely still.

Where were those damned Sidewinders and Hank?

Stay focused.

The light thump of a footfall in the snow, then another, sent another tingle up her spine.

Were they being attacked? No, she would hear it.

FOCUS!

Hel's teeth! Working alone was so much less complicated.

A Slayer's life, of necessity, was a solitary existence. Her grandfather had instilled that notion in her more effectively than any other.

I know, Afi.

She knew, yet instead of attacking whatever was outside of the tent, here she crouched, worrying about her three companions. She would have made it to the barn by now if …

A snuffling sound, followed by thumps of erratic footfalls, came from the other end of the tent.

She gripped her swords, watching the shadow of a white grizzly loom up the tent wall, and then back down as it sniffed along the ground near the edge of the tent. It pushed against the canvas with its snout, and then rose tall again.

It could stand on two feet *and* four? What in the name of *Hel*?

She'd happened upon many strange and awful creatures, but it was rare to see any that possessed the traits of both animal and human.

It lumbered to a nearby tent, dropped to all fours, and began sniffing at the ground again. She peeked through the flaps, watching as it picked at the body of one of the *caper-sus* Boone had dispatched earlier.

Her muscles tightened as energy surged through her, the urge to slay the beast driving her now.

She prepared to lunge, envisioning sinking both of her blades deep into its flesh.

Yet she waited, watching.

The white grizzly lifted the man's saggy, limp body by one arm, sniffed at the gaping mouth and then dropped the body.

Why? It didn't like the sme—

The grizzly stomped on the torso, grabbed one of the legs, and began wrenching it back and forth until it started to tear free. One more hard pull and the leg ripped away from the body with a sucking *crack!*

Clementine stared out through the flap, fascinated as it stripped the flesh from the leg with its claws until nothing but a few pieces of bloody muscle clung to the bone. The beast held the leg up by the foot, chasing the flopping femur with its mouth until it grabbed the bone in its teeth and began crunching loudly.

Good Valhalla! She needed to strike while it was distracted, but …

The creature continued eating its way up the leg and dropped the foot, the only part that it hadn't stripped of skin and flesh.

Suddenly it stopped.

Rising up on two legs, it sniffed at the air. "*Scharfrichter.*"

It spoke! Not only that, but it spoke the German word for "Slayer." For her. Or her kind.

Potzblitz! It knew she was here.

The white grizzly tipped its head back and loosed a screaming howl that echoed through the valley.

It was calling others, she was sure. It was time to kill!

Thwp! An arrow was suddenly sticking out of its chest.

Thunk! A knife bounced against the side of its head and fell away.

Clementine cleared the tent and lunged toward the white grizzly, blades first.

A blur of sheepskin and dark, shiny metal streaked toward the distracted beast.

"Aaaah!" Boone leapt, raised his blade, and swung with both arms, slicing the meaty neck clean through with one blow. His feet hit the ground and skidded in the snow, landing him on his rump.

"*Dritt.*" Clementine let her arms drop, her blades hanging loosely in her hands.

"Hot damn, Booney! Helluva swing." Rabbit trotted up to Boone's side and held out his hand to help him up. "Landing could o' been better."

"Cut right through that fucker, didn't I?" Boone took Rabbit's hand, panting but managing a grin.

"Ugh." Hank pulled up beside them and wrinkled his nose at the oozing lump of white grizzly head.

"Boone." Clementine watched the three of them, her head tipped.

He jerked, apparently startled by her voice. "Clementine. See what I did?"

"I see." She poked the headless carcass with the toe of her boot. It seemed the Sidewinders still didn't care much about leaving a trail to follow. Or the art of stealth. "What should we do with it?"

"Huh? Do with what?" Jack scraped at the snow with his boot. "There you are." He stooped to pick up his knife.

"Why should we want to do anything with it?" Boone asked.

"Aw, I see it," Hank said. "Miss Clem, your preference as to sending them back to the ground. Hide your handiwork, so to speak."

Clementine nodded. At least Hank had learned some things.

Jack sheathed the knife. "More comin', I expect. Don't see the point right now in grousing about who kills what."

"Are we really worried about that here?" Boone grimaced at the sticky goo on his sword. "This whole valley is obviously a nest of your *others*. Besides, Hank and Rabbit imprudently used their firearms." He winked at Rabbit.

"We always need to worry about concealment." Or … perhaps Boone was right. This valley was crawling. And more trouble was undoubtedly on the way. "They're not 'my' *others*."

Jack scanned the ridgelines. "They keep howlin', talkin' to each other. And we ain't even got to that barn to take a gander inside yet."

Hank pointed the tip of his bow at the center of the town. "I saw a few more *caper-sus* roamin' the streets, Miss Clem, but I think if'n we can get out behind the barn, can't see none of us that way. Unless you are thinkin' we cut and run."

Cut and run? Clementine shook her head. Hank apparently still had some learning to do, too. "Tent to tent, over to the right, then across that small clearing to the trees, out behind the barn, like you said."

"Clear the tents or sneak through?" Boone's voice was breathy with excitement. But Clementine still heard hesitation as well.

"Best to be stealthy. If the gunplay went unnoticed, that is. It's possible that it was heard and there is a search going on." She glanced around, checking for signs of more trouble coming their way. "But the echoes in this valley make it difficult to determine a location. So, we proceed. If anything sees us, we kill it," she said flatly.

She hadn't forgotten the large number of *Draug* that had disappeared into the barn. Normally, she would push forward in such circumstances, even though others might consider it foolish. But here, now, there were just too many in that building. They would almost certainly overrun her and her companions. And then there was the matter of *El Vaquero*, as Jack called the *other* that had been rounding up the *Draug*. She needed a better idea of what *El Vaquero* was before she committed her crew to a fight. Past clashes with all manner of beasts reminded her of too many horrific possibilities.

"So kill whatever we see," Jack said. "Got it."

"Rabbit." Boone backhanded him in the chest. "She said—"

"I heard, I heard. Funnin' is all I was doin'." Jack twisted his bandolero back and forth, resetting it on his shoulder. "You set, Hank?"

"Rarin'."

"Then let's light a shuck. Booney'll be along shortly. He needs to over-contemplate the situation a little longer." Jack winked at Clementine.

She smiled back.

Boone elbowed her arm lightly. "Jealous 'cause he doesn't have the equipment to contemplate a cricket."

"I contemplate you can ruminate more than a cow in a field of dry grass. I contemplate that."

"I contemplate a hunk a jerky 'bout now." Hank rubbed his belly. "My bucket's empty."

"We eat later." The urge to keep moving tickled at Clementine's neck. It was rarely a good idea to stay in one place too long in a situation like this. "Did you find out anything with Ludek's map, Boone? You've studied it more than a few times now."

"That man—is he a man?" Boone waited for Clementine's response.

"Does it matter?"

"I suppose not. Anyway, he sure put some time into it."

"He drew a wagonload of trees." Jack shook his head.

Clementine scoffed slightly, searching the ridgeline.

"What have you got against maps?" Boone pulled the map from inside his coat and held it out for her to see.

She didn't look. "I don't need a map. I've got these." She pointed at her eyes. "And this." She pointed at her nose. "And if that isn't enough, I've got this." She pointed at her head.

"I get the trees," Jack said. "They're pretty. Must be hundreds of 'em on there. Take a man a good while to do that. I mean … but stumps?" He snorted.

Hank squinted at the map. "Had some time, prob'ly, sittin' and watchin'. I'da maybe done one lasso around all them buggers and scribbled 'trees' in the middle of it. Ain't gonna draw ever' single one."

"That'd make more sense. And no stumps." Jack pointed at the stone table Ludek had drawn in the clearing. "Not for a Sunday meal, I expect."

Hank wrinkled his nose. "You reckon they really strap folks on that thing? Cut into 'em, maybe?"

"Like for sacrifices, maybe?" Jack asked.

"Fer skinnin' Jack Rabbits?" Hank side-eyed Jack.

"Strap down a Hank Varney and cut up some Varney vittles." Jack's grin was devilish.

Clementine huffed. "*Gottverdammt!* We don't care about any damn stone table."

"Looks more like an altar," Boone suggested. "Or maybe for sitting when you're tuckered from a walk."

His wisecrack fell on the ground and died. She shot daggers at him with her eyes.

He paused, watching her, then folded the map and tucked it away.

Smart man, she thought, since one more remark from him or his *amigo* and she'd be serving Sidewinder for supper.

"We should get moving, boys," Boone said, still watching her with a good dose of caution crinkling his eyes.

"Now he's all fired and ready." Jack smirked, glancing between her and Boone, then sobered. He nodded, serious now. "Okay. On the move then. Kill it if it squawks."

"Tent by tent," Hank added. "To that stand of trees over yonder, then the back of the barn."

"Good." Clementine stood tall and took in the entirety of their planned route.

The collection of tents and canopies and lean-tos were every manner of shape and size, erected with poles and predominantly animal skin or canvas. The grouping as a whole had been assembled in a way that avoided any pleasing pattern whatsoever. Smoke drifted in long lazy lines from the few pits that were more embers than campfires. No one had tended them for some time.

She guessed the number of structures at fifty and didn't like it. There were too many dark shadows and obscured sightlines. Any number of things could be out there. And while she could usually sense the presence of danger, this ability was nearly useless when her adversaries numbered more than a few. Such as now.

She frowned back at her companions, the need to protect them making her hesitate in the hunt. For now, she had to temper her compulsion to deal with the infestation.

* * *

Rabbit, Boone, and Hank followed Clementine from shelter to shelter. They found cover inside the tents or up against thick evergreen underbrush as they moved closer and closer to the barn. Rabbit assumed the inhabitants of this makeshift village were tending to business in the enormous building or elsewhere, since they had met no resistance to this point.

They were positioned to make the dash to the stand of trees at the back of it when Clementine stopped abruptly and took refuge in one of the larger tents nearby. This afforded Rabbit the opportunity to take stock of their surroundings.

The disrespect for nature and decency here disgusted him. The streets of Deadwood were occupied by those besotted with the coarse tawdriness pervading the frontier, yet somehow retained a few of the elements of a civilized society. Slagton, at least this part of it, was a stinking, gruesome collection of grime and waste and tattered canvas. If ever society had existed here, it was overrun now by a pestilence.

Rabbit pushed the thoughts from his mind and focused on Clementine. Her eyes were dark, fierce. She crouched, still as cold stone as she studied … what? The air? She watched the tent above them, her gaze sliding along its length and down the opposite end. He understood that now was not the time for horseplay or witticisms. Her intensity had obviously spread to all of them, almost as if they could feel it radiate from her. *He* could, anyway.

"We won't make it to the barn," she said quietly, maybe to herself.

His heart fluttered in his chest as he looked back and forth between Boone and Hank. "What—"

Clementine silenced him with her palm, then raised her finger and twirled it in a circle.

Shit! He knew what that meant.

They were surrounded.

Surrounded by what, he didn't know, but probably not *Draug*. They were noisy bastards without a care of making their presence known. So *caper-sus* then, and *El Vaquero*. And white grizzlies. And who knew what else. Might as well throw in a few *Bahkauv* and a *Höhlendrache* to boot. A glance at Hank's pale face and wide eyes dropped a rock in his stomach. Hank understood, too. Rabbit patted Hank's shoulder and gave him a nod.

Boone studied the canvas tent from one end to the other, probably looking for some sign of what had Clementine spooked. His hand gripped the handle of his scimitar.

Rabbit looked back to Clementine to see her shaking her head at him.

"What?" he mouthed.

She pointed at his waist.

He glanced down, realizing he was holding his Colt with the hammer cocked. He couldn't remember drawing it from the holster. He raised one palm toward her and slowly, silently lowered the hammer, holstered the pistol, and then drew a throwing knife from its sheath. He'd rather blaze guns than knives, but now wasn't the time to push that thought.

Snow muffled footfalls from outside the tent raised the hair on his neck. He leaned over and pulled the Bowie knife from its sheath on Hank's belt and put it in Hank's unsteady hand, giving him a firm nod. He gripped his own Bowie and held it up between them, shaking it while gritting his teeth.

Hank straightened, puffing his chest. He gave Rabbit one good nod and held his knife up next to Rabbit's.

More footfalls, closer now. And murmurs, human, but not quite loud enough to understand.

Boone's black scimitar joined the others. His stern stare and slow nod reassured Rabbit that he was in the fight.

Rabbit's glance at Clementine was less reassuring. Her eyes, black as coal now, were fixed on the end of the tent, her twin blades held to her sides and pointed forward. Could she see through the canvas? Or just sense the creatures on the other side?

They were all hunched but standing now. Somehow Clementine looked bigger than all of them, more menacing. On second thought, her presence and appearance was definitely reassuring.

A shadow grew and fell away across the canvas.

Then another.

The voices were hushed, the footfalls faint.

Why didn't Clementine attack?

The silence now was worse than any of the noises before. Rabbit thought he could hear Boone's and Hank's hearts booming in their chests. His own was slamming against his ribcage. *It's intolerable!* It was all he could do to keep from lunging through the canvas and having at the first thing he came across.

Swoosh thunk!

The canvas shook and sagged along one side.

"They're cutting the ropes," Boone hissed.

Thunk! ... Thunk! Two more ropes cut. The tent poles pitched toward each other under the weight of the canvas. It began to collapse in on the four of them, billowing gracefully toward the ground.

"Drop your packs!" Clementine's swords began flashing, spinning in a complex series of circles and arcs, shredding canvas. Long strings and bits of canvas flew.

"Cut the canvas!" Boone's sword was at work now, too, slicing through the material like hot metal through tallow.

A long slender blade sank through the canvas, narrowly missing

Rabbit's shoulder before being withdrawn.

"They have swords!" he yelled.

He joined in with his Bowie, cutting at the canvas.

Another sword sank through canvas directly above Hank's head, but Hank's Bowie, in the middle of an arcing slice, clanged against the blade, deflecting it in front of him. He pushed out with his knife, forcing the tip of the sword away, and back toward the attacker. It pierced the canvas like a knitting needle, and Rabbit heard a grunting sigh outside the tent. Blood seeped through the canvas and ran down the blade. The attacker's shadow slumped. Hank had knitted his foe to the tent with his own sword.

The canvas was in full collapse now, and it was time to get out from under it and go to work. As near as Rabbit could tell, Clementine was free and dispatching whatever was within reach, judging by the screams.

He thrust his knife through the fabric and ran it over his head, past Hank, as far as he could reach. He'd lost track of Boone but getting clear of the tent was the first step to finding him.

The canvas slipped down over his shoulders and dropped to the ground. He and Hank were standing in the middle of *caper-sus* … How many?

"Eight left, Jack!" Clementine shouted.

"Argh!"

That was Boone!

"Seven! Well done, Boone! Behind you!" Clementine's stern, strong voice bolstered Rabbit's resolve. He instinctively raised his Bowie and blocked a dagger aimed at his chest. Before he realized, his pistol was in his hand. Again.

Boom! BoomBoom!

Three more dropped.

"Damn it, Jack! No guns!"

"Sorry, Miss Cl—" The apology was drowned out by the deep, steady bray of a horn echoing off the cliffsides.

"Dritt!"

"What the hell was that?" Rabbit put his back to Hank and pointed his pistol at anyone who advanced on him.

"They're calling reinforcements. Jack, you've really done it." The heat in Clementine's voice warmed his cheeks.

A white grizzly galloped into view and skidded to a stop, knocking two *caper-sus* to the ground.

Two more beasts appeared, showing the same disregard for the *caper-sus*, and took up positions in the circle forming around them.

Clementine and Boone moved closer to Rabbit and Hank, blades pointed outward.

"Why aren't they attacking?" Boone spoke quietly, but loud enough for Rabbit to hear.

The *caper-sus* were obviously eager to finish the job, yet something was holding them back. They held their places, except one white grizzly, which paced and growled at them.

A dull, distant thrumming began building to the south. It was difficult to see over the *caper-sus* surrounding them, but it seemed to be coming from the direction of the barn.

"They called the *Draug*. Or something worse." Clementine scanned the circle around them.

"*El Vaquero*," Rabbit stated. "Good. Let's take care of that bastard right now."

"They're holding us here," Clementine said.

"For what?" Boone stood ready at Clementine's back. "If they want us to stay, we shouldn't."

The white grizzly stopped pacing and snarled at Rabbit.

"I know you. You're that bastard that bushwhacked us on the trail." Rabbit nodded at Hank. "I'd know that snout anywhere."

"Yer makin' him mad, Jack Rabbit." Hank moved closer to Rabbit, sliding around his side so that they stood back-to-back.

"Fuck him." Rabbit bared his teeth at the beast and barked. He'd been simmering in a big pot of revenge since the day they'd been attacked by the varmint.

The white grizzly howled and shot toward him.

A whooping cheer rose up from the *caper-sus* with a "Get 'im" and "Watch this" thrown in.

Rabbit wasn't ready. He lurched sideways, raising his Bowie knife, but his heels slid out from under him in the packed snow. He stumbled, trying to regain his balance, but there was no stopping it now, he was going down.

The beastie was already in the air and descending on him by the time Rabbit rolled onto his back and thrust his Bowie high, hoping the bastard would skewer itself on the sharp steel.

Hank lunged, arm extended with his knife slicing through the air in front of him, and crashed into the beast directly over Rabbit's head. The blade sank into the grizzly's shoulder, followed quickly by the bulk of Hank smashing into the handle of the knife, driving it farther into the creature. They tumbled over and away from Rabbit in a jumble of arms and hairy legs and teeth.

Squeals and cries filled the air from both Hank's victim and the *caper-sus* thugs surrounding them.

Rabbit jumped to his feet and raced toward them, knife raised. But the white grizzly had already righted itself and was shaking violently, attempting to dislodge Hank and the knife in its shoulder.

Hank flopped about like an empty potato sack in a strong breeze but held on with both hands.

"Hank, let go!" Rabbit raced toward them. *Clementine, do something!*

The beast rolled, crushing Hank beneath it.

Hoots and whoops and shouts rose up from the circle of *caper-sus*. Rabbit swiped at its throat with his knife, but a giant, white fur–covered paw smashed into his face, knocking him onto his back.

"Hank!" Rabbit noticed the leather strap of Hank's quiver was wrapped over the handle of the knife stuck in the grizzly's shoulder.

He's caught up on the knife!

The beast crouched and launched into the air, dragging Hank with it, and landed on a *caper-sus*, mashing him flat on the ground. It bolted, trampling two more *caper-sus* before disappearing between the tents while Hank still held on with both hands.

"Hank!" Rabbit leapt to his feet and started after the white grizzly, but the *caper-sus* closed the opening.

He felt warmth ooze down across his lips and onto his chin, realizing it was blood from the blow to the face he'd taken from the beast. He drew his pistol, but his watery eyes afforded him only blurry targets.

Where the fuck were Boone and Clementine?

He fired off a round, and another. Then it occurred to him, for all he knew, he might be shooting at his companions.

He whirled, looking for Boone's black scimitar or Clementine's glinting, spinning blades.

Crack! A bolt of lightning shot through his skull.

Darkness closed his vision.

Nothing.

Four

Rabbit groaned. "Uncle Mort! Stop bangin' that pan! It's makin' my head pound."

Boone's stomach fluttered. "He's waking up."

He kneeled next to Rabbit and leaned in close. He'd been unconscious for some time, and Boone's anxiety had been building every minute of it. He was well aware the longer a person was knocked out, the more likely they'd wake with something wrong with their noggin. If they woke at all.

"Rabbit."

"Uncle Mort?" Rabbit raised his hand and put his palm on his forehead. "You sound like Booney."

His words were crackly with barely enough wind behind them to make it past his lips.

"Rabbit. It *is* me. Can you open your eyes?"

"I don't want to."

"Try anyway. Slowly," Clementine said as she knelt beside Boone.

Rabbit's eyes slowly opened, but only a crack, then squeezed shut again. "No." He abruptly sat up, "Hank!" Then he groaned and fell back into the snow.

"Take it slow, *amigo*."

"Hank," Rabbit said weakly. His eyelids remained shut.

"I know." Boone glanced at Clementine. "We know."

"The white grizzly." Rabbit opened his eyes slightly and grunted his way upright.

Boone nodded. "Yeah."

"Where is he?"

Boone shook his head. "We didn't get the chance to track him down."

"Yet," Clementine added.

"Sheaaat. We gotta shuck and find him!" Rabbit pushed to standing, but began to reel.

Boone steadied him with a hand on his shoulder. "Not just yet. You can barely stand."

"Yes. 'Yet.' Right now." Rabbit jerked his pistol and began fumbling at the cartridges on his bandolero.

"*Den fordømte pistolen.*" Clementine shook her finger at Rabbit. "You brought the horde down on us with that thing."

Rabbit shook the pistol at her. "I save lives with this 'thing.' "

"It's a menace. You're a menace with it!"

"I'm a menace?" He squinted sideways at Boone. "I'm a menace?"

"She said, 'You're a menace *with* it.' "

"Same thing. Now you're on her side? Why didn't you two stop that bastard from makin' off with Hank?"

"We were busy." Boone dropped his chin.

"You gotta be shittin' me. I might be a *menace*, but leastways I was tryin' to save Hank while you two were off gazin' into each other's eyes."

"Slow down, Rabbit." Boone could feel his anger rising, but he knew Rabbit felt responsible for their predicament. That he'd failed Hank. "You need to stop flappin' your meat and listen a little."

Rabbit clenched his jaw and said through gritted teeth, "Fine. Talk."

Clementine nailed Rabbit with a glare that was about as cool as the snow under their feet.

Boone cleared the snow from a downed tree trunk and forced Rabbit to sit. "First, tell us what happened to the two of you. After the white grizzly attacked."

"Don't know much. I was cracked on the noggin, if you remember." Rabbit's furrowed brow smoothed, but Boone still measured some amount of disgruntledness in his voice.

He stared at Rabbit.

"Don't treat me like a *niñito*, Booney."

"Did it bite Hank? Claw him?"

Rabbit shook his head. "I recognized that fucker from the trail. Remember? Outside of Deadwood our first time comin' in?"

Boone remembered it. It seemed like a lifetime ago.

"It was him. I think he recognized me, too."

Boone aimed a raised eyebrow at Clementine. She didn't seem surprised. "He's carrying some grudge with him, I imagine."

"I know I am," Rabbit said.

"Then what?"

"I, uh, I mighta insulted it."

"How?"

Rabbit bared his teeth. "Barked at it."

Boone shot another look at Clementine, this time with both eyebrows raised.

She squeezed her lips together and shook her head.

Rabbit peeked up at her, his expression sheepish.

"It attacked then?" Boone asked.

"Came right at me, in the air, just like they do."

"So why didn't you handle it?"

"I uh …"

"Out with it."

"I slipped, okay? I fell right on my ass."

"Sounds like you."

"Not now, Booney."

"How's the head?"

"Thumpin' a little, but gettin' a little better already."

"Clementine's poultice."

Rabbit nodded to her. "Thank you, Miss Clementine."

"Then?" Boone pushed on.

"I was on my ass and the grizzly was pert near on top of me and in flew Hank. I'll tell you, he was flyin'. Caught it in the shoulder with his Bowie, then knocked it catawampus when he followed up with his whole self. Skewered it like a holiday roast." Rabbit slowly shook his head. "Took the vigor outta that beast just like that. Least for a little bit."

"But it didn't bite him," Boone stated.

"No. Not that I saw." Rabbit waved his hand out in front of him. "Got up and skedaddled. Hank was lassoed to the handle of his Bowie that was stuck in the fucker's shoulder. Strap on his quiver all wrapped around it somehow."

Boone took a moment. "He wasn't bit or clawed."

"He might be alive," Clementine said, articulating his thought.

"Your head good to go, *amigo*?"

"I'm a little dizzy, but I can shoot, er, uh, I can go to work with my knives." Rabbit turned to Clementine. "Miss Clementine, I am sorry about my lousy disposition. I swear, that pistol was in my hand before I even knew, but I'll do better."

Clementine sat beside him and bumped her shoulder against his. "I'm awfully worried about Hank, too. It's got me unsettled. I'll try to keep my temper in the future. We need our wits now." She paused, shrugging. "Besides, you're the deadliest I've seen with those 'lead pushers,' and I'm not entirely sure relying strictly on blades is what we need now. Maybe a combination of both will win the day."

Boone watched a smile creep onto Rabbit's face. It made him smile, too. That was exactly what Rabbit needed right now, especially coming from Clementine.

Clementine continued, "I would like to suggest something, though."

"Shoot." Rabbit chuckled. "Get it?"

"I get it. I think you believe that your strength lies in your guns."

Rabbit nodded.

"It's my opinion, that's not entirely true. Your strength is in your speed and accuracy."

Rabbit nodded again, slowly this time.

"I don't think I've ever seen anyone, human that is," she clarified, "move as quickly as you. And the way you size up a situation and act. Between that and your speed, you handle circumstances no other man could, including Boone. It has served you well and will continue to, I believe."

"I don't know why you had to bring me into it." Boone was starting to feel a little trodden upon.

Rabbit sat up straight and his smile widened. "Thank you, Miss Clementine. What you're sayin' is I need to make a good choice when to use what, far as knives and guns."

"Partly."

"Use prudence," Boone added.

"Talk about bringing names into it."

"Not that Prud—"

"I know, Booney, I know. So what happened to the two of you? Beggin' your pardon Miss Clementine, but why didn't you help Hank?"

"You didn't see, I guess," Boone said. "But once that white grizzly rushed you, all the others started in on us. We had our fill of *caper-sus* and the other two grizzlies. They both went for Clementine, like they knew she was the real prize. The *caper-sus* too, really."

Rabbit looked from Boone to Clementine and back. "Take any damage, either one of you?"

"Not a whip," Boone answered. "Like I said, they went for Clementine. You wouldn't believe her, Rabbit. I've never seen anything like it, including what we know already. It's just not human, what she did. I hardly caught a glimpse of her, let alone those two blades she's got there."

Rabbit's eyes widened as he stared at Clementine. "Amazon. Like I said."

"I got a couple turned toward me, but I don't think I helped much."

Clementine's gaze locked onto Boone's. "You helped."

Boone's head spun a little. He wasn't sure if he actually had, but maybe. "Those white grizzlies are real bastards. They work together. Like wolves, only smarter."

Rabbit shook his finger in the air. "That bastard recognized me. And when I barked, it really boiled over."

"Remembered you stuck it once before. Like you said, it held a grudge." Boone squatted beside Rabbit. "One came right at Clementine. But she had, I don't know, three or four *caper-sus* on her already. Blades were swinging this way." He twirled his hands out in front of him. "She spun around …" He stood again to properly show Rabbit what he'd seen. "Twirling swords like this." He extended his arms fully, still twirling his hands. "*Caper-sus* couldn't get close, or they'd get chopped into little *caper-sus* chunks." He lowered his arms. "That's when I started in for the one coming from behind. Didn't think she saw it, but she kicked back like this." He pushed his right leg as far as he could out behind him, teetering somewhat. "Caught the second grizzly in the jaw. Slowed him some."

Rabbit grinned. "I bet it did."

Boone stood upright and waved his hands in front of him. "Didn't even think she saw that one behind her." He stared at Clementine for a moment, still in awe. Then he returned to acting his story out. "Down on her knee as she pushed one sword up through the jaw of the one in front. Spun around on that knee," he said, tipping as he attempted the move, but caught himself before going all the way over. "Swung the other sword around like lightning and lopped the head off the one behind her, like it was never supposed to be there in the first place."

"Holy Moses!" Rabbit's jaw was slack now.

"I got too busy to watch after that."

Clementine shifted on the log, stretching one leg out. "You're better with that sword than you give yourself credit, Boone."

"Well, thank you, Clementine, but I don't know." Boone was sure he didn't help much at all. He'd been tempted to throw down with his pistol just as Rabbit had, truth be told.

"You went for the *caper-sus* I didn't have time for. You knew it without me telling you."

"That's true, I guess. I could see you were in it with those two grizzlies."

"And that's one of your strengths." Clementine smiled back and forth between them. "I'm lucky to have you both."

Boone stared at her again, his gaze probably lingering too long, but he surely enjoyed the sight of her smile. Especially after staring death in the face more than once so far today.

"So you got 'em all then?" Rabbit stood, resting his hand on Boone's shoulder while testing his balance.

"All of them that were around us, but there was a whole army, practically, coming, we could hear it. The sound of it scared the shit out of me more than anything. More grizzlies and *caper-sus* and a couple of other things Clementine didn't recognize."

"Sheaat."

"Yeah. So, we hauled you up and skedaddled."

Rabbit turned a complete circle. "Where?"

"In the woods behind the barn. Clementine found us this hideaway. Rock outcroppings over there." Boone swept his hand to the south. "Thicket of bushes and brush there. In a small basin with some downed trees. Pretty well protected."

"We'd be wise to keep watch, though," she told them. "I'm sure we were followed. This forest must be crawling with *others* and *caper-sus*."

"Right. We should be out after Hank anyway. Your head ready for that, Rabbit?" Boone searched his eyes. He didn't like what he saw. Pupils too big and a little too jittery.

"I'm good to go."

"Did you see which direction the bastard took Hank?"

Rabbit pursed his lips. "To the east, I think. Toward the pond, south of the main cluster of buildings."

"Shit. That takes us right by the barn." Boone rubbed his hat back and forth on his head to scratch an itch. "Maybe back up north through the tents and then east. It's afternoon now. We'll lose the sun pretty soon."

"Maybe better in the dark." Rabbit grabbed his hat and gingerly wiggled it onto his head. "Smarts a little."

"Jack, you're swooning." Clementine stood up from the log, her forehead lined with worry.

"From lookin' at you, handsome Amazon," Rabbit joked, then quickly sobered. "I'll straighten out, Miss Clementine. If they're tortur …" Rabbit stopped. "Hank needs rescuin'. We're the party that's gonna do it."

"Don't take this wrong, but you're a liability right now." Her worry lines deepened. "At least until you get your balance back."

"He'll be okay," Boone assured her. "Who knows if Hank has that kind of time. It's already been a while. We need to go."

Boone wasn't actually sure if Rabbit was up to it, but there would be no stopping him. He'd seen his *amigo* in worse shape and still handle business. This was Hank, after all.

But Clementine didn't move. "What is it, Clementine? You're hesitating."

She chewed her lower lip.

"I'm okay, Miss Clementine." Rabbit stood up a little straighter. "Hank's waitin'."

Still, she didn't budge, which was odd, considering how eager she'd been to push through the snow and anything else in her path earlier.

"You appear to be a woman facing a dilemma." Boone adjusted the pack strap digging into the meat of his shoulder.

"We can't go out there yet," she told them.

"We can." Boone hadn't known Clementine to turn down a fight. "What about Hank?"

"If Hank is dead, we can't help him. And if we get ourselves killed, that'd be pointless, wouldn't it?"

"We ain't gonna get killed, Miss Clementine."

"You didn't see what's out there." She pointed toward the forest, frowning at Boone. "You did. And we didn't see everything, we can be sure of that."

Boone knew better than to believe Clementine's newfound caution was a product of fear. "What is it exactly that has you spooked?"

"I'm not spooked."

"Okay, what then?"

"Listen, I'm as concerned about Hank as the two of you. But I'm also concerned about the sheer numbers of *others* we just witnessed. Fifteen or twenty is manageable. Two or three hundred is decidedly an issue. You must agree with that."

"Agreed." It *was* an overwhelming number. Of anything, let alone *others*.

"There are countless creatures searching for us in this forest," she continued making her case. "I've masked our tracks and scent from them. That should last for a while, at least until the real trackers are summoned."

Boone took this point as well. "It might be better if we wait a little longer—maybe they'll give up the hunt."

Clementine stepped closer to Rabbit, examining the back of his head. "And Jack isn't at full steam, either. We'll all need to be at our best when we make our next move."

After casting a scowl toward the trees, Rabbit nodded.

Good. Rabbit's head was clear enough to listen to reason. Judging by the look on his face, he was more interested in setting out for Hank right this very minute than sitting on his ass. Hell, Boone would like to go find their partner, too. Who knew what they were doing to Hank. Or what they'd done. He dared not let his mind wander into that particular quagmire.

"And then there's the—what was it, Jack? *El Conquistador?*"

"No. Those *hombres* were assholes. He's *El Vaquero*, The Cowboy, since he was herdin' the *Draug* around like they were cattle."

"Right. *Vaquero*. I don't know his sort. He might be the one my benefactor is concerned about."

"Your benefactor?" Boone asked. "You mean Masterson?"

"Yes. And if this *El Vaquero* is the concern, he's not one to be taken lightly. We'll need to be extra careful if an *other* of that rank is roaming around Slagton. That would mean this area is a full-fledged infestation on the level of a usurpation." She pushed a pile of snow around with her boot. "I'm not sure how to handle this."

They were silent for some time, each contemplating their next move.

Rabbit scoffed and turned away. "It's a sad day when a man can't ride out to help an *amigo*."

"We'll get him, Rabbit. He's out there, waiting for us to find him." Boone wished he believed it.

A heavy, sad silence reigned after that, and a deeper chill settled into their little dell as the sun sank behind the tall trees surrounding them. Boone's bones ached from the cold.

"First light then?" Clementine asked as darkness blanketed them.

Boone's nod mirrored Rabbit's, and they began to prepare for another night in the cold under the flickering stars without their friend.

Boone knew that none of them would sleep much through the long stretch of darkness ahead of them, made especially intolerable in the absence of a fire. "I'll take the first watch."

What seemed like a month of nighttimes later, Boone watched as the first glow of morning began pushing the bleak, frozen darkness across the sky.

He'd taken two watches. Clementine had taken two as well, both agreeing Rabbit needed as much rest as he could manage. The elixir Clementine had concocted worked reasonably well, considering the circumstances.

By the time the sun was making a proper appearance, they were packed and ready to head out. Rabbit deemed himself fit and fine, and ready to find a Varney. Clementine concurred. Boone, too, although a warm bed in front of a crackling fire sounded mighty appealing, along with some fresh, warm biscuits. Better yet, a steak.

They had decided to head some way north, then east in the direction Rabbit had seen the white grizzly disappear with Hank leashed to its side. They'd begin the search, tent by tent, and tree by rock by river.

"You need to ride on my back, Rabbit?" Boone joked, but he would have done it had his *amigo* needed it.

"Sure, but you need saddle train—"

"Hush!" Clementine held out her palm, then pointed into the forest. "There's something out there."

They dropped to their knees and waited, watching.

A shadowy figure moved under the trees, roughly the shape of a man. Boone couldn't make out features, but it was clear that whoever it was—or whatever it was—was coming straight toward them.

"I guess they know we're here now," he whispered.

He heard the *whiz-click* of Rabbit's pistol and grabbed his sword.

Five

W ho's this now?"
Rabbit felt his skin prickle. "Uncle Mort." He turned to see his
uncle's ghost hovering behind him, decked in his normal winter
duds, a sheepskin-lined leather duster and heavy wool pants. "Nice you
could grace us with an appearance."

Boone shook his head. "Not now, Rabbit," he whispered.

Clementine glanced at Rabbit. Her gaze drifted behind him for a
second, then back to the approaching stranger.

Rabbit would give his left nut if it meant Boone could see their dead
uncle. He was damned tired of being the only one who could chatter
with the old codger. Or was it that the old codger wouldn't chatter at
anyone else? Either way, it was downright irritating. And that Boone
refused to accept the fact their uncle was back from the dead made it
even more irritating. At least Clementine and Hank believed him, even
if they couldn't see or hear him.

Uncle Mort floated in front of Rabbit. "Still coming. You best have
your weapons ready, boy. Might be nothing, better to be ready, though."

"I can't see through you, move over." Rabbit leaned to the side to
see around the wavy, partially transparent apparition.

Boone backhanded his shoulder. "Pay attention."

The figure was closer now, but still in the shadows. Rabbit could
almost make out a nose and eyes. His heart fluttered in his chest. If he
fired his pistol, who knew what kind of creatures that would call down
on them. He holstered his pistol and reached for one of his knives. If he
could just see …

Clementine stood, a smile spreading across her face. "It's Hank."

A man stepped out from under the trees.

It was indeed!

Rabbit and Boone ran the few steps to their companion.

"You son of a polecat!" Rabbit grinned, grabbed Hank by the shoulders, and shook him hard.

"You look like you've been dragged through a muddy slush puddle and hung out to dry in a blizzard." Boone slapped Hank's back. "At least you're alive."

"Near as I can tell. Surely is a satisfaction to my eyes to see you fellers."

"Not hurt?" Rabbit stepped back. He held back the urge to jump in the air and whoop like a rodeo cowboy. Instead, he shook his finger at Hank. "Out all night. You've got some explaining to do, mister."

Chuckling, Hank hustled to Clementine and wrapped his arms around her. "Miss Clem, for a while there I thought I weren't gonna see you again. It was a sorry thought."

"A sorry thought, indeed." Clementine hugged him back. "Glad to see you and that bow are still in one piece."

She led Hank to a nearby log, sitting next to him while Rabbit and Boone surrounded them.

"No hug for the uncle, I guess." Uncle Mort put his hands on his hips.

"Quiet, Uncle Mort," Rabbit said, turning to Hank. "How are you alive? Did you kill the white grizzly? Where did it take you? Did you see *El Vaquero*?" Rabbit couldn't help but want to know everything at once.

"Let him talk." Boone waved Rabbit off. "Tell us, Hank. What happened? We thought you were dead, but I can't see a scratch on you."

Hank breathed deep. "I ain't dead. How much you tell 'em, Jack Rabbit?"

"Everything up to that bastard grizzly draggin' you away."

"Yep, well, stuck him good, but somehow my ding-dang quiver got wrapped around the handle of my knife. You prob'ly saw that part. Don't know how that happened. Call me Mr. Luck, I guess."

"I don't know if I'd count that as luck." Rabbit sat down next to Hank, handing him a hunk of jerky.

" 'Spect ain't luck after all. You prob'ly saw too, I was a floppy rag stuck on that critter. Hoo hoo, squashed a *capers-man* on the way outta town!" He bumped Rabbit's shoulder. "I'll take that as a plus one on my *capersy* count." Apparently Hank had adopted Rabbit and Boone's game of keeping count of the adversaries he'd defeated.

A burst of laughter erupted from Rabbit. The good cheer of Hank's return warming him in spite of the brisk air. "Okay. Fair enough."

"That critter dragged me around one tent then through another …" Hank pursed his lips. "It's in my mind we went through a tent, anyway. My eyeballs was shook around a fair bit, makes for fuzzy recollectin'. Not sure what I seen and couldn't."

Rabbit wasn't entirely sure he was following Hank's tale, but it didn't matter. It didn't appear to matter to Boone either. "Fuzzy like your scruffy chin," Rabbit said.

"Aw, Jack Rabbit." Hank smiled at each of them. "Surely am glad to see you three." His face went blank for a moment. "Thought I was dead."

Clementine squeezed his shoulder. " 'Bravely and gladly a man shall go, till the day of his death is come.' " She glanced at Boone. "That's from *Hávamál*, an Old Norse poem. Not quite as witty as your Samuel Clemens, though."

Hank tore off a bite of jerky with his teeth. "Don't rightly know which direction we was headed, I was gettin' banged up the whole way." He rubbed his hip. "Through a campfire."

That explained the sooty black streak up his side.

"Lucky me it was dead out. Anyhow, I got to thinkin' this critter is taken me somewheres or he's gone plumb crazy, 'cause he weren't stoppin'. Either way, I prob'ly ain't gonna be happy about where he stops."

Clementine nodded while frowning. Rabbit felt the same as her about Hank's story so far.

"Well, I got to thinkin', I gotta stop this runaway train or get my car disconnected from the engine somehow. So I start pullin' on the knife. Weren't easy, bouncin' this way and that. Knockin' my noggin on its jaw ever' now and then." He gingerly touched his head and then felt around up top. "Tarnation. Lost my hat."

Rabbit shook his head. Hank was fortunate he hadn't lost more than just his hat.

"So there I was, one hand, no hands, one hand, no hands, on that knife, wigglin' it when I could. Hands slick with blood. Musta been stuck in the bone, 'cause it weren't comin' out. Hurt somethin' awful I gather, 'cause the critter starts in wailin' like a woman poppin' a baby … Beggin'

your pardon, Miss Clem."

"Stuck into the bone, no doubt." Uncle Mort stood in front of them. "I went hunting once, got my tallywhacker stuck in a—"

"That's enough, Uncle Mort." Rabbit sent a glare at his uncle, who folded his arms and pinched his lips together.

When he focused back on Hank and Clementine, he saw the corner of Clementine's mouth curl up, along with one eyebrow. "It's fine, Hank," she said. "Keep going."

"I wiggled it," Hank continued. "I pulled on the quiver strap. I never been so stuck in my life."

"Isn't that the damnedest." Boone scratched his chin absently. "Couldn't extract that knife. Huh."

"Nope."

"I would've thought you could unwrap that strap from the handle of the knife." Rabbit noticed a line of dark stains up the sleeves of Hank's red coat, but they looked to be washed mostly away.

Hank aimed a finger at Rabbit. "I'da thought that too. Anyway, 'bout this time I'd had my fill of gallivantin' and decided I'd swing m'self over the critter's shoulder and take the weight off that strap, then I could pull it free. I got my feet lined up, bounced once on the ground, kinda like you see those fancy trick riders do on horses. Did that and rolled up over its shoulders." His hands were fully involved in telling the story now, just like Boone's had been last night. "So there I was, ridin' the critter backward like and all of the sudden *CRASH*! Dumb beast ran smack-dab into a tree."

Boone's and Clementine's eyes were big, probably the same as Rabbit's.

"No how!" Rabbit slapped his knee in disbelief.

"How! And that ain't all. My caboose slid up its neck and clobbered that very same tree." Hank shifted on his seat, grimacing. "Good thing I got my best paddin' back there. So, that knocked the bugger out. I slid the quiver free."

"That killed it?" Clementine asked.

"Nope. Almost. Had to push with my foot, and pull and wiggle with both hands, but I brung that knife free."

"Took the head then?" Boone winced.

Hank nodded. "Weren't pretty. Never is. You all are aware, ain't my favorite part of my job."

"Why'd it run into the tree? Was it loco?" Rabbit asked.

"Maybe. But I think it was more somethin' else. Near as I can tell, when I rolled up on it, my lucky coat got wrapped around its whole head. Covered up his peepers. Hoo! Couldn't a done that if I tried."

"It's official, Mr. Varney, you are a lucky man." Clementine punched his arm. "I guess we need to update our plans. The Hank Varney rescue venture is canceled."

"Wait." Rabbit raised his hand. "How'd you get back here? How'd you find us?"

"And why did it take all night?" Boone added. "How were you not seen?"

Hank grinned wide. "You thought that white grizzly ride was the interestin' part, wait till you hear this."

"Anyone worried about the horses?" Uncle Mort asked, pretending to sit on the end of the log next to Rabbit.

"Not now, Uncle Mort," Rabbit said without looking in his uncle's direction.

"Ho there, Uncle Mort! Good to see ya … hear … well, glad you're here. You been listenin' to my story?"

"Go ahead, Hank," Rabbit urged. This was better than any dime novel about pirates he'd ever read.

Hank paused. "I met a fellow."

"What?" Out here? Just meandering around the backside of Hades? He had to be kidding.

"I said," Uncle Mort answered, "someone should tend the horses."

"Not you, Uncle Mort! Hank, what'd you say?"

"Heard me right. I met a man. Maybe a man. Turns out, my big ride, somebody was watchin'. Hidin' somewhere's nearby."

"Tell us," Clementine said. Rabbit could hear the misgiving in her voice.

"He scurried on over quick," Hank explained. "Collected me up. Made it known we needed to skedaddle before any rough types show'd up. Pointed at the barn and made a face. Somethin' about him, I just trusted and went along. He took me to a cave in the cliff, opposite side of the valley over there." Hank thumbed to the east. "Comfy, for a cave anyways. Warm enough. Food."

Rabbit turned to Boone, mirroring his slack-jawed expression.

Clementine just looked plain bewildered. "Hank …"

"I know, Miss Clem, don't trust nobody. But he's different. I think he can help us. And he needs our help, too."

"Who is he?" Boone's brow was furrowed now.

"Near as I can tell, he's a lookout for Slagton. This whole area, maybe."

"Near as you can tell? What does that mean?" Clementine asked.

"He don't speak. Grunts some, makes a funny moanin' sound but can't talk. I think he had his throat cut but he lived through it. Got a mean-lookin' scar from here to here." Hank ran his finger from under one ear to the other. "I think something in that barn did it, but I ain't sure about that part."

"You're shittin' me. Hank, if you don't beat all." Rabbit laughed. "Leave it to you to find a pal in Slagton."

"Hoo hoo! Yep. That'd be me."

"And you think he can be trusted?" Clementine still had a healthy dose of misgiving in her voice.

"I'm sure of it, Miss Clem. He don't like those critters in the barn, or anyone in Slagton for that matter."

"Can you get us to him without being seen? Can he help us get in that barn?" Clementine pressed.

"I can get you to him. No tellin' if'n he'll get us to the barn. He don't like it, that much is for certain."

"Isn't this a bag of nails." Boone turned to Clementine. "Do we trust this stranger?"

"It's a fact he knows how to avoid the critters in this valley," Hank insisted. "He tried harder than me to stay outta sight. More'n that, I get a feelin' in my gut, Miss Clem, we can trust him and we need him." He nodded once to put an exclamation point on it.

"Okay, Hank." Clementine didn't sound convinced.

Rabbit wasn't either, and he was sure Boone wanted to go read his fresh copy of *Tom Sawyer* by a warm fire. "Tough luck, Booney."

"What?"

"Got time for the horses now?" Uncle Mort cut in, hovering next to Boone. "They were fidgetin' like you when you fell asleep near that ant hill. Remember that?"

Rabbit did remember. "Learned a lesson that day, didn't I?" He chuckled. "When'd you last see the horses, Uncle Mort?"

Boone shook his head. "Rabbit's lost his mind."

"I don't know."

Rabbit rolled his eyes all the way from one side to the other. "Don't know, he says."

"Don't you roll your eyes at me, boy." Uncle Mort floated right up face to face with him. "Time doesn't have purpose for me now. Not easy to keep track and no real urge to try."

"It'd be helpful to those of us on our side if you could try."

"Rabbit."

Rabbit ignored Boone. He stood. "Besides," he said, dusting off his backside, "Hank gave 'em oats enough for at least three days."

"I did that," Hank confirmed, standing as well. "Uncle Mort got a concern, does he?"

"They ate through those," Uncle Mort said.

"Now how did you know that?"

"I've been keeping an eye. Nobody else was." Uncle Mort harrumphed. "I carry more concern for those horses than you, apparently."

"Uncle Mort," Rabbit growled between gritted teeth.

"Rabbit!" Boone called.

"Huh? Oh. What is it, Booney?"

"Can we go?"

"Uncle Mort's expressin' concerns about the horses. Bein' truthful, I'm carrying concern too. Those white grizzlies crawling everywhere."

"They'll have to wait." Clementine gathered her pack. "Let's get moving, Hank. Don't fret, Jack. Fenrir will look after Dime and the others."

That notion did help Rabbit feel better. The immense black Morgan was more animal than most could handle.

Boone shouldered his pack and fell in behind Clementine and Hank. "We'll get to this cave, Rabbit, then a couple of us can strike out and gather the horses. We need the supplies they're carrying anyway." Boone looked straight up. "That suit you, Uncle Mort?"

"Should do," Uncle Mort answered as if Boone could hear him. "I'll head back to keep the rascals out of trouble."

Rabbit watched as Uncle Mort float-walked into the forest. "He's not up there, Booney. He said that'll do." Rabbit lined up behind Boone, adjusting his heavy pack so that his shoulders carried equal weight, and they were off. "You didn't tell us how you found us, Hank."

Boone looked back over his shoulder, probably making sure Rabbit was coming. "We watched Clementine cover our tracks once we reached the forest. Pretty thorough job, I'd say."

Hank stopped and turned. "Miss Clem, she does a baker's job of cookin' in the kitchen when she covers tracks."

Rabbit shot a raised eyebrow at Boone. He figured that was a good thing.

"Ain't probl'y not a soul could track her, 'ceptin' me. Beggin' your pardon, Miss Clem, but I known you long enough now." Hank swished his hands to the right, then around in circles. "She leaves tracks, in a real Miss Clem way. Leaves a pattern to see. Leastways I can see it."

"Hank!" Clementine animatedly dropped her lower jaw and put her fists on her hips, feigning indignation.

"Sorry, Miss Clem," Hank said sheepishly. "Doubt no one else couldn't see it. Just looks like blowed snow lessen you know what to look for."

She laughed. "Don't you feel bad, you ol' bloodhound. I'm actually glad I can count on you to find me if I'm in trouble."

"Surely can, Miss Clem." He turned and continued to pick his way through the forest. "We'll head back same way I came. All the business seems south near the barn now, since we riled them buggers yesterday. We better put a candle to it. Looks like bad weather's on our tails."

Hank's strong sense of direction and Clementine's adeptness at finding cover had them across the valley and fording the stream that meandered near the foot of the eastern cliff without mishap or unwanted attention. Rabbit wasn't at all fond of crossing water that would freeze up solid if it sat still for a minute, but he'd be damned if he'd complain about it if Boone could take it without squawking.

The sky darkened considerably with thick gray clouds as they trudged along. The wind had a bite to it now. Hank was right, a storm was on their tails.

They stood for a moment, shoulders hunched against the cold, watching Hank scrunch his lips while he studied the cliffside.

"Right along … let's see." He followed the top of the ridge to the south with a finger. "Right along … there." Hank pointed, then quickly put his hand down and glanced at the barn, which was mostly obscured by landscape and trees. "No sense sendin' signals to those what might be watchin'."

"That *arroyo?*" Rabbit studied the sharp-walled valley perpendicular to the main valley. They were too far north to see any appreciable distance into it.

"Yep." Hank nodded. "I'd call it a gulch. A cut. Ravine maybe."

"Your friend's cave is in there?" Clementine asked.

"Yessum."

"Is it a dead end?"

"It may be, Miss Clem, but looked to me it just might have a way through to the east, if'n we need it. Ain't sure though."

They started up again. Hank led them along a meandering arc in the general direction of the ravine, no doubt to confound anyone, or any *thing*, that might be hunting them. Boulder to scrub to tree they slipped, staying out of the open as much as possible, until they stood at the mouth of the ravine.

"You were right, Clementine. It looks like only one way out." Boone squinted as he scanned up its length.

"Like *Arroyo Palada* back on the ranch."

"That a thing, Jack Rabbit?" Hank asked.

Rabbit nodded. "It's a dead-end canyon we would use to corral strays. Longhorns, pigs, horses."

"Don't forget chickens," Boone added.

"Damn porch perchers. Just when you think you got 'em, they'd go that way." Rabbit stuck his left arm out. "Happy to eat 'em on Sundays."

The mouth of the gully in front of them was, by Rabbit's estimation, about fifty yards wide. The rough rock walls grew closer and closer as it wiggled back away from the cliff edge. Mostly too steep to climb or hold snow or ice, the walls reached a hundred and fifty or so feet into the air, as did the cliff all along this part of the valley. The narrowing floor ascended up and away into the cliff, reaching the level of the plateau above them some two hundred yards away.

Rabbit could hear a small stream tumbling through rocks under the snow somewhere near the center of the *arroyo*. The abundance of boulders, rocks, and sharp outcroppings, as well as the steepness of the walls, left him with the impression that only deer and coyotes could scale the sides.

"You're right, Booney. It looks like a trap. Anything catches us unawares, we're stuck like fritters in molasses."

"It's up that cliff there." Hank jutted his chin at the southern bank.

"Tucked away ... can't see ... where was it now." He continued tracing the outcroppings. "There it is. That right there. Hidin' behind that rock."

Rabbit saw the outcropping but no sign of a cave entrance. "Don't see it."

"Me neither," Boone agreed.

"Gotta get closer. It's hid real good."

"Are you certain about this, Hank?" Clementine obviously wasn't.

"Yessum."

They clambered up at a diagonal, being that it was too steep for a straight vertical climb. Up and up, over rocks and small scrags, until a faint trail began to reveal itself.

"Here. I knowed it. Right here." Hank grinned with satisfaction.

They stood before a sheer rock face with an opening large enough to fit two abreast and upright. Tuffs of tangly, scrubby brush billowed from each side of the opening, not quite obscuring it.

"Good spot." Clementine squinted into the darkness of the cave. "I couldn't see this at all from below."

"I oughta go first, maybe." Hank stepped up to the entrance and pushed aside the brush. "Ho there. Inside! It's me, Hank."

Rabbit muffled a chuckle with his hand and leaned toward Boone. "Like he's here to play cards," he whispered.

Boone grinned back. "Sunday visit."

A long slender arm with a massive human-looking hand suddenly appeared and seized Hank's arm. He was gone, yanked inside the cave in less than a breath.

Rabbit had already jerked Boss from its holster and started toward the cave by the time his thoughts caught up with him.

Clementine, who had been behind him, was somehow now in front with both of her short blades held ready to strike. "Hank!" She rushed toward the cave. "Hank!"

"MissClemdontkillim!" Hank's strained voice came from just inside. "I think he's worried we'll give up his hideout."

Clementine took another step closer. Rabbit was right behind her. A glance at Boone confirmed what Rabbit already knew. He'd taken up a position to the side, pistol drawn. Boone always had him covered.

"Hank?" Clementine motioned with a sword for Rabbit and Boone to follow and disappeared into the dark opening.

A short unlit tunnel led to a cavern somewhat smaller but very much like the one in the Bloody Bones mine where they'd battled the sharp-clawed *Bahkauv*. A small, tended fire in the back corner lit the stalactites hanging from the ceiling, lending them the appearance of drippy, glowing chandeliers. Stalagmites thrust up from the ground, some meeting with the stalactites from the ceiling to form columns. Angular rocks lay strewn across the entire cave, some as tall as and much bigger around than a man. The Bloody Bones had shone with a crystal brilliance that dazzled the eye. Here a dreary palette of grays and tans seemed to soak up the light from the fire, leaving a bleak, shadowed tomb. The smoke from the fire was almost enough to persuade a cough.

"Least there ain't no *Bahkauv*," Rabbit whispered to Boone.

Hank appeared from the shadows, holding both palms up toward his companions. "Ain't no critters. Don't kill nothin' in here. Leastways right now. Come over here."

He led them to the fire, where a figure sat hunched, poking at it with a stick, its back to them.

"This is our new …" Hank paused. "I don't know whatch'd call him. Friend maybe. *Amigo*, if'n you're a Sidewinder."

Hank's friend rose and faced them in the dim firelight. Rabbit took a step back. "He's a foot taller than you, Booney." That would put this *amigo* at over seven feet. But skinny as a train rail. Hell, he probably outweighed the man by half as much again.

Rabbit took a closer look north of the square shoulders at a too-large head that reminded him of a fresh-cut block of ice. The angular chin, jaw, and forehead looked to have been chiseled from the stony cliffs surrounding them. Below the stranger's neck, unusually long, spindly arms and legs connected to his slender torso.

Even though Hank's rescuer was plainly dressed in rope-cinched canvas pants and a too-short-in-the-sleeves wool coat, Rabbit had a suspicion this was no plain *hombre*. Nope. If his height was somewhat irregular and his lankiness even more so, those hands were downright improper. The fingers were barely distinguishable from the rest of the hand in this feeble light—or maybe he didn't have fingers, just huge, meaty fists that equaled the size of a man's head.

"Hello," Boone greeted the cave dweller with an outstretched hand.

Clementine didn't move except to sniff the air and narrow her gaze. The stranger drew back.

"Shaking hands is a human convention," Clementine said in a wary voice. "Not all *others* are accepting of it, or are even aware of what it means. It might be interpreted as a challenge or aggressive. Try this instead." She dropped her chin to her chest for a moment, looking down, and then raised it again and met the stranger's eyes.

"That's customary? Noddin'?" Rabbit had seen plenty of nods throughout his travels. Were some of those folks *others*?

"Yes. You are displaying that you are willing to take your eyes off your counterpart, while at the same time offering up a weak position by showing the back of your neck. It's a sign of trust."

"I don't like it." Rabbit had no reason to trust someone until they earned it.

"It's like shaking hands, then?" Boone turned toward their new partner and dropped his chin to his chest. "Oh, I see." He raised his chin. "Right hand, because most people are right-handed. Weapons are usually carried in your favored hand. It's to show you aren't carrying weapons and you come in peace."

"Exactly," Clementine confirmed.

The stranger dropped his chin for a moment, returning the greeting.

"Well, I can shoot with both hands, so there's that." Rabbit dipped his chin anyway. There was no sense in riling anybody. "Howdy, pard."

The *other* grunted and shifted from one foot to the other.

"I'm thinkin' that fancy steppin' means 'Hello.'" Hank grinned. "He did that to me, too, last time."

"How do you figure that, Hank?" Rabbit asked.

"Context, mostly."

"Context." Rabbit chuckled. "Couldn't get his name, though?"

"Anders." Hank pointed at the stranger.

The stranger groaned and murmured a raspy string of almost words. Rabbit snickered. "Sounds like he said no."

"See? Context," Hank said.

"Sounded like gibberish," Boone chimed in.

"Boone is right." Clementine finished out the round of opinions. "He probably speaks a different language anyway."

Rabbit took a step closer. The thick scar on the stranger's scrawny neck ran under the entire length of his jawbone, which was oddly squarish enough to keep Rabbit staring longer than he knew he should. All other features—nose, ears, and eyes—were flattened against the block of his head. "That's a bad scar. Don't think I'da lived through that one."

The stranger rasped out a few more garbled, non-words.

"Said a healer saved him." Hank came closer.

"I know," Rabbit said. Huh? How did he know? There was something odd about this fellow aside from his physique.

"What are you two on about? It's gibberish." Boone seemed perplexed.

"It is for me, too." Clementine joined Rabbit.

Hank stuck his finger in the air. "Nikolai."

More raspy mumbles.

"I think he's sayin' his name, but I'm not gettin' it." Rabbit took off his hat, roughed up his hair, then replaced the hat.

"Me neither, Jack Rabbit."

Rabbit glanced at Clementine, finding her frowning at the ground, looking lost in thought. "Miss Clementine, you're wearin' the look of disquiet. Somethin' eatin' at you?"

"Well …" She paused long enough that Rabbit almost asked her again. "I think I might know what this is. Boone, you don't understand anything he's saying, is that right?"

"Nonsense," Boone replied.

"That mean you do understand him, Booney?"

"No, when I say 'Nonsense,' I mean he's babbling."

"I understand him. Hank understands him."

"Clementine doesn't. And I don't."

The stranger moved slowly around Boone, studying him, making him shuffle with discomfort.

"My amma taught me many things," Clementine said. "She had shelves of old dusty books and through the years I studied from almost every one of them. There were books about all sorts of things. Things that could be used to heal and things used for killing, and just about everything in between. Herbs. Plants. Animals."

From what Rabbit had learned over the short time he'd known Clementine, her grandmother had been a hard-driving teacher, much like Uncle Mort. He imagined little Clementine was much better at focusing on reading and writing than he had been. There'd been a creek nearby filled with fish distracting him to no end most school days.

"And there were other books, too," Clementine continued. "Books that were strange to me then, but not so much now. They had stories about *others*, both creature and human-like, friendly and not so friendly."

The stranger's focus moved on from Boone to study Rabbit.

Rabbit started to smile but then stopped and froze. There was no telling what might offend this character.

"Jack can understand our new friend, so can Hank." Clementine repeated the facts, as if making a list in her head. "Boone and I can't."

"Talkin' to Booney's like talkin' to a bullfrog, croakin' all the time." Rabbit sniggered.

"Keep it up, and your tombstone'll say, 'Here Lies Jack Fields, Good for Nothing but the Onions He Peeled.'" Boone smirked at him.

"That don't even rhyme, brushtail."

Clementine ignored them, and continued. "Most people are born with innate abilities. Some people live their entire lives without even knowing it. I think Jack's ability to understand this *other* has something to do with being able to see and hear his uncle."

"Not this again." Boone folded his arms.

"Hush, Boone," Clementine scolded. "Who knows what other abilities Jack has or how he can use them. He needs *der Lehrer*."

"What I need is a whiskey and a blanket." Rabbit figured he'd be happy with only that.

"*Der Lehrer*. A teacher, to help him develop his abilities. He may be capable of powerful manipulations, but he must learn how."

Rabbit's mind raced. He liked the sound of being powerful. He could, after all, see and talk to a ghost. "First thing? Make Booney bray like a donkey."

"Hoo hoo. Aw, Jack Rabbit. You'd do no such thing."

"Rabbit, I'm gonna lop your ears." Boone backhanded him in the stomach. "What about Hank?"

Clementine turned to Hank. Her head tipped and she smiled. "I don't know. I've never met a … man who can do the things he does." She patted his shoulder.

"Me'n Hank are special." Rabbit straightened up and put his thumbs under his armpits.

"Hank's not 'mean,'" Boone teased, his eyes glinting.

"What I'm getting at," Clementine interrupted, "is that we are beginning to see your abilities. Boone hasn't been put in a situation where he's had the opportunity to use his, if he has those talents."

Dang. Maybe Boone didn't have any. Maybe he would never see

Uncle Mort. The thought tore at Rabbit's heart. "Booney—"

Hank broke in with, "You was sayin', Miss Clem, about your amma and her books."

"Right. One of the books on *others* discussed some of the abilities I might come across as a *Scharfrichter*." She smiled. "That's a name my amma didn't use for me then, but one that I am growing to like more and more."

Rabbit was familiar with that name. It meant hunter. Or was it executioner? In any case, it meant she was an official stone-cold killer.

Clementine turned to Rabbit. "You should remember, I told you we might meet with an *other* that is capable of controlling your mind, at least to some extent."

Nope. Rabbit hadn't remembered.

"Right," Boone said.

"I think our *amigo* here is one of those. Fortunately, Hank was right. I don't sense he means us any harm."

"How do you know he doesn't mean any harm?" Rabbit didn't like the idea of *anyone* poking around in his thoughts, let alone an *other*.

"I think he would have controlled you and Hank otherwise, possibly turned you against Boone and me."

"Hey now, there's a question." Boone pointed at Clementine. "He can't get in your head?"

"I'm a *Scharfrichter*. It's impossible." She frowned slightly. "At least I think it's impossible. It hasn't happened yet, anyway."

"Oh. But why is …" Boone stopped, as if trying to decide if he wanted to know the answer to his unfinished question.

"It's part of my natural defense, I guess," she answered anyway.

The tall stranger finished studying Rabbit, slapped his back with his massive hand, and moved on to Clementine. Rabbit coughed, feeling like he'd been clobbered with a sledgehammer.

"He likes you, Jack Rabbit," Hank said.

Rabbit knew that, too. Goldurnit. It was ding dang strange.

The stranger quickly finished his study of Clementine and went to crouch by the fire again.

"What should we call him? He needs a name." Boone scratched absently at his chin. "*Amigo?*"

"What? *Amigo?*" Rabbit shook his head. "Gotta be different for a guy like that. Besides, we don't know he's a friend yet. How about Horace.

Horace the Horrible." Rabbit laughed. Horrible Horace. Sounded like one of those bare-fisted boxers he'd heard about back east.

Boone shrugged. "Good as any. At any rate, it's time to lay some plans. We need to help Horace and then he helps us, right, Hank?"

"Sums it up, Boonedog."

Clementine growled softly. "If it gets us to that barn, then let's find out what he needs."

Six

*C*lementine paced a circular path through the rocks and stalagmites in the cave. She tugged at her collar. The itch to keep moving—to hunt and slay—had the back of her neck tingling again. It was the same itch that had spurred her into action since she was young. Both welcome and annoying, often at the same time, it elevated her energy and mood, but it also made her restless.

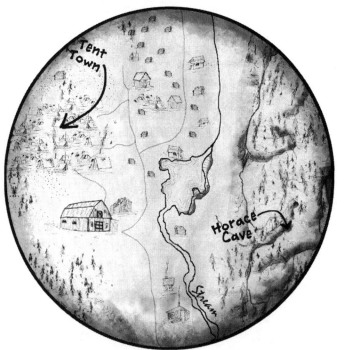

She shot a frown at Hank's new friend over by the small fire. Surprisingly, he was a chatterbox, something Hank had neglected to tell them. Grunting, groaning, sighing, rasping out vague wisps of words foreign to her, and even throwing in a whistle here and there. Horace's hand and facial gestures were so animated, Clementine could almost follow along with what he was telling Hank and Rabbit, who sat across the embers from him.

The two men had spent a number of minutes doing their best to interpret Horace's ramblings and relaying them to her and Boone, yet still hadn't come to the subject of his need for help. Luckily, Horace had offered a pot full of tea that was passably good. That, a cold biscuit, and a piece of jerky from her pack, and her rumbling stomach had been quieted.

Boone sat back against a boulder, watching her circle with mild amusement playing at the corners of his eyes. She stopped in front of him, crossing her arms. "Isn't this getting to you? We have less than three hours of daylight left. We should be out there doing something—anything. Not just sitting here."

"I don't think we're going anywhere today." Boone sat up, his gaze brightening as it traveled from one side of the cave to the other. "We should go get the horses. This cave is plenty big enough, and Horace has oats and hay stocked over in the corner."

No! She had to get to the barn. She had to cleanse Slagton. Masterson had made that clear at their last meeting. After that, perhaps he would calm down and stop issuing threats, give her some room to breathe so she could figure out how to put a stop to the corruption spreading throughout the Black Hills. It was a safe wager that the key to finishing her work in this godforsaken place had everything to do with what was inside that *verdammt* barn.

Boone stared up at her with one raised brow. "I know that look, Clementine."

"Wir verschwenden Zeit, verdammt!" she growled.

He smiled. "I only recognize one of those words, but I can take a guess at the rest." He stood and brushed off his pants. "Think about it. We don't have enough daylight left to get to that barn. We don't have any plan for when we get there, and Horace is still grunting and croaking without clearly indicating what he needs."

Clementine glanced toward the cave opening. Actually, sneaking to the barn in the night might be easier for them. Except for the white grizzlies patrolling the area. She had a feeling those creatures could hunt well at night, especially with their keen sense of smell. And who knew what else might be waiting out there? She turned back to Boone. "What, then? Am I to sit and wait by the fire?" She scoffed. "And here I am with no needlework to pass the time."

His smile widened. "We have just enough daylight to get to the horses and start back. Then we can go through the tricky part in the dark."

"What's the tricky part?"

"The horses. We need to cross the valley in the dark. The horses are too big to risk moving across in the light."

"Holy shit, Booney," Rabbit said, looking their way over his shoulder. "You ain't gonna believe this."

Boone ignored him, his focus holding on Clementine. "Hour and a half over and up the cliff where we came down. About the same coming back. The sun will be down about the time we hit the valley floor on the return. I'm concerned about our mounts. Rabbit and Hank are too. And apparently Uncle Mort. Are you?"

"Of course." The logic behind his plan was sound, damn it. While her need to strike out for the barn and slay the vermin undoubtedly holing up in there had her fingers tingling, she was worried about Fenrir, too.

"Plus, all the weapons and supplies are in their packs." Boone kept working her. "We leave now, there'll be just enough light for the horses to navigate that landslide we came down. Get to the valley floor, sun's down, we can hustle back here. You like working at night anyway."

Clementine did prefer reconnoitering at night when it was easier to stay hidden. And she did want the weapons in Fenrir's packs. She huffed. "Fine! I'll wait even longer to complete the task I came here to do."

Hank, Rabbit, and Horace all looked her way.

"You two," she said, eyeing Hank and then Rabbit. "Keep listening to Horace and find out what we need to do for him." She grabbed Boone by the arm. "Come on. Get your backside moving. We've got horses to fetch."

By the time Clementine and Boone returned to the cave with the horses and Hank's mule, Fred, the sun had long since set. The twinkling stars did little to illuminate their path back to the cave. The sliver of moon didn't help either, except to create beautiful gleaming crystals across the thick blanket of snow beneath their feet.

They had arrived to find that the horses had pulled their lead lines free by untying the quick release knots Hank always used to secure them. If ever the horses had a need to run, a firm tug on the rope and they'd be free. Hank had told Clementine he liked using the special knot, even though both Nickel and Dime could untie most with their lips and teeth, and Fenrir could and would simply bite through the rope. However, while the horses had been roaming free, poor Fred the Mule stood hitched yet with his head low, facing the horses in the distance. Clementine had to chuckle at his obvious despondence over being left behind.

The horses hadn't wandered far, probably searching for food after eating the oat bags empty. They were sticking together, and at least somewhat near Fred, which was comforting to Clementine. Strength in numbers.

The Sidewinder's dead uncle, Morton, was there, too. She'd suspected he would be, since she had been eavesdropping while Jack talked to him earlier.

When Boone and she had first approached, she'd seen Morton dancing back and forth, waving his arms at the horses, attempting to herd them toward Fred.

Jack had been right about Morton being genuinely concerned about the horses. In fact, he'd spent several long-winded minutes chastising Clementine for taking so long to come for them.

She hadn't argued with him. He was correct. They were engaged in dangerous business, and the forest around Slagton was a perilous place for a horse or mule, day or night.

She found it curious, though, that Morton hadn't let on to Jack that she could see and hear him as well—an ability she'd realized on Christmas morning when Morton first appeared to her. Something must have brought about her sudden capacity to communicate with the dead, but she wasn't sure what. It was an odd thing. Quite bizarre. Maybe it had more to do with a shift in Morton's abilities rather than her own.

Clementine had heard of communion with the dead, but it had always been in a tale or fable. Even her amma and afi, who'd experienced much in their long lives, hadn't mentioned witnessing any such occurrences. If they had, it would surely have been part of her lessons.

In any case, Morton was talking to her now, too. A lot. Before Christmas, he had been directing all of his chattiness at Jack. Today, while they'd rounded up the horses and prepped for the return trip to the cave, he'd babbled so much she'd struggled to carry on a conversation with Boone. No wonder Jack was so exasperated with his uncle.

With the horses safe in the cave, Rabbit and Hank had taken the time to properly greet their mounts with head bonks and good brisk neck scrubs before unstringing their packs.

Boone's estimation of the time it would take to retrieve the horses had been spot on. An hour and a half to cross the valley, and then navigating the landslide at dusk. His time-predicting accuracy might come in useful.

They'd arrived to find that Hank had started a pot of herbs simmering. Clementine thought she could smell sage, but she wasn't sure what else. As she warmed her hands over the fire, Horace offered to throw in a lump of meat that none of them could identify. The musky, sour smell of the meat was almost strong enough to put her off her supper for the night. Hank kindly turned down the offer, so Horace had taken the hunk of flesh to a corner of the cave where he chewed at it energetically. Hank instead fetched a few potatoes from the food pack Fred carried and sliced them into the steaming broth.

"Soup's ready." Hank fetched tin cups from Fred's pack as Clementine and the others, in the absence of stools or chairs, chose sitting rocks to place near the fire.

Clementine plunked her rock down and sat, turning to Jack. "You three talked for a long time. I'm interested in what you know now." She tilted her head toward Boone. "And we don't."

Jack's brow furrowed.

"Puts a burden to my mind," Hank said as he returned with the cups.

"We had to figure things," Jack told her. "It's kinda like seein' pictures in our noggins, right Hank?"

"Yessir, Jack Rabbit."

"Sometimes we don't see the same thing," Jack explained.

Hank nodded. "Most times."

"That valley down there …" Jack pointed toward the cave entrance. "Well, we got us a pickle of a problem, Miss Clementine."

She'd thought as much. From her conversation with Boone on the trip back, she knew he believed the same. It was obvious from their trek back across the valley. Clementine would have been comfortable with creeping through the group of tents to return to the cave, but Boone had insisted on taking a more circuitous route, well north of the tents and shacks and cabins. Partway along, she'd joked that his plan must be to backtrack clear to Deadwood to recruit help.

"Some of the things we're pretty sure of," Jack continued, bringing Clementine's focus back to what Horace had shared.

"Cabins are full." Hank poked at the fire, then stirred the potato soup with the same stick.

Rabbit grimaced. "What Mr. Ash Soup is sayin', is nearly all of the shacks and cabins down there are habitated with *others*. Horace didn't call them that, but Hank and I think that's what he means."

"That's right." Hank nodded again.

"Anyway, all sorts of 'em down there. Lots in some, couple three in others. But most of them buildings are gonna be a problem for us."

Boone groaned.

Clementine wasn't surprised. What worried her was what kind of *others*. "Keep going."

"Some sound to be *Bahkauv*, but I don't know for sure. Not too many, so they probably won't slow us much. White grizzlies. Lotsa things we couldn't figure. That's when me an' Hank started in on the worries. Horace showed us things that I ain't afraid to say curdled my blood some."

"Right in my body." Hank stirred the steaming soup with the stick again. "Like to be my blood froze up."

Rabbit thumbed at the pack Fenrir had been carrying. "I hope you got the weapons for this, Miss Clementine."

"A zoo!" Boone blurted out. "It's like somebody is keeping a damn zoo!"

A shiver climbed her spine clear to the base of her skull. This might be a bigger task than she'd first thought.

She met Rabbit's worried frown. "It's resources. Reserves for a battle." Clementine had come across something similar before, deep in the forest surrounding a mining village in the Carpathian Mountains of eastern Europe, or at least the remains of it since she'd arrived after what appeared to have been a brutal, bloody battle. "They're spread out. It means we don't need to face them all at once. Or we might be able to get to the barn without facing them at all."

That was unlikely, but the Sidewinders and Hank had big round eyes at the moment. A dose of courage would not go amiss.

"Miss Clem," Hank said, his face puckered. "Horace said gettin' to that barn is on the other side of undoable. There's a thing about that barn you—"

"We should tell her about that other thing first," Jack interrupted.

"When you say so, Jack Rabbit." Hank dipped a tin cup into the potato soup and handed it to Clementine.

She thanked him and took a sip. It was bland, although not horribly so. But it was hot, and that made up for the lack of everything else. "The best soup I've had in two days, Hank."

"Only soup in two days, Miss Clem." Hank grabbed another tin cup and dipped it. "Horace over there got his throat cut. We all seen it. He'd be dead 'ceptin' he's—"

"*Other*," Boone finished for him and took the cup Hank held out to him.

"Co-rect. The beastie what done it sounds to be a cantankerous bugger. Happened a ways up the crick on the other side. Holes up in a shack. Horace tried and tried to get the best of the bugger, but happened t'other way round ever' time. Got a bunch of little critters millin' all around that shack. Easy enough to do them in one by one, Horace says, but when they get to conglomeratin', that's a problem. Makes it nigh impossible to even get a whack at the shack. Ol' Horace is beside himself about it. That bugger in the shack stole Horace's weapon." Hank's brows knitted as he turned to Clementine. "Here's the thing. He says his weapon there can handle the beasts in this valley."

So could she with *Ulfberht* in her hands. She thought of the number of *others* she'd seen in and around Slagton so far. Then again, having some help might be welcome.

"Seems to me he said 'tool,' not weapon." Rabbit sipped at his cup of soup.

Clementine had met many kinds of *others*, from evil and chaotic to honorable and good, and everything in between, but the mention of a specifically tasked weapon piqued her interest. She stared over at Horace, contemplating a suspicion, before turning back to Hank. "Did Horace give you an idea why he's here in Slagton?"

Hank glanced at Jack. "Can't quite get that straight, Jack Rabbit an' me."

"Did he indicate anything that gave you the impression of an agent? Or sentry?"

They both looked confused.

"Keeper? Watcher?" she pressed.

"Watcher. That's it, Miss Clementine!" Rabbit grinned at Hank. "See, we were close. We thought he maybe meant peepers or somethin'."

That made sense. And he was likely here in Slagton for a certain purpose. "He keeps an eye on that barn?"

"Yep," Hank and Jack said in unison.

"Well, all of Slagton, we figured," Jack added.

She nodded once. "He could be some kind of sentinel."

"He said there were more like him but they're gone." Jack ran his finger across his throat, then he glanced at Horace. "Oughta not do that, I suppose."

"Some are kilt, he said," Hank told Clementine. "Some disappeared. He don't know if'n those ones are still alive or hidin' or kilt."

It was more and more evident that Slagton wasn't merely a stable in which the smoky ghost they'd seen earlier kept his pets, much like Masterson and his herd of *Bahkauv* in the Bloody Bones mine. *El Vaquero*, as Jack called him, wasn't simply playing at regional control. He was amassing more forces than one Slayer could possibly put down alone. This was looking like a major assault on Masterson's sovereignty.

Not only that, Slagton was almost assuredly a *porta magna*—a doorway to the darkness. Something her amma had warned her about often during her schooling.

A gateway.

Her grandparents had called them *Leitungen*, or conduits. In Clementine's opinion, this was a more accurate description, since if used correctly one went in a gateway, traveled through the darkness, and came out somewhere else. A predetermined exit. Not every region had such a doorway, but she'd suspected for some time now that the Black Hills did, especially considering Masterson's reputation and station. His Guardianship would not be of a placid or inconsequential territory.

"More potatoes, Miss Clem?" Hank's question snapped her attention back to her companions.

"Yes, Hank. Thank you." She handed her cup to him.

Boone and Jack continued to watch her from under the rims of their hats, their faces full of questions.

"Something to tell us?" Boone asked and then sipped steaming broth from his cup.

Should she tell them of her suspicions about Slagton? Here? Now? Of course there was no chance of convincing them to return to Deadwood without her. Better if they knew what they were facing. "Yes."

Horace had finished the hunk of mystery meat and rejoined them at the fire, setting himself down next to Clementine.

"You remember I thought the Bloody Bones mine was the entrance to a gateway?"

All three nodded. Horace rocked his head back and forth slowly, appearing to be listening.

"Does he understand me?" she asked Hank and Jack.

"Think so, Miss Clementine. Mostly understands us, I think. It's disconcertin'." Jack tipped his cup and emptied the remains of potatoes and broth into his mouth.

Boone smirked. "I don't understand Rabbit."

"You'll understand my boot in your caboose, you flea-bitten milk wagon pony." Jack stuck a fist toward Boone, but his eyes twinkled.

"Uncle Mort's milk wagon pony? That's a compliment." Boone chuckled. "Jugs was a helluva pony."

Jack sat back and scanned the cave. "Say, where is Uncle Mort? Didn't come back with y'all?"

Clementine almost answered, but held her tongue. Morton had told her he needed to return to Deadwood to "check the edges," whatever that meant, and to take his evening constitutional. But he did promise he'd be back "in a shake of a lamb's tail" to help with their predicament. She wasn't sure how he could help in his ghostly form. Perhaps he meant corralling his two scrapping nephews—or at least one of them.

"You tell us, Mr. Ghost-talker," Boone replied.

"Booney, I hear the regret in your voice. Don't fret, just because your mind don't have the strength don't make you useless. I can think of lots of stuff for you to do. Come here, warm up my feet."

"Better yet, I'll tan your hide. You think I want to argue with you—oops, I mean Uncle Mort—all the time like you do? You think I want a part in that?"

"You do."

Boone paused. His head sank forward a little. "Yeah, I do."

Jack's expression softened. "Sorry, Booney. I wish you could, too."

Clementine had been biting her lip through the whole exchange. "Are you two finished?"

"Yes, ma'am," they both said, sheepishly.

She sloshed the bit of soup left in her cup. "I believe there truly is a gateway somewhere in Slagton. And I think it's in that barn."

Horace stared at Clementine, seemingly transfixed. He uttered a gravelly string of syllables.

"I think he's figured you for somethin' special, Miss Clem."

"I'm gettin' that too, Hank," Jack agreed.

"If that isn't an understatement," Boone chimed in.

Clementine stared back at Boone for a moment, then glanced toward the fire. She hoped the others couldn't see that his compliment had her cheeks warmer than before.

Horace jumped up and ran to a corner of the cave. His bent-over, loping, bouncy gait and dangling arms was almost amusing. His colossal hands were entirely out of place on his body.

Jack snickered and tipped his head at Horace. "Got some ol' fashioned sarsaparilla in his get along."

"Jiggle in his wiggle," Boone added.

Clementine cleared her throat loudly. "I said, I think there's a gateway down in that valley." Given their apparent lack of concern, she was pretty sure her three companions didn't understand the danger they faced.

"Miss Clementine, I ain't never had a good understanding of that," Jack said. "What the hell is a gateway exactly?"

"I'll tell you what I know. I haven't had any experience with gateways. I haven't gone through one, or even seen one. I only know what my grandparents taught me, and anecdotal things I've heard since then." She had their full attention now. "Under the right circumstances, there are those who—"

Horace loped back, reached toward Clementine, and offered her a flat stone. She accepted it and held it toward the light of the fire to better see it. Actually, it wasn't stone at all, but a clay tablet covered with markings she did not recognize. Not hieroglyphs or Latin. If she were to guess, it was a combination of hieratic and demotic, or some other very old language in any case. How strange. Unfortunately, her amma had concentrated her studies on Latin and more contemporary Western languages.

She looked at Hank. "Will you thank him and ask its significance?"

"You can thank him yourself, Miss Clem. He understands."

"Thank you, Hor …" She realized she still didn't know his real name. She smiled. "Thank you."

His mouth curled up on each side, but it somehow wasn't right. His big, sad eyes widened. Was he trying to smile back but didn't know how?

Horace rasped and grunted.

"I don't understand what he's sayin'," Rabbit said. "You get it, Hank?"

Horace drew a circle in the air and then shook his huge hands in the middle of it.

Hank's forehead crinkled as he watched, then shook his head. "Kinda like when he told us his name. Can't make sense. Nothin' to grab hold of." He leaned toward Jack. "Did it sound …"

Clementine's focus returned to the tablet as Hank and Jack deliberated Horace's meaning. Who was Horace? If he truly was some kind of sentinel, then he must be highly regarded. Those who were assigned to a gateway and its surroundings were special in some way. Judging by what she'd learned, there weren't many things more important than a gateway. Actually, her amma had taught her that those who watched a gate had no master, but rather felt a calling to their task. Did the tablet have something to do with the gate?

I wonder if Hildegard could make something of it. Or Ludek, or Miss Hundt. She turned the tablet this way and that in the firelight. *And why did Horace give it to me, of all people? Hank had said that Horace thought I was special somehow. Was Horace talking about the fact that I'm a Slayer? Or is it something else?*

"Clementine." Boone's voice brought her focus back.

She looked up from the tablet, meeting his dark gaze. "Yes?"

He leaned closer. "You were going to tell us about gateways."

"Right."

Was she to use the tablet for … Stop and focus!

"Gateways are doors. There are two ways that I know of to use them. One, you must actually locate it. Once you have found it, there are rituals used to recite …" She couldn't quite recall the details. "Not rituals, really.

Observances. Adherences." She dug deep into her memories in an attempt to hear her amma's voice. "Procedures …"

"I think I understand," Boone interjected. "The gateway is opened with some type of verbal sequence or concatenation. Once it's open, someone can go through. Does it take anything besides words or sounds, like sacrificing a chicken or a 'Rabbit' or something?"

"Keep it up, Booney. I'll come in the night for you, with my 'Rabbit' weapons."

She shook her head. "I don't know. When I was much younger, I was warned to avoid a village … odd, I can't recall the name. I was traveling from Zürich to … *dritt*, I can't even remember where I was traveling to. But I remember being warned to avoid this village along the way. It was said that an assemblage of *others* was sacrificing humans to facilitate the commencement of travel to realms historical and prospective."

Clementine remembered that part well. It had alarmed her. So much so that she had backtracked a day to take another road that skirted the village, adding four days to her journey. She had been very young then, full of uncertainty that made her weak. Now, she would walk into the village and face the challenge directly.

Boone's eyebrows peaked. "Historical? Prospective? You're talking about time travel?"

She nodded and glanced at Hank, who seemed to be listening but remained seemingly unfazed by the subject. Then again, he was probably just concentrating on the hunk of wood he was whittling while Jack questioned Horace.

"No such thing as time travel," Jack stated, looking her way, dismissing the idea entirely. "A bunch of plumb loco *others* is all."

"Possibly." Until she made it to the barn, she wouldn't know for sure. She finished her cold soup in a gulp.

"Can anyone go through?" Boone continued. "Or just the one that opened it?"

Clementine's piecemeal memory wasn't of much use. "I don't know."

"If I can go through an open gate, what's on the other side?" Jack joined the discussion, apparently done with Horace.

"Like I said, I haven't even seen a gate." She set her cup down. "But I believe it will open to the place you want to go, *if* opened correctly. To a place and maybe a time."

"And if it isn't opened correctly?" Boone was like a bloodhound on the trail of a fox.

"It's said that there is a great darkness. One in which you will wander but never realize your ambition. That's why gateways are best left to those who know how to control them. And before you ask, I don't believe I've ever met anyone who can."

Jack stood and stretched. "You said two ways to use a gate."

"Yes. The second requires someone called *der Mystiker*, who can open the gate for others."

"So this *der Mystiker* can use it?" Jack drew his Bowie knife from its boot sheath and began flipping it in the air.

Horace tapped on the tablet.

Clementine nodded at Horace, unsure what he meant by the tapping, and then answered Jack. "I don't think so. I think he or she … or it only opens a gate."

"*It.*" Jack nodded. "Fine. Long as we're here, let's give 'it' big teeth and claws, like everything else around here."

"I haven't met one," Clementine told him. "I don't know who, or what, *der Mystiker* is."

"Right. And they can send you gallivantin' into the future or the past?" Jack's question was packed full of sarcasm.

She didn't like his tone. "So the story goes."

Horace started to tap the tablet again, but stopped, looking toward the dark entrance of the cave. With a grunt, he took off at a fast lope.

"What the blazes?" Rabbit said, watching after Horace. "Had to pee?"

A tingling sensation shot up Clementine's spine, ending at her fingertips. Odin's eye! They had company.

Seven

*I*t took Rabbit a split second to realize it might be trouble that had Horace spooked. He jerked his sawed-off shotgun.

Clementine's blades were already in her hands.

His weapon held two big shells loaded with lead pellets, which was why it had earned the name *Boss*.

Hers, long and slender steel, glinted in the firelight as she spun them into position.

Rabbit followed as she sneaked from rock to stalagmite, approaching the black-as-coal tunnel leading to the cave entrance.

All was silent but for the scrape of leather sole on rock and the rustle of wool and canvas as they inched toward the mouth and open air. He ran his hand along the jagged rock walls as he crept forward. He assumed Boone and Hank behind him were doing the same, since it was too dark to see the ground. He didn't know if Clementine could, but he did know her vision was better than most under these conditions.

His eyes strained at the blackness, filled with the swirling colors and tiny sparks he saw whenever he squeezed his eyes shut. The feeble moonlight afforded just enough light to catch Clementine's silhouette as she slipped out and to the side of the cave.

He reached the opening and stopped, listening as Boone tiptoed up behind and put his hand on Rabbit's shoulder.

"Hank's right behind me." Boone's whisper was scarcely loud enough for Rabbit to hear. "We should make for that boulder up to the left."

"Okay. You got your sword out?" Rabbit whispered over his shoulder.

"Yeah. It's poking me in the leg. Where the hell is Horace? Hank, you ready?"

Rabbit heard a muffled "Set." He took a deep breath. "To the boulder on three. One, two, thr—"

"Wait." Boone grabbed Rabbit's coat.

"What the fuck, Booney?"

"Shhh. Not so loud."

"What?"

"I thought I heard something over to the right."

Rabbit looked in that direction and caught Clementine's silhouette again. She was waving to them from behind another boulder. "It's Clementine. Let's go. We can cover her flank from that boulder we were headed to." Rabbit remembered the climb up to the cave. It was steep, up the side of the *arroyo*, and littered with toe snags. "Don't go over the edge. It's a long way down."

"Okay."

"Onetwothree*go*." Rabbit took off in a crouching run.

He heard Boone's whispered "Shit" behind him, and then a muffled *thump thump* of Boone's boots in the snow.

Boone and then Hank *oomphed* into him, nearly knocking Rabbit over as they reached the boulder.

Bushes rustled from Clementine's direction.

Scuffling sounds next.

A branch cracked.

Rabbit knew Clementine wouldn't be as sloppy as that.

Swish swish swish.

He knew that sound—Clementine's steel blades cutting through the air.

"Hear that?" Boone sprang to his feet. "Clementine."

Low growls coming from her direction made Rabbit's neck bristle.

Boone rushed toward Clementine, his sword at the ready.

"Booney, stop!" Rabbit hissed. His eyes were beginning to adjust to the meager moonlight.

Boone didn't stop. Rabbit started after him, but Hank caught him by the coat and held tight.

"Wait!" Hank whispered.

The *swish* of Clementine's blades meant she was still at work out in the darkness.

Another growl, this time louder. And clacking teeth.

She needed help!

He felt the air move around him. Something big swooped over his head. Rabbit ducked, his breath catching as the shadowed shape smashed into Boone.

Boone grunted and landed face first with a *whump!*

"Booney!" Rabbit's mind whirled. What the hell was going on?

Hank let go of Rabbit's coat and pushed his backside hard, shoving him to his feet and toward Boone's attacker. "Go!"

Rabbit sprinted toward the shadowy hulk on top of Boone, raising the sawed-off shotgun by the barrels like a club. He swung, hard, slamming it into the shadow beast's head with a solid *thunk*. He rushed forward, bashing into it with his shoulder, knocking it away from Boone.

The creature screeched as he tumbled with it. He pushed at it as the two of them hit the ground, and swung the shotgun again, aiming for dead center of its mass. *Thump!*

It growled and scrabbled to its feet, turning toward him.

Boone lay motionless on the ground next to Rabbit, but he didn't dare look away from the hulking creature now upright before him. It howled toward the sky.

A white grizzly. Rabbit knew now. Maybe it was the darkness, but the beast seemed bigger than any he'd seen before.

He raised his shotgun and took aim. But a colossal paw swooped in from the darkness, knocking the gun to the side as he squeezed the trigger.

BOOM!

Pain shot through his hand and up his arm, but Rabbit held onto the shotgun.

"Jack Rabbit! DUCK!" Hank bellowed.

He dropped to his knees and gawked at the beast in front of him. It was huge, standing on two legs, each the girth of a man's torso. He could see the shape of the bastard. Head, shoulders, arms. Every part of it was too big.

Something whooshed over his head. Was that a branch?

It slammed into the beast's head—*crack*—snapping it to the side where it hung loosely, its neck obviously broken.

The white grizzly collapsed into the snow with a squealy groan.

A blocky, dark figure approached the whimpering grizzly and raised a huge fist high into the air and slammed it down on the grizzly's head. *Crunch!* The sound of cracking bone made Rabbit's stomach flop over.

He stayed on his knees, speechless, panting, until Hank shook the sense back into him.

"Horace saved your bacon from the fire, Jack Rabbit." Hank pulled him to his feet. "You see to Boonedog. I'll go check on Miss Clem."

Hank faded into the darkness, heading toward Clementine.

Horace leaned over and wiped his hand in the snow, leaving it dark with what Rabbit assumed was the grizzly's blood.

Boone grunted and sat up. "What hit me?"

" 'Nother one of them damn white grizzlies." Rabbit took Boone's outstretched hand and hauled him upright.

Horace turned toward Rabbit, grunting and mumbling with more intensity than before.

"He sounds angry," Boone said.

"I think he—" Rabbit started.

In a split second, Horace swung his arm up and knocked the shotgun out of his hand, sending it flying into the night.

"Ow!" Rabbit shook his hand as he tried to see where the gun landed, but it was lost to the darkness.

Boone chuckled. "He *was* angry."

Horace turned away and loped after Hank without a word.

"I'll be." Rabbit rubbed his hand. "I guess that's another 'No' vote on my guns. He took care of that, though." He squinted down at the grizzly. "Horace doesn't take the head, he clobbers it."

"Bloody bastards. They must be everywhere." Boone turned around on the spot. "Where are Hank and Clementine?"

Rabbit waved an arm in the direction of Hank and Horace. "Still over there, I guess. Same direction Horace went. Hank just left a minute before you woke up."

"You see or hear anything else out there?"

Rabbit hadn't had time to listen. "No. Clementine sounded busy. I got a shot off with Boss, so everybody knows we're here now."

"Let's go check on her." Boone plucked his hat from the snow and brushed it against his leg.

"She probably dispatched a dragon and she's collectin' its fire."

"Heh. Yeah. You take a hit after you got that shot off with the sawed-off?"

Rabbit shook his hand. It throbbed. "White grizzly bastard tried to knock Boss out of my hands. Then Horace came along and actually did it."

"We'll look for it when we've got the light."

"How are you feelin'? That fucker knocked you out when he fell on you."

"Noggin is thumping a little. You got it off me?" Boone's tone was casual, which Rabbit appreciated. They'd never fawned over one another. The bond between them was strong enough, there was no need to pack it with a freight wagon full of emotions.

"Yeah. Horace finished the job, though."

"How about that? Horace the head crusher. Now we know what those big, fat paws of his are all about."

"Haha." Rabbit paused. "Booney?"

"Yeah?"

"Glad you're okay."

"You too, *mi hermano.*"

They started out toward their companions.

"You know Clementine doesn't want us using guns," Boone said quietly.

"I know, Booney. It's a mighty strong temptation. Involuntary, I'd call it."

"She won't be happy about it."

"I see your pie eyes catchin' looks at her. You'll smooth her ruffled feathers for me, *chico amante.*" Rabbit snickered.

"Cállate, burra."

"Boone. Jack," Clementine whispered. "Shut up and get over here!"

"Sorry, Miss Clementine." Rabbit backhanded Boone in the gut. "Miss Clementine says be quiet."

Boone punched him back. "Clementine, you okay? What happened?"

"She dispatched a grizzly is what she did." Hank caught Rabbit's hand and pulled him into the shelter of a grouping of rocks and boulders.

"So did Horace. Son of a gun squished its head with his fist." Rabbit made a fist and slammed it into the palm of his other hand.

"Smashed flat," Hank agreed.

"Oh, and," Rabbit whispered, pointing at Horace. "That fucker used us as bait!"

Horace grunted and moaned.

"What'd he say?" Boone rubbed his temple

Rabbit closed his eyes. He let Horace's images and words drift through his thoughts. He was understanding Horace more and more all the time, but sometimes the things he saw didn't make sense. "Said he was sorry. He got caught up ... What'd he say, Hank? Caught up taking care of ..."

"I think it's somethin' 'bout they's small. Bunches of 'em, looks like. Oh. It's the little critters we jawed about earlier. The ones what helped take his tool. Kinda like ugly cats, looks to me."

"Yeah, I see." Rabbit was finding it strangely satisfying talking to Horace. It felt almost natural. "Meek ... Meta something ... You're right, Hank, they are ugly. Sharp parts all over, too. Teeth. Claws."

Hank nodded. "Demon kitties is what they are."

"*Meeklspain.* Think that's it." Rabbit kept trying. "You heard of that, Miss Clementine?"

"No. But whatever they're called, they're still here so we should probably table this discussion until later. I killed two, but there are countless more all over the sides of this ravine. I can hear them." She searched their surroundings, occasionally stopping and aiming her ear in a direction.

"Sheeat. We should get back to the cave." Rabbit didn't particularly mind cats, but the picture Horace put in his head. He shuddered. These devils were ugly.

"I don't know if we—" Clementine went quiet and then in a blink disappeared around a nearby boulder. A moaning growl rose only to abruptly stop. She reappeared and wiped her blade in the snow. "You alerted everyone in this valley again with that damned shotgun."

A wave of guilt made Rabbit wince. He couldn't read her face in the darkness, but he knew she wore a scowl. "That shot echoed three ways to Texas. They'll never know where it came from. Besides, you'll be happy to know, Boss is layin' lost out there somewhere. In the cold snow. All alone."

"Where it belongs." Clementine turned. "We need to clean up. This place is crawling."

"It doesn't matter now if they heard us." Boone came to Rabbit's rescue. "They must have tracked us when we brought the horses back."

"I don't see any *Mekal Spaen,*" she said. "But I do hear them. Horace and I—"

"You ain't gonna go off on some fanciful gallivant, chasin' those critters are ya, Miss Clem? Boonedog, Jack Rabbit, an' me can't even see our friendly personalities in this dark, not to mention the ugly kitties."

Clementine appeared to weigh his point. She sighed. "We can guard the tunnel entrance. That way when they come, we can face smaller numbers of them at once. They may be little, but significant numbers would overwhelm us."

"I'm a bit surprised you don't want to do this now," Boone said. "At night."

"Well, Boone, I would. But then I've got the three of you."

"What?" That didn't follow for Rabbit. "That's more boots kickin' kitty *culo*, ain't it?"

"During the day, yes. But at night, like Hank said, the three of you can't even see your 'friendly personalities,' remember? I'd go with Horace since it's obvious he can see reasonably well, and he can take care of himself."

"Well?" Rabbit pressed.

"You three won't let Horace and me do that, though, will you? Hunt while you wait in the cave?"

"That's … I don't …" Rabbit looked to Boone for help, but got a shrug in return.

"You ain't goin' nowheres without us, Miss Clem." Hank's tone left no room for discussion.

"Right. So, we hole up in the cave until morning. But I'll warn you three right now—there will most definitely come a time where you won't be able to follow me. Get ready for that."

Clementine took off for the cave. After a frown at the others, Rabbit followed, with Boone, Hank, and Horace bringing up the rear.

* * *

Boone sat propped up next to Clementine against the smoothest boulder they could find. The thick wool blanket between him and the unforgivingly hard and cold rock helped keep the cool in the rock and the warm in his backside. Rabbit and Hank were on duty to watch the cave entrance, but judging by the whispers, they were doing more storytelling than watching. They'd retrieved lanterns from the horses' packs and lit the cave properly. If they were going to be attacked, better that they actually see their attackers.

The cave was warm enough for him to shed his coat, and the body heat of the horses had helped in that regard. The horses' vaporous emissions from both ends, however, added to the unpleasant bouquet of mold, rotten meat, smoke, and unwashed Horace that had already permeated the entire cave before the horses arrived. Fred the Mule was a whole different matter. His contributions were especially demanding on the nostrils.

Rabbit and Hank had tried to learn more from Horace, but he had gone silent soon after returning to the cave. They were able to get one thing from him, though: he thought it had been a bad idea to expose his whereabouts to Hank. The lanky watchman sat near the fire, motionless, his focus locked on the entrance to the cave.

Boone had tried resting, but between the odors in the cave, the damp air, and hard surfaces, he hadn't had much success. Neither had Clementine, judging from the way she kept shifting and turning next to him. He'd offered her his shoulder as a pillow when they'd first spread out their blankets and settled in somewhat close to each other, but after a glance in the direction of the others, she'd declined. Yet she had inched closer, explaining to him the move was partly for warmth and partly because he smelled a lot better than anything else in the cave. Then she had smiled at him, and he had seen in her eyes that her nearness was "partly" for another reason. Savoring that smile, he'd leaned back and listened to the sounds around him—the crackle of the fire, more whispering, snorting and rustling noises from the horses, Clementine's steady breathing.

She shifted again, then sat up and stretched her arms overhead.

"Do you actually sleep, Clementine? I don't think I've ever seen … wait. You slept when we got drunk that night we camped, looking for the *Höhlendrache*."

She'd also fallen asleep in front of the woodstove on Christmas Eve while he was reading Dickens's tale, *A Christmas Carol,* to her. She'd looked soft and handsome in the oil lamp light that night, nothing like the deadly, blade-swinging killer she had been since arriving at Slagton.

Clementine grinned. "I was faking it."

"Of course. I should have guessed from your snoring."

She swatted his arm. "You should be sleeping right now. I have a feeling we're going to have a big day tomorrow."

"Who can sleep? *Draug*. White grizzlies. The *caper-sus*. What was that last one Hank and Rabbit mentioned? *Mekal* somethings?"

"*Mekal Spaen.*"

"Right. Never met up with those before?"

"I don't think so. I remember a story about small cat-like creatures. Furless. Ugly, like Hank said."

"At least they sound manageable." Boone was hoping, anyway. Facing something *manageable* sounded good about now. "That was one you took care of tonight, wasn't it? Besides the grizzly."

"Yes. But that was only one." Clementine wiggled and pulled her coat partway over her. "I wouldn't mind one of my chairs from the front room of the Pyre."

"Make that two. So, your story?"

"I was traveling in Germany. I'd been called to a village. Thinking back, it seems like I was always on my way to a village in Germany. Or somewhere in Europe. Anyway, on the trip I stayed at an inn, and while I was eating I overheard one man telling another about an odd-looking woman who'd come to town wearing a cloak. It sounded innocent enough—lots of interesting people travel through places. He went on about a clowder of what he described as *streunende Katzen*, stray cats— homely and hairless, according to him. They were getting into several chicken pens and tearing the birds into little chicken bits. But then the strange woman arrived. After that, he claimed all the stray cats disappeared."

Boone stared at her, contemplating her story. "What's that?"

"What?" She turned her head, meeting his gaze. "*Streunende Katzen?*"

"No. 'Clowder.' What's a clowder?"

"A group of cats."

"Oh. I didn't know that."

She grinned, a teasing gleam in her gray eyes. "Well, now you learned something."

"I can learn things. Back to the foxes in the hen house."

"What?"

"Nothing. Keep going."

She watched him for a moment longer, her gaze warm. Then she looked toward her feet, scraping at the ground with her heel. "I didn't think much of it. But later I learned that there had been an infestation in that village. Another Slayer had been tasked to manage it. I would have liked to have met that cloaked woman. Then again, she might have been a real pain in the ass and full of herself, like Prudence the Rogue."

"That man in the inn used the word 'clowder'? Is that German?"

"No. And no." She glanced his way, teasing again. "Don't get stuck on 'clowder,' or I'll regret using big words."

"Okay. But I know some big words." If Rabbit had said that, Boone would have punched him. "You think what's here outside the cave is the same thing?"

Chicken-killers still didn't seem like much of an adversary to Boone, considering the things they had faced so far.

"Possibly. I didn't get a good look at it."

"You have good night vision."

"Yes. But not that good. And everything is in shades of gray."

"Hmm."

"What?" She shrugged. "I depend on my other senses more at night."

"I see."

"And when I fight, everything seems to slow down and become more clear. Sight, sound, smell, touch. All are more acute. More intense." Her brow lined. "I don't know if that makes sense."

"It makes complete sense. Watching you, it really is like everyone around you is moving deliberately slow. You get three or four moves to their one."

"That's what it feels like to me, too." She nodded. "Like I have an unfair advantage."

"Lucky for you. That along with Amazon strength and tremendous fighting skills. Don't ever get mad at me."

"I couldn't." She reached over with the toe of her boot and nudged his leg. "Maybe incensed. Irate? Irritated?" Chuckling, she added, "That's just the 'I's."

He held his palms up. "Okay, okay. So what happened to the ugly cat? Did it explode? I didn't see any explosion."

"It was hard to tell. I think it dusted. Most lower-level *others* go to dust."

"Hmm. That's not the most interesting thing to watch. I'd like to have seen Augustine go. That sounded dramatic." From what Rabbit had told him, it had been a flashy display to behold.

"It was."

A comfortable silence settled between them for a moment.

But reality hovered in the shadows.

"Can we get to that barn?" Boone asked, serious now. "And if we do, can we handle it?"

Clementine scraped some dirt into a pile with her boot heel. "We have to get to that barn."

"And the gateway." The gateway worried Boone, possibly most of all. "You think Masterson knows the situation here?"

"Maybe. He might not know the extent. He did seem concerned about it."

"We have to help Horace, you're thinking?"

That worried him, too. What the hell took Horace's weapon? Or was it a tool? Could Clementine handle whatever it was? Boone had seen her do some things, but it was always a possibility that they would come up against her match. He'd already made the determination that he'd do whatever he could to protect her, from ugly cats to big, fangy, hairy *others*. It didn't matter. To the death.

"I'd rather not take the time," Clementine said, frowning toward Horace. "But we may need to. Besides, clearing all of Slagton is within the scope of my charge. Now or later. It works either way." Her frown turned to Boone. "My concern is, if we make a ruckus, the residents in that barn, and the shacks and cabins too, may get restless. We don't want to put a stick to the hornet's nest if we can help it."

"I agree. So if we can keep guns out of Rabbit's hands …"

"Exactly."

He nudged her boot with his. "Those ugly cats seem like close-in work anyway."

"About those ugly cats." She made a slightly pained face.

"Yeah?"

"Even dogs or barn cats can be a problem if there are enough of them. And these are *others*. We don't know what they're capable of." She touched his coat sleeve, toying with the cuff. "What if they swarm?"

"Shit. Nobody said anything about swarming."

"What, bees?" Rabbit asked, walking their way. He handed each of them a tin cup of Horace's steaming tea.

Clementine shifted slightly away from Boone.

"Hank's still watching?" he asked Rabbit.

"Yeah, I'll get back there in a minute. What's this about swarmin'?" He looked at Clementine.

"It appears to me that *Mekal Spaen* are a clustering animal." She stood and stretched. "If that happens, whoever they're clustering around is in trouble. We'll need to try and take them individually or in small groups." She gave Rabbit a hard stare. "Quietly."

Rabbit stared back for a beat. "Ohhh. I get ya. Leave my best weapons in their holsters."

"Yes, Mr. Quickdraw. Are you willing to leave your guns behind?"

"No."

"Rabbit." Boone stood, joining in. Although he knew there wasn't much chance in changing the mule head's mind.

"No. I already lost Boss." He pointed at Boone's holster. "You don't go to the Saturday night shindig and leave your dance partner sittin' at home."

"But I don't use my gun. It's only if I'm going to die." Boone glanced at Clementine, hoping she believed him, because he didn't quite believe it himself. He'd become adept at using the scimitar, but it also gave him peace of mind that he was pretty good with a pistol. It would sing, if needed.

"Fine. That's me, too." Rabbit held his right hand up. "Only if I'm dyin'. Or if somebody I like is dyin'."

"I wish I could believe you." Clementine shook her head, but a small smile played on her lips. "You are incorrigible, Mr. Fields."

Rabbit grinned. "I go to bed every night thinkin' that very thing." He bowed and headed back to Hank.

* * *

Rabbit returned to his guard post near the cave entrance to find Hank dragging a stick across the cave floor, scratching lines and zigzags into the dirt.

He slid back down the boulder, sat on his saddle blanket, and watched Hank draw in the dirt. He didn't know what the design was, but it was capturing his attention. "You know what those two are talkin' about over there, Hank?"

"Nope. What?"

"Nothin' is what. Like two young'uns on a date."

"Hmm."

"Think we should try Horace again?"

Hank looked over at their new companion, then shook his head. "Best not rile him. I think he's worked up a batch of displeasure for me."

" 'Cause you brought us here? I'm 'displeasured' at you for bringin' us here, too." He bumped his shoulder against Hank's, took a sip of tea, and glanced at the cave entrance. It had been quiet since they returned; no one and no thing had followed them into the cave. He suspected that Horace had a reputation of protecting his abode, so if there was something out there, it—or they—might be too scared to enter the tunnel.

Hank pointed his stick at Rabbit. "I'm beginnin' to regret it too."

"The adults over there want me to unstrap my pistol." The thought of Boss buried in the snow strummed his heart like a guitar. "Goddammit."

"What's ailin' ya, Jack Rabbit?"

"Boss."

"We'll find it come tomorrow, no frettin' about that."

"Thanks, Hank." That wasn't the only thing bothering Rabbit. He honestly tried to put his guns aside in favor of the knives, but they just didn't suit him like shootin' iron did.

"You're still frettin'."

Rabbit wasn't sure if he could tell Hank. His companion was, after all, Clementine's employee. And friend.

"You can tell me, Jack Rabbit."

"Readin' my mind again, you fortune teller?"

"Hoo. May be."

"You know Miss Clementine wants me to use knives, right?"

" 'Course. You done real good learnin' those pig stickers."

"I've been trying. I don't know. Throwin' knives are a tickle and I'm pretty quick, but they don't feel right in my hand like the ol' ivory and nickel." He patted his revolver.

Hank looked up at the ceiling of the cave. "Noticed it's got a 'US' stamped on the trigger guard."

"You think I took it from the Army? Naw. It's a reject. It got nickel plated and ivory handled and then sold to me."

Hank nodded. "Wondered. I was sure as thunder after lightnin' you wouldn't …"

"Nawp. I'll tell you though, this pistol shoots straighter than anything I ever—well, exceptin' my Sharps. And, well …" He didn't want to admit it but, "Booney's Winchester. That's a helluva shooter."

"How is it some fellas like you come to shoot so good? Not sayin' you ain't a nobody, but …"

"Aw, it's okay, Hank. I don't know why, just come by it natural. I aim. I hit. And I've always had quick hands. People come different, this is how I come."

"Teach me that sometime? Then I'll be worth somethin' in a fight."

Worth somethin'? Hank considered himself to be a burden? That notion made Rabbit's gut heavy. "When I aim my pistol, I kinda act like I'm pointing my finger at whatever I'm trying to poke a hole in. Stop breathing. Squeeze. That's about it. Tell me somethin', Hank. How long have we known each other?"

"Don't know offhand. Few weeks strung out, I guess."

"Yeah. That's what I figure. In that time, you already saved my life … I can't even remember how many times. And Boone's. And Clementine's a couple times, too. You seem to know what a fella or lady needs before they even know they need it. And you can pop a *Bahkauv* in the eye with that twig shooter of yours. At a dead run, mind you. Ain't anybody else I want by my side in a fight beside Boone, Miss Clementine," he paused and put his hand on Hank's shoulder, looking him in the eyes, "and you. I count you as a good friend, Hank."

Hank's eyes went sad puppy. He nodded and pressed his lips together, then cleared his throat. "I got your back to the end, Jack Rabbit." Then he wiped at his nose with his sleeve.

"Same here. Now we'll have none of this talk of not bein' worth somethin' in a fight."

Hank scraped away his dirt drawing with the stick and started another.

They sat listening to the sound of the wind whistling and moaning outside the cave for a while.

Rabbit was confident they weren't followed. If the *Mekal Spaen* had a plan to attack, it was a pretty safe wager it wouldn't be tonight. Or the bastards went to get help.

A familiar stench wafted past Rabbit on its way out of the cave. "Sheeat."

"What is it, Jack Rabbit?"

"The vapors squeakin' out of Fred's posterior are more revolting than those damned *Draug*." He waved his hand in front of his face.

Hank snickered. "Curl yer toes, no doubt. You get used to it."

"No, I don't."

"I got a thought on guns, Jack Rabbit."

"Just one?"

"Cut it out. I think maybe somebody like you—you're meant for both. Knives and guns."

"Hmm."

"Yep. Keep 'er quiet when you need, but I never seen a shot like that one you made out t' the Bloody Bones. Spanned that whole gulch. Whoo wee. Never seen somethin' like it. That kinda thing's bound to come in handy ever' once in a while. No blade to match that. Or arrow."

Rabbit pondered.

"Close in, get to work with the blades."

"Right." It wasn't a new idea. He was pretty sure he understood what Hank was getting at. Leave the sawed-off in the saddle pack.

"That means …" Hank glanced at him. "Put it this way. Could be, you losin' that scatter gun happened for a reason."

"I'm on the wagon with you, Hank. But that double barrel sure has settled its share of disagreements."

"I don't doubt for a second."

"Make Miss Clementine happy, though," Rabbit said. "She believes my strength is in my speed, not in the guns. I don't know. Could be."

"Yep. Don't need no cartridges for a blade, neither. Sometimes can't get cartridges. Or powder or flint."

"*You* can." Hank always seemed to have the good fortune to come into the right ammo for whatever task was at hand.

They fell silent again for a spell.

Flint. Why had Hank said "flint"? Probably used it in the war. "You had a flintlock? In the war?"

"Nope. Let's see. Used a Colt Navy, Remington. Henry rifle. Not all at once, mind ya." Hank tapped Rabbit's shoulder with his finger. "Lucky to get that Henry. Hard to get cartridges though."

"Hard for you is impossible for me."

"Didn't mind losin' that Remington pistol. Always jammin'. Bullets went dogleg, hard to hit anything. Wasn't sorry to lose it. That was lucky in a way, too, 'cause I got the Colt Navy after and that was a fine piece of metal reckonin'."

"Colt makes a helluva pistol. How'd you lose the Remington?"

Hank leaned toward him and whispered, "Damn Monkey did it."

"Uh, what? A monkey did it?"

"No, Damn Monkey did it."

"Yep. That's what I heard."

Hank touched his finger to his lip. "That's right. I carried a bayonet, too. Miss Clem would like I had a bayonet."

"The Remington and the monkey…"

Hank sniggered. "Damn Monkey. I was on a steamer from South America tryin' to get to Virginny—"

"You were on a ship?" That sparked Rabbit's interest. He had been an avid reader of every book and magazine he could get hold of concerning pirates and he was a supporter of privateering in general. Now, to find out Hank was the next best thing, well …

"Surely. Catchin' a ride back to the States. Carrying a load of sugar cane and bananas. Bananas was new then, only 'somebodies' had any idea about 'em."

"What're bananas?"

"See? You ain't a somebody. Hoo hoo, jus' funnin' ya, Jack Rabbit. It's a curious-shaped thing. A kinda fruit, yella'. About yay big." He held out his outstretched thumb and middle finger. "Skinny, curved. Peel the skin off and eat it. Tastes good. Didn't like the feel of it in my mouth, though. Mushy, like a wet piece of bread."

"Oh." Rabbit thought he'd probably stick with apples. "What about the monkey?"

"Damn Monkey," Hank corrected. "He liked sugar cane. Captain figured he stowed away, following the sugar cane. He did like to chew on that cane. We all got friendly with him after a while. He was entertainin', like a review down to the Gem Theater. Kept us grinnin'. Got so's he could paint and scrub the deck. Then the little bugger found the bananas. You never saw nobody peel and eat so many bananas."

"I never saw nobody eat even one banana," Rabbit replied. Maybe he'd like to try just one. "Give him a name?"

"Sorta like. We was tryin' to come up with somethin' clever, then he started causin' banana problems, so's we ended up callin' him 'Damn Monkey.' You know, 'Damn Monkey got to the bananas again,' or 'Damn Monkey dropped the paint brush overboard.' "

"So did he eat all the bananas?"

"No. Had crates of 'em. We locked him up in a cabin. Kept gettin'

out, though. Raided the bananas ever' time."

Rabbit scratched his head at the scene Hank was painting. "What does this have to do with the Remington?"

"Oh, right. I was due in Georgia, so I hopped on a train t' get me there. It was in South Carolina, I heard a porter talkin' about a thief eatin' the bananas and leavin' the skins on the floor of the cargo car. Gotta watch, them peels are slippery buggers. One step and *zshwip*! On your behind. Anyway, knew right then Damn Monkey hopped the train with the bananas. Considered it my duty to corral the little thief, but I couldn't catch him. When I got close, he jumped the train. I had to jump too." He rubbed his elbow. "Still gives me trouble time to time when the air's sticky muggy."

"Did you catch him?"

"Damn Monkey took the jump better'n me. Galloped off in his funny monkey way. Kinda two-legged, but used his itty-bitty monkey fists like feet, too. Sometimes he'd go up on his short bow legs, like a saddle tramp, long ol' arms up like this." Hank held his arms over his head and flopped his hands up and down. "Ever seen a monkey run? Hoo hoo. It's funny. Gets me gigglin'."

If Rabbit didn't know better, he'd suspect he was getting shorn like a sheep. But Hank didn't fib. "Where the hell was he going?"

"Runnin' from me, I'd guess. Don't know why. I snuck him bananas on the boat when the crew weren't lookin'. Thought that made him my friend. Guess not. Liked his freedom I s'pose."

"Right. Can't blame him for that."

"Lotsa bluecoats along the road that day, marchin' on the South. Tents set up ever'where. Damn Monkey goin' in and out, this way and that, them soldiers didn't see a thing. He musta lost track of me, 'cause he went in a tent and didn't come out. I was makin' my way round to the flap, thought I'd catch him inside. Worked my way in back of a group of men standin' there and headed t' the other side when a man yelled, 'You, in the back! The boatman! Stand up straight!' Called me a boatman on account of my hat, I suppose. Well, he was starin' right at me, so I popped up at attention. Pow! A flash of light got me to reelin' and I fell over on my be-hind. Blinded me for a spell."

"Ah. You got your picture taken. Makes you famous. Did you smile for it?"

"Don't smile for a pitcher," Hank told him. "Anyway, a hand

grabbed me by my coat and hauled me up. Jack Rabbit, you'll never believe it. I was standin' face to face with General Ulysses Grant, in the flesh. He asked me if I was fit and then went on with his day. Took my wits a spell t' recover, that bein' General Grant and all, so don't recall sayin' nothin' back."

"Wait just a damned second. That ain't the picture in the loft? The one with you and Grant and all them other fellas in it?" Rabbit distinctly remembered that photograph. It was a rare thing to be photographed with a war general turned president.

Hank pointed at him. "That's the one. Tintype man gave it to me. Said was 'no good' 'cause I was movin' around, blurry. Had to wait is all."

Rabbit sat with it for a minute, trying to keep it all straight. "What happened to the monkey?"

"Damn Monkey. He was gone when I got done with Mr. Grant. Lost his trail. Couple years later I saw a circus parade in the street, different town. Ely-phants and tigers and people. Id'a bet my Colt Navy pistol Damn Monkey was ridin' on that ely-phant's back, wearin' a top hat and a little red suit with gold trim, wavin' his twig of a walkin' stick in the air."

Rabbit shook his head. Boone was never going to believe this. "Hank, you've seen some things. What was—"

Boone stepped up next to Rabbit and looked down at him. "Planning on doing anything today or are you happy working your jawbone?" He kicked Rabbit in the boot. "Morning light is lit."

Monkey tails, he'd forgotten about the time.

He extended his hand for a help up. "I can't help it if Hank is a better talker than you."

Clementine came up next to Boone. "How are we feeling about guns now, Mr. Deadeye?" She raised an eyebrow at Rabbit.

"I'm feeling like they belong on the same ledger as pretty women and good steaks."

Her eyes narrowed.

"Don't be like that." He held his hand up. "Like I said, *only* if somebody is dyin'."

She turned to Boone. "As good as we'll get, I guess."

Rabbit chuckled. "Thing is, somebody is always dyin' when you're around, Miss Clementine."

Eight

A faint glow was beginning to emanate from the tunnel leading out to the ravine. The sun was close to cresting the hillside. Clementine would have preferred to handle the *Mekal Spaen* the night before, but the inability of her companions to see well at night would have limited her speed through the rocks and snow. On top of that, she would have needed to position them safely out of her way, and of course none of them would stay put if she had.

Besides, if she were honest with herself, it was good to talk to Boone for half the night. Not so good for her mental wellbeing, though, especially concerning how much she liked sitting next to him … and that she'd wanted to inch even closer. However, for a short time she was able to forget about the lonely ache that usually accompanied her into dreamland and enjoy listening to the sound of his voice, his laughter, even just his breathing. Never mind that they were in the middle of a hornets' nest sure to face battle again come sunlight.

Rabbit and Hank had already questioned Horace this morning on what they were facing, but he didn't seem to have anything more to share.

She had slain two *Mekal Spaen* last night. They were a nuisance, best handled with sharp steel. Her dual blades were actually called tantos, but it was a crude name for such elegant weapons. Long, not too slender, light and sharp as freshly stropped straight razors. She referred to them as, simply, "the Twins." *Ulfberht* nested nicely in the scabbard strapped to her back, rounding out her arsenal for the day. Since she was unsure what had taken Horace's weapons, and he had remained closemouthed on his thief's description, *Ulfberht* was the safest choice to keep close and handy.

As for Rabbit keeping his gun holstered … if only he would trust his quickness, he would begin to realize how effective a thrown blade could be. She rolled her eyes at his stubbornness in giving up on his guns. She'd deal with that problem when the time came.

"Everyone equipped?" Clementine wanted to get the day started.

Hank looked down at himself. "Bow, quiver n' arrows, pistol, Bowie knife. That about does it."

"You're bristlin', Hank." Rabbit grinned.

Boone patted his scimitar, Bowie knife, and gun, then nodded.

Rabbit patted his dangly bits. "Ready."

"Packin' light today then?" Boone winked at him and clucked his tongue.

"Booney, I'll lay you out, right here." Rabbit twisted his fist in Boone's face.

"Later, sweetheart. I'm busy right now." Boone swatted at Rabbit's fist and then grabbed it and started dancing with him. Both laughed as it turned from dancing to a struggle.

Clementine watched them for a moment, almost breaking a smile. "Okay, okay. Let's get moving, you Matildas."

"No Sharps for you, Jack Rabbit?" Hank looked at the long-barreled rifle leaning against a rock.

"That horse leg is Dime's burden. Or better, Booney, you carry it."

"You carry this." Boone pointed at his own rump.

Horace led them out of the cave and down the side of the ravine, then headed toward Slagton until they turned north along the base of the cliff. He was extremely skilled at slinking, so much so that Clementine struggled to match his stealth. They might as well have not bothered. The whispering, thumping, rackety trio behind her was making enough noise to wake every *verdammt* beast in the valley. She was surprised they hadn't been overrun the second they left the cave.

But they hadn't been. Now, after passing the large pond and a few shacks and cabins along the stream, they crouched under a group of trees near a large cabin. She presumed the place housed whatever creature that had stolen Horace's weapon. Or tool. Scattered about on the snow-covered ground between her and the cabin were gray-black lumps of what she initially thought were piles of dirt or ash. Upon closer inspection, it became clear that they weren't piles at all, but rather *Mekal Spaen*, hunkered down in the snow.

They appeared to be sleeping.

"Five. Seven … ten more there … couple there." Hank counted. "Looks like thirty or so on this side. Can't see 'round the other side."

That many. Damn. Clementine hesitated. If the *Mekal Spaen* awakened and swarmed … or if Clementine and her party made a commotion, everything within hearing distance would be on them within a matter of minutes. Or seconds.

Her eyes darted, searching for any sign of the white grizzlies. Did they kill them all? She couldn't rely on that presumption. No, better to figure the sharp-toothed *others* were around and might attack at any time.

"Grph ghn aahgh," Horace whispered.

Clementine looked to Rabbit for a translation. At the confusion on his face, she turned to Hank, who squat-waddled closer to Horace.

"Don't look him in the … uh … *flavo oculos*." Hank's lips scrunched into a pucker. "What'd I just say?"

"Yellow balls is what I saw," Rabbit offered. "He says don't look at him—I think he said him—in the 'balls of yellow.' " He scratched under his hat. "Hope that makes sense to you, 'cause it don't to me."

"What the hell are you talking about, Rabbit?" Boone moved up next to him.

"I said," Rabbit repeated slowly, "it don't make no sense to me."

Horace grunted, turned, and loped back the way they had come, disappearing around a rock outcropping.

Clementine stared after him for a few seconds, waiting to see if he was planning to return. After a moment, she realized he'd delivered them to the site and left, as if they were freight.

"The fuck?" Rabbit stood, and then crouched down again.

"Did he say anything?" Clementine couldn't decide if she was upset at his desertion or not. He hadn't been a great deal of help up to now.

"Mighta been 'Good luck,' " Rabbit told her.

Hank nodded.

"Just as well," Boone said. "He distracted me."

So, Boone was thinking the same thing she was.

"But still," he continued. "Could have used his hammer hands to clobber a few of these devil kitties."

"Maybe. But I have a plan." Clementine knew it wasn't a good idea to go straight at the cabin. Too many *Mekal Spaen*, increasing the chance of alerting other creatures in the valley. In fact, it was probably why they were around the cabin in the first place, to raise the alarm.

Most important, she didn't know what was in the cabin. Or who. *Yellow balls?* If they were busy dispatching the *Mekal Spaen* outside and were attacked by whatever creature lurked inside ... trouble.

"Of course you do," Boone said, studying her from under the brim of his hat. "Let's hear it."

* * *

Clementine's plan was simple: The small, short ravine to the north of Horace's cave was the perfect place to set a funnel trap. She would stand at the mouth, Boone and Rabbit a little farther on, with Hank playing the bait. As the small gully narrowed, their prey would be packed into a tight group and find it difficult to maneuver. Clementine would act as the trap door that prevented retreat, while Hank would pick up the strays with his bow and watch for any uninvited guests from the vantage point they'd chosen earlier.

Now, half an hour later, she waited for Hank to round the corner of the ravine, her blades up and ready. She nodded to Boone and Rabbit. They waved back, Boone with his scimitar, Rabbit with his Bowie knife. She pretended to throw a knife and then pointed to her midriff. It was important he use his throwing knives first, then collapse in on the group with his Bowie knife.

Her one concern was that the ugly, furless devil kitties would catch Hank before he rounded the corner at the mouth of the ravine. It was a short sprint from the cabin, but if he fell ...

She considered checking on him, then restrained herself. No. Let the plan work.

Hank rounded the corner at a dead run, lifting his knees high to clear the shin-deep snow, his arms pumping like a locomotive. For a moment he was alone, bounding through the snow toward her.

Then she saw it. Not five or ten, but a whole herd of wriggling, furless black bodies, loping and leaping and galloping toward her. There were so many that they fouled each other's strides, tripping and rolling only to regain their stride and continue the pursuit.

As Hank approached her, she saw the fear in his big, round eyes.

"Pass me and turn right, up the hill!" she ordered, stepping aside.

He turned sharply, almost losing his footing. "Plan's workin' so far, Miss Clem!" he yelled as he shot by her, then headed up the side of the gully behind her.

The mass of *Mekal Spaen* advanced rapidly, their snarls and growls growing louder. Blades out and ready, she waited back in the shadows behind a couple of boulders for them to pass by her.

In the daylight, she could see them better. They did look a little like cats. Really ugly, furless cats. With no ears and black eyes. Maybe they didn't have eyes? They must. They looked as if they'd been shaved and mummified, and then unwrapped, exposing blackened wrinkly skin and eyeless sockets in the process.

Was someone controlling them? Or flocking? She would figure that out later.

As soon as the last of the creatures had moved deeper into the ravine, Clementine stepped out from her hiding place and took her position.

A knife sizzled through the air, flying a bit too close to her legs, and stuck into one of the creatures near the back of the pack. The thing tumbled into the snow but continued to writhe and squirm. Several of the victim's cohorts stopped and looked back, catching sight of her.

In a blink, a group on the left flank broke off and headed farther into the ravine toward Rabbit and Boone.

Good. They could handle some of the fiends.

The rest turned, sharp teeth bared, and came for her.

"Take the heads!" she hollered and then started in with her blades.

Thwack! Thunk! Swhip!

Her blades easily sliced through muscle and hacked through bone, the sound of ripping flesh and cracking bone filled the air. But there were so many. A sea of vermin washing toward her. She spun, kicking out, sending those nearest flying backward into the throng.

An arrow sank into an eye socket of one at her feet. *Thwap*! A second sank into another's chest.

The *Mekal Spaen* began leaping at her from farther back in the pack that now surrounded her. "Little bastards!"

A jolt of energy shot through her, leaving her limbs tingling in its wake. Her blades slashed faster and faster, while everything else seemed to slow down. She could sense their attack patterns now, understood their impending movements, knew exactly where to swing her blade a split second before a creature would leap. Her vision tunneled as her senses took over, allowing her to perceive rather than actually see where every last enemy was.

More and more *Mekal Spaen* rushed forward, lunging at her. Her blades sang in blurring arcs and slices.

"Jehoshaphat, Booney!" Rabbit shouted above the cacophony of growls and screeches, over the crunching of bones and squelching of flesh. "She's like a dust devil!"

"Behind you, Rabbit!" Boone sounded composed but strained.

From the lack of panic in their voices, Clementine figured they were getting along fine with their charge of *Mekal Spaen*.

Blood and meat and legs and heads filled the air around her. She kicked and spun and thrust and carved. Her body hummed with exhilaration.

Out of the corner of her eye, she glimpsed Hank approaching her, knife in a hand, held up in front of him, ready to attack.

She turned toward him. "Stay back!"

As she spun back, an outstretched paw adorned with long claws was coming straight at her. A quick flick and her steel sliced through the gut and backbone of the furless beast, cutting it in half. But it was too late. Momentum carried it past her face, the claws raking her cheek.

Anger surged at the stinging pain, and she channeled it straight into her blades. She didn't know how many she'd killed while her mind was focused on slaying one after another, but she was putting an end to each and every one of them.

"Clementine!" Boone's voice pierced through her rage. "Clementine!"

She pulled up and took a deep breath, the smell of the creatures' blood thick around her. The onslaught had subsided. A pile of furless

Mekal-meat and body parts circled her entirely. She would need to climb over them to remove herself.

Or wait.

Those that she had killed first began to dust and disintegrate, making the pile shudder and shift as it sank. Some of the creatures near the top still writhed and howled pitifully in an attempt to escape the mound of death and reach their quarry.

Boone and Rabbit stood outside the piled-up ring of *Mekal Spaen*, jaws slack. Behind her, she heard the footfalls of Hank descending the hillside. He must have scurried back to his position after she'd shouted at him.

She surveyed her surroundings. The *Mekal Spaen* lay strewn about and in small mounds of bodies here and there.

The Sidewinders had been busy, too, but they had moved around a fair bit as they fought. Each of them had been caught by claws on their necks. Gloves and coats and pants protected the rest.

"Miss Clementine." Rabbit grinned wide. "You never disappoint. Say, got hit on the cheek."

She touched her cheek. It still stung. "One of those little bastards caught me." It wasn't a bad wound, not enough to trickle.

Boone made a show of bowing, then raised his hands and clapped softly. "That's the fastest I think I've ever seen you move, and that's saying something. Do you get tired ever?"

Hank kicked at the mound around Clementine. "Let's get you outta there, Miss Clem. Fix up that cheek of yours."

"Hold on, Hank." The pile had collapsed in on itself somewhat. A few more moments and she would be able to hop free.

While she waited, she finished the job on those still living, then leapt free and took care of the rest.

Boone and Rabbit had done a respectable job of taking heads, leaving her only a handful to finish off.

"Some cut tail and scat," Hank said. "Eight or ten, I'm thinkin'. Kinda disappeared back over near the cabin, so we gotta worry about them when we go in." He retrieved the last unbroken arrow from a lifeless *Mekal Spaen*.

"You think we alerted anything with our little dance?" Boone finished wiping his black scimitar in the snow and slid it into the scabbard at his waist.

"I don't care if we did." Clementine decided then and there that she'd had enough of this tiptoeing business. She tiptoed around Deadwood. She tiptoed around the Bloody Bones. And she tiptoed around Masterson. Enough! "Let's go see what's in that cabin."

She stabbed one of the dead creatures Hank had taken out with an arrow. What she really wanted to see was inside that damned barn.

Instead, she was trifling with these *Mekal Spaen,* and now had to deal with some other yellow-balled hindrance in that cabin. All for what? Some weapon or tool that may or may not help them fight their way out of this mess?

"Barging in then? No plan?" Boone's tone was loaded with sarcasm.

She whirled on him. "I'll tell you what, Boone. You stand here and work out how you want me to clear that cabin." She held up her twin blades. "In the meantime, I'll go clear that cabin."

"What'd I say?" Boone frowned from her to Hank.

She turned to Rabbit. "Well? What about you?"

He raised both palms. "I like watching Amazons at work."

She nodded. "Okay then. Follow me or don't. It's up to you."

* * *

Rabbit grabbed a severed *Mekal Spaen* tail, figuring it might be useful after all, and tucked it into his coat pocket. He fell in next to Hank, well out of reach of Clementine's dual swords.

Actually, there probably was no "out of reach" of Clementine when she was on the warpath. It was pretty obvious she was worked up, what with the way she was plowing through the knee-deep snow like a steaming locomotive. Maybe she was still coming down from the fight. Or it could be getting caught on the cheek with a set of claws had her extra riled. Injuries made her grumpy. Rabbit had witnessed this in the past and determined that she thought of them as a weakness. Or failure. As if being injured in a fight meant something must have been done wrong. Hell, he got thumped or cut or bruised all the time and didn't feel like a failure. Who was still standing at the end of the fight was the important thing.

It could be she was annoyed that Horace had sidetracked her from getting to the barn. The whole valley and the teapot and the kettle all knew she wanted into that goddamned barn. And where was Horace? Shucked. That made for an untrustworthy pard in Rabbit's eyes.

He hustled up beside Clementine and wiped at the blood on his neck. It stung. "Got a little scrappy back there for a minute or two."

She nodded. "It did."

"You were movin' fast, all whirly and blurry."

"I was pretty busy."

Her clipped answers were hard to counter. "You were *really* busy. Maybe you didn't notice—no guns."

"I noticed." She stopped suddenly and crouched. "Down."

Rabbit sank to a squat. They were within sight of the cabin. A few trees and saplings dappled the space between them and their destination. He was sure they hadn't been seen.

Hank and Boone squat-waddled up behind them.

"Straight in swinging?" Boone eyed the cabin.

Hank sniffed. "Gotta figure on more of them devil kitties."

"And a white grizzly or two," Boone added.

"Haven't seen a *Draug* for a while," Rabbit chimed in.

"Gettin' to missin' my li'l *Draug* buddies." Hank sniggered, elbowing Rabbit.

Rabbit laughed. "Cut it out, Hank. This is serious."

Clementine turned, hitting each of them with a hard stare.

Hank dipped his chin. "Sorry, Miss Clem."

"There's only one door," she said. "I'm straight in, then Hank. Jack and Boone, you watch our backs. Make sure no *Mekal Spaen* or grizzlies surprise us."

"No," Rabbit said simply.

"Why not?" Clementine looked confused.

Rabbit knew she wasn't accustomed to hearing no. "I go in with you. Hank stays out with Boone."

"Rabbit's right," Boone said. "I should watch your back since I have the sword. It sliced through those *Mekal* things without too much trouble." He eyed Hank. "You're tops with that bow, Hank, but Rabbit is quicker with his Bowie close in. You can load up that bow and pick off anything coming from farther out."

Hank nodded. "What do you think, Miss Clem?"

"Okay. But I'm first in."

"Nobody argued on that," Rabbit agreed. None of them was as fast

as Clementine with a blade, let alone two.

"Let's go." Clementine sprang to her feet and started toward the cabin.

"Wait!" Boone grabbed Rabbit's coat.

She stopped and turned. "What now, Boone?"

"Horace said don't look at something …" He tapped Rabbit's shoulder. "What did he say?"

"What he said was nonsense." Clementine started off again with long strides.

Rabbit followed, sizing up the area as they fast-walked toward the cabin, but he saw no sign of devil cats anywhere. As they approached, he focused on the small structure. One window, a door, chimney. No sign of anyone inside.

An idea occurred to him. Entering through the door—that wouldn't surprise anyone.

The window! He glanced at Clementine. She was ten strides, maybe fewer, away from the door, and he decided on the spot.

"I'm gonna surprise the hell outta all of 'em," he muttered to himself.

He veered away from her and bolted toward the window.

"Jack!" Clementine called in a hushed voice.

"Rabbit! Don't!" He heard Boone take up behind him.

He knew none of them could catch him before he reached the window. He yanked his Bowie knife without breaking stride. Gauging his step … *two, one*, he launched himself at the window.

His elbow slammed into the glass with a *CRASH!*

If he got out of this with a few cuts, he'd be lucky. He flew through the window and tucked tight down into his belly, holding the knife out to the side. Momentum rolled him in a somersault and he popped up at the end, searching frantically for anything to stab.

An odd clacking sounded from the far dark corner and caught his attention, but he was immediately distracted by Boone's war cry behind him. Rabbit turned in time to see Boone fly through the window and crash into him, sending them both stumbling sideways across the cabin.

Rabbit windmilled his arms to keep his balance, but the force of Boone's impact was too much and he crashed to his side on the hard dirt floor. He tried to hop to his feet, but gasped for breath instead. He wheezed, struggling to refill his lungs with air.

The front door blasted open.

Clack clack clack … came from the dark corner still.

Boone screamed suddenly and dropped his sword on the floor. He lurched toward the door but crashed into the wall beside it and fell to his knees. Rabbit reached for him, but Boone bounced back to his feet, still screaming. He stumbled toward the window this time, now convulsing, his arms waving wildly in the air. He fell forward, out through the broken window onto the ground, and then popped up and sprinted frantically out of sight, his screams fading.

What the fuck was that! Rabbit staggered upright, panting to regain his breath. Boone was gone, and now he'd lost track of Clementine.

Clack clack …

"Jack Rabbit!" Hank's silhouette appeared in the doorway. "Miss Clem! I'm comin'!"

Clack clack clack …

Hank rushed forward but quickly froze and stared at something behind Rabbit. His face contorted as if he were both pained and horrified. He started screaming, the same as Boone had, then turned and toppled to the floor. He scrambled on hands and knees back the way he had come, but he missed the door and hit the wall headfirst, just as Boone had done. He felt around, found the open doorway and slipped through, still howling.

Rabbit's head spun. He couldn't decide if he should jump back out the window and go after Boone, or help Hank. Or Clementine … Where was Clementine?

At the sound of boots scuffing over the dirt floor, he looked behind him. She was there, arms out in her fighting stance, her *Ulfberht* sword raised and ready.

But her eyes were closed.

"Miss Clem—"

"Shhh! I need to hear it!" The intensity of her voice raised the hair on the back of his neck.

Rabbit gripped his Bowie knife.

Clack clack …

He looked toward the noise, but the thick shadows made it impossible to see what was there. He took a step closer, flipping his knife into a reverse grip, ready to slice whatever was clacking.

"Don't move!" Clementine commanded.

Clack clack clack …

What the hell was that sound? Rabbit squinted, trying to see what hid in the corner. Two yellowish, milky orbs glowed in the blackness. Swirling white and yellow liquid. Mesmerizing. Capturing him. He couldn't move.

His head filled with images he couldn't comprehend. Fear gripped his throat, making it hard to breathe. The tightness melted down into his chest and pain oozed up into his head. His skin burned. He wanted to tear his eyes from their sockets, rip the skin from his face. The fear was swallowing him. He opened his mouth to scream and it seeped down his throat, choking him. He tried to scream again, but there was no air.

He had to get out.

He had to get out!

But he was sinking into the terror … sinking …

It had him now.

Nine

*C*lack clack clack ...
Clementine really wanted to open her eyes and see the source of
the sound, to measure her adversary. But she kept her eyelids
squeezed shut.

Yellow eyes. Now she understood Horace's warning. They'd stumbled
upon an enchanter or conjuror of some type here in the cabin. The
reactions she witnessed from the Sidewinders and Hank were an
indication of what might happen if she were caught in its gaze.

But she couldn't fight what she couldn't see. Her palms were slick
with sweat, her breaths short and fast.

If you are incapacitated in some way, compensate. Her afi's voice filled her
head, steadying her. *Strength in serenity, Liebling.*

"Strength in serenity," she whispered.

A deep breath later, her heart rate slowed to normal. She focused in
the dark, feeling the cold air from the open door and window slowly
circulating around her. Another deep breath found the odor of dust and
dry-rot coming from the corner of the room. She centered her energy
and listened.

Clack clack clack clack ...

A ploy. It was trying to make her open her eyes and look its way.

Concentrate! A footfall. Then another. *It's moving closer.* A faint rattle of
the breath. *Its head is right ...*

She squeezed the handle of her sword, preparing to swing it in an arc
and bring it up under what she judged would be its chin.

Whoosh!

The air shifted, pushing ever so slightly against her left cheek. A
heavy object was dropping on her.

A weapon!

She swept *Ulfberht* above her head, parallel to the ground, and braced for impact.

Clang! Metal hit metal. Clementine cringed at the sound. Her sword recoiled toward her from the weight of the blow, but she tightened her muscles and stopped its descent before it sliced into her.

Open your eyes, her own voice whispered in her head.

"No!" She kicked straight out in front of her, but struck only air. She faltered, almost losing her balance, but righted herself in time to feel the shift of air on her face again. She ducked and raised her sword.

Clang!

Odin's beard! This would turn into an unwinnable, defensive duel if she didn't do something.

Maybe if I just open my eyes a little, she thought.

That was not a good idea.

Just enough to see feet. To find out its position.

She opened her eyes to a narrow squint. Barely enough to see … two legs and … a skirt?

The conjuror's feet shifted. She knew that fighting stance and what came next. She dropped to a squat, one hand on the dirt floor. *Whoosh!* Something hit the top of her hat, knocking it from her head.

A quick turn on her hand and one foot, and she launched a stabbing side-kick at the conjuror's knee, knocking her attacker back.

Crouch, sword up, spring, THRUST!

Her sword clanged against metal.

It had armor. *Dritt!*

Drop the tip, twist, two hands, swing. Quick!

She dropped the tip of *Ulfberht*, spun on one knee, and used both hands to bring the sword across its knees, completely severing one leg and lodging it deep in the thigh bone of the other.

The yellow-eyed bastard let loose a woeful scream as it tumbled to the dirt floor.

She stood and peered down, blocking her view of its eyes with her arm. "What the hell are you?"

Was it a man? Or the skeleton of a man? It was hard to tell from the remaining leg under the knee-length, dark skirt.

It swung its blade up at her, but she saw the move coming and stepped back. She recognized its weapon—a *khopesh*. She'd wanted one in her collection for as long as she could remember. Its arced blade was reminiscent of a scimitar, but the overall look of it was the blending of a scythe and a sword. The crescent-shaped blade formed a hook at the tip to catch armor or a shield. This was a slicing weapon, just as Boone's scimitar was.

She kicked the blade from its hand and continued to carefully study her attacker as it crawled toward her, leaving two broken trails of dark blood behind.

What in the hell was this creature exactly? The shape was human, but the visible parts of its body seemed to have had the skin flayed away, and then the remains had been desiccated under the hot, dry sun, leaving sinewy muscles and cartilage and bone.

It wore a skirt and an impressively ornate chest plate—or maybe an elaborate necklace. A brown, flat-topped hat that was several inches in height hugged its skull.

The conjuror slumped to the ground, but still it reached for her, rasping out what she quickly figured out was a chant:

Ihk Rah Ha Kep Seht Nefre.
Ihk Rah Ha Kep Seht Nefre."

Rah? Nefre? Those words, from her amma's teachings, an old bloody fable. That was Coptic! One of the languages based on ancient Egyptian.

"Oh no you don't!" Clementine raised her sword and brought it down on the conjuror's neck, cutting cleanly through the dried flesh and bone.

It was her experience that chants never ended well for the one on the receiving end.

The conjuror began to crackle at her feet, like wool on a dry day.

Clementine backed away. There was no telling how this bastard would go. Jagged shards of light spread away from the arms, the torso, the head. Shortly, it was fully engulfed in light. She turned away quickly, right before the crackling intensified into a deafening pop, like report of a pistol. The cabin filled with a sour, unpleasant odor and gray ash fell like snow, coating the cabin floor.

* * *

Open your eyes.
Nope. Boone was steadfast in his refusal to listen to his inner voice.
You've got to get up.
He was fine right here.
Boone opened one eye. He was lying half buried in the snow.
Sit up.
He closed his eye.
Sit up!
He sat up and opened one eye again. The world was moving in ways it shouldn't. Queasiness told him to shut his eye again, but he didn't.

Instead, he opened his other eye and tried to blink away the blurriness. Rolling onto his hands and knees allowed him the opportunity to check his surroundings, even if his vision was fuzzy.

He was in the middle of a valley with a stream cutting through one side near a sheer cliff. At the edge of his vision he could make out cabins strewn sporadically along the stream, but he wasn't sure if he could trust the inhabitants.

His hat was missing.

In front of him something had dug in the snow down to the ground and had scraped at the grass and frozen dirt. He looked at his hands. His gloves were gone and his fingertips were dirty and caked with blood. Oh Christ! He was the one that had done the digging. His stomach turned.

"What the fuck happened to me?" His head throbbed, his fingers ached. Nothing made sense.

Pushing up from the ground, he scanned the area and rubbed his freezing hands together.

"Where am I?"

* * *

Clementine ran her blade through the snow outside the cabin to wipe away the conjuror's dust and charcoal.

"Now, where did you boys run off to?" She looked into the distance, then studied the ground. It was difficult to distinguish their tracks in the trodden snow. There had been so much activity here. Most were probably from the *Mekal Spaen*, but there were other tracks mixed in as well.

There. She saw Hank's boot prints in extra-long strides headed toward the cliff. She followed his trail until she came to the foot of the cliff. There she found Hank nestled in next to a boulder, picking at it.

"Hank! You're alive!"

"Miss Clem!" Hank shook his head like a wet dog. "Got me a humdinger of a headache back there. Can't rightly figure how I find myself here." He scratched at his jaw.

"I'm glad I found you. Have you seen Jack? Or Boone?"

"No, ma'am. I been … well, I don't know what I been doin'. I'm doin'."

"It's okay. You need a little time to recover. You stay tucked in here, I'll go find the Sidewinders."

He nodded. He took up picking at the rock again. "I'm okay, doin' what I been doin'. I'm doin' what I been doin'. I'm doin'," he repeated softly.

She hesitated, not really wanting to leave him, but he was secure for the moment. She headed back toward the cabin and hadn't walked more than a few minutes when she saw Rabbit. He was well south of her, waving his hat in the air. Relief added a bounce to her step as she hurried toward him.

When she was thirty or so feet away, he collapsed into the snow.

"Jack!" She started running.

He had lost consciousness by the time she reached him. She rolled him onto his back. He was soaking wet from top to bottom, his clothes starting to freeze stiff. His skin was so cold. His breathing sounded shallow, raspy.

"Oh, Jack. What happened to you?" She needed to get him warmed up.

She glanced around, debating her next move. It would be an hour trek to carry Jack back to Horace's cave, but only a few minutes to the cabin. She would need to build a fire if she took him to the cabin, but that risked alerting a multitude of *others* to their presence.

And what about Hank? She couldn't leave him picking at the boulders. Not in the cold, with *Mekal Spaen* and white grizzlies roaming.

And where was Boone? Her throat constricted at the memory of him falling back out of the cabin, screaming as he charged off toward the trees. Any number of predators—*others* or not—could have heard him. She needed to go look for him quickly. After seeing the condition Hank and Rabbit were in due to the conjuror's mind games, he might very well need help, too.

That settled it. She hoisted Rabbit up with a grunt and a few curses, slinging him halfway over her shoulder. Great Valhalla, he was twice as heavy as he looked. Was he hiding a cannon inside his coat? She wouldn't put it past him if he could manage it.

"Let's get you inside, Mr. Fields." She trudged through the snow. It would take her only a few minutes to carry him the short distance back to the cabin, then she could begin looking for Boone.

* * *

Boone tucked his hands inside his coat. His fingers tingled and hurt with the cold. So did his ears and nose. He knew he risked frostbite if he didn't get warm soon. He also knew he was in for it when he got his hands warmed up and washed. There was no telling how much damage he'd done to his fingers digging into frozen ground.

Digging frozen ground with my fingers! Am I loco?

He needed to skedaddle, but to where? The cabins nearby were the logical conclusion, but he was weaponless. He could head in the other direction but couldn't see anything but meadow and trees beyond. There was no telling what else was out there. Probably more trees and rocks and meadows. Not to mention things with sharp teeth and claws.

Why was he here?

He took a deep breath.

Entertaining your fear won't solve anything. Somebody said that. Somebody he knew ...

A sharp pain jabbed his left hand. If he didn't do something, he was going to start losing fingers.

It had to be the cabins. He'd freeze otherwise.

"What are you thinking, Boone?" he muttered, looking down at his feet. "Follow your tracks. Even children know that. If you're lost, follow your tracks in the snow."

He found his footprints, which happened to lead back toward the cabins along the creek. He started out and soon spotted two dark patches of cloth not far away.

"My gloves!" He'd never seen such a beautiful sight.

He picked them up. They had somehow become wet and frozen solid. He must have thrown them off before he started digging, but why in the hell were they so wet? It was as if they'd been dipped in the stream rather than just sitting on top of the snow. He stuck them inside his coat next to his chest, the cold of them against his ribs sending a violent shiver through his body.

Where was Rabbit? And Clementine? Hank?

He trudged on through the snow and frigid gusts of wind, listening for other sounds of life—or impending death—over his labored breaths.

* * *

Clementine carefully lay Jack down near the stacked rock fireplace in the cabin. The resulting ash from the conjuror's bursting demise had coated much of the rest of the dirt floor, along with her sword and boots.

She looked around. The cabin was better described as a shack, but meager shelter was better than none. She grabbed the remnant of a dirty blanket from a bed of pine limbs and dried grass and draped it over the window.

She frowned down at the bin of firewood next to the fireplace. The smoke from a fire would be seen throughout the valley, but Jack needed warmth, and quickly, or he wouldn't survive. Besides, she'd seen a few other trails of smoke from fires farther south.

Within minutes, a crackly fire filled the fireplace and the cabin was beginning to warm. She put Jack on the makeshift bed, and then performed a quick examination before covering him with her coat. Physically he seemed fine, much to her relief. While he'd lost a significant amount of body heat, she'd seen no sign of frostbite. She needed to dry his clothes somehow, but bringing Hank back here came first. He could tend to Jack while she searched for Boone.

Before leaving the cabin, she picked up Boone's scimitar from the floor and slid it into her belt. She grabbed his hat, too. She paused in the doorway. *What if I can't find him?* A lump formed in her throat. It was too much. Jack on the verge of freezing to death. Hank's wits scrambled up like breakfast eggs. Boone missing. What if Boone was …

No! She closed her eyes and took a deep breath to loosen the fear tightening her chest.

Afi, help me!

Her afi's voice pierced her panic: *You must control your feelings,* mein kleiner Liebling. *Master the circumstances, not with emotion, but with intellect.*

Yes. That was it. She had to work the problem.

Her panic eased. "Thank you, Afi."

She looked back at Jack. He lay with a frown seemingly frozen on his face, unmoving, eyes closed. When she returned with Hank, she would make tea, or barring the makings for that, at least hot water to warm their insides. Then she'd strike out to find Boone.

She stepped out of the cabin into the gusty, cold Black Hills afternoon and headed for Hank. She prayed to Odin that the *Mekal Spaen*—or worse—hadn't returned in her absence.

* * *

Boone had walked for only a few minutes before he had to stop to rest.

Damn it. Tramping through shin-deep snow was tiring, but shouldn't exhaust him to the point of wheezing. Something had used up his grit.

It appeared that he hadn't lessened the distance to the shacks and cabins, yet he must be closer. He'd made sure to follow his own tracks, so he couldn't have gotten lost.

Maybe he should sit and rest.

No. If he sat, he might never get up.

He tried to take another step only to fall to his knees. "So tired," he mumbled and fell onto his side, welcoming the soft, comforting embrace of the snow.

Sleep. Only for a bit.

His eyelids were too heavy to hold open. Close them, only for a minute …

Darkness.

* * *

When Clementine arrived at Hank's boulder, he was gone.

In his place was a writhing *Mekal Spaen* that swiped at her even though she stood well out its reach. Its back legs were broken, jutting from its body at odd angles, flopping and spasming each time it reached for her. It had been stuck in the chest with a wide blade, probably Hank's Bowie knife.

The sight of the injured creature spurred a mixture of disgust and empathy in her, but mostly disdain. Even injured and close to death, it sought to harm her. Did it even understand what it was doing? Why it wanted to kill her?

A quick thrust of her blade into its skull finished the job she assumed Hank had started. She began reading the ground around her as the ugly fiend disintegrated into dust.

Hank was gone. She knew he would have waited if he could have.

Had they taken him? Dread raced through her, making her pulse pound in her ears.

"List what you know," she said aloud, returning to an old calming trick her amma had taught her as a child. "I know that Hank is capable of surviving winter weather. I know he can fight like a devil when he needs to. I know that he's got a lucky streak a mile wide."

As a matter of fact, his luck was so strong of late, she was beginning to wonder if there was more to his good fortune than even he realized.

"I know that Hank Varney is my friend," she added as a gust of freezing air whooshed past her and shook snow from the nearby pine tree limbs. She shivered and rubbed her arms. "I also know that a muslin shirt is no match for a Black Hills winter day."

She needed her coat if she were going to have to go searching for Hank. She climbed the boulder and looked around her. There was no sign of him.

He wasn't himself when you left, her guilty conscience accused.

Verdammt! She shouldn't have left him.

But she had to find Jack. And Boone.

Boone. Her gut sank. Where was he? Every minute she spent looking for Hank meant one less minute of searching for Boone.

"One thing at a time," she told herself. "Now, what happened here, Hank? Where did you go?"

She began trying to make sense of the tracks around her.

"I shouldn't have left you, Hank," she whispered. Her guilt weighed heavy on her shoulders, along with worry. How could she possibly find him? There were so many tracks, all seeming to circle around and around.

Intellekt, mien Liebling, her afi would say whenever she started to whine in defeat, reminding her to use reason and control to confront her predicaments.

"Concentrate, damn it," she said under her breath, taking another look at the footprints.

The tracks were muddled. "He must have turned, run … I can't read this."

Walking the perimeter of the disturbed snow made more sense. She found boot prints and the tracks of at least two *Mekal Spaen,* all leading back toward the cabin. "You tried to find the cabin?" She could tell by the distance between footprints that he hadn't been running, so it was possible he was following the *Mekal Spaen.*

Or, they were tracking him.

If Hank led them back to Jack … She stopped the thought.

She needed to hurry.

Clementine took long strides through the snow, closing the distance quickly, until the crack of a gunshot stopped her.

She knew that gun. It was Jack's pistol. Reason told her that she couldn't know that for sure, but somehow she did. She leapt into a gallop.

Another shot rang out.

Faster now, until she was nearly stumbling through the snow.

* * *

Crack!

Boone stirred from his favorite spot in the world—lounging in the large, puffy, leather chair in the great room at the ranch where he, Rabbit, and Uncle Mort spent their evenings.

That was a gunshot. He growled, annoyed at the sound, and stood up from the chair. "Quit shooting at the ground squirrels, Rabbit, and feed the chickens. It's supper time, knucklehead."

Crack!

Another gunshot rang out, followed by a blast of frigid air that made him shiver clear to his toes. Damn Rabbit for pulling him away from the warmth of the fireplace.

He opened his eyes, the fireplace was replaced by the harsh mid-day sun, which was made more brilliant by white drifts of snow that seemed to go on forever. His hands ached. Why was he laying on the ground? He grunted himself to sitting, a patch of ice, yanked free of the ground, stuck to the side of his face. He brushed at it, but it stuck fast.

Get up.

He struggled to his feet, his legs wobbling so bad he had to rest his hands on his knees to steady himself.

The terrain was beginning to look familiar. "This is … This is Slagton," he croaked.

Crack!

A third gunshot rang out.

Rabbit needed help!

He stumbled toward the gunshots, but it was difficult to determine the direction, the echoes bouncing off the surrounding ridges confused him. With nothing else to do, he staggered onward.

* * *

Clementine dashed toward the gunshots. As she approached the group of cabins near the center of Slagton, she saw movement outside one of the cabins. She drew closer and began to hear loud chatter along with the moaning of … "*Draug*."

Oh no!

She darted from tree to tree, gaining better and better vantage of the commotion. She counted eight *Draug*. And a white grizzly. That meant there was one more somewhere nearby.

There was something on the ground … humanlike. It wasn't moving. It could be a *Draug*. The others had it surrounded but weren't attacking. As she moved closer, another figure became visible from around the corner of a cabin. It had a gun—

"Jack!" she exclaimed before she could stop herself.

She leapt from behind the tree and sprinted toward him, drawing her twin blades as she ran. She raced for the narrowest part of the stream and vaulted it like a deer. A few more seconds and she was amongst the *Draug*.

"Miss Clementine!" Jack's voice was a welcome sound, but he was weak, judging from the way he swayed in the breeze. He took a few steps toward her, but was still some way off.

She spared him a glance. His skin was pale, his body limp, still draped with her coat, yet he held the pistol on the *Draug*. His gun dipped again as he tried to fire, but it was empty. Or jammed.

"Hank's down," Jack rasped and then collapsed in the snow.

A short distance away, Hank's body lay motionless within the circle of *Draug*.

Where had the white grizzly gone?

The sight of Hank's body unleashed a fire that raged through her. Renewed strength flowed along with the heat, awakening every nerve and muscle, heightening her senses.

She spun her blades, and they began to sing against the putrid flesh of the *Draug*.

They fell quickly, leaving her standing in a mess of flesh and blood.

But not alone.

The grizzly that she'd seen before was creeping toward her, attempting to ambush her from behind. It breathed so loudly she didn't bother turning to face it. She knew where to strike.

Back kick to counter, rotate, lunge, thrust. Simple.

As she bent over to deliver the back kick, a churning, dark gray cloud to the south caught her attention. It traveled swiftly toward her, like smoke riding on a strong breeze. But it couldn't be. The wind was gusting in the opposite direction.

In a blink, the gray cloud was swirling a few short steps in front of her. It began to gather, thickening into the shape of a man—but not a man. It was much too tall. It coalesced into a long, slender torso that broadened outward into massive shoulders and thick, sinewy legs. Its grayish-black skin was stretched tightly over thick cords of muscles and covered with designs that looked familiar to her.

The being's only clothing consisted of a mid-thigh length black skirt decorated with gold embroidery and a gold chest plate. A braided gold necklace hung loosely around its neck. Higher up, a long, narrow snout and tall, pointed ears jutted from its head, looking nothing like a man, but rather that of the hairless head of a canine, locked in a permanent snarl. Clementine took a step back. A very strange, evil canine carrying a staff adorned with the skull of a wolf or some other fanged animal. Yellow-orange eyes glowed from inside its hollowed eye-sockets.

It lifted its muscular arms and spread them wide above its head, as if basking in the awe and reverence demanded simply by its presence.

Distracted by this newest sure-to-be-trouble visitor, Clementine sensed the grizzly lunging for her from behind. She was caught out, the only move left to her was …

Duck! She dropped to her knees, stooping forward. But not quite low enough. A claw grazed along her back as it overshot and soared toward the tall stranger, the sting of it making her wince.

She planted her blades in the ground and pushed up in time to watch the ebony demon-dog reach out and snag the beast in midair, as if it were nothing more than a gently tossed loaf of bread. It gripped the writhing grizzly in both hands, lifted it overhead, and then began to twist, tearing the white fur and skin apart.

The grizzly screeched, gurgled, and then went limp and silent.

Clementine watched, her blades raised but her mind completely absent as the demon-dog ripped the grizzly in two. Entrails unraveled and spilled onto the ground as the smoky canine tossed the grizzly aside, as a bored child would a broken toy.

The sound of footfalls crunching in the snow jolted her back to the moment. She whirled around, bringing her blades to bear, but she was too late to defend herself before the second grizzly slammed into her. Claws raked down her chest, jolting her backward into the snow.

She lay there for a second as pain throbbed along the trails of her raked skin, from collarbone to stomach. Rage followed in its wake.

* * *

Boone was beginning to remember where he was—Slagton, Horace's cave, the cabin with the shadowy figure inside with the yellow, swirling eyes.

He also knew Rabbit needed help. Felt it in his gut. That alone gave him the strength to make a stumbling run to the cabins.

He hid at the corner of a shack and peeked around it. This was where the shots had been fired, he was pretty sure.

Near the next cabin over, he could see a tall man clad in dark clothing. Actually, after a longer look, he didn't think there wasn't much chance of it being just a man. Nearby, a white grizzly crouched next to someone on all fours in the snow. The figure sprung up as he watched. Wait!

"Clementine!" he tried, but managed only a hoarse whisper.

The grizzly dipped back on its haunches, preparing to spring at her. He could see no glint of steel in her hands to defend herself.

"Shit!" He jerked his pistol. This would be one of the longest shots he'd ever tried.

His hands were numb and shook with cold, but he spun the cylinder to free it of ice and pulled back the hammer anyway.

Hurry!

He jammed his finger through the trigger guard. Popping out from behind the shed, he raised his gun and stared down the barrel. The grizzly had knocked Clementine down onto her back and was now standing over her.

Calm. Aim. Squeeze.

Crack!

A split second later, the grizzly howled. It swatted at its shoulder.

Boone bolted for Clementine. He aimed his pistol again as the beastie turned its attention back to her.

What happened to the tall, dark *other*?

He stopped, aimed, and squeezed the trigger again. *Crack!*

The white grizzly howled toward the sky. This time it turned to look at him.

Oh, hell!

The grizzly started in his direction, but Clementine lurched to her feet and lunged after it.

From the corner of his eye, Boone saw a flash of gold.

What was …

A bolt of lightning shot through his head.

His face was cold … snow … darkness again.

* * *

It took Clementine a second to realize it was Boone who'd fired the shots at the white grizzly.

It took scant seconds more for her to slice through the grizzly's neck and look toward Boone, who was some yards away.

The ebony, dog-like *other* that had been in front of her a moment before had metamorphosed and turned back into swirling smoke. She had watched it travel through the air like a churning cloud of flies, which slowed next to Boone. From the swirling smoke, the creature coalesced, towering over him.

Boone gaped up at it.

Before she could yell out a warning, the creature backhanded Boone across the face, sending him flying through the air like a straw doll. He lay in the snow, crumpled and unmoving.

NO! Was he dead? If he wasn't, there was no question it would kill him.

She rushed through the snow toward the tall creature, dropping her blades and snatching *Ulfberht* from its sheath on her back.

This new adversary had to be *El Vaquero*, the one they'd seen from up on the ridge herding *Draug* into the barn. Becoming non-corporeal by swirling into smoke was something she hadn't seen before, only learned about during her training. Her amma had called *others* with special abilities "Eminents." Higher forms of *other*. She had little doubt she was meeting her first.

Clementine was doubtful the Eminent would fall to her blade easily. There was a good chance she might even lose if they were to battle. But she had to try to slay it, even if only to give Boone time to come to and limp away.

As she closed the distance between them, sneaking up from behind, *El Vaquero* approached Boone where he lay on his back in the snow. She sighed in relief at the sight of Boone's chest rising and falling. Bending down slightly, the Eminent lowered its staff, almost touching the skull on the end to Boone's forehead.

She approached as quietly as she could, but it was about to make contact with that *verdammt* staff. There was no telling what might happen when it touched Boone, but she was sure it wouldn't be good for his future.

The Eminent's back was to her. It was now or never. She took two running steps and launched into the air, her sword held high.

The creature turned, shifting back on its heels, and swung its staff up with lightning speed. It slammed into her sword with an ear-ringing *CLANG!*

The vibration from the blow nearly shook her sword from her hands. She flew sideways into the snow, sliding within inches of Boone. Using her momentum, she rolled to her feet and held *Ulfberht* tight, ready to attack.

But *El Vaquero* waited, sniffing the air with its long, dog-like snout. It reminded her of a hound on the hunt, tracking its prey. It continued to sniff at the air until its sunken eyes locked onto her.

"Slayer," it said and snarled at her, giving her a glimpse of a mouthful of pointy teeth.

She gripped her sword tighter, stepping in front of Boone who still lay on the ground.

Pointing its staff at her, the Eminent began to speak in a deep, thundering voice that seemed to shake the ground—and her head. It sounded like Coptic again, or some variation of it. She continued to hold *Ulfberht* between them, waiting for the creature to rush her. Instead, it decomposed into a dark smoky swirl and reeled back toward the conjuror's cabin, where she'd left Jack and Hank.

"What the hell?" She lowered her sword. Why would it go there?

Rather than wait and see, she sprinted after it, sword in hand, leaping like a deer over the snow rather than pushing through it.

The sooty devil flew past Jack and Hank and disappeared into the cabin.

She slowed a bit. "What does it want in—"

Horace's tool!

She raced for the cabin. She didn't know what she was protecting, a weapon or tool, but she couldn't take the chance that *El Vaquero* would escape with something vital to her efforts in Slagton. Not to mention the fact that Horace would probably start breaking things with those huge fists if he didn't get it back.

As she passed Jack, his head raised only to drop into the snow again. She'd need to get him, Hank, and Boone to a safe place. And quickly. But first …

As she reached the cabin, the dark tendrils of smoke gathered outside the door. She slid to a stop, waiting for the Eminent to take shape again. But the gathering smoke swirled up and flew past her driven by a strong wind that made the earflaps on her hat flutter.

She watched as it became faint in the distance until it finally disappeared.

It was heading to the barn.

"*Dritt!*"

Ten

R abbit banged out the door of the cabin and stopped. God, he hated that fucking place. He'd been driven to madness by some glowy-eyed bastard in there and forced out into the snow. To escape? Or had that thing sent him on his way? And why had Clementine found him soaking wet? He'd nearly frozen to death. Was that what the bastard wanted?

On top of that, he'd been scratched and bitten by furless demon cats! This place was straight out of a book about Hell.

Now, Hank had gone off with Horace to retrieve their supplies from the cave, most likely to never come back. But worst of all, Boone was laid out inside, heart almost stopped, probably dying.

Rabbit was going to fucking kill *El Vaquero*, whether Boone died or not.

Boone is dying.

The thought kept worming its way into his head. What the fuck had that son of a bitch done to Boone? Why was his heart slowing down? It didn't even look like anything was wrong with him.

He wiped his hand down his face, feeling like a lit stick of dynamite.

"Jack, get back in here!" Clementine hollered at him from inside the cabin.

Rabbit glared at the door as a bone-rattling shiver ran through him. His body temperature was too low, his clothes still wet in the creases.

"When I'm goddamn ready," he muttered. He couldn't just stand there and watch the man closer than a brother die.

Damned Clementine and her death wish to get to that barn.

"Fucking goddamned *others*!"

If only he and Boone had returned to Santa Fe and taken back up at the ranch. They'd have to deal with an occasional street scuffle or skirmish, maybe even a Pinkerton or two, but at least he understood how that world worked.

But he'd never have gotten to know Hank. Or Clementine.

" 'No guns,' she says. 'Take the head,' she says. Sheaat!" He kicked at the snow. What kind of fighting was this, anyway?

Boone is dying!

What if he does? What then? Back to Santa Fe? Back to Uncle Mort's Ranch? They'd sold it to Carlos, but surely Carlos would take him on as a foreman or some such.

Boone gone.

Rabbit couldn't get away from the thought. He squeezed himself from the despair of it and resisted the urge to run farther out into the cold. To just keep running. To leave all of this *other* business behind.

"Jack!" Clementine yelled again. Something in her voice made his breath catch.

Boone!

* * *

Boone woke to the sound of wind. No, it was a pulsing pain in his temples, a thumping in his ears. His neck was so stiff he couldn't move his head. He tried to shake it out but that made it worse, and caused his vision to go blurry to boot.

"Boone?"

Clementine's voice was soft, encouraging him to open his eyes if only to a squint. Fortunately, it was dim wherever he was. Was it nighttime? No, too bright yet for that. Was he in a cave? He shivered as a cold breeze bit at his cheeks.

"Where are we?" he croaked, thanks to a throat that felt so dry it had to be full of barbed wire.

She leaned over him. "Sit up and drink this."

The pounding in his head threatened to pop his eyes out and blow his ears off as he struggled upright. He was on a make-do bed of pine limbs and straw, with Clementine's coat wrapped tightly around his torso and legs. His tingling, burning, aching hands were making a considerable attempt to take his attention away from his throbbing head and neck.

Clementine handed him a steaming tin cup. "Drink. This will help."

He reached for the cup and realized his hands had been wrapped in muslin. He held them up to her. "What happened here?"

"I cleaned the wounds and wrapped them. Drink."

He cradled the cup in his mittened hands, holding it up to his face to inhale the pungent steam while letting it warm his sinuses. Then he took a sip and nearly gagged before choking down the liquid. "Mmm. Cow plop tea, I wouldn't have hoped."

Clementine laughed, standing upright. "And skunk cabbage, but it'll help you heal."

She walked to the window, the one Boone vaguely remembered careening through. He shivered as another cold breeze fluttered the tattered blanket covering most of the opening.

"Jack, get in here," she hollered loud enough to make him wince. "Boone is awake!" She turned back to Boone. "I need to block this window with something better. Haven't had time for that with all of the excitement."

The cabin door swung open and a silhouette filled the doorway, backlit by the late afternoon sun preparing to say its goodbyes behind the ridgeline.

"Booney!" Rabbit hustled over to him and squatted, looking him up and down and then straight in the eye. "Almost slept the day away, you lazy panhandler." Rabbit squeezed his shoulder. "Good to see you up and kickin', *amigo*."

"Good to be." A stabbing pain shot through his head, making him cringe.

Rabbit pointed at the cup. "Careful with that 'elixir.' It'll tie knots in your belly."

"It will not." Clementine slapped Rabbit's shoulder. "It'll heal you is what it'll do." She pointed at his hands. "They'll hurt for a little while, but with the poultice I used they should heal quickly."

A few sips and Clementine's tea was helping already, or was it that his companions were safe and by his side? Boone glanced around the cabin, taking another sip, enjoying the warm liquid trickling down his throat. Hank was missing. A lump formed in his gullet.

"Hank?" Maybe he didn't want to hear the answer.

"Don't worry." Rabbit put up a calming hand. "He's with Horace.

They're off to the cave, fetchin' our supplies. They should be back soon." He frowned toward the door. "I hope, anyway."

"The horses? I'm missing Nickel about now."

"Hank thought it was safer leavin' them where they are." Rabbit rose and crossed the cabin to the fireplace, poked at it, then threw on a hunk of wood. "Miss Clementine thinks this is a good spot to rest up before we storm the barn. That was her words. 'You must be plumb *loco*, Miss Clementine,' is what I said back."

"Storm? What is it, a castle?" Boone stretched his neck side to side. It was still stiff as a new piece of boot leather.

Rabbit nodded. "Might as well be. Anyway, she says I ain't got the proper motivation. It's my estimation that I'm full up with ..." He paused and bobbled his head before continuing with, " 'proper motivation' to stay a territory away from that barn. No stormin' needed."

Boone studied Clementine. So, she was still fixated on getting in that barn even after the run-in with that tall, dog-headed creature. He would be happy to leave things be at the moment. He was already hard pressed, and they hadn't even tried to get in that barn yet.

"What was that thing we ran into?" he asked, then cringed as another bolt of pain shot from one temple to the other.

Clementine smiled, but her brow was lined with fenceposts. "You'll need to be more specific. We've run into a number of 'things' in Slagton, and we haven't really even started yet."

"Feels like we started somethin'," Rabbit replied.

Boone rubbed his temple. "How about in this cabin? Everything went badlands when we hit this place."

He surveyed the small room. Comforts were minimal. A pine pole and straw bed, fireplace, two stools, a wooden box nailed to the wall as a shelf, and a three-legged table propped against the wall.

Clementine grabbed a stool and sat beside him. "Do you know anything about the ancient Egyptian culture?"

"A little." Boone had read four or five books about ancient Egypt. He particularly liked the one that was illustrated. The ornate and colorful buildings and clothing and armor were a wonder. "Pharaohs and pyramids. Obelisks. Mummies. Gods."

"Do either of you remember anything that happened in this cabin?" Clementine asked. "Anything before you woke up in the snow?"

"No." Boone couldn't. "Except ..." His memory was cloudy, but there were fragments. "I came through the window. That's it." A face with yellow-orange eyes and dark leathery skin flashed through his mind. He blinked several times. *What the hell?*

"What about you, Jack?"

Rabbit scrunched his eyebrows together. "Not much more. It's not clear in my head. Booney went *loco* and ran smack into the wall, then fell out the window, I remember that. Hank came through the door and went *loco*, too. And you were facing off with somethin' in the corner." Rabbit shook his finger at Clementine. "Your eyes were closed. You told me to hush 'cause you needed to hear it."

Clementine nodded. "I'm not sure what the *other* was, but I think it was a conjuror of some kind. It hypnotized you both. And Hank. Or something like hypnosis. You all scattered, so did your wits. All three of you, hysterical."

"Naw."

Boone sighed. Of course Rabbit would deny it.

"Do you two remember when I said that some *others* are capable of attacking you not just physically, but mentally, too?" Her gaze bounced from Boone to Rabbit and back. "And don't forget Horace. How do you think he communicates with Jack and Hank?"

Boone's jaw dropped. "Fucker got in our heads!"

Rabbit's was hanging loose, too. "Sonofabitch." He snarled. "I'll kill him."

"I already did," Clementine said. "That's why we're here in this cabin."

Boone nodded. "Safe enough then, you think?"

"Yes. I'd sooner face whatever comes for us next here where it's warm than head back to the cave. Once Hank gets here with our supplies, I think we'll have the upper hand."

Boone didn't agree. The cave offered better defenses. And it was someplace other than *here*. He didn't like this cabin. It made him uncomfortable.

"You don't agree?" Clementine must have read his expression.

"I don't neither," Rabbit said. "We could put our backs against the wall in the cave. One entrance. Then again, I don't like hidin' from a fight."

Boone couldn't have explained it better.

"Remember the tall, ebony creature that sent you flying through the air?" she asked Boone. "Well, it realized I was a Slayer before it blew away in a cloud of smoke."

Off to gather reinforcements was Boone's guess.

"What 'tall, ebony creature'?" Rabbit asked. "One got away?" He growled. "Probably got a couple hundred devils marchin' on us, then."

"Now I have questions," Boone said. This was too much too soon for his fuzzy mind. "What the hell was that thing, and what does that have to do with ancient Egypt?"

He figured it was better not to mention what he saw, namely the head of a dog on a man's body. That was assuredly the sign of an addled brain. Then again, he remembered something about a drawing of a dog-headed man who'd represented a god of some sort from one of the books on Egypt.

"Make that 'the tall, shiny black creature wearing a gold chain and carrying a staff,' " Clementine told Rabbit. "Oh, and this *other* had the head of a dog, or was wearing a head covering to make it appear that way." She nodded at Rabbit's frown of disbelief. "I don't know too much about the culture myself, but I'm sure he was Egyptian. Or at least he was dressed like an Egyptian. I'm fairly certain he's the one we saw from the cliff. *El Vaquero*, you called him. The other that was waiting here in the cabin looked like an Egyptian priest or conjuror, at least according to the drawings and paintings I've seen of them. He was dressed the same way but with a hat, although his skin appeared to have gone through some sort of mummification process—natural or not, who knows."

Egyptian. That was it! That chain necklace must have been the flash of gold he'd seen right before blacking out. *El Vaquero* must have hit him with the staff.

"Say wha … " Rabbit stood, fixing a raised-brow stare on Clementine and then Boone.

"Egyptian." Boone took over for her. "Ancient Egyptians dressed like that. Some of them."

"No, not that," Rabbit said, focusing on Clementine. "You said dog's head? Head of a dog?"

She bobbed her head once, seeming to understand he needed time to get a grip on the idea.

"The head." Rabbit grabbed his head with both hands. "Of a dog. Here?" He patted the top of his head.

Boone nodded. "A really mean dog with no hair and big teeth. And tall pointy ears. But just the head."

"And the rest of him?" Rabbit pointed at his chest. "Was what? Not a dog?"

Boone thought back to that moment when he'd stared up at *El Vaquero*. "A man, but taller, quite a bit taller, and shiny ebony skin. Bigger muscles than you've ever seen, like they were made out of ropes twisted together. Oh, and yellow-orange eyes."

Rabbit nodded absently. "Right. What was he wearin'? Besides the necklace."

"Well … " Boone paused.

"Wasn't wearin' nothin'?"

"No, a skirt," Clementine said.

Rabbit stared blankly at her. "A skirt. He was wearin' a skirt?"

"That's what I saw, too," Boone told him. "I think that was normal for Egyptians."

Rabbit's stare swung to Boone.

Boone nodded, beginning to see a little bit of the humor in the description. "He carries a staff. Clementine said he was getting ready to touch me with it but she stopped him." He looked at her and smiled. "Mighta saved my life right there."

She smiled back. "That's my job."

"No shit." Rabbit scoffed. "Dog's head and in a skirt. Black as coal, head to toe, but shiny." Rabbit appeared to wrestle with the idea for a few moments, then finally shrugged. He'd apparently come to terms with the description. "Kill 'im?"

"It won't be that easy," Clementine said, frowning down at her hands. "I think he's a higher-level *other*. They're called 'Eminents.' He's possibly the one gunning for Masterson's territory. He didn't like the smell of me, though, which seems logical since he decided to leave rather than fight."

"I do," Boone said, winking at her.

Clementine's gray eyes met his. "Thank you, Boone. Most of the *others* I've met or battled tell me I reek of death." She looked to Rabbit. "*El Vaquero* sniffed the air when I was near. He could tell by scent alone that I'm a Slayer."

"He called you out as a Slayer?" Boone asked. "Why is it logical he'd turn tail?"

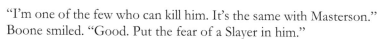

"I'm one of the few who can kill him. It's the same with Masterson."

Boone smiled. "Good. Put the fear of a Slayer in him."

"He could kill me, too, though."

He winced, not liking the sound of that. At all. "You said you killed the conjuror?" He looked around the cabin. "Was it in here? I don't remember anything after jumping in through the window until I woke up out in the snow."

"Wait." Rabbit held up his hand. "You said Masterson's territory?"

A light knock on the door startled Boone.

In a blink, Clementine moved to cover the door, her sword up and pointing before Rabbit could even pull his pistol.

"Miss Johanssen," a deep, hushed voice called from outside. "Please put down the sword with which you are undoubtedly prepared to lance my heart. It is I, Ludek."

"Ludek!" Rabbit hurried to the door.

"Wait." Clementine took a step toward the door. "I'm sensing an *other*, but are we sure it's truly Ludek?"

"I recognize his voice." Rabbit paused, then stepped to the side of the door, clearing Clementine's path. *Ready?* he mouthed to her.

She nodded.

Rabbit yanked open the door, his pointed pistol greeting their visitor.

Ludek smiled slightly at the pistol and then Rabbit. "Mr. Fields," he said with a nod. His angular, pale face looked weary in the fading light. His long white hair was loose and fell around his shoulders. His dark gaze shifted. "Good evening, Miss Johanssen. It is my pleasure to find you alive and well." The knee-length, hooded, gray cape draped over him looked entirely inadequate considering the freezing temperature of a Black Hills evening.

Rabbit grabbed Ludek's arm and pulled him inside, taking a long look outside the cabin before closing the door.

Ludek unstrapped his enormous pack and dropped it on the floor. He turned to Boone. "Greetings, Mr. McCreery."

Boone smiled back, happy to see a familiar face, especially since almost everything else they'd run into in and around Slagton wanted to kill them. "Howdy, Ludek."

"It's sure good to see you, Ludek." The delight in Rabbit's voice confirmed the fact.

"Indeed it is," Clementine said. "But I must admit I wasn't expecting you." She fetched a tin cup, filled it with the so-called tea she'd "brewed" in a dented iron skillet, and handed it to Ludek.

He sipped. "Ah. Exactly what I needed." He set it on the table and began rummaging through his pack.

"Did you walk from Deadwood? The whole way?" Boone blinked several times. His head had stopped throbbing, but fragments of confusing, abstract thoughts kept flashing through.

"Yes," Ludek said flatly. "Here." He threw a wool blanket to Boone, and then another to Rabbit, who quickly wrapped up in it. Then he stood and turned to Clementine. "Forgive my honesty, but you have stumbled thus far in your efforts, *Scharfrichter*, and a new development must be addressed before it is too late."

Clementine glared at him. "And you are aware of my stumbling how?"

"I'm not currently at liberty to say."

"If stumblin' means we got our asses kicked, then I agree." Rabbit pulled the blanket tighter around his shoulders. "I woke up soakin' wet and I don't know why."

"Do not languish, Mr. Fields." Ludek gestured toward his pack. "I have brought you provisions. Meat. Tea and candies from Hildegard, along with a message for Miss Johanssen."

"Shh! Someone's coming." Clementine pointed her sword toward the closed door again, her gaze narrowed, her body poised for action.

Ludek stilled. His head cocked slightly.

Boone sat forward, trying to hear the sound of footfalls, but all was silent except for a few birds.

"Do not be alarmed, Miss Johanssen," Ludek said warily, eyeing Clementine. "I observed Mr. Varney and *der Wächter* approaching from the southeast."

"Hank?" Rabbit glanced back at Boone, his brow lined.

Clementine lowered her sword to her side. " 'The Watcher'? That's his title?"

"Whose title?" Rabbit asked. "Where's Hank?"

"In the cabin!" A familiar voice called from outside, clearly a distance away. "It's me, Hank n' Horace! Don't shoot."

At the sound of Hank's voice, Boone's shoulders loosened. He hadn't realized how worried he'd been for Hank until now.

Clementine looked at Ludek. "I suppose 'Watcher' is fitting."

"What do you call him?" Ludek continued to empty his pack.

"Horace," Rabbit answered, moseying closer to Ludek as he unloaded burlap- and muslin-wrapped packages.

Ludek scowled slightly at Rabbit. "His name isn't Horace."

"Well, we figured, but he's meager on the details." Rabbit sniffed. "The bigger thing is, he don't speak."

Tap tap tap.

The light knocking on the door was followed by a muffled, "Miss Clem, it's me." Hank's voice filtered through the cracks.

The door creaked open a hair. Boone could see an eye peeking through.

"Get in here." Clementine pulled the door wide. "You took too long." She hugged Hank, hurried him in, and then waved Horace in as well, who had to bend to get through the door.

"I was startin' to think I'd have to fetch you from the grave, you ol' cowpoke." Rabbit grinned at Hank.

"Valley's crawlin' with all manner of critters." Hank shuddered. "Stayin' undiscovered took some doin'." His gaze locked onto their visitor, and a smile was quick to surface. "Ho there, Ludek. Pleased as a bee in a honey bath to see you."

"Greetings, Mr. Varney." Ludek bowed to Hank and then Horace. "*Grüße Wächter.*"

Horace subtly nodded back and dropped his load of three packs before squatting next to the fireplace.

"He speaks German," Clementine stated, as if she were writing it down in her book of facts.

Boone started to stand, only to hesitate halfway up as a sharp pain worked its way up his back. He dropped back down on the bed, stretching the kinks from his legs and arms. "And he carries a pack like Fred the Mule."

Rabbit chuckled. "Gotta always have a mule, right Hank?"

Hank nodded. "Wouldn't be no other way."

"*Der Wächter,*" Clementine repeated. "I assume it's his charge to watch the gateway then?"

"He isn't 'charged' with this task," Ludek explained. "As it is with many of us, it is a duty he assumes. He is compelled to do his part in maintaining the balance. It has been so for ..." Ludek seemed to measure his words as he regarded Rabbit, Hank, and Boone. "An exceptionally long time."

What did he mean by that? Exceptionally long. Weeks? Years? Longer? The more Boone learned about Clementine's world, the more questions he had.

Rabbit crossed his arms. "Maybe you can tell us what the hell is going on, and what Horace's duty is, since he was scanty on the subject and left us to face the mind-messin' bastard holed up in this cabin." He threw a few eye-daggers at Horace's back.

"Easy, *amigo*." Boone could see Rabbit was spinning up into a dust devil. "Horace had his fill with that conjuror character. He probably knew he wasn't a match, but figured Clementine was."

"Coulda warned us is all I'm sayin'."

"His name isn't Horace. What conjuror?" Ludek looked to Clementine for the answer.

"There was a creature in this cabin," she started.

"One look in his eyes and you're cracked," Boone added.

"It happened to these three." Clementine pointed at Boone, Hank, and Rabbit.

"Cracked?" Ludek seemed puzzled.

"*Loco*," Rabbit explained. "Off your chump."

Clementine leaned against the wall next to the door. "*Verrückt.*"

"Ah." Ludek nodded. "And not you, *Scharfrichter*?"

"I kept my eyes closed."

A smile spread wide across Ludek's face. "You fought him with your eyes closed?"

"And killed him."

There was no braggadocio in her tone that Boone could hear, only the fact of the matter.

"Hildegard is right about you," Ludek said. "I will use care not to cross you."

Horace approached Rabbit and they stared at each other for a moment before Rabbit shrugged. "He's beggin' pardon for leaving us with the ... What is it? An *hombre* that took his tool? Same as before, right Hank?"

Hank squinted at Horace. "Think he meant 'weapon,' same as before. What took it? Some kinda scout or somethin'?"

"Maybe that. It's a tool he's missin', though." Rabbit sounded certain.

"You two." Boone sighed. "Horace might as well draw pictures in the air."

"Cram sand, Booney."

"*Schlüssel*? A key?" Ludek asked, joining in their guessing game.

Horace lumbered over and laid his meaty hand on Ludek's shoulder.

"It seems you got it right, Ludek." Clementine walked to her pack. "Can you understand him?"

"I cannot. But he can understand me." Ludek studied Horace's neck for a moment. "I see. His voice has been silenced." He frowned at Clementine. "He is able to associate with Mr. Fields and Mr. Varney, but not you or Mr. McCreery, is this correct?"

"Correct. I'm able to interpret his expressions and movements in a limited way but nothing more." Opening her pack, Clementine began to search through it. "We've been relying on his connection with Jack and Hank."

Rabbit jerked in surprise and then whirled toward the fire, his face pinched in a scowl. "About time you showed up," he said to the empty air. "We mighta used your help earlier."

Oh, hell. Boone knew who Rabbit *thought* he was talking to. They were back to this again. "Hey there, Uncle Mort," he said, playing along. "Good to see you."

Eleven

abbit's heart sped up, thumping hard in his chest. "Really Booney? Finally? You see him?"

"No." Boone's face drooped. "I was just fooling, Rabbit. Sorry, *amigo*."

Heat filled Rabbit's cheeks. "Ain't funny, Booney."

"Greetings, Mr. Morton." Ludek bowed in Uncle Mort's direction. "I appreciated your company on the journey here from Deadwood."

"My pleasure, good sir," Uncle Mort said, bowing back. "You've got grit, that is absolute. I would be indebted if you would take it upon yourself to advise Jack here on the merits of courage and resolution."

Rabbit felt the anger well up, warming him from his toes all the way north of his neck until flames shot out the top of his head. It felt that way, anyway. At least it helped overcome some of the chill in his bones. He wanted to berate his uncle, but what would be the point. He growled in his throat, "Thanks for that, Uncle Mort."

"Have we decided on a strategy?" Clementine broke in, looking up from her pack. She was obviously anxious to get moving, the same as always. "Shall we start with the—"

"Wait a damn minute!" Rabbit pointed at Ludek. "You see my uncle?"

Ludek looked at Uncle Mort. "Of course." He shrugged. "Hildegard and Miss Hundt do as well."

Boone shook his head slowly. "Damn, Ludek. Just when I was beginning to think you might have a level head."

Rabbit's heart was back to pounding again, this time aiming to break out of his chest. He wasn't alone! He wasn't *loco*! He hurried to Ludek and grasped both of his shoulders. "He talks to you even? What about

Miss Hildegard?"

Ludek nodded. "Yes to both." He glanced at Uncle Mort. "He has been consistently expressive ... verbally."

"I have things to say," Uncle Mort said, hooking his thumbs in his suspenders.

Rabbit stepped back from Ludek, recognizing a certain amount of indignation in Uncle Mort's voice.

"I meant no offense, Mr. Morton." Ludek tipped his head.

Uncle Mort snickered. "I suppose I do tend to twaddle from time to time."

"You think?" Rabbit loaded his question with plenty of sass.

"Listen, boy. I talk to help you understand a thing."

Rabbit scoffed. He recognized that "boy." It meant Uncle Mort was beginning to lose his calm. But he was feeling ornery after almost freezing to death while Uncle Mort was off gallivanting between Deadwood and Slagton, so he pushed a little harder. "And then you keep talkin' right on past it. Just like Booney."

"Hey now, don't start in on me." Boone raised his bandaged hands in front of him.

"Boy, keep it up. You're on your way to the woodshed." Uncle Mort reached out to grab him by the ear, but missed again and again, his hand swiping through Rabbit's head with each attempt.

Rabbit cringed at the sudden, cold ache in his upper teeth. He waved his uncle away. "We're waaay past that."

"Ludek, you said you have a message from Hildegard?" Closing her pack, Clementine stood, her hands planted on her hips. The question was for Ludek, but she was drilling holes in Rabbit with her stare.

"Apologies. I do." Ludek clasped his hands together in front of him. "You must abandon your plan to directly attack the outbuilding."

Outbuilding? He must mean the barn. Rabbit watched Clementine's gaze darken and harden as it shifted back to Ludek. Her brow lowered while her upper lip curled into a snarl. She looked almost feral. He backed up farther until he was standing beside Boone and Hank.

Ludek raised one hand. "Please consider." He must know there was a chance of him losing that hand in the next few minutes if he wasn't careful. "Hildegard has weighed the information relayed by Mr. Morton along with evidence gathered by me and developed a plan, or rather a suggested sequence of events to guide you."

Rabbit figured that Ludek and Hildegard knew enough to be real careful when they dealt with Clementine. She wasn't just headstrong, she was an Amazon. A killer, and well equipped to carry out her task. Crossing her could be hazardous to one's ability to stay upright, and to the health of everyone nearby, too. Treading lightly was a necessity, especially when she was in … what would he call it? A frenzy? More like a killing frenzy? Boone had called it "bloodlust." It made Rabbit downright fidgety to think it, but she said it herself. She wasn't in complete control when her temper was up.

"So, Hildegard presumes to counsel me on the execution of *my* tasks?" Clementine moved over to the fire, glaring down at it.

"Ludek's got a sound plan, Clementine." Uncle Mort had been quietly floating along each of the four walls in the cabin, through the bed, the table, a stool, and the wall shelf, but now he joined Clementine at the fire. "I can help you reconnoiter."

He could help … Rabbit could have used some help from his uncle before he'd burst into this cabin and run into that glowy-eyed conjuror. Rabbit glowered at him, but Uncle Mort paid him no mind.

Ludek lowered his chin. "Hildegard," he started, then hesitated. He must be choosing his next words carefully. Rabbit sure would be. "*We* presume nothing."

Clementine inhaled deeply, but remained silent, still watching the flames.

Boone opened his mouth to speak but Rabbit quickly jabbed him in the ribs with his elbow, eliciting an "oof." Boone scowled at him and pushed him away but remained silent. Good. Now was the time to stay quiet.

Ludek was trying to reason with a thunderstorm. How many times had he been in this position with other Slayers? Rabbit had heard things that hinted at long-lived *others*. As far as he knew, Slayers lived a regular human life span—unless they were taken out by the beasties they hunted, but how old was Ludek?

Uncle Mort shifted to the other side of Clementine. "Don't give Ludek conniptions. He's here to help, young lady."

Her head turned slightly in his uncle's direction. Hold up! Did she just look at Uncle Mort?

"Clementine." Boone tried again before Rabbit could stop him. His tone was reassuring, gentle.

She hit Boone with a fierce glare, lightning flashed in her eyes. But then her face softened. She took another deep breath, turning to Ludek. "I apologize. You understand what I am."

"I well do." Ludek held her gaze.

Rabbit sized up the situation. Ludek seemed to know exactly how to handle an agitated Slayer.

"The gate must be closed," Ludek continued without emotion.

She nodded once.

"I am sure you have guessed that is the task of *der Wächter*." He looked over at Horace, who bowed at the mention of his title. "I am sure you are also aware it is useless to slay *Draug* and *Höhlendrache* and *Bahkauv* …" Ludek continued with several more German-sounding names Rabbit didn't recognize. "You will make little progress toward cleansing this territory until *der Wächter* accomplishes his objective."

For the first time, Rabbit began to feel that he and Boone truly had become tangled in a net without a knife to cut themselves free. Was Hank feeling the same way? He spared him a glance. The mule skinner stood expressionless, arms folded across his chest, appearing ready to wrestle an alligator if that's what Ludek and Clementine threw at him. Hank's determined, calm demeanor helped Rabbit bolster his own confidence.

"We must retrieve," Ludek started, then paused, his chin lifting slightly. "*You* must retrieve the key."

"*Verdammt!* I knew you'd say that."

"There are other Watchers in Slagton," Ludek continued in his calming tone, as if they were discussing the day's weather. "They and I will assist you if we are able. However, without the key, it is impossible to stop the transferences, and the infestation will spread."

"The barn is infested," she said.

"And will continue to be if the gateway remains open," Ludek countered.

Uncle Mort floated directly in front of Clementine. "You must understand that helping Horace is the next logical step, girl."

"Horace doesn't need—" She stopped abruptly, casting a glance at Rabbit. Then she sighed and looked at the ceiling, muttering something about Odin's eye.

Rabbit gawked at her. What just happened? Did she talk to his uncle?

"Wha … Wait! Miss Clementine?" Rabbit strode over, pointing at

Clementine before coming nose to nose with his ghostly uncle. "Did she just talk to you?"

Uncle Mort's focus drifted away from Rabbit, then he floated a little higher until he was no longer eye level. "I'm starting to get tuckered. Maybe time to do the edges."

Rabbit went on tiptoes. "No you don't. Look at me."

Uncle Mort obeyed. "Fine."

"Did she talk to you?" He thumbed in Clementine's direction. "Can she see you?"

Uncle Mort pursed his lips.

"Yes," Clementine blurted out. "Okay? Yes. I talked to him. I can see and hear your uncle."

Rabbit grinned and frowned with his whole face as a flurry of emotions—surprise, happiness, and relief—rushed through him. His pulse pounded. Finally! He turned toward Boone. "You see him?"

Boone shook his head, looking depressed for the fact. "No, I don't see ghosts. But I guess now that Clementine can, and Ludek and Hildegard can, I'm the odd man out."

"You and me, Boonedog."

"You can't, Hank?" Rabbit asked. "Still?"

"Nope." Hank seemed perfectly happy with the situation.

"Good." Boone rested his hand on Hank's shoulder. "That makes me feel better."

"You didn't tell me, Miss Clementine." Rabbit felt indignant and let it show in his voice.

She shrugged. "I didn't tell anyone."

"How long?"

She exchanged a look with Uncle Mort. "Since Christmas morning."

Christmas morning?!! "So up on the flat? In the cabin with the *Draug*?" Rabbit tested her.

"He wasn't with us then."

"Down in the tents, during the dust-up with the white grizzlies?"

"No, Jack. He wasn't there, either, and you know it."

"I was watching the horses," Uncle Mort defended. "Since nobody else seemed to care."

"Hush, Uncle Mort." He smirked at his uncle. "Lotta good that did, by the way."

"He was there with the horses when Boone and I retrieved them, does that ..." Clementine started, but then shook her head. "Listen, we can't waste time accounting for your uncle's presence every minute of the day. I can see him and I can hear him, the same as you. It's time to move on." She returned her focus to Ludek. "Let's presume I can clean out the barn and perhaps find this key at the same time."

Ludek clasped his hands in front of him. "Please concede to reason, Clementine. You must help *der Wächter* first."

"I believe I am being completely reasonable." Clementine folded her arms. "I think it's entirely possible that what the Watcher needs is in the barn."

"You'll be overrun," Ludek countered.

"I'll be careful."

"Careful and foolhardy may meet, but always fail as bedfellows," Ludek's voice dipped, sounding more growly now.

"The twain shall rarely meet," Clementine shot back.

What? Rabbit rubbed the back of his neck. He was prepared to hold a grudge against Clementine for withholding the fact that she could talk with his uncle, but her conversation with Ludek was distracting him from her comeuppance.

"Miss Johanssen!" Ludek snapped, a vein pulsing in the middle of his forehead. For a split second Rabbit could swear that his eyes bulged slightly and his pupils elongated to dark vertical slits, looking almost snake-like. Then Ludek blinked, and his features settled back to normal. "It would be wise to diminish their numbers prior to moving on the stronghold. You know battle theory, *Scharfrichter*, better than I. If you attack, the outlying forces will collapse on your position and overwhelm you." He indicated toward Rabbit and the others. "Overwhelm us, really, since we will be forced to fight with you."

Clementine sighed, long and loud, cursing at the ceiling yet again.

Ludek waited, hands behind his back, looking as if he had all the time in the world. Had Boone seen Ludek's eyes do that snake trick, too? But Boone was frowning down at his bandaged hands. Hank was watching Clementine, his brow one big, furrowed mess, while Horace still worked the fire.

"Makes sense to me," Uncle Mort said, joining their conversation whether they wanted him to or not. "You don't take all the snakes out of the nest at once. Lure them out, one by one. Exterminate the beasts sure, but do it little by little. Save your strength. Whittle away at them."

He waved his hand toward Rabbit and Boone. "I for one don't want to see my boys harmed due to overzealous intentions. Not you two, nor Hank, for that matter. Always have the superior han—"

"All right, all right, Morton." Clementine shook her head, a hint of a grin on her lips. "There's no question why Boone and Jack chatter like squirrels. They learned from the best."

"Hey!" Boone held up his hands in surrender. "No reason to be insulting. Rabbit can't help flappin' his lips."

"I hear you squawkin', Booney." Rabbit snickered.

Horace rose from his squat by the fire, stood next to Ludek, and began grunting and whistling through his teeth.

"His new buddy," Rabbit whispered to Boone. "Talkin' to him when it's me an' Hank who can understand him."

Boone chuckled, nodding, but his eyes seemed dull, edged with confusion or doubt or something.

Hank scratched above his ear. "Horace says the barn's too busy."

"Of course he does," Clementine said.

"Says there're trouble spots down south, in the cabins down there," Hank continued, "*caper-sus* an' such dug in."

"Does he know why there are so many *others* coming through the gateway?" Clementine asked, looking at Horace instead of Hank.

Hank shook his head. "No, didn't say."

She returned to Ludek. "How about Hildegard? Any message to relay about the Eminent? Is he Masterson's problem and not mine?"

Ludek's head tipped as if he hadn't heard her correctly. "You saw an Eminent?" At her nod, he pressed, "You're sure?"

"As certain as I can be after a brief encounter."

Ludek frowned. "There is no message other than '*Sie müssen dem Wächter helfen.*' "

"What does that mean?" Rabbit asked.

"I need to help the Watcher." Clementine growled about the task.

"What did the Eminent look like?" Ludek asked her. "I do not believe I observed one here."

"Very tall, muscular, shiny ebony skin with the head of a *canis*," Clementine said. "Like one of the ancient Egyptians. He can transmogrify into a gaseous state and travel that way."

Ludek's eyes narrowed. "Transmogrification is extraordinarily uncommon."

"That's what I thought, too."

"Interesting. There is some record of Egyptians using alchemy to transmute metals and occasionally biological entities, but I do not recall any related occurrences that describe transmutation of a human or an *other*."

Clementine bit her lip. "You're right, transmutation might be a more appropriate term. Either way, his clothing resembled that of the ancient Egyptians, at least the drawings I've seen."

"He's not human," Boone interjected, wincing as he stretched his back.

"Dog's head," Rabbit blew out a breath. "That's just *loco*."

"I will discuss this with Hildegard," Ludek said. "It is unlikely that a manifestation of an ancient Egyptian has occurred here, although many creatures may use the gateway or be sent through."

"I suppose I'll need to speak with Masterson about this." Clementine sniffed. "If we make it back to Deadwood."

Ludek scoffed. "I would not list cooperation among Masterson's assets. He is accustomed to treating others as underlings, I think. Hildegard and I avoid him for this reason, among others."

"I don't blame you," she said. "I would be happy to avoid him too, if I could."

Horace moved in front of Hank and grunted.

"Miss Clem, he says we should start on the ridgetop above his dwelling. He's seen … uh …"

"Images of ghostly activity," Rabbit translated, still not certain how he knew what Horace was trying to say, but he just did.

"Yep," Hank continued. "Goin's-on up thereabouts. He thinks we should stop the spread."

"Tighten the boundary on those buggers." Rabbit stared at Horace. "Keep 'em to Slagton, so it's manageable again. Down south, too—*capersus* down there. They herd the … the travelers?"

"He already said that," Clementine grumbled.

"We could head north along the base of the ridge," Boone suggested, limping over next to Clementine. "Find a way up, then back south along the top of the ridge, swing around down near that lake, then up into the forest to the east of the barn. Come in at the barn that way, like we were going to originally. Clean up any of these 'travelers' along the way."

Boone's plan made sense to Rabbit since it would make Horace *and*

Clementine happy.

"Do you have the map?" Ludek asked. He finished his tea, leaving the tin cup on the table.

"Yep. I've added a little here and there." Boone pulled the tallowed paper from his saddlebag and unfolded it. "This cabin. Horace's cave."

Ludek studied it. "I'm pleased you find it useful."

Seeing the map reminded Rabbit of the hundreds of tree stumps.

"I would like to see that, too." Clementine held out her hand.

"Why so many stumps?" Rabbit blurted out. He couldn't help himself. He really wanted to know why Ludek had spent so much time drawing them.

"Yeah, what is it with you and those stumps?" Boone handed the map to Clementine.

Ludek raised one white eyebrow. "I—"

"Never mind that, Jack," Clementine stared down at it. "Ludek, do you recall a pathway up anywhere along this bluff?"

He studied the map for a moment and then pointed. "Here. There is an animal trail up this ravine. It will be somewhat arduous here. And here. But it should be passable."

She ran her finger farther down the ridgeline. "You're right, Boone. We should be able to follow the ridgeline south to the lake, then head west."

"Good." Boone pulled a twine-tied linen bag of biscuits from one of the packs and began handing them out.

Horace cringed away from Boone's outstretched hand and stood with his back to the fire, staring at the biscuit. He croaked at Hank. Awful images of smashed animal heads and bloody chunks of meat filled Rabbit's thoughts. "That's how you hunt?" he whispered, grimacing as the revolting visions kept coming.

"Says he's huntin' later. He'll get his own vittles." Hank's eyes were wide, his face a bit paler than normal. He must be seeing it all, too.

"Listen here, Horace," Rabbit started, meaning to put a stop to the repulsive images Horace was forcing into his head.

"We'll head out in the morning then," Clementine cut him off, still focused on the map. "These three," she said, waving toward Rabbit, Boone and Hank. "They need at least that long to recuperate. Will you be with us, Ludek?"

"No. I will leave tonight with *der Wächter*." He turned to Horace. "I assume you will want to search for your attendants. We could communicate your activities to any we can find. Perhaps they might aid in the eradication of the scourge that afflicts this valley."

"Horace says he's a Watcher, not a warrior," Rabbit told Ludek. He would argue the point after seeing the big-fisted Watcher smash the head of a white grizzly flat.

"He'll clobber the whomper what needs whompin', head to heels." Hank's face pinched into a pucker. "What'd I say?"

"Ho-boy, Hank!" Rabbit laughed. "Train went off the tracks on that one." He slapped his knee and then winced, immediately regretting it. Apparently he'd taken a bruising there, too.

Boone grinned. "What the hell are you talking about, Hank?"

"He'll whomp whoever's doing the whomping?" Rabbit tried.

"He doesn't want to fight, but he will." Ludek concluded. "So it is. Horace and I will be off, then."

Rabbit cringed at the thought of Ludek, or Horace for that matter, spending the night out in the frigid, blustery Black Hills night. Especially with countless *other* buggers out there with them.

"I'm not comfortable with you going out there, Ludek," Clementine said. "Shouldn't you stay here? We'll all set off in the morning."

Ludek shook his head and smiled. "Your tea has revived me, Clementine. Thank you. I will be—how is it said here—dandy? I'm confident that *der Wächter* will be fine as well. We will try to contact his attendants and then scout the area. You need not worry about intruders, at least for this night." He strapped his pack over his wool cape and opened the door. "Good evening Clementine, Boone, Hank, Mr. Fields."

Rabbit pulled the blanket tighter around him as a cold gust of air rushed through the open door. Why the formality with only his name? "Just call me Rabbit."

"Rabbit, then." Ludek waited as Horace plodded out the door and then followed him out, closing the door behind him.

"Now what?" Rabbit asked, noticing Uncle Mort had disappeared as well. Maybe he was going with Ludek, too. Would have been nice of the ol' codger to let somebody know his plans.

Clementine leaned back against the closed door. "Now we rest. I have a feeling tomorrow might be even more troubling than today."

Twelve

It had been a comfortable night for Clementine, considering the condition of the little one-room cabin. The storm had blustered through the cracks and crevices of the cabin most of the night, and there was only one bed, which they'd agreed Boone should use since he was in the worst shape of all. He bucked the idea, initially, but the pains in his head eventually forced him to lie down again.

She had made him drink another cup of tea, this time full of herbs to help him sleep. His headache had her looking into his eyes more than once in the feeble firelight, checking his pupils for signs of a worse injury, but it was too dark to see for sure.

With the blankets Horace and Hank retrieved from the cave, along with the extras that Ludek had brought in his pack, they each made nests to settle into for some much-needed sleep. Jack took her up on the offer of the same tea she'd given Boone and soon drifted off, but Hank declined. He was feeling back to his old self, much to her relief. Hank stayed up later with her, stoking the fire as he often did back at The Pyre before leaving her for the night so that they had to feed it only two more times before dawn.

She'd woken a short time ago to the sound of a dull thud on the roof, leaping up from the blanket and peeking outside only to find the culprit was a falling branch. Otherwise, the night had been uneventful. Certainly, she had Ludek and Horace, and possibly the other Watchers standing a perimeter, to thank for that.

Back inside, she checked to make sure the poultice she'd applied to the scratches on her chest and back was doing its job. The lacerations were healing quickly. The time she'd devoted to learning her amma's recipes had been well spent.

Careful not to wake the others, she sat on one of the stools, thinking about her grandparents. She hadn't properly understood the love and devotion she'd received from both of them in her younger years, mixed in with all of her training and schooling. Or grasped how extraordinary the gift of their knowledge was. Or realized how fleeting her time with them would be.

Shaking off her melancholy, she stretched her arms and shoulders, wincing at the tenderness of the spot where her foe's blade had gone deep almost a fortnight ago. She was a quick healer, especially when it came to injuries from *others*. It was one of the innate gifts that came with having Slayer blood.

Another peek out the door found the landscape bathed in the gray light of early dawn. The sun would soon rise on the crisp Black Hills morning. She knew what to expect as soon as she stepped outside—painfully cold air would assault her nose and throat and lungs like thousands of tiny sharp daggers. This was nothing new. She'd been raised on the coast of the Norwegian Sea, and that was without doubt a harsher environment than this. But that didn't mean she enjoyed the discomfort of a frigid morning.

The next few days would most likely be spent without shelter or a hot meal. If she lived through them. There was always that dark cloud in the back of her mind, especially more so with the amount of trouble they'd stumbled into since arriving at Slagton. She sat back down on the stool and made an effort to ease her mind by silently reciting bits of wisdom from her afi.

Hank rose a short time later, gathered his cooking supplies, and started in on a hearty, aromatic breakfast. She finished her meditation, enjoying the aroma of pungent coffee and pan-fried fatback sizzling over the fire.

Jack and Boone were still sleeping, though Jack was starting to toss and turn, showing signs of awakening. She stood over Boone for a moment, studying him. His injured hands would take a little more time to heal before he could grip his sword well, but she had a feeling he'd suffer the pain if killing needed to be done.

What had that conjuror done to him? Why had it sent him off to dig in the frozen ground? He'd ripped two fingernails completely off and torn most of the others. They would heal in time, but his fingers would be bothersome for a while. Not that he'd let on about his pain. Poultice and wrap were the best she could do here, and that was enough.

"Miss Clem, you want I should wake the Sidewinders?" Hank whispered, joining her next to Boone. "My way of thinkin'? Best not to push our luck stayin' in one place too long." He handed her a tin of coffee too hot to hold in one hand for long.

If Clementine had learned anything, it was to listen to Hank's "way of thinking," unless it interfered with her way of thinking. He had an uncanny way of knowing the what, when, and where of a thing.

"Yes," she replied in a quiet voice. "We should get moving. A quick breakfast, then up the ridge."

Hank drooped his head. "Maybe, better if'n we send these boys back to Deadwood. I got a feelin' this is gonna get dangerous for them. Dangerous for us, too, but we can handle it. Them Sidewinders might be … it don't … what I'm sayin' is—"

"Gee, Hank," Jack said from behind them. "If I didn't know better, I'd think you were trying to cut us loose."

Clementine turned to find him propped up on his elbow.

"Aw, Jack Rabbit. Worried about you two is all. You ain't accustomed to these things."

"I'd argue that point," Jack parried. "Given the last few run-ins we've had with Miss Clementine's 'friends,' I'd say we're pretty damned accustomed."

Clementine frowned back at Boone. If Hank was worried, then there was definitely a reason to be concerned. The problem was, there was absolutely no chance Jack or Boone would abandon her. "These two stubborn mules won't go back to Deadwood. And the *others* around here aren't my friends."

"Not goin' nowhere," Jack agreed.

"You know why?" She shifted her frown to Jack, wanting to prod him a little.

"Because the Sidewinders are worth their weight and a welcome and necessary part of any demon-fighting posse," he answered with an excess of self-assurance.

"Well, my answer would include words like 'willful,' 'contradictory.' Hmm, 'recalcitrant.' "

"Okay, Miss Pessimistic." Jack stood, stretching. "You went decidedly contrary on the subject."

"Mulish. Dogged. Opinionated." She teased him a little more, fighting a grin.

"Bull-headed," Boone added, sitting up in the bed.

"Shut up, Booney, you're fraternizin' with the wrong side."

"Troublesome. Bothersome. Flaps the lips alot," Boone continued.

"She means you, too, dunderhead." Jack leaned down and poked Boone in the sternum.

"Hoo hoo. Jack Rabbit can be a rabbit-rouser, all right." Hank handed tin plates of fried fatback and biscuits along with cups of steaming coffee to each of them.

"Follow Hank's lead is all I do." Jack took the tin plate and sat next to Boone on the bed, mashed the biscuit and meat together, and jammed a bite of it into his mouth.

"I assume we'll be headed for the barn, just in a roundabout way." Boone eyed her as he took a bite of biscuit. "Hank! You soaked this in fatback grease." He groaned in appreciation. "Will you marry me?"

Clementine nodded. "At the risk of sounding dramatic, my concern is to cleanse this area. I believe the infestation centers on the barn. My concern is not to run errands for a Watcher. He has his responsibilities, I have mine."

"Seems they overlap, currently." Boone stopped chewing and winced, putting the heel of his hand on his forehead, his eyelids fluttering.

The headache appeared to still be bothering him. *He probably has a little bit of yesterday bouncing around in there.* Maybe. Or maybe not. She studied Boone for a moment, replaying the battle with the Eminent, suspicion flitting through her mind. It disappeared as quickly as it had come, but left behind a ball of tension born of worry. That headache could mean a bigger problem than his sore hands, especially when it came to fighting for his life.

"Perhaps," she said, keeping her concern for his health to herself for now. "But I'll follow my path. Whether it incorporates Horace's wishes, I can't say. Besides, I do agree that going straight for the barn is foolhardy. There are simply too many adversaries between it and us, especially if that Egyptian Eminent is part of the mix. We'll thin the herd, so to speak."

"Fair enough," Boone said, blinking a few times and then returning to his plate of food. "You agree, Rabbit?"

It appeared his headache was fleeting. She'd have to watch how often it recurred today, and keep track of the intensity as best she could without calling him out on it and worrying Hank and Jack.

"Line 'em up. I got a grudge against that ebony character in particular, though." Jack made a finger gun and shot Boone with it.

It was cavalier of Jack to think he could simply kill the Egyptian Eminent, but she expected it from him. And he did possess a speed— no, a quickness—that belied the fact that he was human. His ability to measure a situation and respond to it as quickly as he did was almost inhuman. He also healed unnaturally quickly. She would like to believe it was due to her skill with tinctures, balms, and poultices, but it would be naïve to think it was wholly her doing. And his ability to communicate with his dead uncle and Horace reinforced the idea that there was something about him she didn't understand. She'd seen many inexplicable things in her travels, so adding Jack to the list wasn't a stretch.

"Let's get movin', Miss Clem." Hank's appeal jarred her from her thoughts.

"Okay, Hank." She gobbled up the last of her crispy fatback.

Hank took Clementine's tin and held his hand out for Boone's and Jack's. "You boys ready to hoof?"

"Horny toads, Hank. Tryin' to have a breakfast is all." Jack shoved the last of his biscuit sandwich in his mouth and drained his coffee cup, handing both tins to Hank.

"I'm good to ride," Boone added. He tested his grip on his scimitar and winced a little.

* * *

Boone's fingertips hurt. Ached.

Lunkhead. Digging in frozen ground is a good way to lose your fingertips.

He shifted his grip slightly on his scimitar. *Thanks for that. Like I don't know.*

As if the damage to his hands wasn't enough, the conjuring bastard that got into his head had left remnants. At least that's what he figured was happening. Strange things, like fragments of thoughts, had been worming through his mind since he'd woken up in the cabin, surfacing occasionally to interrupt his sensibilities, setting his nerves on edge. Not only voices, but impulses. Ideas. Compulsions.

Slayer.

He tried to brush aside the hot rush of anger that came with that thought, making his eyes burn.

She will kill you!

The Slayer.

He rubbed his eyes.

Kill her!

"Stop," he said quietly.

He looked over to see Clementine watching him. He gave her a small smile and set his scimitar aside, and then began rolling blankets and stuffing them into his pack. It was probably best if he kept these strange notions to himself for the time being.

Boone helped as much as he could with bandaged hands as they packed up the provisions and weapons Hank and Horace had retrieved from the cave. He kept his mind occupied, pushing out the disturbing thoughts. *Some cold, fresh air is what I need.*

They were ready to set out within an hour. With the additional supplies Ludek had brought, each was obliged to carry an extra-large pack. Clementine had suggested that they leave a few of the blankets behind, but Rabbit was loath to part with anything that had something to do with keeping warm. Boone couldn't blame him after his own experience the previous day.

Outside the cabin, his ears rang in the quiet. Steamy breath in the damp cold was to be expected but the quiet was not. It was absolute. Not a bird sang. He would have expected at least the caw of a crow or screech of a hawk.

The trees and underbrush were still as gravestones, the breezes of a fitful afternoon having not yet commenced. The storm had passed, leaving in its wake a bright sun and stray, puffy clouds that betrayed with the appearance of a warm spring day. Instead, winter welcomed them with crackly, cold dry air and a thick blanket of powdery new snow covering the ground and trees.

Boone couldn't decide which was worse: wet, heavy, drippy snow that offered a degree of warmth; or the fine, fluffy, powdery snow that indicated bitter cold. The latter gnawed at patches of exposed skin and irritated his nostrils with each stinging breath. It did seem to clear his head some, though.

Rabbit gazed up at the sky and hugged himself, then he scowled at Hank. "I do recollect you sayin' something about spring bein' around the next bend." He pulled on one of Boone's pack straps and adjusted the load, which felt surprisingly lighter. Then he turned back to Hank. "Well, I been down a good stretch of winter road and I ain't seen no bends at all, let alone one with a blade of green grass or buttercup at the other end."

"Hidin' under all this snow, prob'ly." Hank grunted as he helped Clementine with her pack, pushing on it and retying one of the straps. "Besides, weren't me said so, it was ol' Fred's tail."

Boone turned, along with the others, to stare at him.

He stopped his busy-ness and stared back. "What?"

"Fred's tail?" Rabbit sniggered. "Can't wait to hear this one."

"You ain't never heard of ol' Fred's magical tail?"

"Here we go." Rabbit folded his arms and smirked at Hank.

"You don't believe in magic, Mr. Ghost Talker?" Clementine goaded Rabbit.

"Well, sure. Some kinds. Take that McCuddle's—"

Boone grinned. "That elixir is a lot of things, but one thing it's not is magical." His head was feeling better and better. Cold fresh air was what he'd needed. All those strange thoughts were probably just leftover dreams from a restless night and whatever was in that tea Clementine had insisted he drink.

"Is so," Rabbit shot back. "You need to percolate it is all. Take the blinders off when you gander at the world." He stretched his arms wide. "It's a wondrous place, Mr. Analytical."

"Let's go, gentlemen." Clementine headed northeast, plowing through the foot of fresh, powdery snow, toward the base of the cliff.

Hank fell in behind her, widening the trail she had started, with Rabbit following. Boone brought up the rear.

"About Fred," Rabbit prodded.

"He surely can blaze a trail, but there he is, safe and sound in Horace's cave." Hank trudged along. "This powdery white is for the deer. Gets down in my boots."

"Hank, you're gettin' a snowball down your pants if you don't tell me about Fred's tail," Rabbit threatened.

"Oh, right. His tail shakes a little this way when it's gonna rain." Hank shook his backside to the right. "And a little that way when it's gonna snow." He shook his backside to the left. "Just gotta ask him."

"Usin' whinnies and haws?" Rabbit asked.

"Yep. And it goes like this when the sun's a gonna shine." He gyrated his hips to make his backside go round and round.

Rabbit burst into laughter. "Horses an' mules shake their tails all the time. Don't mean they're magical occasions." He was getting snagged up in one of Hank's twirly tales, and Boone was going to do his level best to stay clear of it.

"Fred does it special."

Rabbit grinned back at Boone. "Like Estella down at the Hacienda Hotel."

Boone had danced with Estella a time or two in Santa Fe. She had a decidedly appealing wiggle and jiggle right around her mid-section and up a little from there, too.

"Special how?" Rabbit was fully hooked.

"Helps if'n he's drunk."

How would being drunk help Fred? "Okay then." Boone felt himself getting hooked, too.

"Yep. Barley an' hops is what does it. That's my thinkin' anyway." Hank took a few quick steps to keep up with Clementine.

"Brings out the gift of prognostication?" Boone couldn't keep himself from asking.

"Yessiree. Uhh. That means he gets hunches?"

"Sure," Boone answered. "Just weather? Or other things?"

"He gets all sortsa hunches, but he's particular good at weather."

Clementine halted abruptly and scanned the face of the cliff above them.

"You see somethin', Miss Clem?" Hank gingerly stepped up beside her.

After a short pause, she pointed at the top of the cliff. "No. We're here. This is where we go up."

Boone studied the cliff. It had collapsed in a landslide, much like the one they'd navigated down two days prior. They were about half a mile east of there now.

"Should be easy," Rabbit said from beside him. He traced a trail up through the rocks with his finger. "Up that slope, that's where Rabbit breaks his leg; through that pinch between those boulders is where Rabbit is gonna break his arm; then over that hump. That'll send Rabbit tumbling to the bottom to die, or start all over again. Oh, and see that straight up climb between those two outcroppings? That'll kick Rabbit's a—"

"Rabbits *are* delicate," Boone interrupted.

"Delicate as a sidewinder, you bullwhacker." Rabbit flicked Boone's hat and took off after Clementine and Hank, who had already started toward the cliff.

Half an hour later, they had worked well up the steep, craggy slope, blazing trail through deep, snag-hiding powdery snow. Small avalanches assaulted them constantly. If not for the snow, Boone was certain they would have made short work of the climb, but the two steps forward, one step back rule was impeding their progress.

That, and Boone couldn't help but occasionally put his back to the cliff and admire the view across the valley. Outside of the malevolent forces he knew waited for them there, it was a beautiful view. Truly. He was able to see beyond the cliff defining the other side of the valley, to rows of ridgelines and peaks rolling regularly across the landscape as far as he could see.

It reminded him a little of the Pacific Ocean, which he and Rabbit had gazed upon while camping along the coastline south of San Francisco a few years back. The ocean was much flatter of course, but the blotchy blacks and greens and blues of the trees seemed a close cousin to the dark, roiling ocean waters. The snow-covered hills and tree tops were a reasonable likeness of the frothy, angry whitecaps that dotted the surface of the Pacific until they finally met with the sky, how far away Boone couldn't tell. He remembered the incomprehensible size of the ocean. The absence of mountains and rock and soil. The lack of any footing or firm ground had made him uneasy. A boat or ship no matter how big would still be too small to measure against the vastness of it.

At that point, he'd decided that firm land was his purview. Rabbit could have his pirate ships and sea monsters, and Boone would be happy to welcome him back whenever his *amigo* made port.

Oddly, that unease he'd felt next to the ocean had returned now. Here. The lack of firm footing. The feeling of being consumed by the vastness. Was it simply a remnant of the conjuror's manipulation of his thoughts? Or was it something more? One misstep and he would fall into the deep dark ocean, or into an existence foreign to him, and be lost forever, swept away like a tiny speck in an immense vortex of—

"Booney! Git yer hind end movin'. We'll leave your butt on this hillside." Rabbit's voice came from some way ahead of him behind a group of large rocks.

He shook the unsettling thoughts from his head. *What the hell was that?*

He started to turn back toward the hillside but spotted a black dot lifting from a tree out in the valley, maybe a quarter mile away. It was a crow, he knew, partly because of its size but mostly because of the series of caws it issued as it climbed into the air. It would have been unremarkable except for the fact that it was the first sign of wildlife he had seen or heard since they left the cabin. The sight of the bird lifted his spirits. He hadn't realized, but there had been little evidence of normalcy since leaving Deadwood, and the lack of it had affected his disposition.

"Hello, Mr. Crow. It seems the skies belong to you today."

He watched two dark dots appear from behind a billowy gray and white cloud and begin circling above the crow.

Hawks? No, too big. Their wingspans must be wide as a freight wagon is long! And too fast. Black as the crow.

The longer he watched, the surer he was they weren't hawks or falcons, or even eagles.

Suddenly, one collapsed into a stoop, followed quickly by the other. They fell on a trajectory that intersected with the crow.

The crow, realizing the threat, began a steady staccato of squawking cries, swooping and diving and turning in an attempt to evade its attackers.

The ambush was fast and well timed. As the first reached the crow, it extended its legs and snagged the doomed bird. The other banked into a tight spiral and crashed into the first. They tumbled through the air, flapping their great wings until finally they separated and flew toward the ridgeline to the south.

Boone strained his eyes to see them. They were each carrying something in their claws. They must have torn the crow in two, each escaping with a piece of the prize. He watched them until they disappeared behind an outcrop farther south on the cliff edge. The same direction he and his companions were headed.

"Boone!"

"What?" Boone looked over his shoulder.

Rabbit had descended into view and had both hands in the air.

Boone glanced back to where the giant raptors had disappeared, and then at Rabbit again.

"Dammit, Boone. What in the name of Peg Leg Pete are you doin'?"

He pointed. "Did you see that?"

Rabbit shrugged. "What?"

"That … those …" Boone took a breath to smooth out his tied-up tongue. "A crow? Over there?"

Rabbit dropped his chin and settled into his "You gotta be shittin' me" face.

"A crow just got torn apart by …" What actually were those things? He needed to get a hold on his wits. "Damnedest thing. Two hawks took a crow out of the air and tore it apart."

Rabbit raised an eyebrow. "Hawks don't hunt together. They're loners. Any hawk I ever saw, anyway."

"I'm not shittin' you."

"Okay, okay. But we gotta get movin'. Miss Clementine ain't waitin' for stragglers, which means Hank ain't waitin' for stragglers neither. *I'll kill you.*" Rabbit waited, his hand outstretched.

Boone frowned up at his *amigo.* "What did you say?"

"Come on, Booney. I said let's get movin'. Miss Clementine and Hank ain't waitin'."

Boone watched Rabbit for another second. He could have sworn he heard …

Goddamned conjuror!

He took one last look at the valley below. "One strange thing after another," he said to himself and trudged up the hill toward Rabbit.

* * *

"Is he coming? What's taking so long?" Clementine was doing her best not to burst. Boone had lagged behind all the way up to the top of the ridge, slowing their progress at every step. She was about to go back and try to carry him up the incline.

"Still gettin' the rocks in his noggin squared away, I'd guess," Hank said, his back to her. He'd spent the last few minutes bent over, looking for any tracks that might tell them which way to proceed. She'd prefer they aim toward the barn, but she knew Hank and the Sidewinders were riding along Ludek's side of the fence.

Was Boone's head still hurting? After they'd left the cabin, he seemed to perk up, showing no signs of pain. Although he hadn't quite been himself either. His gaze often seemed glazed rather than sharp. And his movements weren't quite right, jerky at times rather than smooth and confident. How long would it take the conjuror's hold on his mind to fade?

Jack and Hank seemed to have shaken free and returned to normal. Why not Boone?

"Miss Clem, these here might be signs. Somethin' musta' been up here during the squall. Tracks are partial covered."

"You said 'squall'?" Clementine was well aware of the meaning of the word. It was sometimes used to describe a short storm, but generally it was a distinctly nautical term.

Hank glanced sideways at her. "Did I? Jack Rabbit and his pirates, I suspect." He frowned off to the south. " 'Storm' is what I meant to say." Then he swept his hand toward the south. " 'Spect we'll be off thataway, like we planned."

As Hank's "thataway" was in the general direction of the barn, Clementine nodded.

Rabbit crested the ridgeline, tugging Boone along with him. "Come on, you ol' donkey, get your hind end up here. Miss Clementine and Hank are waitin'."

Boone smacked Rabbit's hands. "Off! I'll give you a few ideas where to put those."

"Try to help a fella and he bites, just like an ornery mutt." Rabbit turned his back on Boone and tromped up next to Hank. "He's hungry, I think. You got the ash cakes, right Hank?"

Clementine watched while Hank tried to reach around to his pack before turning his back to Jack for help.

"Clementine." Boone reached her and sagged until his hands were resting on his knees. He took a few big, puffy breaths.

"Are you okay?" She touched his shoulder, checking if he was shivering from the cold, then squeezing hard enough to feel if his muscles were trembling from the climb. Neither was happening. Most likely, the ordeal the previous day had drained his stamina and he needed more recuperation time.

She looked at the conjuror's other two victims. Jack was unnaturally resilient, his quickness to laugh and unlabored breathing showed that. And Hank? Good fortune followed that man. One would never know he'd been dragged through the trees by a white grizzly a short time ago. But Boone lacked both of those traits.

"I'm fine. Just need to catch my breath."

She nodded, believing him. Mostly. She patted his shoulder before stepping back to give him some space. "That's fine. It looks to be generally level now for a while."

The terrain to the north was indeed flat, with only trees adding any relief. To the east another ridgeline scrawled north to south. Their destination was to the south, though. If they stuck close to the edge of the cliff along the Slagton valley, only minor hills and rocky outcrops interrupted the shallow glens and draws they would need to traverse. The evergreens were exceptionally large, but well-spaced with no undergrowth to present hardships in their passage.

"Here, Booney. Eat this." Rabbit handed a crusty cornmeal biscuit to his friend.

Boone took it without a flippant reply and stuffed it in his mouth.

A prickle of unease feathered down Clementine's spine. She couldn't shake the notion that something was wrong with him. Then again, she'd never seen him hurt before like this, both physically and mentally.

"Yer gonna want some water to wash that sawdust down, Boonedog." Hank handed him a canteen.

Boone nodded and took it, standing upright again. After a few gulps, he wiped his mouth with his coat sleeve. "Okay. Enough hen-pecking. I'm ready." He wiggled under his pack, then jutted his chin out. "This way, right?"

Clementine eyed him for another moment, trying to see if there was some sign of ill health she'd missed before, but then shrugged. Maybe she could convince him to let her check him over closer when they stopped to camp for the night.

"That's right," she said and headed south, taking long strides to get out in front of the crew.

* * *

Rabbit's stomach ached with worry. Something was wrong with his friend.

They'd been walking only a few minutes and twice Boone had stopped to look up into the treetops, as if frozen by the rustle of the needles and branches in the erratic breezes that had kicked up since they'd reached the top of the ridge. A pat on the back and a "Hey, Booney" was all it took to break his trance, but still it bothered Rabbit since Boone seemed to have no idea why he'd stopped or what he was looking at.

After he'd started hearing Boone mumbling to himself, he'd decided to stick close.

They followed the cliff edge. Rabbit occasionally prodded Boone along until, having walked for half an hour, Clementine abruptly stopped and held up her open hand. She scanned the pine trees to the east. Rabbit looked too. His eyes weren't as sharp as hers, but maybe if he concentrated …

Nope. Nothing. She was looking at nothing.

"There," she whispered and pointed into a thick grouping of aspens.

Rabbit squinted at it but still saw nothing but patches of white and brown and black mixed in the shadows. He looked to Hank and shrugged.

Hank pointed at his eyes and shook his head.

"It's eating," she told them in a hushed voice. "We might be able to pass by if we're quiet."

"Pass by what?" Boone asked.

"A white grizzly."

"Sheeat," Rabbit muttered. "Can't these characters send along something new?" What was he saying? "Wait. No doubt somethin' else would be somethin' with more teeth and bigger claws. No thank you."

"We'll sneak by, but we need to stay on guard for the partner."

"Why are we sneaking? Why ain't we killing?" Rabbit knew well enough that an adversary avoided usually meant a future problem.

"The noise might sound the alarm. We're downwind, so it won't smell us. Come on." Clementine led them closer and closer, always with an eye on the white grizzly.

As they snuck from tree to tree to the south and east, Rabbit began to see what Clementine saw, movement in a cluster of aspen trunks. The white grizzly was well camouflaged by the snow and white bark of the trees.

To sneak past, they would need to come within a stone's throw, and Rabbit didn't like it. He resisted the urge to jerk his pistol.

They had the upper hand. The advantage of surprise. Who knew what the situation would be later. "Let's kill it," he whispered.

Clementine stopped, turning to glare at him, then pointed to her ear.

He nodded and watched the grizzly, chilled by the crunching and grunting. It really was eating! But what? What was it crunching on? Bones?

It suddenly stood on its hind legs. Rabbit reached for his gun, but then pulled his hand away, taking a deep breath.

It was a big fucker, probably at least ten feet top to bottom. Bending down, it pawed at the ground and pulled up on … was it a deer leg? He wasn't sure. The piece of prey was so badly mangled he could only make out the bloody flesh with a length of white bone protruding from the end. The pile of meat and guts on the ground in front of it didn't help him identify the animal. He hoped it was a deer anyway. The alternatives were even less pleasant. The big bastard picked at the flesh with its claws, peeling it away from the bone.

"You seen this before, Miss Clem?" Hank whispered when they paused behind a stack of boulders.

"Yes, when we were down in the tents."

Rabbit looked at Boone to share the "holy shit" scene, but Boone was focused on the ground in front of him, wearing a bewildered look on his face.

Oh hell, not now, Booney. Stay focused. Rabbit scrubbed his hand down his face. He returned to the grizzly, watching as it peeled and scraped at the bone, removing almost all of the flesh.

"Never seen …" Hank covered his mouth with his hand.

The beast froze, and then stuck its long snout in the air and sniffed. *Shit!*

But Clementine was right, they were downwind. There wasn't any way it could smell them, could it?

The grizzly looked in their direction.

Clementine grasped the handles of her twin short swords, her body clearly ready to lunge.

After a few seconds of seemingly staring directly at them, the creature refocused on the freshly cleaned bone. It began taking long licks, bottom to top, as if enjoying a piece of rock candy.

Rabbit grimaced. He still couldn't make out what type of animal it was eating, but the femur and tibia were still held together by ligaments and certainly looked like those of a deer.

As he continued to watch, both mesmerized and horrified, the grizzly stuck a knobby end of bone into its mouth, grabbed it with both paws, and bit down, breaking off a shard of bone. Then it started chewing. Another crunch and grunt, and it began gnawing on the jagged bone still held it its paws.

"Jehoshaphat, that's repugnant." Hank face was pinched tight. "Makin' me look upon such a thing."

Rabbit's belly churned. It was already bothering him, what with Boone being out of sorts. Now, with the *CRUNCH! CRUNCH! CRUNCH!* of teeth on bone, he was struggling not to lose what was left of his breakfast.

"Stop it stop it stop it," Boone mumbled.

Clementine waved them forward. "Keep moving."

Rabbit grabbed the shoulder of Boone's sheepskin coat and tugged him along behind Clementine. He didn't want to follow her. Not anymore. Not after watching that white grizzly tear flesh from bone. What he really wanted was out. He wanted to scurry straight back to Santa Fe and sit on the porch with Boone and Uncle Mort. He wanted to eat Isadora's tamales and drink her sarsaparilla and tell stories until midnight like they used to do.

Hank was right. He and Boone didn't belong here.

* * *

Boone's head throbbed.

Strange visions flitted through it, only to be replaced by stranger ideas.

Every time he tried to focus on sensible, lucid thoughts, they were pushed aside by intense feelings of fear and hate that spurred even darker thoughts.

Shadows overhead pushed down on him. *I'm in a barn?*
That's impossible. I'm in Slagton—

He blinked, the shadows fading as the light grew brighter. *Am I in a dream?*

"Booney." Rabbit was shaking him by the arm. "We're past the white grizzly. He didn't see us."

"Grizzly …" He didn't remember anything about a grizzly. There'd been … something … on the way … Deadwood.

The dark silhouette of a man with the head of a dog suddenly filled his vision. A staff with a skull on the end descended toward his forehead.

He'd seen this before.

He'd been here before.

His gaze locked on the staff. He recognized it.

Clementine … She was coming for him, her sword leading the way.

Kill the Slayer! Kill her!

He reached for the handle of his sword, squeezing it, pain stabbed at his hand.

Thirteen

"*C*an you tell how many were here?" Clementine studied the tracks leading up to the edge of the cliff and then peered up at the darkening sky. It looked like snow was moving in again.

"It's a clutter, Miss Clem." Hank tilted his head. "They was here for a little while, diddlin' around up here, after the snow fell last night, mostly. Disturbs my quietude to think they was up here watchin' us, who knows how long."

"Same here."

She and Hank stood on a bluff that soared above the cabin they'd slept in the night before. Jack and Boone had stayed back in the trees to rest—in actuality to allow Boone to rest and gather his wits. Jack just didn't want to let his *amigo* out of his sight.

Boone's condition was worsening quickly. If it continued as it was, she was going to have to *try* to send Boone and Jack back to Hildegard in Deadwood. They probably wouldn't go, but she had to try.

She couldn't take the chance of Boone losing his head in the middle of a skirmish. Maybe Hildegard could diagnose and remedy whatever it was that ailed him. Whether his sporadic headaches and bouts of confusion were simply a matter of a head injury he'd sustained when the Eminent backhanded him, or if they had something to do with the conjuror's mind games.

Both ideas had her frowning at the horizon, dread heavy in her heart. What in the hell had happened to him? If it was the conjuror's doings, why was Boone steadily getting worse instead of shaking it off, like Jack and Hank? Why hadn't the conjuror's spell dissipated after she'd killed it? The darkening sky reflected her thoughts more and more when it came to Boone's condition.

"They milled," Hank continued, pulling her back to the task at hand. "For a spell, anyhow, then somethin' shooed 'em off thataway." He pointed toward where Boone and Jack waited.

She squatted, examining the prints in the snow, the way the smaller ones were grouped around the larger ones. She started to see a pattern. Hank was right, there were a number of creatures here. Not white grizzlies. Not humans. Not *Mekal Spaen*.

"Here. This was a big'n. He kinda just stood here, over t' here, then back again." Hank shuffled back and forth, following the tracks he was describing. "Few times more, right on the edge of the bluff. Ain't no better spot to lay eyes on our little abode last night." He scowled down at the cabin, then back at the ground. "Then off over there. Into them trees, looks like."

"And the others?" Clementine had an idea what made the tracks, and it wasn't one of Horace's associates.

"Lotsa smaller goblins. Lighter or smaller. Traipsed all over this bluff. Antsy little goblins. Lotsa claws like always. Maybe not so little. Then off, same as the bigger fella."

So, they'd been spied upon. Since the tracks were fresh, who—or whatever it was—had been here after the storm had passed. "I don't know exactly what creatures made these tracks, but I know why they're here."

"How's that, Miss Clem?"

She stood, glancing back toward the trees again. "It was a bounty hunter."

Were they being watched right now? She hadn't sensed anything yet, but she'd been distracted by Boone's troubles since leaving the cabin.

"Sounds disagreeable." Hank pursed his lips. "Judgin' by the name of it, I suppose I should be distressed by the news."

"We all should be."

The last thing they needed right now was a bounty hunter trailing them. They had enough problems with the *other* pestilence swarming this valley and the surrounding hills.

"Not some of Masterson's pack." Hank sniffed. "Probl'y not enough luck in my day for that."

"The hunter may be Masterson's charge, but I doubt it." Why would he hire a bounty hunter *and* a Slayer? "Either way, I have to find and slay it now, whether it's here for me or not. We don't need the hunter adding to our headache when we're busy fighting something with sharper teeth."

Hank had brought up a good point, though. What if it were Masterson's charge? She'd already killed some of his *Bahkauv* "pets," provoking his ire and threats.

She shook away the thought. It didn't matter. If Masterson had agents here, he should have told her. Barring any other instructions or information, she would be the one deciding how to conduct her business.

It gnawed on her that following the tracks would lead them away from the damned barn.

"Let's go get the Sidewinders and see who made these tracks. It should be …" She paused to measure the size of the bigger footprint with her own boot, grimacing at the size of it. "Interesting."

Harrowing was probably a better word for what they might find. Bounty hunters often were not easy kills.

She sniffed the air as she headed back to Jack and Boone, scanning the trees and the shadows beneath them, listening for the crack of a limb or any other sound that could mean it was time to draw her sword.

Since they'd cleaned the *Draug* out of the first cabin they'd come to on the way to Slagton, Clementine had been vigilant. A foe might lurk in the quietest crack of a breaking branch or swish of wind-blown snow. She constantly scanned her surroundings for the next attacker, her blades ready for a fight. But she hadn't done enough. Hadn't prepared enough. The conjuror had caught her unawares, and all three of her companions had paid the price for her mistake.

It's not your fault.

And yet it was. She hadn't prepared them enough. She hadn't listened to what Horace had been trying to relay. She'd been so hell bent on getting to the barn.

She shouldn't have let them come to Slagton.

They insisted on coming.

Her lapse in judgment and patience could be the death of them. No, *would* be.

She stopped suddenly, clenching her fists. This constant battle with guilt was wearing. She needed to maintain her focus.

"Miss Clem? You okay?" Hank drew up next to her.

"Hank …" Her throat constricted, making the words she was about to say even harder to get out. "I think I've killed Boone and Jack," she whispered, her gaze meeting his before dropping to her feet. "And you, too."

"Oh, now, Miss Clem." He rubbed her shoulder. It was surprisingly soothing. The tightness in her throat eased. "I'm tough as pine bark and meaner'n a badger with a meaty bone. I ain't gonna let nothin' happen t' you or the boys."

She shook her head. "I shouldn't have let them come."

"Them two didn't give you no choice. The Sidewinders got more hard iron in 'em than a set of locomotive tracks."

He was right about that. She blew out a shaky breath, shifting to a more pressing issue. "There's something wrong with Boone. We need to watch him."

"I know'd it. Didn't wanna say. Conjur fella, you figure?"

"Most likely."

"It weren't easy gettin' outta my head. Fluttery little things holdin' on t' the edges of my thoughts. Truth to it, I'm surprised Jack Rabbit got away so quick. That buzzard stirred through my noggin like he was whippin' up eggs for Sunday breakfast."

"Why is Boone getting worse?" She didn't expect an answer, just needed to voice her anxieties out loud.

"Don't know." Hank hung his head. "Didn't do my job."

"It's not your job to watch out for those two, Hank."

She'd thought she was the one watching out for everyone, and here Hank was doing the same thing.

"Is so my job," he said, his gaze narrowing. "Just like watchin' out fer you. Partners take care of partners." He patted her on the back. "We should get moving before these tracks get covered."

"Right. Time to hunt a hunter."

Hank looked at the sky and grunted. "Don't got long, then we're chasin' our own tails."

She let Hank lead them back to the Sidewinders.

It was obvious the bounty hunter did not expect to be hunted. Neither it nor its underlings had made any effort to conceal their numbers or hide their tracks. This showed a confidence that made Clementine's ability to focus on the task at hand even more important.

Rarely was a single hunter commissioned. Usually two, three, or even more were enlisted to enhance the competition. Generally the quickest, luckiest, or most ruthless won and collected the quarry. It was only natural to assume that she was the target. Slayers usually were.

It was a vicious game. One that a Slayer could easily lose.

The question was, who set this particular game in motion?

* * *

"Can't get that sound outta my head, Booney. Ain't ever seen nothin' eat bones before." Rabbit wrinkled his nose.

"Mmm."

"That all you got, Booney? Mmm?"

Rabbit twisted his gloves one way and then the other, taking his anxiety out on the leather. Boone hadn't spoken since Clementine and Hank left. When Rabbit forced him to look into his eyes, Boone might as well have been looking at the rolling hills of Wyoming.

"Damned Clementine," he muttered. Somebody needed blaming and she was at the top of the list, even though the blame wasn't hers to carry.

"Fuckin' conjuror." His blood boiled for the bastard that did this. He wanted to scream, but tamped it down, channeling the rage into a promise to avenge his *amigo*.

Boone stood quiet and motionless, staring at the ground.

Hank and Clementine had been gone for fifteen minutes, and Rabbit was getting more impatient with each and every one of them. They needed to move. Or stay. Or find Ludek. Maybe he would know … *Goddammit!*

He felt so helpless. Boone's mind was drifting away and there wasn't a thing Rabbit could do. There was no one to reason with or fight or shoot. What if Boone— *No!* He stopped himself. Somebody must know what to do. If Clementine didn't, Ludek, or Miss Hildegard might. Or that highbinder Masterson. Somebody would, even if it was at the end of a gun barrel.

"Yo! Jack Rabbit! Thisaway." Hank was standing next to Clementine forty yards south. He swooped his arm up and over his head.

Rabbit saw Clementine turn to Hank and shake her finger at him. Hank raised both palms to her but then swooped his arm at Rabbit again.

"Let's go, Booney. They're callin'." Rabbit grabbed Boone's arm and dragged him toward his companions. "He hasn't said a word, Miss Clementine," he told her when he got closer. "Maybe Ludek knows what to do." Rabbit tried to fan the little flame of hope he was holding onto.

"He might. But there's no telling where Ludek is and we need to follow these tracks before it snows." Clementine didn't look at Rabbit, instead she scanned the ground and then the forest to the east.

"I'll help you take care of him, Jack Rabbit." Hank stepped up beside Boone and put his arm around his shoulders.

Boone slowly turned his head and stared at Hank, but he remained silent. A long look at Boone's pale, emotionless face sent a shiver through Rabbit.

"Almost like somebody else is lookin' at me, Miss Clem." Hank leaned away from Boone but didn't move his arm. "Needs a little more time is all." His tone didn't reassure Rabbit at all.

Clementine stared into Boone's eyes, studying them. Her knitted brow didn't help Rabbit feel any better than Hank's demeanor had. "More time," she said and quickly turned away, making a show of searching the forest.

"You hidin' somethin' from me, Miss Clem?" Rabbit wasn't letting her stonewall him.

"No. I think maybe Hank is right. He needs more time." But she wouldn't meet his gaze. "Let's see where these tracks lead." And then she was off, studying the ground as she went.

"Who needs more time?" Boone leaned over into Rabbit's view.

What the hell? "Boone? You with us?" Rabbit couldn't believe his eyes and ears. Boone was back. A little sickly looking, but he was back.

"What does that mean? Where else would I be?"

Clementine rushed back to them, her attention on Boone.

A grin spread across Hank's face. "You had us in a conniption, Boonedog." Hank unwrapped his arm from Boone's shoulders. "You feelin' up to snuff?"

"Yes, how do you feel, Boone?" Clementine took him by the chin, leaning in, playing doctor.

"What are you all talking about? I'm fine." He frowned, pulling slightly away from her, and then measured each of them with a suspicious squint. "Are we going after the hunter or not?"

"You know where you are?" Rabbit asked.

"Cut it out, Rabbit."

Rabbit squinted at him.

"Fine, we're on the ridgeline above Slagton. Clementine and Hank just got back from checking out some tracks. We're going to follow them, right, Clementine?"

She hesitated, her gaze narrowed with a suspicious glint. "Right." She took a step back from him, her eyes locked onto his face. Then she seemed to shake off whatever had been bothering her and turned to Hank. "You lead for now. Everyone be prepared. We don't know what we'll be facing, if anything."

Hank started off, following the tracks east away from edge of the cliff and Slagton. Rabbit fell in behind with Boone beside him. Clementine brought up the rear, and Rabbit had a feeling she was keeping an eye on all of them. She was, after all, the only one who hadn't been affected by the conjuror.

He cast a glance back at her. Yep. She was a good distance back, but the apprehension visible on her face told him he was right. She was watching.

They hadn't gone far when Hank suddenly stopped and turned. "It occurs to me, Miss Clem. These tracks, bein' blatant as they are, there's a middlin' chance this is a trap."

She nodded, her lips pinched thin, but indicated for Hank to keep going.

Hank shrugged and trudged along.

Rabbit, however, wasn't so sure he was taken with the idea. He slowed and let himself fall behind Boone as he plodded through the snow, until he was alongside Clementine.

"Uncle Mort once said to me 'Son, you're going to meet folks, all they want to do is use you for gain; and you're going to meet folks you might be tempted to use. Either way, they aren't your *compadres. La amistad por encima de todo, hijo.*'" He glanced at her. "You know what that means, Miss Clementine?"

"Should I?"

"Yep. Right now might be a good time to know what that means."

"Jack …"

"Friendship above all." Rabbit watched for a response but none came. "You know why I say that?"

"Maybe." Clementine avoided eye contact.

Rabbit continued. "You wouldn't be using Hank and Boone and your ol' pal Rabbit as bait, would you?"

She stopped and stared at him. "Yes."

Before he could do more than blink, she headed off again.

"Well, I guess it ain't the first time I been used as bait," he said as he caught up with her.

"How do you say 'trust' in Spanish?"

Rabbit understood the point she was making. "Is your meanin' trust in? Or is it believe in? Two different things."

"Hank knows the stakes and he knows I have him covered. I think you can handle it, too. You've had a peek into my world and you chose to accept what you saw."

He'd seen some things that he didn't want to accept. "*Draug* growing big? Don't accept that."

"Of course."

"Or something changin' into somethin' else, don't accept that neither."

"You know what I mean."

He did. She had Hank, him, and Boone covered, he believed that a surety. "I know, Miss Clementine. I know. I'm out of sorts is all. What with Boone actin' all peculiar and that conjuror character gettin' in my head, it's disconcertin' not controlling my own self. The scoundrels we're after, well, feels like they're gettin' worse. Meaner. I'm startin' to wonder if we got the goods to do this. Not you, mind, but the three of us. I'm startin' to see your point, we might be a distraction." It pained him to say it.

She slowed her pace, lowering her voice. "I've fought beside the three of you a few times now, and in all honesty it has had its advantages and disadvantages."

"Miss Clem, you comin'?" Hank and Boone had stopped twenty yards farther along.

"One minute, Hank." She turned back to Rabbit. "I have to watch out for the three of you, and that distracts me to some extent."

Rabbit loathed the idea of being a burden to anyone, excepting maybe Boone.

"I see the look in your eye," she said. "But keep listening. It's also true that you three, each of you, have saved my life. I have a strong sense that we are all meant to be here. Together."

"You mean we were all destined to meet up in the Black Hills?"

She nodded. "I'm not sure if it's destiny or fate or dumb luck. And I'm not sure if there are others who are part of it. Ludek. Hildegard. Even Mr. Beaman and Amelia. I'm not even sure if someone else is controlling us in some way."

"Uncle Mort, me, Boone. Fate. Hmm." The implications were stirring Rabbit's brain. He wasn't sure whether or not he liked the idea. No, he didn't like it.

"I'm not sure of anything. Having seen the things I've seen ..." She trailed off.

"Worth ponderin', for sure." He still wasn't sure how they'd come to the subject, considering he was preoccupied with caring for Boone.

"Short of that, you Sidewinders and Hank have made things more interesting around here."

"I think your *other* buddies are doing a fine job of that."

She punched his shoulder lightly. "They're not my buddies." She glanced toward the others. "Listen," she said, whispering now. "I think we need to keep a close eye on Boone."

"Some reason other than the obvious?" He looked ahead at his friend. Boone talked animatedly but quietly to Hank, appearing to all the world completely normal.

"You remember Hank and I came back from checking those tracks?"

"It was ten minutes ago, so yeah …"

"Let me ask you this. Do you know what we're tracking?"

"Uh … I gathered it was something needin' sorted out."

"Yes. What kind of *other*?"

"What are you getti—"

"Boone knows. He said it, 'hunter.' How did he know that? I didn't tell the two of you when we got back."

"Sheeat." Rabbit skidded to a stop. "How did …"

"I think he's not alone. That there's someone or something in his head with him." Clementine rested her hand on his shoulder. "I think the conjuror affected him somehow, left him vulnerable to influence. We need to watch him."

"Okay, but how do we help him?"

"I don't know yet." She sighed. "But things like this are usually never permanent."

Rabbit didn't know if she was blowing smoke or not. He chose to believe she was telling him the truth, but he didn't like that she'd used the word "usually."

"There's something else," she whispered.

"Something …"

"Don't look, but up in the tops of those trees …" She tipped her head almost imperceptibly. "Two *aerioccisor* have been watching us since we left the ridgeline."

What? Two *whaf*? What the hell was an *airy awk sizor*?

Clementine must have read his questions on his face. "*Aerioccisor*. They look like ravens but are much bigger. Their heads are featherless, skinless gray bone with small, beady red eyes. They're common among bounty hunters."

"What the hell are they doing here?" Rabbit really wanted to take a peek at them, but resisted the temptation.

"Watching us. Spying. They'll attack if we provoke them. Otherwise, they will simply watch. They are the eyes of the bounty hunter. It knows we're here."

Dread prickled the back of Rabbit's neck. "Let's kill the fuckers."

Clementine's brow furrowed. "How should we do that? And before you answer that, you should know that they like to eat their prey while it's still alive by tearing off pieces of flesh but leaving the organs."

"Jumpin' toads." He quickly took stock of their weapons. Clementine was strictly close range with her swords. He had his throwing knifes, but the hunter's "eyes" were easily a hundred feet up in the trees. Straight up. He tickled the handle of his pistol with his fingertips.

"No, Jack," she growled, her nostrils flaring.

"I know, I know." He peeked up at the big birds through the gentle, fine snow that had begun falling.

Once again he found himself longing for his Sharps, but of course Clementine wouldn't allow that anyway, same as his pistol. Boone didn't have anything long-range either.

"Oh!" He looked back to Clementine. "Hank's bow and arrows." It was unlikely Hank could shoot that high, but maybe …

Suddenly, both raptors dropped silently from their perches, disturbing the snow piled precariously on the branches as they passed. They fell like stones until within a few feet of the ground before extending long wings and swooping out through the trees, flapping their wings in perfect unison.

Rabbit watched them swerve and pitch through the trees on their great wings, finally disappearing into the veil of falling snow.

He turned to Clementine. "You sure those ain't vultures?"

"If you want to think of them that way, be my guest, but these vultures will attack you given the opportunity or incentive or provocation. And if they do …" She shook her head, frowning.

"I suppose we need to follow—"

From the corner of his eye, Rabbit saw movement in the shadows farther ahead. Squat, winged shapes, he wasn't sure how many, six or eight maybe, scurrying between the closely spaced tree trunks. Clumps of snow fell from the trees. He looked up into the branches. There was movement there, too.

As quickly as it started, the movement stopped and all was still again, excepting the hushed whisper of snow landing in the needles and branches, and the soft crunch of Hank and Boone's footsteps as they approached.

"Uh, Miss Clementine, did you see that movement in the trees?" Rabbit blinked several times, wondering if he'd actually seen anything move after all.

She nodded and slowly drew her twin blades.

"You two see that?" Hank whispered. He and Boone sounded like horses tromping toward them.

"Shhh." Rabbit scanned the trees but still nothing moved.

"Vultures," Boone said.

Rabbit eyed him. He hadn't seen the other creatures? "They aren't vultures. Miss Clementine called them somethin' else."

"Shhh!" Clementine's creased brow had him pinching his lips.

She motioned them all in closer. "The hunter is nearby. Its underlings—or goblins, as Hank is calling them—are swarming all through this part of the forest. Mind the trees. They're up there, too." She looked at each of them with worry-lined eyes. "I'm afraid this really is a trap."

Fourteen

B oone tried to focus on what Clementine was telling them about something and something ... goblins, did she say? Every thought sent a bolt of pain through his head, and he couldn't shake the smoky image of those pointed ears and snout. *El Vaquero.*

It talked to him, whispered ideas, urged him to do things. Disturbing things. He fought against it, trying to use sheer will to maintain control, but he struggled to concentrate on anything for more than a few seconds.

Boone couldn't let his companions know. That was important above all. They mustn't know.

* * *

Clementine had two pressing problems, besides the fact that it had started to snow. One, deciding on how to properly deal with Boone. She could only hope that his cursed condition was temporary. And two, figuring out how to manage a bounty hunter and countless "goblins" in its charge. She knew neither the hunter's abilities nor its limitations, but she had a feeling she'd be finding out soon.

She needed a plan. If they were to continue on, she suspected they would see many of the goblins' tracks break away from the main trail. The creatures undoubtedly would be trained to come back around to either flank her group or to sneak up from behind and herd them forward into the ready and waiting arms of the hunter. That was assuming the hunter thought they would be frightened into fleeing toward it.

They would not, of course.

Predictability—likely a weakness of this particular hunter as it often was with others she'd come across over the years.

Unpredictability. Definitely one of her strengths.

She knew what to do.

Without looking at any of the men, she told them, "On my signal, I want the three of you to drop your packs and walk back the way we came. Don't run, walk. Quickly. Like I said, mind the trees. If you find yourself underneath one of the goblins, wait. When it drops, sidestep, then keep walking all the way to the cliff."

"Miss Clem," Hank said. "I ain't leavin' you back here."

Jack snorted. "No chance."

As usual, her companions were loyal to a fault.

"I'm not staying here, for goodness's sake." She frowned their way. "I'll be right behind you to clean up anything that tries to chase us down. Ready?"

Jack and Hank nodded.

Boone stared into the snow at his feet.

"We've lost Boone again," she said, her chest tightening. But now was not the time to worry about him. They had bigger problems directly in front of them.

"We got him," Jack said, taking one of Boone's arms and indicating for Hank to grab the other.

Clementine nodded. It was now or never. "Go."

They started off toward the cliff, dragging Boone along.

Clementine waited for the onslaught, blades ready. The wind kicked up and the snow pelted the side of her face. Trees shivered and swayed, the gusts whistled through the pines. She sniffed, unable to smell anything but fresh, cold air.

Within a minute, the gangly creatures began to appear in front of her, standing knee-high on four spindly legs, snorting and growling. They looked more like gargoyles than goblins with their primate-like bodies, bluish-gray coloring, and tall pointy ears. Or were those horns? The flesh covering their faces was stretched tight, giving them an almost skeletal appearance, including sunken nostrils and eyes. Spines protruded from their arms and legs, like the stiff bristles of a well-worn brush.

She swore under her breath. She'd learned a lesson long ago about fighting against small, spiny creatures. They could be deadlier than the big ones, claws and teeth notwithstanding.

Clementine watched as several began galloping through the snow under the trees to catch up with Hank and the Sidewinders, who were plodding due to Boone's incapacity. The goblins scuttled along in disordered, meandering lines. A few began to rear up on their hind legs, doubling their speed.

Fortunately—or not—the majority began to close in on her rather than the men. Their movements were chaotic under the pines, making it difficult to judge their numbers. Scurrying from one tree to the next, hiding momentarily, then scurrying to another. Zigging and zagging, swerving, stopping and starting. It was disorienting, especially with the snow now blowing and swirling. She had a feeling their sporadic movement was part of their attack strategy.

"Git your goddamn butt movin', Boone!" she heard Jack holler. "Fuckers are snortin' everywhere!"

"Weapons!" she yelled, swishing her deadly twins, warming up her arms.

She glanced their way, catching sight of Jack's and Hank's Bowie knives in their hands. But Boone was slumped to the side, leaning heavily on Jack. His sword remained sheathed.

Hel's realm! They could have really used his blade.

"These goblins are straight outta my nightmares!" Hank wailed.

"What's that poking out of their fur? Cactus spines?" Jack yelled back, his voice was slightly higher now.

"Don't let them touch you!" Clementine shouted. She eyed one of the goblins that was galloping through the snow toward her while the others held back. "The spine tips might be poisonous!"

The goblin slowed as it closed in, lips pulled back to show an ugly set of tiny fangs rimmed with black gums. Silvery eyes glittered from the depths of sunken eye sockets. It arched in the middle, a ridge of spines rising out of the fur.

She swung one of her blades at the creature, but it hunkered down and collapsed its spines. The blade skipped along its back as if she'd swung at a sheet of steel.

Clementine drew her sword back to swing again, but the spines were still flattened. She cocked her leg to the side and kicked it, sending it flying into the trees.

She ducked instinctively and stumbled back a few steps as something swooped low over her head. Had an *aerioccisor* returned? It wasn't an *aerioccisor* at all, but a goblin. She stared as it glided toward Hank.

"Look out from above!" she yelled. "They can fly!"

Jack looked up just in time. He hauled Hank and Boone to the ground as it flew low over them and then touched down twenty feet farther on.

To their right, three more goblins were descending on the group from the trees, while more rushed forward on the ground to join those already closing in on the three men. At least one was on the mark for sure.

Shit, with Boone dragging anchor, Jack and Hank were going to need her help.

"Change of plans," she called, the back of her neck prickled.

She heard the rustle of footfalls in the snow behind her and whirled with her blades raised. Another goblin was coming fast, its spines flattened, its jaws wide. She stepped back and kicked out, catching it in the chest in midstride, sending it reeling backward into a tree trunk.

She raced toward the men, propelled by a fresh rush of fury. She raised her blades above her head and prepared to start taking heads. If they wore armor, she would pierce it. She leaped over a rock stabbing up through the snow. If they attacked from the air, she would gut them from below. If they …

Strength in serenity, she heard her afi's voice as she slid to a stop a few feet behind Hank.

She stilled, drawing in a deep breath of cold air. Her fiery anger was quickly snuffed, replaced by a cool, calm strength. Her head cleared. Everything slowed around her. A goblin rushed at her, but she knew exactly when to swing.

Ready … *Swish Crack!* The spines shattered under the force of her blade. She shoved the steel down through flesh, and then bone, and finally through air. The goblin instantly turned to gray ash that blended with the falling snow.

A lesser, she thought. *No special technique needed.*

As quickly as the notion occurred to her, she was preparing for the next two goblins gliding down on them.

Steady blades … Swing, stab in the underbelly, slice. *Poof!* Duck! Turn and swing up again, slice through the wing, stab hard though the spine armor. *Poof!*

She shielded her eyes as the ash fell from overhead.

At the sound of another coming from behind, she kicked back, connecting with a body much heavier than a goblin.

"Oof!"

Hank! She turned to him, but another goblin dropped from above. Her blade sliced through the air. *Crack!* She knocked it to the ground, where it stumbled sideways with one wing dangling from a strip of bluish-gray flesh, its spines still flattened. *Swish. Crack! Poof!*

She spun back to Hank, who was on his knees in the snow. He was gripping the handle of his knife, the blade stuck into the throat of the goblin she'd tried to back kick.

"Get up, Hank!" She reached down and hauled him to his feet.

"Bristly bastards are pulling back!" Jack joined them, holding Boone by his coat collar.

"We need to head for the clearing we came through earlier," Clementine said, eyeing another goblin in a nearby tree that appeared to be preparing to take flight. "They can't attack from the trees there."

"I think I'm done, Miss Clem." Hank's exasperation showed on his face.

"Are you hurt?" Clementine began to pat him down, checking for injuries.

"Not done for. Done. When a man comes up against giant, flying, horned goblins runnin' on two legs, that's it. Done."

"And covered with spines full of poison, don't forget." Jack searched the trees surrounding them. "We should skedaddle."

Boone suddenly pulled away from Jack.

He drew his scimitar and swung it high, turned and aimed—at Clementine!

His eyes were dark as a moonless night, his face pale and drawn.

"Boone!" Jack yelled, reaching for him.

She shoved Hank aside as Boone began to slice downward, aiming for Clementine.

She crossed her blades above her head, blocking the blow. *Clang!* She squeezed Boone's sword between her deadly twins and twisted, wrenching the scimitar from his hands. With a flick, she flipped it toward Jack, who caught it and promptly dropped it.

He rushed forward and wrapped his arms around Boone from behind. "What the fuck are you doing, Booney?"

Boone reached for his knife and tried to lunge at Clementine, swiping in the air between them, but Jack held firm.

Clementine cocked her arm. "Boone! Stop!"

He bared his teeth and snarled at her, almost *Draug*-like. He tried to lunge at her again and again while Jack strained to hold him.

She stared into those dark, dark eyes, looking for signs of the man who'd sat next to her in Horace's cave, laughing and talking in the firelight. But he wasn't there.

"You're not Boone," she said.

He lunged again, savage, breaking free of Jack's hold.

She let loose a lightning bolt of a punch. Her fist slammed into his jaw, and he crumpled to the ground.

Instantly she regretted it. Not Boone! Great Odin, what had she done.

"Why'd you do that?" A mixture of horror and fury flashed across Jack's face. He dropped to his knees next to his friend.

"You like to broke his jaw, Miss Clem." Hank squatted next to Boone and helped Jack turn him over.

"We need to move." Clementine grabbed Boone's knife and scimitar, tucking the first into her boot sheath and the other into her belt.

As Jack and Hank struggled to get Boone upright, she sized up their predicament, trying to ignore the ache in her heart. They still needed to make it to the clearing. From there she could face the hunter, if he presented himself, without worrying about flying goblins attacking from the damned trees.

"His jaw seems okay." Hank sent her a sidelong glance. "Helluva swing, Miss Clem." But there was no reverence in his words.

Jack nailed her with a hard glare before returning to attending Boone.

Neither Hank nor Jack were happy about the force of the blow. Frankly, she wasn't either. Her Slayer instinct had taken over. *Kill or be killed* coming into play. It had saved her more times than she cared to count.

She sighed. She would need to atone for her misdeed later. Right now, they had to move.

"Get him up," she said, watching the trees around them. Movement in almost every direction was making her twitchy. "They're coming back. We'll need to bind his hands when we get the chance."

Jack spit and sputtered, looking as if he would fret himself into a puddle on the spot.

She reached out and grasped the front of his coat, pulling him in close. "He's going to be okay, Jack, but we need to move."

Clementine wasn't sure if she believed Boone was ever going to be okay again, though. Not because of her punch, but due to whatever had a hold on his mind.

Rabbit and Hank lifted him and wrapped his arms around their shoulders while Clementine kept watch. The goblins were beginning to rally, darting through the trees, fluttering up into the branches. Most of their movements were blurred by the falling snow.

"Where's your master, you little bastards." She pointed toward the clearing. "Go!" she ordered Hank and Jack.

They took off at a fast walk, half dragging, half carrying Boone between them. It wasn't far, but it seemed too far.

She glanced back. The trees seemed clear of the flying menaces now … *Wait!* Several spiny goblins were climbing on the opposite sides of the trees, attempting to remain unseen.

"I see you," she growled.

Clumps of snow dropped from several trees back the way they'd come. More were coming. Before the creatures could ambush her, she took after the men, hoping to make the clearing before the spiky devils could drop down on them again. This time, there would be too many in the air to cut down by herself.

They arrived at the clearing minutes later, Clementine watching their backs as Hank and Jack struggled with Boone. The large peninsular meadow above the Slagton valley was precisely where they had been only a short time ago. The middle of the clearing was thirty yards from the tree line to the east and at least forty yards to the edge of the cliff on the north, west, and south. There would be no sneaking up on them here, but there was also a decided lack of cover. Which direction to go from here was an easy decision to make.

"Toward the cliff," Clementine yelled. "Away from the trees!"

A quick look back made her curse. The goblins were coming, but it was difficult to determine numbers due to the heavy snowfall. To make visibility worse, gusty winds were blowing up the cliff and over the top, blowing the snow into a turbulent whirl, whipping the icy particles at her face and eyes. The tracks they had followed earlier were already wind-whipped and mostly snow-covered.

The spiny goblins seemed to be slowed by the deeper snow of the open ground, giving Clementine and the men more time to reach the cliff. Several feet farther, she turned and looked behind them again.

There was something else coming through the snow.

She shielded her eyes with her hand. Two figures were headed for them, human-like, approaching from the southeast. Did bounty hunters work in pairs? Not in her experience. There were many, but they hunted solo.

She squinted into the snowstorm.

One of the figures was extremely tall and slender, with long limbs.

The other … Ludek! And Horace!

Thank Valhalla! She could use their help.

Hank and Jack stopped and looked back, staring at the approaching figures, shielding their faces against the wind-driven snow.

"It's Ludek and Horace!" she shouted. "Keep going! Closer to the edge!" She wanted the three of them well away from the trees and flying menaces.

"Clementine!" Ludek called as he approached. "There is a hunter here!" Had he too seen the tracks before the snow hit?

"I know!"

"You mustn't let the acolyte's spines pierce your skin." He stopped beside her, breathing hard, his blade drawn. "The venom will affect the mind and possibly kill. Perhaps not you, *Scharfrichter*, but do not leave your fate to chance."

"You was right, Miss Clem," Hank said when Clementine, Ludek, and Horace joined them near the edge of the cliff. "Them goblins is poisonous." He huffed. "Jack Rabbit, we need to put Boone down. My back is killin' and I don't want a handful of Boone when I need to be holdin' my knife."

Jack nodded and they lay Boone in the snow, his gaze lingering on his friend for a moment. "We'll get you outta this, Booney."

Horace grunted and waved his massive hand toward the tree line.

"The acolytes are coming." Ludek raised his sword.

"Acolytes?" Hank waved his Bowie toward the trees. "You mean those li'l goblins?"

Ludek glanced at Hank and then Clementine. "I would say they are more akin to gargoyles than goblins."

"Same here," Clementine said. "But Hank named them first, so goblins it is."

"Have you seen the hunter?" Ludek asked.

"No. He's waiting for an invitation, no doubt." Clementine would be happy to oblige.

Shadowy figures began to appear at the edges of her vision, once again swerving and veering this way and that, quick, then slow, on two legs, then four, then two again. Their distraction was working. Clementine fought to keep her attention on anything that might be an indication that the hunter was near.

"Bugger got my LeMat!" Hank took after a goblin that had snuck up behind him. Waving his knife in the air, Hank disappeared into the blowing snow.

"Hank!" Jack started after him.

"Jack! You stay right where you are," she said. "We don't need two of you out there."

"Hank!" Jack called again, staying put. "Git back here!"

Clementine watched as another goblin darted in, its spines flattened into armor, and bashed into Jack's legs, knocking him to the ground. He popped back up, but the goblin had already vanished into the foggy falling snow.

"Fucker got my pistol, too!" He picked up Boone's sword and began swinging it clumsily at the air.

The goblins tightened closer around them.

Clementine backed toward Jack, Ludek, and Horace, the four of them surrounding Boone's still form. She and the others began kicking and swinging at the spiny creatures as they came at them from every direction.

Horace smashed two, and Ludek's sword clanked and clanged off too many to count. In the midst of it all, Hank scurried by with one on his tail. He was out of Clementine's reach, but fortunately Horace had very long arms. He clobbered it hard enough to send it sailing over the edge of the cliff.

"*Scharfrichter*, you must draw the hunter out," Ludek called as he swung at another.

"How?"

"Step away from our group. If he's here for you, then you must present yourself to him. We will manage."

She hesitated, loath to leave her friends, especially Boone, who was still unconscious on the ground. But Ludek was right. She tossed one of her blades to him and tucked the other in her belt.

"Keep those things off me," she said, unsheathing *Ulfberht* and gripping it in her hand.

She broke through the ranks, knocking goblins aside, slashing others into ash, more than willing to introduce the evasive hunter to German steel. The snowfall had lessened enough for her to see farther into the trees. She pushed at the wind toward the tree line until finally a figure strode into view, coming straight for her.

She faced the bounty hunter. Alone.

As it approached, its features became more distinct. Armor covered most of the hunter's body, looking particularly thick over the arms, shins, and thighs, and perfectly positioned to deflect a sword strike. A tight-fitting helmet covered the upper half of its head, down the nose and across the cheekbones, giving its eyes a sunken shadowy darkness. Maybe she could aim for the mouth or neck, possible vulnerable spots. Its spine was likely armored as well. It might take a few blows to break through and sever.

The hunter stopped several feet from her and began tapping its armored fingertips together, as if eager for battle. Then its teeth began to chatter, mouth spreading wide in a grotesque grin.

So be it. She raised her sword, planting her boots in the snow. Her blood simmered, her focus zeroing in on the hunter's weak spots. The commotion of the others battling behind her faded.

The hunter circled slowly, drawing closer, coming into full focus, teeth still chattering. The sound reminded her of shuffling ivory dominos. No. Of her amma, shaking her linen bag of small animal bones before dumping them on the table to interpret the arrangement.

Upon closer inspection, she realized its armor wasn't armor at all, not in the sense that she'd thought. It was more like bone. Fingers, arms, legs, everything—covered in a type of exoskeleton, similar to a crustacean enveloped in gray-white bony shell. Its arms and legs articulated oddly, like a blending of man and crab, not unlike the crabs she and her afi caught in the Norwegian waters when she was a girl.

Where in *Hel's* kingdom had this hunter come from?

Straps of metal secured curved blades that ran the length of its forearms and extended beyond its bony hands. She would need to parry the hunter's leading attacks without fail. One miss and those blades would cut her to ribbons.

It stilled, sniffing the air. "Huntress," it said, a hissing sound mixing in with chattering teeth.

The hunter had picked up on her scent. There was no use playing games. "Who sent you to collect this bounty?"

"*Malveaux.*"

What? Was that French? Who was Malveaux?

"*Zahlung ist fällig.*"

"Payment is due for what?" The hunter appeared to have an agenda, and Clementine was completely baffled about what it was. "I owe no payment."

"*Die Verwüstung von Malveaux.*"

"The devastation of Malveaux? What the hell are you talking about?"

She spared a glance at her companions. Hank had rejoined the others, and they appeared to have things in hand with the goblins. Boone was struggling to stand, but no one had noticed.

Meanwhile, the hunter continued circling. It stuck both arms out, lifting and lowering them quickly, as if shaking out a rug—or slicing through flesh. The blades on its forearms slid out further and clicked into place, adding another foot to its reach.

The hunter crouched, but didn't lunge. Clementine wasn't sure if it was preparing to charge or delaying her for some reason?

"Enough!" It was time for *Ulfberht* to sing.

Lunge, roll, onto the knees, reverse twist, swing and ...

Dritt! She couldn't see her finishing move.

If the last part went badly, she would be left vulnerable, and it was unlikely this adversary would waste an opportunity.

"Miss Clementine!" Rabbit called out. "Over here! Quick!"

Clementine glanced over to find Rabbit with Boone's scimitar, hacking at a goblin clamped onto Horace's leg as he writhed in the snow next to Boone, who was still struggling to get up. Ludek was busy fending off several goblins, and Hank was running from another. Horace tried to stand and clobber the creature at the same time, but faltered.

The hunter would have to wait.

She raced toward them, slashing at goblins as she passed through their ranks, leaping over bloody carcasses. She rushed in swinging at the one attached to Horace's leg, lopping off its head with one brisk blow.

Poof! It turned to ash.

Horace tried to stand but collapsed to the ground.

Something grabbed hold of her ankle. Boone held her ankle and she watched as he drew his knife from his belt and brought it up to stab her through her boot. *What in Hades?* She kicked free, catching him on the forehead with her heel by accident. His body went limp, and the knife dropped from his bandaged hand.

Damn it! She'd have to deal with him later.

Nearer the cliff, Ludek roared like a riled bear, chilling her to the bone. She paused and turned his way. He battled three goblins, who appeared to be coordinating their attacks.

She glanced back at the hunter. It was advancing on her, still folded into a crouch, ready to leap.

"Not yet!" she told the bastard and flew toward Ludek, praying to Odin that the hunter and his goblins would believe Boone to be dead and leave him alone.

She skidded up next to Ludek, spearing a goblin in the haunch as she arrived. It wailed and squirmed on her sword until she jerked it free and brought the blade down on its neck.

Ludek kicked another, sending it over the edge of the cliff.

Clementine's neck bristled. *Down!*

She dropped facedown onto the ground a split second before the hunter's long blade hissed through the air over her head.

Roll!

She flipped onto her back as another of its blades stabbed the ground where she had been a moment before.

Ludek lunged at the hunter, only to be knocked aside by a bone-covered forearm.

Clementine rolled again and pushed to her feet, but the hunter kicked out, landing a bruising blow to her chest that sent the breath rushing from her lungs. She flew several feet backward before crashing to the ground. Her sword slipped from her grip, landing a few feet away.

The hunter was on her before she could find her footing. Gasping for air, she reached for the knife sheathed at her boot.

It stepped down on her wrist, pinning her hand to the ground. "Payment is due, Slayer."

"Payment for what?" she wheezed. "Malveaux? I don't even know what that is. And would you pick a damned language!"

"For the massacre you wrought." It pointed the tip of its blade at her. "My contract will be fulfilled."

"Miss Clem!" Hank yelled, his tone high with fear.

The bounty hunter drew back the blade to strike, its hold on her wrist loosening just enough.

She yanked her arm free and started to swing her leg, aiming for the hunter's knee. If she could knock it off balance …

Thump! Thump! THUMP!

Horace galloped into her vision right before his massive fists smashed into the hunter's back, sending it soaring over the edge of the cliff. But Horace wasn't stopping. He slipped and slid on the snow and ice, his long arms windmilling wildly as his momentum carried him toward the cliff's edge. He tripped over a rock jutting out of the snow and stumbled forward, grasping wildly at a small bush.

Clementine shoved to her feet and threw herself at him, hoping to catch onto one of his arms, his coat, something.

"Nooo!" Ludek yelled. Out of the corner of her eye, Clementine saw him racing toward Horace, but a goblin rushed into his path, slowing him.

She dove and reached for Horace as he slipped over the edge, their fingers almost touching as he stretched his huge hand out toward her.

But then he was gone.

"Horace!" she cried and pushed up onto her knees, crawling after him. She peered over the ledge, praying he'd grasped a snag or root protruding from the cliff face. Instead, she watched in horror as he plummeted through the air, his arms and legs flailing, until he disappeared into the veil of falling snow.

Clementine closed her eyes, her throat tightening. *Oh, Horace!*

"Look!" Rabbit yelled from right behind her. "That fuckin' hunter can fly."

She opened her eyes. The hunter had indeed spread large, leathery wings it must keep tucked away under the ridge of spines on its back.

It could fly. *Potzblitz!* It surprised her … but not much, not after the things she'd seen.

Ludek joined Jack and Clementine, her sword in his hand. He tugged her upright and then gave her *Ulfberht*.

"They're following their master," Ludek said, pointing at the goblins racing toward the cliff. "Twenty. Thirty. Possibly more."

"Up on two legs and movin' like a herd of spooked cattle. We know those little bastards can fly." Jack spat over the edge.

The three of them watched as one goblin after another raced toward the cliff and leapt without hesitation, following their master over the edge. They jumped, spread their legs like flying squirrels, and drifted along with the gusts of wind.

Hank jogged up next to her and peered over the edge. "You think Horace made it through, Miss Clem?"

She frowned down at the whirling flurries below. "He might be an *other*, but I don't think so. There were rocks at the bottom, remember?"

Hank looked at Ludek, his brows raised in hope, but Ludek shook his head.

Meanwhile, in the distance Clementine could see the dark shape of the bounty hunter as it glided through the falling snow. She glared after it for several more seconds until it disappeared into the white.

Fifteen

Rabbit insisted on being the one who bound Boone's wrists. He'd be damned if he'd let anyone else. It was one of the hardest things he'd ever done. But after attacking Clementine twice, there was nothing else to do about his *amigo* until someone figured out what or who was in his head.

Clementine stood directly over Rabbit. "Make those tight," she said as she sheathed *Ulfberht*.

"Don't tell me," he snapped back. Anger and despair at their predicament had him grinding his teeth. "You and your goddamn *others*." He immediately regretted saying it, but not because of Clementine. "Sorry, Ludek."

Rabbit stood and looked the pale-faced *other* in the eye to make sure his apology held sway.

Ludek squeezed Rabbit's shoulder. "Do not trouble yourself, my friend. Facing *ein Jäger* is always distressing." He looked toward the cliff's edge. "It undoubtedly survived and is gathering the remains of its troops somewhere in the valley below."

"Those goddamn—what'd you call them? Acolytes? Annoying little cusses. Oh! I gotta find my pistol. Saw the little goblin drop it right around here." He started kicking at the snow. "Lost Boss, can't lose little Bang Bang, too."

Clementine gathered her twin blades and joined Ludek. "Do you know what the bounty hunter was talking about?" Rabbit heard her ask Ludek. "What is 'Malveaux'?"

Rabbit looked up from the snow long enough to see Ludek frown. "He said, 'Payment is due.' Regarding Malveaux? Correct?"

"Yes." Clementine nodded.

Rabbit circled a bit farther out. There were so many tracks in the snow. He decided to return to where he'd been when the pistol was taken and start from there.

"Maybe did a job for this 'Malahvoe' character and didn't get paid?" Hank offered.

Rabbit glanced over at the three of them.

"Possibly." Clementine's gaze narrowed. "But what does that have to do with me? And he used the term 'devastation of Malveaux.' Devastation?"

Rabbit checked the tree line for any signs of life, in case a white grizzly had come to join the bounty hunter party, but everything was still. Where the hell was his pistol?

"The use of the word 'devastation' would indicate that Malveaux is a place, rather than a being," Ludek said. "But that is an assumption we cannot currently make."

"If we presume that Malveaux is a place, can we also presume that it is in France?" Clementine asked, then answered herself, "No."

"No," Ludek agreed. "But I have heard of no such place in this land."

A dark spot in the snow caught Rabbit's eye. There it was!

"Gotcha!" He scooped up his pistol, rubbing it against his leg.

He heard Boone grunt and hurried over as his *amigo* rolled onto his side.

Rabbit kneeled next to him. "Booney, your jaw hurt? I'm sure Miss Clementine didn't mean to kick you in the face so hard." He glared up at her guarded expression.

"Put away those eye daggers, Jack," she growled and then turned her back on them.

Hank joined him and together they hoisted Boone up to his feet. He was unsteady but kept himself upright in spite of his bound hands.

"Ho there, Boonedog." Hank bent slightly so he could look up into Boone's eyes. "Got yer noggin on straight?"

"I'm fine. Got a headache." Half of his face squinched in pain. "Think I lost my hat."

Clementine had kicked him too hard, damn it. Rabbit sucked a breath in through his teeth and blew it out. *In with the good, out with the bad*, his uncle had said it countless times to help Rabbit control his anger.

"Right here it is, Boonedog." Hank left Rabbit holding Boone up and jogged over to the black, bullet-holed hat. He brushed it off as he returned and then gently pushed it down on Boone's head. "My hat's missin'. Prob'ly lost it for good when I took that white grizzly ride through the trees."

"I must return to Deadwood with news of the Watcher's passing," Ludek said, joining them. "It is good to see you on your feet, Mr. McCreery." He turned to Clementine. "We will need to find a solution to counter the Watcher's absence."

Clementine frowned. "A solution?"

"Perhaps Hildegard or Miss Hundt will have insight concerning *der Jäger* as well," Ludek continued. He arranged his blades in his belt and looked at the sky. "Without encumbrances, I anticipate arriving at The Dove by sunset if I leave now."

"*Eres un lobo duro*, Ludek." Rabbit rested his hands on Ludek's shoulders. "You watch your butt out there."

Ludek chuckled. "*Que es duro?*"

"Nice, Ludek." Rabbit nodded and smiled. "You speak Spanish. It means 'tough.' You, my friend, have an extra helping of tough." He actually liked the white-haired *other*, strange eyes and all.

Ludek replied in Spanish, "*Gracias, amigo. Tú también.*" Which had Rabbit smiling even wider. Ludek turned to Hank. "*Eres un lobo duro, tambien.*" He winked at Rabbit. "Boone, we will see you mended before this is finished."

"Yeah, okay." Boone's face was still lined in pain.

Ludek turned to Clementine, saying in a lowered voice, "I will inquire after a cure for Mr. McCreery."

Her back was still to him, but Rabbit heard her say something under her breath. What it was, he didn't catch, but the words sounded German.

Ludek replied, his voice equally hushed, ending with what sounded like *in tooten*.

She nodded once.

"And I will bring help," Ludek told her, speaking louder and in English. "I now feel that this task is beyond the abilities of one Slayer." He didn't wait for Clementine to agree or disagree before heading off to the north. Several steps later, he stopped and faced them again. "Stay alive. It would be disheartening to attend your services."

With that, Ludek jogged off through the trees and out of sight.

"Was he serious? Disheartenin'? Services?" Hank looked insulted. "Like bury us dead in the ground services?"

"He was ticklin' your feet is all, Hank," Rabbit said. Or maybe not. It was hard to tell with Ludek. "What I'd like to know, when he says help, what does that mean exactly?" Not many names came to Rabbit's mind. Only one did, as a matter of fact.

Clementine still faced the forest, hands on hips. What was she thinking?

"Miss Clem?" Hank tried.

She raised one hand but didn't turn around. Her shoulders quaked slightly, followed by a sniff.

Was she crying? Did Slayers cry?

The knot of anger in Rabbit's chest loosened.

"Rabbit, free my hands." Boone's gaze darted between Rabbit and Clementine. "Why am I tied up, anyway?"

A leery look from Hank told Rabbit how he felt about setting Boone free.

"Booney, I'd like nothing better, but you took a run at Miss Clementine. Twice."

"I did *what?*" Boone gaped.

"We gotta work the problem." Rabbit avoided looking into Boone's eyes. "Get you straightened out."

"I don't remem ..." He groaned. "I ... I think it's gone now. I certainly don't feel that way now." Boone tried to move in front of Rabbit and look him in the face.

Guilt squeezed Rabbit's windpipe. What if they couldn't help him? He turned away, struggling to breathe due to his despair. His *amigo* was getting worse.

That fucking, cocksucking, sonofabitch conjuror!

Clementine had killed it, leaving Rabbit at a loss. What was he supposed to be mad at? And where in the hell had Uncle Mort gone off to? He could use his uncle right about now to help him carry this hopelessness.

Clementine sighed loud and long. She turned around, looking at them with red-rimmed eyes. "Go grab your packs. I have a plan."

* * *

Boone gritted his teeth against the demon consuming his mind.

Something was lurking below the surface of his consciousness. A monster waited. He didn't know what it was or what it looked like or why it was there, but he could feel it holding him so tightly that he struggled to breathe. Biding its time. Holding him down. Controlling him.

Boone grappled with it, bucked it. But he was stuck at the bottom of an inky-dark well with no rope to free himself.

He had to get out and warn his friends. Warn Clementine. But he was being suffocated, pinned down, his mouth filled with tar whenever he tried to speak.

You will kill her, the gravelly voice ordered, filling Boone's head with a thick cloud of dark smoke that blocked out every last bit of light.

I will kill her, he heard his own voice whisper back in the dark.

* * *

Rabbit didn't like Clementine's plan. Not even one little bit.

He didn't like splitting up. Didn't like what he and Hank might face without her help. Didn't like being separated from Boone, especially in his condition. Didn't like any damned part of their circumstance.

But he agreed to it.

Clementine's reasoning was sound. He and Hank would set out south and scout along the ridgeline until they reached the lake, or "pond," as Hank called it. It looked like a lake to Rabbit, but Hank had pointed at Ludek's map and said, "That ain't a proper lake. Anyone what set his eyes on Bigler Lake would call that there a puddle, or if they was real generous, a pond."

Rabbit didn't care. He just wanted Boone back.

Meanwhile, Clementine would stay with Boone and the two of them would come along more slowly behind them.

Clementine was adamant about her being the one to watch him. For one thing, she was a healer, and she needed to keep a close eye on Boone to make sure his injuries didn't worsen. For another, she explained that Boone might use Rabbit or Hank against her. If there were some dark force controlling Boone that could possibly reach out to snare others' minds nearby or not, Rabbit was too emotionally involved to defend himself mentally or physically, and Hank was too kind.

Rabbit hadn't liked leaving his *amigo* with Clementine, especially since she'd not only punched him, but kicked him, too. But she'd promised Rabbit she wouldn't hurt Boone again, she only wanted to help him.

As they headed south, Rabbit looked back several times, nearly turning around twice.

It would have been nice if Uncle Mort had stuck around to keep an eye on Booney and Clementine, but no, Mr. Unreliable was off who knew where doing ghostly who-knew-what.

"You think she'll really be only an hour behind us?" Rabbit didn't mind letting his concern show.

"She said it, she'll do it. Don't you fret, Jack Rabbit."

A short hike later, they'd reached the ridgeline above Horace's cave. A wave of guilt washed through Rabbit. Horace had fought beside them, taken care of them, saved their lives. He'd been a good companion.

Hank lowered his chin, his expression somber. "It was a short acquaintance, but I'd count him a friend. A man needs his hat at a time like this'n, to hold while speakin' kind words about the departed."

Rabbit nodded, pulling off his hat and holding it. "Horace was agreeable. Not so pleased he used us to get his job done."

"Needed doin', Jack Rabbit."

"Used us as bait, is what he did." He was getting worked up, but caught himself and softened. "Anyway, don't matter. You're right, he coulda been a friend, if circumstances were different."

Rabbit slapped his hat back on and peered over the edge of the ridge. It wasn't a ridge, really, more of a bank. "We could probably negotiate our way down to the cave."

"What's in yer mind?"

"Visit the horses an' Fred." He wanted to make sure that Dime was fed and healthy, but he wanted to look for Boss, too. Laying in the snow wasn't good for a shotgun, after all.

"We don't have time," Hank said. "Them horses is fine. Plenty water. Day or two without food ain't gonna hurt 'em. Fred'll complain at me is all."

If Rabbit accepted that point of view, Dime would make him pay for sure. But he knew their mounts were safe. They'd be fine. "Sorry, Dime. Hank's right. We've got business." But he sure would like to have Boss back in the holster.

They continued south but stayed back from the ridgeline since neither of them wanted to be part of an avalanche triggered by trekking too close to the edge. On top of that, it was important to remain unseen by the inhabitants roaming Slagton's one street, if it could be called a street. More like a muddy trail through the center of Hades.

When they did stop behind a tree or bush to peek down at the town or the barn, which due to its size remained visible the majority of the time, the street was always occupied by enough critters to make Rabbit want to double-check that his pistol was loaded and ready to fire. They were too far away to actually see the features of anyone roaming down there, but he felt confident in branding them as *other*, and he wasn't excited by the idea of facing more and bigger claws and teeth. It would be a hard fight to get past them and reach Clementine's barn.

Who was he fooling? It would be impossible to reach, especially if there were more conjurors in there. Even Clementine and Ludek weren't sure what *El Vaquero* was or what havoc he was capable of. It did help Rabbit's confidence that he'd turned tail once he got a good sniff of Clementine.

Rabbit gazed down on the town. "Just watching them has my skin crawling. They don't move right."

"Like watchin' a circus," Hank said, slurring around a hunk of jerky. He didn't even bother to take a peek at the town.

"Ain't you a might curious what's in that town?"

"Naw. We know." Hank started counting on his fingers. "We got *Draug*, an' *caper-sus*—say, we ain't seen any *caper-sus* for a spell." He took another bite of jerky. "Then we got … what was it? Devil kitties, and prob'ly those goblin fellas now." He huffed. "Stole the LeMat. Irks me." He counted off another finger. "Then there's … hmm, white grizzlies yet."

Rabbit wrinkled his nose. "Revoltin'. Strippin' flesh off and crunchin' on the bones."

Hank shook his head like a dog fresh out of the water. "Can't get that sound outta my noggin."

"Crunch crunch. Like the sound of breakin' bones, but slurpy somehow. Yuck." Rabbit shuddered.

He turned away from the ridge and sat next to Hank on a downed tree, working a piece of beef jerky between his teeth. The meat had barely enough spices to reach the level above shoe leather, but his hungry belly didn't care.

"Miss Clem said that man-dog—" Hank started.

"Egyptian Eminent, she called it," Rabbit corrected. "But let's just stick with Egyptian. Easier on the tongue."

"Right. The Egyptian. She said he was gonna touch Boone with that stick he was carryin'. Touch him mind you, not hit him."

"Yep, that's right." Rabbit hadn't seen the creature, but Clementine and Boone gave good descriptions. Anything that could turn to smoke had his attention.

"What you suppose woulda happened if'n he'd touched Boonedog?"

Good question. "These *others* everywhere around here do all sorts of *loco* things. Sheeat. Mighta turned him into a *Draug* or somethin'."

"Turn to smoke. That don't sound like a normal *other*."

"Normal *other*." Rabbit chuckled. "That's funny." He took another bite of jerky, remembering something from the last time they'd sat and jawed for a bit. "Say, you didn't finish the Damn Monkey story."

"Yep, I did."

"No."

"Yep." Hank backhanded Rabbit's shoulder. "Did too."

Rabbit punched Hank's arm. "Didn't, 'cause I don't know what happened to that Remington pistol."

"Oh, that pistol?" Hank shrugged. "Forgot it on the train."

Rabbit snorted. After that long-winded tale about the monkey ... Ol' Hank. His stories always meandered to a different destination than anybody could ever guess. He started thinking about Hank coming from South America in that tale. "How old were you when that happened?"

Hank scrunched his lips together tight and squeezed one eye shut. "Let's see, I musta been ... Let's see." He scrunched up his nose, too. "I was ... Hmm. Railroad. Nevada. Lousi-annie in there 'fore that." For each memory, he tipped his head one way and then the other. "Boston. Quebec. That's an oddity. 'Fore that, it was ... After crossin' ... No, that was about the time, wasn't that ..."

Rabbit watched as his face became more and more scrunched and twisted. "Hank."

His face loosened. "Yeah, Jack Rabbit?"

"How old are you, really?"

He dipped his chin and looked up sheepishly at Rabbit. "I can't rightly remember." He shrugged. "Anyway. Miss my Remington. Ooo! Almost forgot. We got *Höhlendrache* and *Bahkauv*. *Bahkauv* queen don't count, bein' she's just one. So that's one, two …" Hank counted on his fingers again. "Uh …" He threw his hands in the air. "Keep losin' count."

So did Rabbit. "Time to go, Hank. Miss Clementine is coming up behind us. I don't expect she'd be too happy to catch up."

* * *

Clementine stood still as a stone, staring up at the sky. The next few minutes would be some of the hardest she had ever faced.

"I still don't understand why we didn't go with Rabbit and Hank." Boone stood a few feet in front of her, frowning down at the tracks the two men had left behind. "We should go, no?"

To look at and listen to him, he seemed absolutely Boone, nothing more or less. But there was something wrong. Terribly wrong. She could feel it when she had to reach out to steady him as they trudged through the snow. Something under the surface that sent fingers of unease scratching up her spine. Something that wanted her dead judging from his attempts to stab and cut her.

"Uncle Mort used to say, 'Time wasted is time wasted.' " He chuckled, turning his back to her. "Yeah, that wasn't one of his better aphorisms. It's just saying the same thing twice. He thought he was being clever."

Clementine swallowed past the lump of sorrow in her throat.

Oh, Boone. A tear threatened to run down her cheek before she swiped it away.

Ludek had confirmed what she'd feared most before he left. She had no choice, not while stuck out here, too far from help. Time was her enemy, and Boone was almost out of it. Almost lost for good. His bouts of clarity were growing farther apart and shorter.

She took a deep breath through her nose, focusing inward to find her strength. But there was no inner serenity to be found. The frigid air burned her nostrils. It took her all the way back to her early childhood in Norway. She thought of her afi and amma, their comfortable but small cabin on the hillside that descended to the sea. Of her time learning how to use her instincts to guide her and training to fight for her life.

"Or is that a maxim," he continued. "I can't remember the

difference. Time wasted is time wasted."

A cold, calm determination filled her. It had to be done. It was the only way. She could do this. She was a Slayer after all.

Now!

She slowly circled around behind Boone so as not to alarm him, grabbed his shoulders and yanked him backward. She used her body weight to pull him down fast and slam him hard onto the ground, knocking the wind from his lungs. He gasped for air as she straddled his waist, her weight and legs keeping his arms pinned to his sides. She squeezed her thighs as hard as she could and then pressed her hands firmly over his mouth and nose.

"You cannot have him," she told the darkness hiding behind his eyes.

Boone bucked and writhed under her, but she held tight. Confusion and fear swept over his face. His eyes pleaded with her to stop, then widened as panic took him. Then the shuddering started.

She looked away, unable to watch the life drain away, sobbing, "Leave him!" over and over.

His movements slowed, convulsions weakening. He hadn't recovered his strength after the last few days of too little sleep and food. His life force had been sapped by the conjuror.

Finally, his body stilled, the muscles relaxing under her.

* * *

Rabbit could swear his toes had frozen, broken off, and were rattling around in his boots. But that was nothing new in the Black Hills.

The trek south had been tiring, the snow was deep enough to make walking a struggle, but uneventful. It seemed the forest was devoid of any living animal, or they were smart enough to keep quiet these days. Three times Hank and he had hidden from the hunter's raptor spies as they soared along the ridge and then circled methodically along the valley floor, across and back, across and back, searching for them, he had no doubt.

He figured the hunter was very much alive and under the impression that they had descended to the valley floor to pursue it. At least he thought that was what a hunter would believe.

Actually, chasing after that bastard was the last thing he or Hank wanted to do. After a short discussion at one point in their trek, they'd both decided that cutting beef in the Chicago slaughterhouses would be preferable to facing that bounty hunter and those goblins again. But they knew the truth of the matter at hand. There was better than an even chance that they'd face the sonofabitch again.

The ridgeline had gently descended for the last half hour of their journey until finally, as they approached the pond-lake, it dovetailed into a flat valley out to the waterline. The creek that had been narrow enough to hop across farther north was much too wide and swift to ford here. Luckily, after a short search along the shore and then upstream, Hank spotted a bridge in respectable condition.

"I don't think we should cross that bridge, Jack Rabbit, unless we hightail it to that cabin over yonder."

Rabbit knew what Hank was thinking, at least partly. Before he made his home in Deadwood, Rabbit would have thought the valley Slagton sat in was pretty, but unremarkable otherwise. Now, knowing what he knew and having seen what he'd seen, he hated it. To his mind, there was a dirty devil—no, a bunch of no-good, ugly dirty devils in every cabin or shack and behind every tree in the whole damned valley. And giant, murderous birds with flesh-ripping beaks and claws, too. Nope, he didn't like this place at all.

"I'm agreeable to that notion," he told Hank. "The first part, anyway. I don't savor the idea of traipsin' across that flat. We'll look like a couple of buffalos on a winter prairie." Rabbit surveyed the valley floor surrounding them. "I see three cabins, one with smoke. Wait, what I mean to say is I see a choice for Hank and Rabbit. Almost dead, pretty dead, and really dead." He pointed at each cabin in turn.

"Hoo hoo! Jack Rabbit, you make me laugh." Hank nodded at the closest cabin. "Big sharp teeth there." Then the second closest. "Big sharp claws." And the third. "Uh, big, hmm. That's all they got, big teeth and claws. Ain't so bad."

"How about big sharp swords and muscles and surly dispositions?"

Hank snorted. "We ain't gonna get deceased, Jack Rabbit. I'll tend you fine."

"And who's tendin' you?"

"Miss Clem. She's comin'."

And Boone. It was about the sixtieth time he'd thought about his *amigo* in the last hour. That must have shown on his face, because Hank reached out and squeezed his shoulder.

"We're gonna get him fit, Jack Rabbit. Don't you fret."

Rabbit wasn't so sure, but he felt a little better anyway. "You're a good friend, Hank."

"Sure am." Hank slapped him on the back. He squinted toward the cliff behind them. "Ain't no sign of Miss Clem and Boonedog. Well, back to the trees or out to that cabin, you decide."

He wasn't prepared to make that decision.

"Jack Rabbit, look at this." Hank frowned up at the sky to the north. "Them vultures is headin' this way again."

* * *

Tears rolled down Clementine's face as she stared down at Boone's lifeless body.

What had she done? Her chest tightened, her own lungs aching for air. A fog closed in around her, dizziness took her balance.

Strength in serenity, my Liebling. She heard her afi's voice, as strong and real as it had ever been.

"I can't." She covered her face with her trembling hands.

You must be brave, not for you, but for those who cannot be.

Lowering her hands, she nodded.

Gather yourself, Clementine. This time it was her amma speaking.

She pushed to her feet and hurried to her backpack.

Concentrate. List the steps.

She grabbed the tincture she had placed in the uppermost pocket of her pack and rushed back to Boone. Kneeling beside him, she pulled out her knife and freed his bound wrists. Okay, she was ready.

One. Clear the mouth.

Done.

Two. Pour the tincture in the mouth.

"What if it doesn't work?" she whispered.

Strength in serenity.

She shook the panic from her hands.

You must try.

She blew out a breath and uncapped the tincture. Forcing his mouth open with her fingers, she drizzled the tincture onto his tongue.

Three. Wrap your hands around the back of his neck and pull up to clear the throat.

She pulled. His head tipped back, his mouth opening wider.

Suddenly his upper body convulsed several times, and a thick cloud of black smoke swirled up out of his mouth.

Clementine pitched back in surprise, landing on her backside in the snow. She watched as the smoke formed a cloud above his head and then lengthened into a long slender stream, like chimney smoke blown across the sky by a lazy breeze. The smoke gathered speed as if it had a life of its own, and then dove down over the edge of the cliff out of sight.

Odin's beard! It worked!

It took Clementine a blink to recover her wits before she scrambled back over to Boone. There was no time to waste now.

Four. Massage the upper neck to aid the tincture in its travel down the throat.

She did, silently sending requests to Valhalla for help from the legions of Viking warriors watching over her.

Now. Calm yourself. You must help his heart find harmony with yours. You must be aware of and in control of your life force if you are to share it with him.

"Impossible!" Clementine looked quickly all around her, wishing her amma were actually kneeling next to her instead of just speaking in her thoughts.

Taking a calming breath, she quieted herself.

She began to hear the faint *thump, thump, thump* of the blood rushing through her ears.

Begin.

She leaned over Boone and placed her hands on his chest. Pushed down, let up, pushed down, let up—matching the rhythm of her own heart.

"Come back, Boone," she whispered. A tear rolled down her cheek and dripped onto his chin. "Come back to me."

Sixteen

*B*oone shielded his eyes from a dazzling light that seemed to pass right through him.

What? Where am I?

"Santa Fe sunsets can be brutal on the eyes, eh Boone?"

That voice! Boone squinted but couldn't see who it was, the light had flashed him blind.

The steady *creak, creak, creak, creak* of a rocker he knew well set the rhythm for a symphony of croaking frogs and buzzing cicadas in the cottonwoods down by the creek.

He was home.

The chores were done. He'd need to get to bed early. In the lane out front of the ranch house, a freight wagon was loaded and sat ready for its journey. An early start would see him home tomorrow evening. Rabbit would be back by then, too. He wondered if Rabbit and Carlos were having any trouble rounding up the ponies from the Chupadero Plain where they'd spent the month grazing on the thick grass that grew along the Pecos River.

"Didn't expect to see you here, boy. Not yet anyway."

Creak, creak, creak, creak.

"I finished my chores. Why wouldn't I be here? Say, you want a beer?" The sun was sinking lower, a half circle visible on the shoulder of Los Greigos Mountain. Boone had probably watched it disappear near that mountain a thousand times on this very porch in this very rocking chair, but never did it seem more beautiful than it did right now.

"It's time for you to go."

"What? To bed? Sun isn't down yet. I'll get up early, don't worry. Get a good start in the morning."

"It's sure good to talk to you again, Boone. One of the few things that's been hard about this." His uncle still didn't look at him but touched the center of his chest.

"I've been seeing you all day long. You feeling okay, Uncle Mort?"

"It's time to go now."

"Go where? Chores are done, remember? You want me to check the edges?"

"She's calling you back, boy. Best you answer."

"I …" Boone's head was beginning to ache.

"One thing before you go." Uncle Mort turned toward him, his eyes sad and serious. "Don't go in that barn. Not down the hole."

Boone looked at the barn across the yard. It was covered in shadow now with the sun almost down. "I was in there not half an hour ago. What are you on about, Uncle Mort?"

Morton leaned closer. "Don't go in that barn." Before Boone could respond, he whispered, "She's calling, go on now." He leaned even closer and shoved Boone's forehead with his palm. Hard.

A burst of light blinded him.

* * *

Rabbit high-stepped over the snow since it was easier and quicker than pushing through the knee-deep fluff. The idea of getting caught out by the hunter's raptors spurred him to move faster than he would have otherwise.

"Keep up, Hank. Those fuckers are comin'."

The raptors had circled south more quickly than Rabbit had anticipated, cutting them off to the east and the safety of the tree line they'd left behind. They'd determined the closest cabin to the west was their only chance at finding shelter before the buzzard bastards were on them.

Hank, who was not as hoppy as Rabbit, pushed through like his mule, Fred. Hank and Fred were slow together, but they always reached their destination. The problem now was time. There wasn't any.

"Hank, I swear. It'd be quicker to put you on my back. You're as slow as Fred."

"Don't go malignin' my mule, you hoppin' long-eared Jack Rabbit."

Rabbit would have been offended, but it was Hank, after all. "You gotta work on your insults, baggy britches."

"Quit makin' me talk. I'm winded." Hank huffed.

The raptors were close, maybe close enough to see them but maybe they only had good vision straight down. He could hope. The cabin was still at least a hundred yards yet.

After a few more steps, he cursed under his breath.

They wouldn't make it. Rabbit headed for one of the larger clumps of grass poking through the snow a few yards away. "Over there, Hank. We'll burrow in and hunker down."

The clump was actually a thicket, more than big enough to conceal the both of them. They'd settled in not long before the raptors soared overhead, silent but for the occasional *fwoop* of a wingbeat.

"Furry long-eared rodent," Hank whispered.

Rabbit snorted and slapped his gloved hand over his mouth. "Cut it out, Hank," he murmured through his glove.

They watched as the raptors reached the shore of the lake-pond and turned back north and west, circling slowly.

Rabbit figured they probably hadn't been seen. "Your aspersions are gettin' better, just a little, you flea-bitten wang doodle."

Hank's shoulders started bouncing. "Hoo hoo."

Rabbit poked him in the ribs. "Shhh."

"Okay, okay. Stop pokin' me, it tickles. You think it's safe?"

"Yeah, we should get to that cabin."

"Not back to the bridge?" Hank thumbed over his shoulder.

"You want to go back across that white desert with those raptor bastards roamin' the skies and who knows what else down here on the ground?"

"Not really."

"Let's go then," Rabbit said. "We gotta be ready. Who knows what's in there, but it's only one little cabin. Can't hold that much badness." Rabbit was trying to reassure himself as much as he was Hank.

"Could be a beasty what gets in your head, or—"

"Pull the reins on that thought right now." Rabbit could easily come up with a list of nastiness they might say "howdy-do" to in that cabin, but he'd be damned if he'd backtrack.

They sneaked across the last patch of treeless, snowy desert and hunkered down along the side of the cabin without a window. It was dead silent inside. No snoring, no talking, not even the scrape of a chair or footfall.

"Wait here." Rabbit whispered, and crawled around the corner, finding a window protected by a pair of closed shutters.

He peered inside. It was dark and smelled of death, even from outside. He crooked his neck to see farther into the room. A fire crackled and popped in the fireplace. Lumps of something, on the floor ... bags of ...

No! Bodies! Jehoshaphat!

He cupped his hands around his eyes to shield them from the gray afternoon light.

One, two, three, four, maybe a fifth in the corner. None of them moved. They were piled up as if they had all decided to collapse where they'd stood. Faint light seeped through the cracks of the ill-fitting door on the opposite wall, but even with the firelight, it was too dim to see any details on the bodies. Hell, Rabbit wasn't even sure if they were human.

A shadow passed in front of the door.

Someone, or some *thing*, was alive in there!

He quickly dropped down and out of sight, scrambling back to Hank.

"Somebody's in there." Rabbit whispered into Hank's ear for fear of being overheard by the giant fanged monster he just knew was in the cabin.

He threw down his glove, jerked the Colt from his hip, and listened, waiting for a drooling, sharp-clawed bogeyman to round the corner of the cabin and eat them alive. Judging by Hank's big round eyes, he was waiting for the same thing, Bowie knife ready.

* * *

A shock blasted through Boone's body like he'd been kicked by a mule. He opened his eyes. Clementine was leaning over him, eyes shut, repeatedly pressing on his chest. The look of fear and tears on her cheeks told a story he probably didn't want to hear.

"Are you ..." He grunted as she continued to push rhythmically. She didn't seem to hear him, she muttered something under her breath over and over. "... uh and Hank ..." *Grunt!* "... and Rabbit ..." *Grunt!* "...

uh … okay?" He tried to sit up while she was on top of him but didn't have the strength. "Would you stop that?"

Her eyes opened, growing wide as she stared down at him. She leaned down, nearly nose to nose. "Boone!" Her voice was filled with excitement and disbelief.

"Am I lucky? Or are we in a frying pan?" He checked around them. He was laying in the snow. They appeared to be alone near some trees and rocks.

Clementine jumped to her feet but continued to gape at him. "You're alive!"

"And so are you. Makes me lucky, I'd say." He sat up and grinned. Something bitter and slightly rancid, on the back of his tongue, made him want to spit. "Blah, what did I eat?" He scooped up a handful of snow and ate it, washing the taste from his mouth.

Clementine walked away from him, shaking her hands by her sides, back to muttering again. Maybe cursing.

Boone pushed to his feet and brushed the snow from his backside. He put his hand to his forehead. It ached some, felt bruised.

"You're upset," he said, watching her. "Is it Rabbit again? He irritates me for the fun of it, I swear."

Clementine turned, her hands balled into fists, and started back toward him with a purpose in her step.

He couldn't figure whether she was angry or temporarily *loco*. He back peddled and raised his hands defensively. "Easy now, you got a head of steam we'll both regret in another second. You want me to bob Rabbit's ears?"

She didn't slow.

What the hell? "Whatever it is, we can—"

She grabbed him by the lapels of his jacket. "You scared me to death, Boone."

Before he could figure out what she meant, she went up on her toes and kissed him. Hard. Nearly bruising. She pulled back too soon and looked up at him, tenderly cupping his jaw while smiling through watery eyes.

"I did?" he whispered, basking in the warmth of her gaze.

"Yes. Very much." She linked her arms around his neck and hugged him tight. Then she kissed him again. Softer this time, with an ardor that soothed and enflamed at the same time.

When she pulled back, he stared down at her lips. "You did me, I mean it was me that was … with you lumbering at me like that …" He paused and pointed over Clementine's shoulder. "You were coming at me, I was here … I was on the ground there, earlier." He pointed at their feet. "Uh, then something … something happened here is all I'm saying and …" He stopped and took a breath, focusing back on her smile. "Ah, hell."

He wrapped his arms around her and pulled her close, like he'd thought about too many times to count. He kissed her, taking his time and doing it right, savoring everything about her.

When he broke the kiss, he stared down at her, feeling winded. One of these days they were going to explore these warm feelings when they weren't bristling with steel blades. "Now what?"

Clementine shrugged, taking hold of his wrist. "Let's go."

* * *

Rabbit's heart thumped so loudly he was sure it could be heard at the north end of the valley.

They sat back to back, him on his ass in the snow, Hank squatting with his Bowie knife pointed at the corner of the shack, for what must have been three hours. In Rabbit's head, anyway.

It was actually closer to ten minutes. But his hand felt like it would break off if he touched it and was surely frozen solid to his pistol. His backside wasn't in any better shape.

"Fuck it." He made the decision to lower the pistol, roll over to his knees, and stand, wobbling on his noodley legs. "Get up, Hank, or they'll find you just like that in the spring."

Hank grumbled but didn't move. He rose part way, but tipped sideways and landed in the snow. "Squatted too long. Ding dang knees locked up on me. Give a codger a hand."

Rabbit loosened Hank's grip on his knife, took it, and then grabbed his hand, checking the corners of the cabin every few seconds for that damned monster.

With a grunt from each of them, Hank was standing but not sturdy.

Rabbit leaned him against the cabin. "Work those knees," he whispered. "We gotta go 'round and see what we can see."

"Or," Hank started, pausing to flex one knee then the other. "We wait for Miss Clem and Boone to show."

Rabbit clenched his fist. Boone. Where was the end of that predicament? Was it with Boone right as rain or something else … enough of that. But it was a problem Rabbit couldn't think through to the end, and it caused him more distraction than he cared for, considering where they were.

"Think the ol' dogs are in workin' order again, Jack Rabbit."

"Surprised they work at all, considerin' you're creakier than an old freight wagon. Whole valley can hear you stand up." Rabbit winked.

"Surprised your mouth is, uh …"

Rabbit held his hand up. "Don't." He shushed Hank then and listened for any sound from the cabin. "Nothin'. Let's go. Kick the door or slow like?"

"You make more noise than a—"

"Okay, we'll kick it. You on one side, me on the other. Stay clear till I have a chance for a looksee. A man's silhouette in a doorway is the best target there ever was."

He hunkered down and squat-walked to the door. Hank followed, creaking and popping along the way. They flanked it as Rabbit had planned. He tested the door with a nudge, then shoved it hard. It banged against the wall and swung back around, threatening to close again.

Fuck it! He jumped in, crouched to make a smaller target, ready to kill anything that moved.

Nothing did.

He scurried through the room, avoiding the bodies on the floor, checking the corners for a killer.

Nothing. The cabin was clear.

Rabbit stuck his head out the doorway and took a good look at the valley. The barn and Slagton proper were far to the north. A hummock ran northwest to southeast between them, so the town wasn't even visible. There was no sign of anyone fleeing the scene, big toothy monster or otherwise.

"Let's get inside, Hank." Rabbit knelt near one of the bodies. "This body's still warm. Close the door, will ya?"

Rabbit checked the other bodies. All of them were warm. The fire had the cabin temperature well above that of the frigid air outside, but not *that* warm.

This whole situation raised the hair on the back of his neck. "All these buggers just got eradicated real recent." It must have been the shadow he saw move when he was peeking through the window. "Slippery bastard departed without even sayin' goodbye."

"Who done it?" Hank asked the same question Rabbit was asking himself.

He handed Hank his Colt. "Watch that door, partner. I'm gonna check these characters a little closer, see if we can figure out who or what got them demised."

All of the dead men were well outfitted with heavy wool coats and pants, and well fed, too. Although there was no sign of food in the cabin.

Rabbit focused on the body closest to him. There were no immediate indications of the cause of death. In fact, he saw no wounds at all on the torso or limbs. Squatting, he pushed the jaw this way and that, looking for any signs of trauma and noticed a pool of blood had collected on the floor under the man's head. Peering closer, he saw a trail of blood dripping from a half-inch puncture wound just underneath the man's ear.

After checking the other men for wounds, he rose. "All killed the same way. Thin-bladed knife, right under here." He poked a finger in the soft spot between Hank's jaw and ear. "Straight into the brain. Quick, probably."

A more thorough search turned up a few coins and a standard array of gun belts and pistols.

And one more thing that didn't surprise Rabbit at all.

"Look what we got here." He pulled the ring from one of the men's fingers and held it out to Hank. "They all got 'em."

Hank kneeled beside Rabbit and took the ring. "*Caper-sus.*" He put it on to test the size.

"Think it's a good idea, puttin' that on?" Rabbit asked. "Might be it's magical. Might send you off somewhere we can't find you."

"I'm gonna use the magic for good. Looka that." Hank held it up for Rabbit to see. "Fits."

Rabbit nodded. "You should take it off. Somebody might get the wrong idea about you wearin' that." He scanned the dead men again. "Thin knife used to kill. Dead *caper-sus* everywhere. If I didn't know bett—"

He stopped short at the sound of a faint thump behind him.

"Play dead," a quiet, smooth voice said next to his ear.
Before he could catch his breath, lightning shot through his head.
Darkness followed.

Seventeen

lementine and Boone followed Hank's and Jack's tracks down the receding ridgeline to the transition from forest to grassland and found themselves at a bridge crossing the stream. She could see that a bridge was necessary here since the stream had gathered momentum and volume as it neared the lake. The two men had headed toward the lake and then up the stream to where they stood now.

Across the valley were three shacks, the southernmost almost hidden in the trees. North, a few small cabins sat along the stream, and a hummock extended across the valley obscuring Slagton and, more important, the barn. Perhaps she and Boone could approach from here, hidden from view by the rise. But she was nervous about what she couldn't see. If it was more flat grassland, then they would not have the benefit of cover. Or worse, her moves had been tracked or anticipated by the Egyptian Eminent, and he was waiting just out of sight on the other side of the rise with an army of *others*. She didn't fancy that idea.

Her afi would advise against advancing in that direction, she was sure. "Let's go see what's beyond that rise."

"Clementine," Boone said calmly.

He seemed back to his old self, perfectly Boone. More than that, she *sensed* that he was back to normal. The presence that had troubled her had dissipated, along with the black smoke that left his body. She was certain now that it was the Eminent who had taken Boone, and that worried her. If he was able to control her companions, that was potentially one more problem—or rather three—with which she would need to contend.

Maybe not. Hank and Jack had recovered from the conjuror's effects relatively quickly. So, the Eminent wasn't so powerful that he could control all of them at once. That, or it was possible only Boone had some susceptibility to his control. Only him, since she was immune to mind control. She appreciated that particular ability now, even more than she had before all of this.

"Clementine."

"What?" She was still looking north.

"The tracks head west. We should go west, not north."

He was right, of course. But the barn was north.

"They might need our help," he added.

"*Verdammt*. I know, I know. Can I trust you with this?" She held up his black-bladed scimitar.

"Yes." His voice carried his frustration. He snatched it from her hand and slid it into the scabbard strapped to his side. "You think the hunter is still alive?"

She pointed north, toward the sky.

He squinted for a few seconds. "I don't see anything."

"The hunter's raptors are up there. I can't imagine they'd be doing that if the hunter were dead."

"Verdammit," he said.

"*Verdammt*," she corrected.

She really wanted to see over that hummock. A look wasn't really going to hurt anyone. She would just like something to use for cover.

"I'm going to take a look up there. You stay here if you want." She set off to the northwest, along the southern base of the hummock, past a small thicket of grass, the last good cover on her side excursion to see Slagton. Hank and Jack had come this way too, in fact. Their stride had lengthened. "Long strides. Straight into the thicket. Hmm."

"Cover," Boone said simply.

Clementine searched a little way in each direction. "No other tracks but the two of them, toward the cabin over there." She looked at the sky. The raptors were black dots against the blue sky now, slowly circling farther and farther away.

"From the air. Hiding from the hunter's raptors, I suppose?" Boone squinted at the sky.

"That's what I'd say. The raptors are headed up the valley, searching in a pattern."

"So they'll eventually turn south again. Gives us a little time anyway." Boone winced. "What am I saying?" He pointed at her. "That doesn't mean we have time to gallivant north to satisfy your curiosity."

"Yes it does. The raptors are still looking, so they haven't found anyone yet, and we need to know how pressing the threat is to the north. Is there a horde of *Draug* on the other side of that rise waiting for us?"

"If there is, I'm not feeling inclined to deliver myself to them."

"Come on, Boone. Aren't you curious?"

"I'm not the inquisitive type when it comes to *Draug*. Or, for that matter," he said, starting to list on his fingers. "Hairy monsters with big teeth, giant putrid eggs, goddamn conjurors, or surly Pinkertons. I leave all that to Rabbit. Give me a buckboard and a pretty view."

"I'm your pretty view." She playfully batted her eyelashes at him, then got serious. "We need to know what's going on up there."

"I wish Uncle Mort was here. He could go take a look."

"You said Uncle Mort." Jack was the one who talked about his uncle's ghost being around yet, not Boone. Had something happened when she'd killed him?

"Did I?" He looked surprised. "Things have changed a little bit in my head. Which gets me thinking—"

"Uh oh." She chuckled.

"Stop it. It gets me thinking regarding just what happened back there on top of the ridge. One minute I'm helping take down a hunter—whatever he's hunting is probably you. The next I'm …" he trailed off and frowned at the ground, shaking his head. "I can't …" After a second or two, he came back. "Then, I was on my back with you pushing the air outta me. Were you trying to kill me, or what?"

"*Helping* might be an overstatement." Clementine smirked at him. Better to turn the conversation than spend the next hour defending her choice to kill him. That would come later.

Boone covered his open mouth with his hand in mock offense. "You dissect my soul with a thousand sharp knives, you wicked woman."

She glanced at the cut marks on her boots, sliced by one deranged freighter with a Bowie knife; and the real irony, he wasn't even aware of what he'd done. "Let's just take a peek over that rise."

He threw his hands up in mock exasperation. "Fine. You wear me down. Since you're itching to go see your freaky Slagton circus, let's go."

"It's not my circus."

It wasn't more than three hundred yards along the hummock before they were crawling the last few steps to the top. Patches of dry grass poked through the snow, certainly not enough to hide anything more than a rabbit, and certainly not the Santa Fe type. They hadn't yet reached the top for a view, but already the clamor of the town was evident. It didn't match the racket of Deadwood and it was definitely of a different quality. Moans and snarls and howls carried on the wind had widened Boone's eyes considerably.

"It sounds like the devil's barn dance up there." Boone's squeaky tone made her laugh. "I don't find this the slightest bit funny, Clementine. My feet are wet, my hands hurt, my head aches. And look at that." He pointed at the sky. "Sun is near gone. This little shindig of yours isn't my idea of a pleasant Saturday night."

"Is it Saturday?"

"Clementine, I swear."

"Okay, okay. We'll head back, but I'm getting a look first. It's important."

She crawled the last few feet to the top of the hummock and raised her head just enough to see the town.

"What do you see?" Boone asked in a loud whisper. He hadn't followed, but he had drawn his sword. "Do I need to kill something?"

The barn was a quarter mile away, but still easily visible, along with a few cabins and shacks dotted along the path of the stream. Beyond the barn, she could see some tent tops as well, and many of the buildings that made up the better part of Slagton. Along with the howls, she could hear laughter now that her head was above the top of the hummock.

The whole area north of the barn was alive with movement. Smoke rose from torches and chimneys in long wispy trails. The town had come alive. She guessed that the failing light was the stimulant for what were mostly nocturnal inhabitants. That and the word was probably out that there were unwanted visitors in the area. Namely, a Slayer and her companions.

Evening shadows masked much of the goings-on in the town, but Clementine was certain of one thing—the barn was the center of activity. White grizzlies, *caper-sus*, and many others she didn't recognize entered the barn as if it were the local saloon.

"Clementine, what do you see?" Boone crawled up next to her and peered over the top of the hummock then quickly scampered back down to the base.

"Clementine, get down here!" he whispered. "They'll see you."

"Wait." She took one more look.

There was no sign of the Egyptian Eminent anywhere, but there were many human shapes milling around town now. At least they looked human. The hunter's raptor spies had made their turn and were headed back south again. She slid-crawled down the slope to Boone.

"What the hell is going on up there?" Boone was pacing a short route, out and back.

"Looks like a shindig." Now she really wanted to see what was going on in that barn.

He stopped and hit her with a *You-gotta-be-shittin'-me* stare. "You're making me ask, is that it? Okay, I'll play. What are you thinking?" Boone's voice still carried a significant amount of agitation.

"I need to consider this a little more. If I could talk to Ludek, that'd be good."

"I'm Boone, not Ludek."

"That's why I want to think about this more." When he continued to give her that same stare, she added, "Boone, I'm not sure what's going on here."

The snow and trees in the distance were turning gray with the dusk.

"We should get to those cabins," she continued. "We'll need cover from the raptors. They may have good night vision, and I don't like the idea of just us two facing that hunter and his goblins."

* * *

Hank groaned and flopped onto his back, rolling onto Rabbit in the process.

"Ugh. Hank, take it easy. You're squishin' my nethers."

Rabbit lay wedged between his companion and the cold body of the *caper-sus* he'd taken the ring from earlier. His hands were bound behind his back, and so far he'd been unable to free himself.

"Hank. You gotta move."

Near as Rabbit could figure, some scofflaw had been waiting in the rafters, jumped down, and clunked him and Hank on the noggin. Again. One more splitting headache and he was liable to start holdin' a grudge against noggin clunkers.

Hank groaned, longer this time. "Feels like my head's got a splittin' wedge drove in it."

"Roll over that way. This character over here's got more ferment to him than an overused privy."

Hank bumped and jostled to sitting, kneeing Rabbit in his side in the process.

"We gotta get these ropes off, Hank. Somebody comes, we'll be like a couple of Sunday chickens trussed up for roastin'."

"These here ropes are tight. Somebody know'd how to tie a knot. Say, you read that sailor knot book I give ya?"

"Hank, we left Deadwood right after Christmas. I ain't had the chance ..." Rabbit read the puppy-dog look in Hank's eyes. "My plan is, read cover to cover, soon as we're back in Deadwood."

Hank smiled wide. "I know'd it. You're gonna love it, Jack Rabbit."

"Right now, I'd love it if you could get us free of these ropes."

"I got an idea about that. Wiggle your hind end this'a way. I'll work on yours, you can work on mine."

"Buy me a whiskey first."

"Hoo hoo. Jack Rabbit, don't make me laugh. It's hard to breathe with my arms wrapped up behind me."

Hank turned on his side, exposing the ropes wrapped around his wrists and forearms.

Rabbit squirmed and bounced until they were feet to head and started working on the knots on Hank's ropes.

"Whoa. You tryin' to work ropes or tickle my hindquarters?"

Rabbit poked Hank's hip. "Don't get excited. If I was fixin' to get fresh, you'd know it."

The door swung open. "If anybody is tickling any hindquarters, it's gonna be me." Boone stood in the doorway, grinning.

"Booney!" Rabbit's heart jumped up his throat at the sight of his *amigo*.

Boone squatted. "You two want us to wait outside, or are you done horsing around?"

Clementine stuck her head in the doorway. "I don't know, Boone, it might be a show to see."

Hank bumped and writhed and craned his neck to catch a glimpse of Clementine. "Miss Clem! Shine my boots! I'm happier than a weevil in a cotton boll to see you."

"Me too, Hank. Whatcha doin' there?" She stepped into the cabin, her attention getting caught up by the dead *caper-sus* littering the floor. "I assume this isn't your work since both of you are somewhat incapacitated."

"No, ma'am. We come on this mess." Hank elbowed Rabbit in the ribs.

"Oof! Hank, hold still. You're like a badger in a gunny sack over there. Booney, hurry up with the knots before Hank breaks one of my ribs." Rabbit watched his *amigo*, wondering if he was talking to the good old, regular Boone, or the bad new Boone that had tried to kill Clementine.

He looked to Clementine with the question in his eyes. A nod and a smile from her told him the answer.

So she'd somehow straightened him out. No doubt there was a story behind it.

Boone cut the knot and pulled the ropes away from Rabbit's hands, then began working on the ropes around his ankles.

"I know what we've been up to." She edged her chin at Boone. "Tell me about you two."

"Not much to tell." Finally free, Rabbit sat on a stool and rubbed his wrists. "Got here. These *caper-sus* characters were already buzzard food."

"Still warm though, Jack Rabbit." Hank sat up and rubbed his wrists too. "Tied too tight, ask me."

"Thinkin' back on it, that shoulda been a clue." Rabbit knew he hadn't been thinking things through real well since Boone started trying to kill the wrong people.

"Clue to what?" Boone toed each of the bodies laid out in the cabin.

"Bodies still warm but no sign of anybody nearby." Rabbit looked up at Boone. "Seems we shoulda seen somebody crossin' that winter desert out there if the bodies were still warm."

"I'd put my money on the killer still being around when you two got here." Clementine tapped her lips with her finger.

"Yeah. Weren't that simple though, Miss Clem. See, we checked the cabin, no one nowhere's we could see."

"Jumped out of the fire?" Boone probably thought he was being funny.

"From the rafters," Rabbit corrected. "Right behind us when we were lookin' over the *caper-sus* boys." He pretended to clunk Hank on the head with a club and clucked his tongue. "Like a doctor on a house call. Both of us."

"What's that now, Jack Rabbit?"

"Doctor on a house call. You know. Out." Rabbit pointed at the ring on Hank's finger. "Got a curled one, whatever that means."

Clementine examined one of the dead men, cutting open his shirt with one of her blades. A large *caper-sus* burn scar covered his chest from nipple to nipple.

"He was special. I'm betting all of these men are." She turned his head left and right, poking her finger in the knife hole under his ear. She cursed under her breath. "I know who did this."

* * *

Boone knew who she meant. "Prudence."

Clementine nodded.

"You're basing your opinion on what, exactly?" Boone knew Clementine was probably right, but he wasn't one to jump to conclusions, especially conclusions he didn't like.

"The way the bodies were arranged. The fact that they are *caper-sus*. The ambush on Hank and Jack. I don't believe many could get the jump on Jack like that. Nor Hank, for that matter. But mostly, the manner of execution, and I use that word specifically. It's rare to come across a single person who can put down five men, and I have to assume that these men were skilled fighters."

"Why?" Boone kept pushing.

"Look at the circumstances. Three cabins, arranged in a triangle. This shack and the two others are quarters for sentries."

"Like Horace?"

"Possibly. I wish he were here to ask if he'd quartered in one of these cabins. If not, perhaps other sentries were here, but were driven away or killed. I think it's safe to assume these *caper-sus* are newcomers guarding something for the Egyptian."

"Why down here? The barn is pretty far north. And why three?" Boone was getting interested in Clementine's theory now.

"I don't know. Ludek didn't mention two more Watchers, but he did mention others hiding about. It sounded like Horace had assistants. They might have been occupying these cabins and then the Egyptian arrived and sent everything *skjevt*. Chased the designated guards … attendants?" She shrugged. "Chased them away or killed them."

Rabbit pulled absently at his beard. "Like the folks working at a train station. Selling tickets an' such. Makin' sure nobody jumps the train."

"Something like that. It's just a theory. I'd really like to talk with Ludek and Hildegard right now."

Boone had no reason to doubt her theory. It made sense. "Okay, so let's assume that you're right. What is Prudence doing here?"

Clementine shrugged. "I don't know. She followed us. Or Ludek. She can sense where the trouble is. Maybe Masterson sent her to dispatch me when the job is complete. He has a low opinion of my abilities, and I've defied him more than once. It's not out of the realm of possibility that he wants to make an example of me."

"Fuck Masterson." Boone felt like spitting at the thought of Masterson double-crossing Clementine. Now he had a new worry to contend with. "You think she'd do it?"

"To understand Prudence, you must understand a Slayer." Clementine scratched at the table with her fingernail. "You've all seen me in a fight. When a Slayer goes into battle or senses danger, things happen that we can't control. Innate things." She looked pointedly at Boone. "You like to call it bloodlust. I don't, but that may be the only way you know how to describe it. It happens to all of you too, under the right circumstances. If someone shoots or swings a blade at you, a rush of energy and heightened awareness surges through you, yes?"

The three men nodded.

"I think it's the same for me, but with much more intensity. It's almost as if someone else has taken control. Everything around me moves more slowly than normal. I can dodge a blade or bullet because I not only see them coming, I can sense them. I can sense things near me without seeing them. I'm stronger, quicker. I see the path forward. But with that ability I lose some amount of control, and impulse takes over."

Boone had more or less witnessed exactly what she was describing.

"I feel compelled to cleanse the malevolence from a thing. From places, people, *others*, deep in here." She touched her sternum. "I've tried controlling it, but I'm not sure how successful I've been. Nor am I sure I should be. Am I limiting my abilities by trying to control them? I don't know."

Boone read the frustration, or was it regret or sadness, on her face. Being a Slayer was indeed a burden. It fell to her, alone. Knowing that pestilence would spread unchecked should she fail. Being the outsider, the one that didn't fit in, no matter where she went.

"It's been a lonely existence for you," he realized out loud. He wanted to reach out to her, tell her she wasn't alone anymore.

She looked at him, her forehead drawn. But as her look turned into a stare, her expression softened, eyes darkened. She leaned toward him.

"What's that got to do with Prudence?" Rabbit asked. On occasion, he was an oblivious sort.

Clementine blinked and shook her head slightly. Boone could practically see her defenses rising, the Slayer taking back the reins. But a wry smile lingered on her lips as she turned her attention to Rabbit.

"I tell you this because Prudence is like me, but with one big difference, I think. I bear the burden of guilt by being a Slayer, because of the things I do. Sometimes the guilt is overwhelming. For her, I don't believe there is any guilt at all. It's been evident every time we've crossed paths with her, even here. She killed those *caper-sus* men without one bit of compunction. They might have been redeemable, but she didn't care. It was the same in Galena, and probably in countless other towns and villages where she has done her work."

"So you might give it a thought—an order to kill another Slayer," Rabbit said. "Prudence probably wouldn't. Are you sure this was her?" He seemed to be catching on to what she was saying. His tone had softened considerably.

"Pretty sure. The position of the bodies, a thin blade to a vital organ or the brain. We've seen this before. Efficient. It's a Slayer's work." She looked at Hank and then Rabbit. "The fact that you two are still alive. That in particular is a message for *me*."

"What? I thought you said she had no compunction," Boone said.

"She doesn't. You two aren't alive out of the goodness in that woman's heart. What would have happened if she'd killed you two?"

"You'da kicked her hind end to California and back," Rabbit growled.

"You'd be hoppin' mad, that's for sure," Hank added.

"Right. She doesn't want to force me into a situation like that, at least not yet. But she also wanted to show me she could."

"That little biddy," Rabbit growled again.

"I never." Hank wore his indignation right on his face. "What'd I do to her?"

"That," Clementine continued, "and she probably thought you have the potential to be useful in the future. Otherwise, she wouldn't have tied you up. Or maybe she would have, just to humiliate you."

"I thought I liked her a little bit." Rabbit was wearing a thick layer of indignation, too.

"I never did. She scares me." Hank got up and poked at the fire. "If I see her, I might tip my hat but I ain't gonna say 'Howdy-do.'"

"You don't have a hat, and at least she didn't take your pants. That's something." Boone grinned.

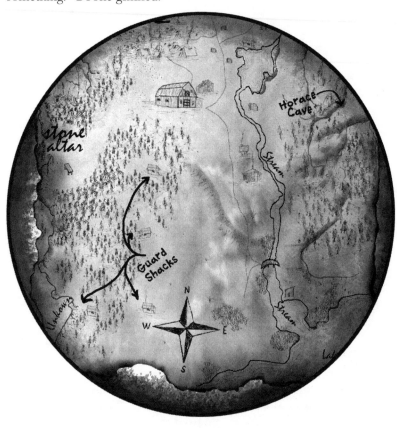

Eighteen

Night had descended on Slagton valley while Rabbit and his companions discussed Prudence and *caper-sus* and *others*, as well as where they were headed next. They made the decision to hunker down in the cabin and wait until morning before moving on.

Since a fire was burning when Hank and Rabbit had arrived, none of them saw any reason to let it burn down now. It would make for a warmer night than sleeping under the stars.

While Hank put together a stew of potatoes and jerky with a pinch of an herb mix he called "Momma Marabell's," Rabbit helped Boone and Clementine move the *caper-sus* bodies outside. He was in the same mindset as everyone else, preferring to take a chance on the bodies being seen over spending the night cozied up to corpses.

An hour later, Rabbit's belly was full of potatoes and broth. "That was fine, Hank, filled my belly proper."

He had to wonder how a man could make such a fine stew out of three or four ingredients. He'd sat and watched Lupe sprinkle and dump fifteen different things into her *mole*. It was good *mole*, though.

"Anything for you, Jack Rabbit."

"Say, Miss Clementine, I've been wantin' to ask, how'd you clear Booney's head out? Thunk him on the noggin?" Rabbit winked at her.

"What I'd like to know is, did we decide?" she asked. "We're going to take a look in that barn, right?" Clementine veered right off course, and Rabbit was well aware of it.

"We didn't decide," Rabbit replied. "We can go see what's in your barn tomorrow morning, but first, answer my question."

"If you saw what I saw up there in Slagton around the barn," Boone said, "you'd hightail it back to Deadwood on the first horse going by."

Boone nodded in agreement with himself then sat down beside the fireplace, pulled out Ludek's map, his lead pencil, and started in on another round of updates.

"I didn't see." Rabbit's frustration was growing. "What'd you do to Boone?"

"Didn't Ludek suggest we leave the barn for now and cull the herd instead?" Boone got in the way again.

Clementine took a sip of coffee from the tin Hank handed her. "There hasn't been much herd to cull, from what I've seen. Prudence seems to be one step ahead of us. I'm more curious than ever about that barn. Why is it so busy in there? It has to be the gateway, right?"

It felt to Rabbit like everyone was purposely ignoring his question. "What. Did you do. To Boone?"

"Miss Clem?" Hank joined in. "Might we could head west a little, into the trees over there and then north, up behind the barn like we done tried from the other direction, before we got roped into Horace's affairs?"

Clementine nodded. "That should work."

Rabbit threw his hands up.

Clementine considered him for a few moments, then she cocked her head. "I killed him."

"You don't want to tell me, fine. Probably Slayer trickery of some sort anyway."

"Hoo. Miss Clem." Hank slapped his knee. "Hope you don't never feel like savin' me thata way. That might hurt my feelings."

"I could never hurt you, Hank. Now Jack, on the other hand," she said with a teasing glint in her eyes.

"Cut it out, Miss Clementine." Rabbit wasn't done on the subject, but for some reason she wasn't ready to spill beans. Okay. He'd find out what happened. He pointed at Boone. "Don't suppose you remember, right?"

Boone shook his head. "Not much. Uncle Mort …"

Rabbit sat up. "What about him?"

"He … I don't know. I just can't remember."

"All right, Booney. You're in with Miss Clementine then. Let's have a joke on Rabbit."

"It's not like that. I just can't remember is all." Boone's look was sincere, Rabbit knew it.

"Okay, Booney. When you do, let me know. Miss Clementine ain't gonna, I guess."

"Jack …"

"Never mind. Time to rest my candles." Rabbit was getting plain tired of things always going Clementine's way. Of her always calling the play. It made him feel weak, like a donkey on a lead rope.

"I put out your bedroll in that corner, Jack Rabbit, next to mine. I'm thinkin' I need some shuteye too."

Clementine stood and stretched. "Boone, you should get some sleep, too. I'll take the first watch. Hank, you can take a turn in a few hours." She opened the door a crack and peeked outside. "It's quiet."

* * *

Boone woke early from a fitful sleep. He'd dreamt of his uncle and Rabbit, Clementine and Hank. None of those had been what he would consider bad dreams. But the one with the canine-headed bastard had been. The son of a bitch had bashed his skull with his staff and started to eat his brain. Rabbit had woken him before *El Vaquero*—or was it the Egyptian?—had finished the job.

The sun hadn't crested the eastern ridgeline, but Boone decided sleep was no place to hide these days. What had the conjuror done to him? He remembered now that it all started in that cabin, when the conjuror stirred his brain. But it was the dog-headed bastard that seemed to take up residence in his noggin, at least until Clementine had worked her magic and kicked him out.

Or had she?

Rabbit sat down beside him, holding a tin cup. "Sleep a little bit more, Booney. I'm still awake. Hank makes a stout cup of Arbuckles'."

"I would, *amigo*, but those dreams are killing me."

"What kinda dreams?"

"Dog head."

"He's a fucker."

"Yeah."

"Still can't remember what Miss Clementine did to make him clear out?"

Boone peered over at Clementine. She looked to be sleeping, but she probably wasn't. "Can't remember much of anything until … Rabbit?"

"Yeah?"

"One thing I do remember, I think." He paused and looked Rabbit in the eyes. "It's gonna sound odd."

"Tell me."

"I have a memory of sitting on the front porch with Uncle Mort." Boone squeezed an eye shut.

"That's no *thing*. I got lotsa memories like that."

"No, you don't understand. I was all of a sudden sitting with him watching the sunset. You were off collecting the horses from the Chupadero Plain. It's like it just happened."

"That was a pretty sight, horses runnin' wild. The oxen not so much. Shit stuck to their haunches."

"Yeah. Anyway, it was …" Boone closed both eyes, trying to remember. "It was … it was like I woke up there, all of a sudden."

"So you think it wasn't a real recollection then?"

"No. But it sure seemed real." The memories were coming to him in fragments. "Talked about a freight ready to go the next morning. Then he pushed my forehead—"

Boone opened his eyes and searched Rabbit's face for answers, but of course he would have none.

He continued, "Like Uncle Mort sent me back from—"

"I killed you." Clementine pushed up on one elbow from her bedroll, her gaze steady on him with not a single teasing glint in it. "I told both of you that earlier."

It came rushing back now. Flat on his back, arms pinned. The horror of her hands over his mouth and nose. The searing pain as he tried to draw air, as if his lungs were filled with glass shards. The anguish on Clementine's face as she looked down at him with tears in her eyes.

Then fear, and searing pain, then nothing.

Rabbit watched him, eyes narrowing. His expression must have drawn the picture for his friend.

"Holy shit! You did kill him!" Rabbit's jaw dropped open, his face a combination of disbelief and anger. He rose and fisted both hands.

"Rabbit!" Boone knew he was about to do a stupid thing.

"Jack Rabbit! Simmer down." Hank was up now, too, at Rabbit's side.

Clementine stood and approached Rabbit. "I had to. It was the only way." Her lower lip trembled. "It was the hardest thing I've ever done." She grimaced down at Boone. "I'm so sorry."

Boone slowly got up, ready to tackle Rabbit if he made his move. But Rabbit's fists relaxed, and his whole body seemed to shed the tension that had brought him to his feet.

"How did you know to do that?" Rabbit whispered.

"Ludek said it was the only way." Clementine ran her hand down her face. "I don't know if he meant for me to revive Boone, but that was my plan all along."

Anger, shock, bewilderment, held Boone's tongue tight. He took a deep breath. Everything still seemed to work fine. He took another deep breath. Yep. Lungs were working. She'd killed him? Suffocated him? He put his hand on his chest. Yep, heart still beating.

Rabbit strode to the fire and back. "Why didn't you tell us? Never mind, I know. But how do you know it worked?"

"I don't, for sure." Clementine crossed her arms. "But he seems normal."

"Do I?" Boone wasn't sure now. He blew on the palm of his hand, the warmth of it was comforting.

"When he ... expired, black smoke came out of his mouth, and it ..." she hesitated. "Well, it flew away, over the cliff toward Slagton."

"Wind took it?" Rabbit asked.

"No. It flew. With purpose. Just like the Egyptian did."

"So this Egyptian fucker was in Boone?"

"I think so. Or part of him. Or it had some influence over him. I don't know."

Now Boone really wondered if he was back to normal. He started poking parts of his body, his arm, belly, leg. His head hadn't stopped hurting since he woke up with Clementine sitting on him. Did the potatoes in the stew really taste like potatoes? Now he wasn't sure about anything.

"Looks normal. Sounds normal. I think he's normal." Hank took Boone by the shoulders and stared in his eyes. "Brown. See, normal. I think. Hoo hoo! Jus' funnin' ya, Boonedog."

"Thanks, Hank." Boone punched him on the arm.

Rabbit laughed. "Brown. So he's still full of shit." He raised a finger at Boone. "You said you sat on the porch with Uncle Mort. He pushed you on the forehead and you came back?"

Boone nodded. It was as real as anything he'd ever experienced.

Rabbit turned to Clementine. "You think Booney really saw him? That happens when you die?"

"I haven't died, so I don't know. I would think it's possible though, especially since you and I can see your uncle."

"I'll be." Rabbit grinned at Boone. "It's about damn time, Booney. Now he can pester you, too, if you can hear him."

"I'm looking forward to it." Boone actually would be, if he thought it was real. Right now he wasn't sure.

"Leaves me odd man out, I guess." Hank sank to a squat and poked at the fire. "Suppose we should get a move on, Miss Clem?"

"Yep." She clapped her hands together. "Slaying knows no schedule."

"Up to the other cabins, then, check on them too?" Rabbit began packing up his bedroll.

"No. I already checked them. It's the same as here. Five *caper-sus* in both of them, all executed the same way."

Clementine must have gone out during her watch. "You left us here, unprotected?" Boone was poking fun at her, masking his concern over her exploring alone.

"Three big strong men," she said with a teasing smirk. "I assumed you'd be fine for a few minutes."

"So, Prudence then." Rabbit stated rather than asked.

"Yes, Prudence. She's a busy woman." Clementine's frustration carried over into her tone.

They were ready to head out after filling their bellies with biscuits and fatback. Clementine had worried the smell of cooking food might alert the *others* of their presence and said as much to Hank, but after she breathed in the meaty, smoky aroma, she surrendered and ate three thick slices.

Clementine led the way once out of the cabin and headed northwest, toward the forest behind the barn. Boone knew Clementine was still focused on it, even though Ludek had suggested they cull the *others* that had invaded Slagton and driven out the citizens that lived there.

He wondered how far Prudence had gone—how far she would go— to undermine Clementine. Or was she truly monomaniacal in her quest to cleanse the Hills. He shrugged. It didn't matter. She had culled the invaders. He just didn't know how much of the task she had completed and what her plans were going forward.

They passed between the other two cabins, headed for the woods. Both structures were quiet, with no fires burning. Boone shuddered at the fact that there were ten dead men inside those buildings.

He caught up to Clementine, who was within a few steps of the tree line in front of them. "You think Prudence plans on cleansing all of Slagton on her own?"

"No. She knows, as well as I do that there are other forces at work here. It would be nice to know if Masterson sent her, but even that doesn't really matter." She paused as they stepped under the canopy of trees to listen, then continued on, deeper into the forest. "Prudence is aware that I will use every means available to me to fulfill my task. She is also aware that you three are with me. I suspect she knows that the Watcher is most probably dead, and that the Watcher's companions are possibly hiding out there somewhere." She swirled her hand over her head.

"She followed Ludek," Boone realized.

"Yes. I think it's likely. Either that or she followed us, but I don't believe she could have done that without my knowing. Ludek was carrying a double load and moving fast. I doubt he could stay hidden from her, even if he tried."

They came into a stand of trees that were twisted and sickly and dying. A little farther on, all of the trees were dead.

"This don't seem right, Miss Clem," Hank said quietly. "This feels like bad luck to me. What's it called?"

"A bad omen." Boone rubbed his stomach. The roil in his guts told him Hank was right.

"Playin' with my guts a little, too, Booney." Rabbit scowled.

"We'll get through this quickly," she said. "We know the barn is less than a quarter of a mile north and east of here. Let's push through."

Clementine, being Clementine, quickened her pace, disallowing any discussion on the subject.

She was right, not more than a few minutes later, they came upon a clearing along the western edge of the valley. The western ridge, which had been hidden by the trees, loomed high into the sky in front of them. It was close to what Boone had expected, since they had seen the whole of that ridgeline from the opposite side of the valley.

What stood directly before them, however, was definitely a surprise.

From the opposite ridgeline, the clearing in front of them had remained hidden in the trees. According to Ludek's map, there was an altar in the middle of this clearing. But what Boone saw wasn't an altar at all.

Clementine stopped at the tree line. A gap in the forest permitted a view of the barn, which sat a few hundred yards to the northwest.

"What the hell is that?" Rabbit pointed at the group of stones directly in front of them, arranged in a circle roughly fifty feet in diameter, each standing about ten feet apart and four feet high.

"It looks like some kind of astrometric dial." Clementine craned her neck to see better. "It's not what Ludek drew on the map."

"They're still buildin'. Lookit there." Hank pointed at two square stone foundations, ten feet on a side. They sat at the edge of the stone circle on each side of a path leading toward the barn.

"Let's go take a look." Clementine scanned the whole of the clearing before heading toward the center of the circle.

"Dammit Boone!" Rabbit backhanded him in the arm.

"What'd I do?" Boone watched Clementine for a second and then took off after her. "We might as well have rings in our noses if she's going to keep leading us around like this," he said over his shoulder, trying to keep his voice down.

Hank was right beside him, following after Clementine.

She went straight for the flat round rock at the center of the circle.

Boone and Hank, with Rabbit trailing, followed her until she suddenly raised her hand. "Stop." And then put her hand to her stomach.

"What is it Miss Clem?" Hank approached another step.

"My stomach. It feels like it's being turned upside down and shaken."

"Maybe you should get out of there." Boone beckoned to her.

"Come on, Miss Clementine, off the stone." Rabbit stepped forward onto the rock. "Feels like hoppin' hotcakes in my belly." He jumped off the rock.

"Maybe you're right." She rejoined them and stared at the round flat rock again. "This looks familiar to me. Wait!" Clementine rummaged through her pack and pulled out the small stone tablet Horace had given her in the cave.

Boone saw the connection. There were similar figures, or drawings, carved in both. They were in concentric circles on the round stone but seemed chiseled into haphazard groups on the tablet. "Whaddaya know about that?"

"This is something I've not seen before." Clementine seemed mesmerized by the figures. "This may well be …" She trailed off as she began to walk the perimeter of the circle, weaving in and out of the stones.

Boone wandered too, studying the standing stones making up the circle, careful not to step on the center stone. They looked like they'd been placed a very long time ago, formed with rudimentary tools into roughly rectangular shapes. Snow had melted or been brushed from their tops. Lichen covered most of their surfaces.

The stone path leading to the barn, too, was devoid of snow, and looked well-worn. But the two square structures on each side near the circle were still in the process of being built. One was about his height, the other almost as tall, but it was obvious the construction wasn't complete. Unlike the weathered stones of the circle, the fit and finish of these square and oblong blocks was exceptional. It was difficult to see the seams. He'd rarely seen such craftsmanship.

Stone chips and dust lay scattered about the bases of the pillars and the snow had been scraped and scuffed and compacted all around both. A wide footpath led to the cliff not a hundred feet to the west where the outlines of two fifty-foot-tall obelisks had been chiseled into the granite wall. The work looked to be about half done.

What happens when they finish?

Boone's eyes blurred and the image of *El Vaquero*, standing between the erected obelisks, arms extended toward the sky, filled his vision. He was making sounds Boone didn't recognize as words, but it was obviously a language. His voice was unnaturally deep and resounded as if he were in a canyon. The obelisks beside him seemed different, cut from orange-brown sandstone rather than the gray granite of those being cut from the cliff nearby.

Suddenly, *El Vaquero* stilled and looked straight at Boone …

"Booney, look at this, ain't budgin' at all." Rabbit's voice cut through his thoughts, the vision of *El Vaquero* fading. Boone turned, staring as Rabbit pushed on one of the stones with his foot.

What was going on? Boone rubbed his forehead. He nodded at Rabbit, but his thoughts were on what he'd just seen. The place *El Vaquero* had been standing had looked different. The area surrounding it was different too. The terrain, even the obelisks were different. Were there more of these places elsewhere? More worrisome, was *El Vaquero* still in his head?

Boone drove the thought away and focused on the pillars instead. From where he stood, he could see that the well-formed blocks used in the construction of the pillars had been quarried from the lower part of the cliff.

"Clementine, come here." Boone watched Hank and Rabbit push and pull on the stones that made up the circle.

"What is it?" Clementine stopped next to him.

"These pillars are still under construction. And the blocks they're cutting and shaping to build them are totally different than the shaped rocks that form the circle. Different time period, different masons. The pillars are being built meticulously, the circle blocks are just roughly shaped and well weathered. Measured in thousands, not hundreds, of years. What I mean to say is that circle looks really old, but someone has been working on these pillars recently. What did you call this again?"

"Astrometric dial. But I'm not sure that's what it is."

"Oh?"

Rabbit and Hank joined them. "Those things don't move for nothin'. Like they're buried way down in the ground, like Hank's butt."

Hank wrinkled his nose at Rabbit.

"I think this may have something to do with Horace." She held up the tablet. "See the markings, many are the same. Either Horace was making or carrying a record of that center slab." She pointed at the round, flat rock. "He may have had multiple duties or tasks during his time here other than just being a Watcher. I think those cabins we just came from are meant to house sentinels of some kind," Clementine continued. "But *caper-sus* aren't sentinels. The Egyptian Eminent ..." she paused, looking up at Rabbit. "Or *El Vaquero*, if you prefer."

Rabbit shrugged. "Either way."

"Right. Well, he has clearly made some big changes, and he's putting his mark right here." She pointed at the pillars.

"*Caper-sus* are just men, right, Miss Clementine?"

The heavy thrum of big drums sounded a slow beat that echoed off the valley walls.

"Oh fuck! They got us!" Rabbit's eyes practically popped out of his head.

"Easy, Jack." Clementine held out her hand, looking toward the barn. Boone's gaze followed hers.

A commotion started up near the barn. Boone watched for a few moments as figures began to appear, some from the direction of the tents, some from the cabins and shacks in town. A number of them disappeared into the barn, while others formed into a line that seemed to be heading right toward them.

"They're coming this way." Boone's heart banged against the inside of his chest.

"We better skedaddle, folks. Which way, Miss Clem?" Hank's eyes darted back the way they'd come, then at the patch of forest to the north.

She didn't move, but continued to watch the scene. "It looks like some of them are carrying spears. Or staffs. And tools. Hammers, maybe chisels." She turned to Boone. "They're coming to work, fifty at least. We should go."

Nineteen

After ten long seconds of debate, they decided to go north, into the thicket of dead trees up against the cliff, which was exactly what Clementine had wanted.

West, the cliff blocked their escape, and since the barn lay to the northeast they weren't going that way. If they went south like Jack and Boone wanted, they'd be sequestered in that forest indefinitely. Or forced to backtrack around to the east and waste another day. Plus, that was grassland, with precious little cover from the hunter and its raptors, or anything else that cared to track them down with the intent to kill them.

Deep in the trees, she chose a spot up a shallow rise leading to the cliff, within a thicket of dead bushes and small trees that provided good vantage of the goings-on in the clearing, around both the obelisks, and the quarry. If they were seen, the closely grown trees would hinder an attack, and to appease Boone, they had chosen an escape route up the cliff. Or, they could take a swifter route north around the bottom of the cliff, but that would put them in view of the tent town. She liked neither, but there was definitely no going south.

Of course, the barn lay not far to the northeast. She still wanted to know what was going on in there.

The four of them hunkered down and watched as a line of workers filed into the clearing and took up their tasks. Clementine counted ten guards stationed around the edges of the clearing, each patrolling a section of the perimeter, pacing back and forth thirty or so steps in each direction. Their appearance was similar to that of the Egyptian Eminent in dress, though they were less impressive in size. Their headdresses more closely resembled that of the conjuror. Their staffs were adorned with large hooks, much like shepherds' crooks. She was sure they were actually blades, and if an unlucky fellow found himself wrapped about the neck with one, well …

Jack leaned closer to Boone and whispered, "You said those are obelisks?"

Boone nodded. "If this Egyptian *El Vaquero* character chooses to mimic Egyptian culture, the obelisk is one of the most symbolic monuments he could build."

"Miss Clem. Here come the Bone Crunchers." Hank dipped his head at the clearing.

"Did I miss something? What's a 'Bone Crunchers'?" Boone asked the same question Clementine had been thinking while he scanned the clearing below them.

"White grizzly. Jack Rabbit calls 'em 'Bone Crunchers.' "

"Since they crunch bones all the time," Jack explained.

"Guess that fits," Boone said. "I don't see … Oh, I see. Shit. Five?"

"Six. Busy little fuckers. Not so little I guess." Jack growled at them.

If there were white grizzlies sniffing around—or Bone Crunchers—then they might have a problem staying hidden thanks to the wind that seemed to keep shifting direction. Clementine couldn't tell for sure if they were upwind of the beasts or not. She reached for her pack.

"Clementine, what are you doing?" Boone peered into her bag along with her.

"I've got an extract in here that will mask our smell." She had concocted it in anticipation of situations precisely like the one they currently faced.

"Good idea, it looks like those Bone Crunchers are starting to sniff around." Boone followed one with his finger as it began nosing around the north side of the clearing near the perimeter.

Clementine pulled two small bottles and a rag from her pack. She shook a few drops from each bottle onto the rag and rubbed the rag on each of them. "That should do it."

"Look." Boone directed her attention to the cliff wall behind the clearing. "I bet those square things are pedestals for those."

Clementine nodded, staring down at the workers, masons, and she didn't know what else, that were crawling over the side of the cliff like ants, defying gravity. They looked four-legged rather than two. They scampered up and around, some carried short metal rods and others had

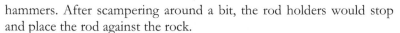

hammers. After scampering around a bit, the rod holders would stop and place the rod against the rock.

"Chisels," Boone said softly.

He was right. The hammer carriers bashed their hammers against the chisels. *Clang!* Four teams worked that way, scurrying around on the rock face, setting the chisels and clanging away.

"They're cutting the obelisks from the hillside." Clementine maneuvered to a position beside Boone better suited to watching them work. "I wonder how they plan on moving them into position."

"Those are good-size obelisks. And that's granite, I think. What could possibly lift them onto the foundations?" Boone asked.

Jack grinned at Hank. "We could."

"Easy," Hank added, making a circus strongman muscle with his arm.

Other masons worked alone in a separate area cutting smaller, rectangular blocks, while laborers carried them to the foundations for the stone layers.

"Miss Clem, look." Hank pointed toward the barn.

She saw a tall figure striding toward the clearing. For a moment she thought it might be the Egyptian, about the same height, muscular, black skin; but as the stranger approached, it became obvious this was something different.

"Looks like he's floating on somethin'." Jack leaned toward Boone. "He ain't floating, is he?"

"It's *Mekal Spaen*," Clementine answered for him. She didn't like the little devils, but they were nothing more than nuisances. Then again, the distraction they caused might be enough to turn a fight.

"Same thing at the conjuror's shack. Pets?" Boone wondered.

"Maybe they're good at tracking," she said. "Like bloodhounds. Or maybe just for distraction. Who knows." Clementine didn't concern herself with them. She was more interested in what must be the overseer of the work crew.

"Devil kitties," Hank growled. "Foul-tempered little cusses."

"*Mekal Spaen*," Boone repeated.

They swarmed the newcomer's feet, indeed lending the illusion that he was floating on a pool of black liquid. As they came closer, they began to spread out in front of him as if looking for something.

"Is he controlling them?" Boone asked.

"Undoubtedly." Clementine watched intently, trying to …

The skin at the base of her neck prickled.

She looked over her shoulder.

Nothing was there.

She turned forward, but sensed something up the slope behind her. It niggled at her, distracting her from the commotion below in the clearing. Each time she turned to find it, she saw nothing. If someone or something was there, it was well practiced at concealing itself.

"If that ain't some kinda costume on that fella." Jack whistled softly.

"That yella and blue skirt would look right fine on you, Jack Rabbit." Hank chuckled.

"You can be my dance partner, you big strappin' man." Jack puckered his lips and sent a kiss in Hank's direction.

"Shirt looks kinda like your bone breastplate, Hank." Boone tapped Hank's chest. "I can see his face. He's wearing a mask? He looks like a big cat."

"I can't tell." Clementine shuffled sideways and concentrated more of her attention on the hillside behind them. Something was definitely up there. She could hear it breathing. She rested her palms on the handles of her twin blades, glancing back at the clearing below and then Hank and Jack.

"What's this one called, Jack Rabbit?"

"Hmm. Carryin' a staff, like almost everybody else in Slagton, with a cockeyed hammer on the end. Got some kinda short whip in the other." Jack tapped his lips with his finger. "Looks like a boss man."

"Looks like a cat head on a man. Tall, pointy ears. Maybe a mask, maybe not." Hank helped with the description. "Not a boss man though. That's Mr. Egyptian, ain't it?"

"And a cat-o'-nine-tails," Clementine added before turning her focus back on the hillside behind them. "Probably to incentivize the workers."

"Foreman, then. Oh, how about cantankerous cat?" Jack said, snickering. "He wants to be a cat, maybe we should call him Mr. Buttons."

Clementine risked another glance down at the clearing. The foreman stopped between the foundations for the obelisks and looked up and down each, then uttered a string of deep, thunderous grunts and barks that sounded nothing like any language she'd ever heard. The workers redoubled their efforts, their frenzied pace giving the clearing the

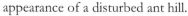

appearance of a disturbed ant hill.

"Definitely some kind of foreman," Boone concluded.

Hank elbowed Jack. "That put the fear in 'em."

"Shh." Clementine searched the hillside behind them again, noticing a blur of movement ten yards up the hill. One sniff at the air confirmed her suspicion. "*Dritt,*" she whispered, then in a commanding but not too loud voice, she added, "Come out, Prudence."

* * *

"What? Prudence?" Rabbit wasn't sure he heard Clementine right. "She's here?"

His heart fluttered and his palms sweat, even though his gloves were doing a poor job of keeping his fingers warm.

Prudence was just about the only person he'd ever met that could make him uneasy and excited at the same time. She was mysterious and deadly and amazing, all at once. Boone had made it known it was his opinion she was plain mean and deadly, certainly not one to fool with.

"Prudence," Clementine said in a loud whisper. "Stop slinking about like a rodent in the trash."

It was Rabbit's experience that Clementine didn't waste niceties on Prudence.

The rogue Slayer must have been close, because within a couple breaths Prudence's knife was at his neck.

His heart thumped like a steam engine piston, but he'd been on the tender side of weapons before. "You might try sayin' 'Hello' instead of pokin' a man with a pig sticker. You'd make more friends that way."

Boone and Hank readied to lunge at Prudence, but had wits enough to check their aggression, undoubtedly knowing full well advancing on her might provoke her to action.

"Perhaps I've made an error in judgment by allowing your companions to live," she told Clementine.

"Oh, stop it, Prudence. If you wanted them dea—" Clementine raised her hand for silence.

A glance below found the foreman looking in their direction. He fixed his gaze but for only a moment, then continued his survey of the area.

They all relaxed, including Prudence. She sheathed her stiletto and stepped away from Rabbit, scowling as she looked over each of the men. The contempt on her face was unmistakable, and intensified when Rabbit winked at her.

In her boots, canvas pants, and buttoned-up wool cape, she could easily be mistaken for a man. Even more so since she had a hat jammed down over her hair. But there was something elegant in her moves, like a high-class saloon girl, only hidden under several layers of clothes. Rabbit smirked. A deadly dancer.

She let her glare rest on Clementine. "I see my work is made more tedious and annoying now that you have arrived with your pathetic collection of wastrels."

Boone put his hand on his chest. "Boys, I think I stand insulted."

Rabbit snorted. "That's fine. Happens sooner or later, everywhere I go."

"I ain't ever been in 'Sulted.' West of here, is it?" Hank kept his expression blank.

Rabbit stifled a snigger and nodded his approval at Hank.

"This isn't the time, Prudence." A small crack in Clementine's voice told Rabbit she was holding onto a laugh as well.

Prudence huffed. "Fine." She turned her attention to the clearing.

"Too many for you." Clementine seemed to be reading Prudence's intentions.

"Perhaps. But here there are two."

Clementine paused, then answered, "No."

Prudence approached Clementine and took cover behind a leafless bush. "Why do you always contradict me?"

"It is my intention to reach that." She pointed at the barn.

"Incorrect. Once again your intentions are misguided. I wouldn't be surprised if you practiced ignorance and the art of remaining woefully inadequate to the task. My fleeting hope imagined you, in the most generous sense, capable of gleaning the smallest fragment of experience from your escapades with your pets." Prudence shook her head and looked skyward. "By now, chance alone should have afforded you a modicum of knowledge and wisdom. You are, however, adept at one singular thing."

"What's that, Prudence?" Clementine seemed unaffected by Prudence's diatribe.

"You are supremely accomplished at deflecting opportunities to better yourself."

Clementine smirked. "Do you know how you are supremely accomplished, Prudence?"

"I am accomplished in many things."

"You are proficient, in the extreme, at talking a person into a stupor from boredom."

"Clever. Meanwhile, a *portail* sits not a stone's throw away, in need of cleansing. Yet here we are, discussing your ineptitude."

Clementine shrugged. "You're doing all the talking."

Rabbit put his hand to his mouth to stifle another snigger. Boone didn't stifle his so well.

"What is it that makes you think that is a gateway?" Clementine didn't take her eyes from the clearing where the foreman was moving from one group of workers to the next.

"What else could it possibly be?"

Clementine had already mentioned her suspicion that it was the gate. What game was she playing with Prudence? Rabbit wondered.

A distant *snap* brought his attention to the clearing. A man—at least it looked to be a man—lay on the ground, covering his face with his forearms. The foreman raised the cat-o'-nine-tails high and whipped it at him. Snap! The man howled and began crawling until he was far enough away to rise to his feet. He lifted the stone he had been carrying and waddled quickly toward the pedestals, cowering away from the foreman. The foreman squawked and pointed his staff at the worker but appeared to be speaking to everyone else. He swung the staff in an arc and then planted it on the ground with a hard *crack!* The workers quickened their pace.

What an asshole. Rabbit felt a fire light in his belly. "Can't abide pickin' on the little guy."

"It's not so bad, though," Boone said. "We don't like *any* of these guys."

Well, Boone wasn't wrong about that.

"Do not move," Prudence said quietly, frowning up at the sky. "The bounty hunter's eyes are upon us. If we are quiet, I do not believe they can hear us at this distance."

Clementine immediately looked up. "There. The raptors. They've been searching for us since they attacked us on the opposite side of the valley."

"Bastards," Rabbit whispered. "Sure like to bag me one of those boys. I'd build a pillow outta that sonofabitch."

"That is an—" Prudence started.

"Airy-awk-sizer," Rabbit blurted before she could finish.

Prudence raised an eyebrow at him. "Correct. Elderly man, let fly your arrows to pierce the hearts of those foul beasts of the sky."

Hank, Boone, and Rabbit stared at each other.

"I think she means you, grandpa." Rabbit pointed at Hank.

"Never me. I ain't elderly." Hank squinted at the sky. "Too high, anyways. Never clip 'em."

"Then let me." Prudence held out her hand.

Hank pursed his lips. "No."

Rabbit wasn't sure if Hank was upset by the disparaging comment about his age, or if he didn't want anyone else using his bow.

Prudence dismissed him with a wave of her hand. "The presence of these raptors does not surprise me." She leaned closer to Clementine. "Did the bounty hunter speak?"

"How did you know ..." Clementine paused, then continued, "Yes. He called me Slayer. His cause seems to be restitution for something called 'Malveaux.' "

Prudence nodded almost imperceptibly and watched the raptors circle their way north.

"The devastation of Malveaux," Clementine added.

Prudence spared her a look. "It is doubtful you are his prey. You simply stumbled into his path."

"You are aware of his obligations?"

Rabbit watched Clementine with a lot of respect and a little amusement. By his account, she was doing a baker's job of not clobbering Prudence, but was, rather, dressing her down.

"I have been made aware." Prudence turned her attention back to the clearing. "I will dispose of him in time."

"How do you know?" asked Rabbit.

Prudence pointed at the foreman. "He commands the workers."

The foreman stooped, examining something on the ground. He picked it up. A rock? It looked rectangular. He turned and started toward the barn, his *Mekal Spaen* swarming with him.

"We figured that already." Rabbit had lost sight of all the Bone

Crunchers. They might be surrounded by them, for all he knew. Luckily, they now had two Slayers to deal with that problem. Then again, there were plenty of others in this valley to keep even two Slayers busy.

"I understand that you prefer to loiter here with your peons rather than experience the exhilaration of battle." Prudence dipped her chin. "I cannot appreciate your sentiments, but I wish you well."

Rabbit was pretty sure she didn't wish Clementine well.

She scanned the slope behind them and then skittered back up the hill, disappearing into the undergrowth.

"Prudence," Clementine called, but there was no reply. "*Verdammt sie!*"

"We should follow her?" Hank asked.

"We should not."

From the gritty sound of Clementine's voice, Rabbit expected smoke to pour from her ears.

"Well, what the hell is the fool planning to do?" Boone asked.

"She's going to take on each and every man and creature down in that clearing." Clementine turned to Rabbit and Boone. "I want you two and Hank to work your way as far as you can up this hill, staying under cover." Scowling down at the crew working diligently throughout the clearing, she looked as if she wanted to spit. "I have a feeling it's going to get busy down there."

She looked them square in the eyes. "No matter what happens, do not go down there. Promise me."

"Where are you going?" Boone sounded either hurt or confused, Rabbit couldn't tell.

"I've got to follow that foreman."

"What? Why?"

"Because I put Horace's tablet down and that bastard just picked it up."

"Oh sheeat!" It slipped out before Rabbit could stop himself. He put his hand over his mouth. "Sorry," he said through his fingers.

"Jack!" Clementine's stern but quiet voice and hard look reminded him of the scoldings he'd received from Uncle Mort.

Where in the hell was his uncle anyway?

"I'll be back in a few minutes," Clementine said.

Boone's brow furrowed. "I don't like it. We'll go with you."

"No."

"Why?"

Her gaze narrowed. "You are still having visions, aren't you?"

"How do you know?" Boone looked away. "Maybe."

"I suspect the closer you get to that barn, the stronger the visions. Am I wrong?"

Boone hesitated. "Well …"

"Then I'll go with you," Rabbit volunteered, but he realized as soon as he'd spoken it that meant leaving Boone behind.

Clementine cocked her head slightly. "Really?"

"You're right. I'm not leaving Booney."

"Hank can stay with you two. I'll be back as soon as I can."

Hank shook his head. "No, Miss Clem. I'll not be leavin' your side."

"You'll stay here, Hank. I need to go now. I can't let that bastard get too far with that tablet." When Rabbit and the other two didn't move, she pointed toward the slope behind them. "You three get up that hill now!"

In a blink she was gone, across the hill toward the barn, using trees and brush for cover … with Hank trailing behind her.

* * *

Boone and Rabbit agreed on an upturned stump farther up the hill at the base of the cliff as their cover. They had an even better view here, being higher up the side of the valley. The entire clearing and beyond was visible. Everything around them was dead, trees and undergrowth, bordering the astrometric dial, or whatever it was. To Boone, it looked almost like everything had been killed intentionally.

Leaving Clementine and Hank to it didn't sit well with him, though, and judging from Rabbit's grumblings, he wasn't pleased about sitting this one out either. But if Clementine was right, the closer he got to the barn, the more *El Vaquero* held sway over him.

The workers were still busy below, cutting and stacking the dead trees as firewood. Boone couldn't figure out why they would bother to do that here, around the circle. There was obviously some purpose that he was unaware of.

"There she is!" Rabbit pointed at the group of laborers chopping away at the edge of the clearing closest to them.

Boone rubbed at his eyes. His vision blurred. It was starting again. Black swirly smoke solidified into the Egyptian. This time, *El Vaquero* simply stared at Boone. His mouth moved. He was speaking, but Boone heard nothing.

"Boone." Rabbit was shaking his shoulder. "You get another one?"

He nodded, the vision fading.

"Gone now?" Rabbit turned Boone's chin to take a closer look at him. "Your eyes ain't black like before. Maybe we just need to shake that bugger out every time he tries to come back."

Boone hoped so.

"I ain't gonna let him take you again, Booney. Don't worry. Look down there. This'll take your mind off that canine bastard."

Boone scanned the clearing but saw nothing more than he had before. "I don't see anything unusual down there."

Rabbit's jaw dropped. "You don't?"

"You know what I mean."

"Look along the tree line, this side of the clearing. She's got her back to that tree, hidin'."

Boone squinted, following along the clearing … there, he saw her, blade drawn. "Got her."

They watched as two of the workers near her stopped chopping to look in her direction. Those farther away continued their labor.

"She must have made a sound that only those two characters heard." Boone shifted, leaning out from the upturned stump. Should they do something? No. Clementine was right, it was best to remain hidden if possible.

The two workers Prudence had alerted moved slowly toward her position, axes raised. They couldn't possibly see her, hidden as she was. Before they probably even knew to be afraid, she had grabbed one and slid her blade up under his chin, pulling him into a fall that took him behind the tree. The other didn't have the chance to swing before her blade had pierced his brain as well. She hauled him behind the tree and then covered both bodies with snow.

The rest of the workers continued chopping and stacking wood, hewing and hefting stone, oblivious to what had just happened.

"Quick as Clementine." Rabbit whistled low. "Maybe quicker."

Boone had watched Prudence in action before, taking on foes with much sharper claws and teeth. She'd moved like the wind then, too.

"Guess they weren't *others*. Maybe *caper-sus* then." Boone didn't feel particularly bad about that. Even if they were men, they had made their choices.

Rabbit raised a brow at Boone. "She's good."

That was an understatement.

He watched as Prudence worked her way toward the cliff at the back of the clearing, using trees and boulders as cover to do her work undetected. Two more, then another, and another.

"She must be evening the odds," Boone said. "There's no way she gets very far before someone sees her." He was impressed with her quick, quiet efficiency. He couldn't help but respect her skill.

"She's like Clementine, only a little different somehow," Rabbit observed. "She's quicker, no doubt, but you watch her, you can tell she'd be in trouble if a beasty got a mitt on her, specially a big one—a bear, say. A bear could whomp her."

"Maybe. How would a bear get hold of her?" Boone knew what it was like to face a bear, but he'd not done it without his Winchester. The same fight with a blade would be a whole different matter. "If a bear got a jump on her, got her pinned, yeah, no way she's strong as a bear. Maybe a brown bear. Now take a grizzly bear."

"Well, yeah, not a grizzly. I mean, Clementine may be strong as grizzly bear, not Prudence though. She's strong more like a brown bear, or a black bear. Not a grizzly bear." Rabbit nodded. "Clementine could work her way round a grizzly and out of it. Prudence? No. Buttered and sliced into little Prudence pieces, served up to the fuzzy little bear cubs."

Boone nodded. "Now a Kodiak bear, though, that's an entirely different matter."

" 'Course it is."

A branch cracked in the tree behind them.

Twenty

*C*lementine slowed her pace, trying to keep Hank at her elbow. If they were attacked from behind, he would be vulnerable.

She growled in frustration.

"What's that, Miss Clem?" Hank puffed.

"Nothing. Try to stay with me, Hank."

She took a deep breath, but her teeth remained clenched.

Odin's spear! He was making enough noise for Fred the Mule to hear back in Horace's cave.

On top of that, the foreman had taken her tablet and hurried to the barn, arriving there before she could catch him. She might have overtaken him but for Hank, who'd insisted on coming with her no matter how many times she told him to go back to the Sidewinders.

They were nearing the tree line and would soon lose their cover, but then it would be just a few short yards to the back of the barn.

Clementine had spotted a ladder leading to the hayloft door. If Hank would stay at the edge of the trees, she could sneak to the ladder unseen. Once inside, she had no idea what to expect, and that's what worried her, especially if Hank stubbornly followed her once again.

The skin on the back of her neck prickled, her hands and fingers tingled. *Dritt.* She stopped and plucked her short swords from inside her coat. There was no need for *Ulfberht.* It was only white grizzlies. Two of them, flanking her. She'd faced enough of Jack's Bone Crunchers now to know what sensations they spurred and how they smelled—vaguely unpleasant, no doubt due to rancid meat stuck in their teeth.

She chanced a quick look over each shoulder. Hank, behind her and to the left, knew enough to stop and draw his knife. Good. The Bone Crunchers were already too close for his bow. No matter, she didn't want him in this fight.

"Hank," she whispered. "When I turn, I want you to drop to the ground on your back. If they attack you, use your knife. I'll help you as soon as I can." She moved her head enough to see him nod.

She heard them advance—or felt it. She was certain that they were coming from two directions. A two-pronged attack, a pincer.

They think they have the advantage. A slight swish to her left.

One was in the air!

Wait ... turn! Slicing uppercut.

The Bone Cruncher's head landed with a thud, its body following quickly behind.

The other howled and leapt.

She estimated its trajectory ended right on top of Hank. *No!*

But she was wrong.

He rolled and stuck his knife straight above him, eyes closed. She would have laughed if there hadn't been sharp teeth and claws involved.

She lurched forward and to the side, focusing her momentum into her blades. A strong, hacking chop followed quickly with the other, both sinking through the neck of the beast as its feet hit the ground. She forced her blades in opposite directions, each slicing through half of the neck until the head fell away. Something twanged in her shoulder—her old injury flaring up again.

Hank grunted as he stood, and brushed the snow from his pants. "Ever'where, these damn Bone Crunchers." He made a face. "My mouth. Sorry, Miss Clem."

"Shh." Clementine cleaned her blades as the remains of the Bone Crunches turned to a dark syrupy liquid that sank into the snow. "We still need to be careful." She rolled her shoulder slowly, working out the kink.

"Right." Hank squeezed his lips together.

Within minutes, they were standing next to the last tree between them and the barn, only yards away from what had been her goal for the last few days.

Finally!

"Stay here, Hank. I'm going over to that group of trees to the south. I need to see what's going on around the front, then I'll be back and I'm going right up that." She pointed at the ladder to the hay loft.

"I don't think so, Miss Clem. I'm coming, at least up that ladder. I got to."

"You are not. Especially not in that red coat. Half the *caper-sus* in Slagton will see you without even trying."

"At least up that ladder, Miss Clem. I ain't talkin' back. Across the way there too, I should go."

"I'll be able to cross that clearing without being seen. You won't, and I don't know what's in those trees. If it gets bustling, I'll whistle for you."

"What kinda whistle? Like a bird? Or callin' a dog?"

"I can do a red-tailed hawk. You stay here."

Tears formed and threatened to roll down his cheeks. "I thought I was …" but he didn't finish his thought. "If you think it's best, Miss Clem. I'll cover you with my bow, far as I can. Lessen you think that ain't needed neither. But I ain't lettin' you go in that barn alone." He looked anywhere except at her.

If she kicked a puppy on the cold, dirty streets of Deadwood, Clementine wouldn't feel worse than she did right then. She almost changed her mind. Almost.

After a deep breath, she continued on with her plan. "Good. I like the thought of you with your bow, watching my back."

He nodded once and unslung his bow from his shoulder, but he still didn't look at her.

She didn't like leaving it this way with Hank, but it was either have him wait in the relative safety of the tree line or possibly lose him in a battle he was not equipped to fight. She wouldn't risk the latter.

She moved in stealth with ease, feeling both liberated and heartbroken, across the clearing and into the stand of trees to the south, to a concealed spot with a good view of the doors at the front of the barn.

She was able to keep her eye on Hank until the last few yards. He had been peeking around his tree, his attention on her, until she lost sight of him. If he'd experienced the same sort of tension as she had after he was out of her sight, then she understood his trepidation at letting her break away, even if for a few minutes.

There was more activity around the open front doors of the barn than she had hoped for. It was not unlike a well-patronized saloon in Deadwood, its visitors coming and going, some in groups and some alone. The sounds, though, were wholly different. Growls and howls and groans, while faint at this distance, emanated from the barn. If she were honest, it was a little nerve-racking. Darkness within the doors prevented her from seeing an appreciable distance into the building.

Worse yet, there was no sign of the foreman or her tablet.

Dammit! She could either count the tablet as gone or enter the building and take her chances. She might be able to isolate and incapacitate the foreman, and then retrieve her tablet. She'd also be able to get a good look at what exactly was going on in there.

So, there it was. Her plan remained intact, and simple. Get into the barn. And somehow convince Hank to wait for her in the trees. She'd tie him if needed.

A quick skitter across the clearing and she was back to where she'd left Hank. But he was nowhere to be seen!

Verdammt! Had a Bone Cruncher sniffed him out?

Wait! He was probably on the other side of his tree, hiding.

She forced her heart down out of her throat and back into her chest. She rounded the tree, but Hank was not there.

"Fuck!" she growled.

She stilled and listened, sniffing the air. There were no telltale sounds of movement in the trees around her or smells of vermin or *other* pestilence. Nothing. Not even a bird.

She looked for signs of a scuffle in the snow, breathing deep to keep panic from overwhelming her.

A lone set of tracks led toward the barn. Her eyes followed them across the treeless field and to the base of the ladder. She looked up.

There, at the top of the hay loft ladder, she watched as Hank's legs disappeared through the open loft door and into the darkness inside.

* * *

A dull thump sounded in the snow behind Boone.

He turned, drawing his scimitar.

Rabbit already had his Bowie out and ready. Boone knew Rabbit wanted to jerk his pistol, but if he did, every bad-mannered creature in the valley would be on them before they could scratch an itch.

"Fuuuuck, Booney!"

The Bone Cruncher eyed each of them and growled. Gobs of sticky saliva dripped in long strings from its gums.

"Way too familiar right here." Boone stepped slowly away from Rabbit.

"Just like when we got to Deadwood. Don't much feel like relivin' this particular part." Rabbit took a step away from Boone.

The Bone Cruncher swiveled its head back and forth, keeping its milky eyes on both of them.

"On you. I'll take his head as he goes by." Boone started raising his sword ever so slowly.

"You better, else he'll take mine."

"They can't turn in the air."

"I know. Wait for the jump." Rabbit's eyes were big, but they were focused.

Boone knew his *amigo* would be taking a chance with their plan. He couldn't miss or Rabbit was dead.

Rabbit began waving his knife at the beast, first with small movements, flashing the shiny steel at it, then bigger with elaborate arcs and stabs.

It growled again and gnashed its long, spiky teeth at him.

"Good," Boone said. "Keep doing that, it's working."

"Good for you," Rabbit shot back. "Not so good for Rabbit. It's pissing off the cocksucker."

"I got him, Rabbit. You just watch out for his sidekick. Always in twos, these fuckers."

"Ah shit. Always makin' the day better for ol' Rabbit, ain't ya? Maybe I should ride him like Hank did, break him like a pony."

The ugly beast screeched and leapt at Rabbit.

Boone crouched and pushed hard, lunging up and toward Rabbit. As he came down, he leaned forward, putting the weight of his body behind the swing. The scimitar sliced cleanly through flesh and hardly slowing as it severed the Bone Cruncher's spine.

Boone followed through, burying the blade deep in the snow. He would leave nothing to chance when it came to protecting Rabbit. He landed on his feet and watched as the headless body crashed into the ground and slid down the bank before coming to rest against a dead tree.

He looked at Rabbit. "Guess he didn't want to be broken."

Rabbit sidled over to Boone and put his arm around him. "Booney, I like you. You kill monsters good."

"I like you too, Rabbit." Boone grinned. "I kill monsters *well.*"

"Couldn't stop yourself, ya scurvy dog."

"Watch for that other one." Boone wiped his blade in the snow, but didn't re-sheath it.

"Right. Say, I wonder how Prudence is doin'."

Boone kept his attention on the surrounding trees, his imagination making an enemy of every gust of wind rattling the tree limbs or distant sound echoing up from the clearing below.

"Damn." Rabbit tapped Boone's shoulder. "Lookit. She's gonna get caught out if she don't—"

A screeching scream filled the clearing and probably the whole damned valley. It was joined by two, three, four more, all around the circle.

Boone glanced down to see Prudence standing at the bottom of the cliff, near one of the partially completed obelisks in the cliff wall. Multiple bodies lay at her feet, he couldn't tell how many. The masons scampered to and fro over the face of the cliff, either too scared to attack her or just plain confused about what was happening. Most of the woodsmen, pedestal builders, and workers that were left scattered into the woods. But not the guards. They were rushing toward Prudence, weapons drawn. A few woodsmen, axes held high, were rushing toward the Slayer, too.

Movement off to the side caught Boone's eye. Two workmen were headed up the trail toward the barn.

"Shit!" Boone knew if they got back to Slagton, the fire would really start. "Rabbit, we gotta catch those guys before th—"

Rabbit took off, bounding down the hillside, dodging trees and bushes, before Boone finished his sentence.

Boone chased after him, not quite able to keep up. He watched Rabbit unsheathed one of his throwing knives mid-stride as he broke through the trees and into the clearing. Rabbit skidded to a stop, cocked his arm, and took aim.

A guard appeared in the periphery of Boone's vision, heading straight for Rabbit at a dead run.

Rabbit had time only to look over his shoulder before the guard thrust his crook-headed spear at him, jamming it into Rabbit's back. He tumbled forward, the blow so quick and hard that he didn't have time to extend his arms and catch himself.

Boone pushed harder. He wasn't far behind, but not close enough to be of any use to his *amigo*.

Rabbit's face smashed into the ground, but he still held his knife.

"Ahhhh!" Boone screamed, trying to get the guard's attention.

But the guard ignored him.

To Boone's surprise, Rabbit flipped onto his back and extended the Bowie knife into the air, slashing frantically at his attacker.

With a flick of his staff, the guard sent Rabbit's Bowie knife flying. It landed in the snow a few feet away.

"Ahrrrg!" Boone was close now, but Rabbit would be dead in less than a moment. Should he slice or thrust? He raised the sword up over his shoulder, instinct decided for him. Pulling forward on the handle of his scimitar, he drew it down the guard's back.

In a flash the guard arced the staff up over his head and down in front of Boone's blade. The scimitar glanced away with a *clang*! The guard snapped the staff up, breaking Boone's hold on his sword before connecting with the underside of his jaw. A loud crack echoed through Boone's head.

His vision blurred, but he managed to keep standing. He scanned the ground, looking for his blade, but he couldn't see it. He had to do something. He reached for his pistol just as the guard pivoted, swinging his staff around. It caught Boone in the jaw again. *Thud.* A shock of pain filled his head. His legs went wobbly, and then he crumpled to the ground as his vision narrowed to complete darkness...

Silence.

A crow screeched overhead.

Someone grunted nearby.

Footfalls crunched in the snow to Boone's right.

Clank! Metal hit stone.

Boone opened his eyes. Still blurry. How long had he been out?

"Fuck you, goddamn back stabber!" Rabbit! He was still alive!

Boone rolled over and jumped to his feet on unstable legs. His vision was blurry around the edges, but he could see Rabbit kicking at the guard's shins and staff. He searched for his scimitar.

There! He lunged and plucked it from the snow, ending up facing the guard and Rabbit, who had drawn one of his throwing knives.

Rabbit let loose with a toss aimed straight at the guard's head. The blade sank into the guard's cheek. He slapped at his face, then roared.

A blur of black and shiny silver swept by Boone and slammed into the guard's back. He rubbed his eyes and squinted.

Prudence!

She spun her long, stiletto dagger as he'd seen Clementine do countless times, shoved it up under the guard's chin, levering it back and forth, stirring his brain inside his skull.

The guard staggered, Prudence withdrew her dagger and jumped down from his back. She wiped the blade in the snow as he collapsed.

Damn. She wasn't even breathing hard.

The guard's body began to smolder, the smoke orange and yellow.

She pointed the dagger at Rabbit. "Get up. They'll be coming for you now after that foolhardy undertaking. Has Clementine taught you nothing?" She darted south then, looking back upon reaching the tree line. "Move!"

* * *

Clementine started after Hank. If she could just get to him before…

Two Bone Crunchers rounded the corner of the barn, sniffing at the ground as they came.

She stopped and slipped behind a tree, running the fight in her head. She could manage the two beasts, but chances were good if there were any others nearby, they would be alerted to the fight. And she didn't know what was on the other side of the barn wall.

Still, if she were efficient …

Her hypothetical battle was interrupted by a group of *caper-sus* rounding the same corner of the barn. Each carried a sword and a wooden staff. Six men in total. Plus the Bone Crunchers. And if one or two of them turned out to be exceptional fighters, or if more were alerted …

No, she would need to wait until they passed.

The Bone Crunchers sniffed at the ground at the base of the ladder and then up the ladder itself. One managed to climb three rungs before falling to the ground on its side. They worked their way, back and forth, following tracks leading straight to her.

Hank's tracks.

Hel's realm!

She crept backward, deeper into the trees and brush as silently as she could, covering her tracks with the wool cuffs of her coat as she retreated. Her concoction to mask her smell should still be working, but if they could smell Hank …

Maybe she could lure them far enough away from the barn, and the *caper-sus*, and then eliminate them without alerting anyone else.

Through the trees, she glimpsed the six *caper-sus* milling around the base of the ladder, watching the Bone Crunchers follow Hank's trail to the forest.

She clenched her fists. Every moment she wasn't in pursuit of Hank was another moment he was in danger. She could attack and take her chances that no one else would join the battle, or wait until her path was clear. Her heart was pounding so hard it seemed it would crack her ribs.

There was no way Hank would last long in that barn. In all probability, he'd already been stuck with a blade or torn apart by Bone Crunchers. Or worse.

The two Bone Crunchers reached the tree she had hidden behind moments before. They sniffed round and round the tree, then stood on hind legs and raised their snouts to howl, like wolves on the hunt. They dropped to all fours again, but didn't follow her path.

The *caper-sus* trudged toward the tree line, swords up. They were close when the Bone Crunchers stood erect again, sticking their noses in the air and sniffing determinedly. Suddenly, they dropped to all fours and bolted north, toward the tent encampment, out of sight in an instant.

Clementine watched as the *caper-sus* stopped in their tracks and stared after the beasts, seemingly dumbfounded. They drew together in a tight circle, animatedly discussing something. Clementine couldn't hear more than sharp tones, though she was pretty sure she heard a "fuck" or two in the conversation.

Within a few minutes they were off, trailing the Bone Crunchers. Judging by their scowls, not a one of them seemed happy about the turn of events.

After waiting not quite long enough to make sure her path was clear but as long as her concern for Hank allowed, she sprinted to the barn and began scaling the ladder to the hay loft, skipping every other rung. At the top, she eased her head inside the loft door and paused, waiting for her eyes to adjust.

The foul smell reminded her of the stink of The Pyre on hot, sticky summer days. Barks and snarls and squeals and moans assailed her ears. There was little doubt a hellish menagerie awaited her down below.

Clementine crawled forward on the plank floor, just enough to bring her legs through the loft door and out of sight from below. She crouched there, surveying the loft before moving farther in, hoping that Hank hadn't been taken to the main floor.

The loft was two thirds the length of the barn, the opposite end being open to the floor below. Hay had been relegated to a small, loose stack in the corner to make way for mounds of antlers and piles of animal parts. Bones, rams' horns, hooves, and what looked like bloody claws that had been ripped from creatures she did not know.

What held her eye were the many stacks of animal hides, most as tall as her. It was impossible to discern how many different creatures had been slain, but there were definitely a great number of deer hides in the stacks. The hides had not been cleaned properly, and pieces of flesh still clung in many places. Blood oozed in thick rivulets down the stacks and pooled on the floor planks. Undoubtedly it was seeping through and dripping on whatever was below.

Fox hides, cleaned and dressed, hung from the walls, leaving little room to hang anything else.

"We like foxes, I see," Clementine whispered. "Now I really hate you, whoever you are."

Thump thump thump ...

She drew her swords. The sound had come from the shadows on her left. Something was with her in the loft, over near the haystack, she was sure. She held still, hunting the sound. *Thump thump*. This time she saw movement.

It's in the hay.

Hank!

If it wasn't him, she didn't have time to waste being careful now. She shot across the loft, rounded the stack of hay, and skidded to a stop.

There, doing a poor job of wiggling its way into the stack, was one of the bounty hunter's raptors. The beast reminded her of a vulture but was much bigger.

The raptor faced her and squawked, wings slowly flapping, then stretched its long neck out and snapped its six-inch-long hooked beak at her. It was much more grotesque to look at close up than it had been far away in the sky. Fleshy nodules covered its bald head. The thing's neck jiggled and flopped and sagged when it moved. A putrid odor hung in a thick cloud around it.

An arrow extended prominently from one of its eye sockets, the barbed steel tip and a short length of shaft protruding from the back of its head at the base of its skull.

Hank.

"You'd have flown away if Hank wasn't such a shot." She spoke quietly, even though the racket below was more than enough to drown out any noise she made.

On second thought, this beast wasn't much like a vulture at all, other than the wings. But even those were decidedly bigger than any Clementine had seen before, their span easily obscuring the better part of the stack of hay behind it.

She raised one of her blades. "I'll finish his job for him."

A slicing blow to the raptor's neck dropped the head into the hay. She watched for a few seconds as it decomposed into a gelatinous goo that soaked into the hay at her feet.

"Hmm. Like the Bone Crunchers." She wondered what made *others* return to the earth in their own way. Exploding or decomposing or poofing into a cloud of ash. "I hope you drip on someone's head down there."

Clementine slipped past the piles of antlers and rotting hides and body parts to the other end of the loft where a wall separated her from the open end of the barn.

She lay out flat on her stomach and peered down the ladder hole in the wall to the barn floor below before shrinking back out of sight. She'd gotten a glimpse, but she saw much. There was movement everywhere.

And noise. Shuffling, groaning, snarling, and an occasional command shouted such as "Down the hole," or "Over there," or "By the feet."

The barn floor was divided up into stalls for animals, much like a normal barn. Horses or cows or goats. But most of the stalls were crowded with *Draug* instead.

The stall right below her was full of skinned animal carcasses, big, small, and in between. The hundreds of bulging eyes staring at her stirred up an unease in her stomach. Most of the carcasses were the size of a deer, but it was difficult to tell what they actually were from a glance. Turned out the absence of skin or hide made quite a difference when it came to identifying animals.

Caper-sus had been entering the stall as she watched, grabbing carcasses, heaving them over their shoulders, and carrying them away. The larger animals were carried by two or even three men.

Other *caper-sus* were coming from the back of the barn carrying armfuls of meat and bone, dumping them into the *Draug* stalls. The "fresh meat" whipped the dead into a frenzy. The growling and moaning Clementine kept hearing was the *Draug* fighting for a morsel.

A group composed of what appeared to be mostly humans—probably *caper-sus*—was gathered by the front door, each carrying a ranged weapon. Bows or atlatls or spears, along with some she didn't recognize. The group seemed in oddly good spirits considering the setting.

She dared another peek, poking her head farther down the ladder hole to see back into the barn. The foreman from the gateway pushed his way between the stalls, through the *caper-sus* tending the *Draug*. He stopped beside one man that appeared to be commanding the others. He barked orders, but she couldn't hear them over the general level of noise in the barn. Then the foreman lifted the tablet. The other man's eyes widened, and he pointed at the front door of the barn.

But still, Clementine saw no sign of Hank.

The foreman strutted toward the front of the barn, using his size and arms to spread the *caper-sus* aside as he passed. Clementine pulled back again, for fear he might see her.

She lay on her back for a few breaths, staring at the roof, considering her dilemma. Retrieving the tablet was important, but where was Hank, damn it?

She poked her head through the ladder hole again. Over near the side of the barn a commotion had started. *Draug* in one of the stalls had managed to pack themselves tightly into the corner and were growling and snarling. They tore at something on the ground, and then at each other.

Hank! She squeezed the frame of the ladder to keep from jumping down into the grisly mess below and killing every last thing she could.

She rolled away from the hole and sat up. Her eyes darted, frantic, searching for something, anything to save her friend from that horrible fate.

If she descended that ladder, she would end up just as dead as Hank. There were too many to kill down there. She would be quickly overtaken and then …

It's not Hank.

It couldn't be. She just knew that somehow. He was too lucky to die in a horde of *Draug*.

She took a breath and calmed herself, trying to block out the cacophony down below.

Suddenly, the top of a head appeared through the ladder hole.

She swung, slightly too early.

The top half of the man's head flipped through the air and landed in the pile of antlers. The rest of his body seemed to freeze, his hands still gripping the ladder.

Oh, hell.

She cringed as the body fell away from the ladder, leaning over the hole to watch as it landed on the floor below.

Silence blanketed the barn.

Uh oh!

She hopped to her feet and dashed to the loft ladder, sparing a glance back as another head crested the loft floor.

Time to go!

She scrambled down the ladder, three rungs at a time, and dashed to the tree line. Once safely hidden in a thicket of brush, she paused to catch her breath and ready her blades to kill anything that followed her.

Twenty One

Rabbit stopped to search the trees.

He and Boone had followed Prudence into the dead forest surrounding the stone dial, barely able to keep her in sight as she darted here and there, cutting down any workers that had fled the clearing. She'd headed east, toward the barn but then arced south, using the trees to conceal her hunt.

"I think we lost her," he told Boone. She was just too fast for them to keep pace.

"At least she leaves a trail." Boone pointed his sword at a dead mason, slumped near a tree.

"Like Hansel and Gretel."

"I'd prefer the pieces of bread."

"No shit." Rabbit waited, listening and looking for any sign of Prudence or her handiwork. "She got out ahead of us pretty quick."

"Yeah. Headed toward the barn then south." Boone lifted his hat and steam rose from his head.

"You look like a pot of stew over a red coal fire." Rabbit blew at the steam.

They'd both worked up a sweat. That was dangerous in deep cold, and the Black Hills was deeper cold than any other place Rabbit had been. But he and Boone had good clothing, sheepskin and wool. The chill might be uncomfortable, but he wasn't too concerned about freezing to death. He was, however, concerned about getting stuck or gored or ripped to pieces by all the claws and teeth and sharp steel he'd come across in the last few weeks.

"She get those two characters headed for the barn?" Rabbit asked.

"I don't think so."

"She gave up on 'em then."

"It would seem so, since she's headed south." Boone had his thinking-hard look on. "She must know they'll raise a ruckus, call in the help. That means she's all in."

Rabbit figured that, too. Prudence was intent on riling up the whole valley.

Boone nodded. "Alert goes up, they chase. She heads to the woods. Spread them out in the trees. They can't attack her all at once. Smart."

"Ask me, the part where she gets a whole passel of *others* chasin' her? Not smart."

"Yeah, she went wrong there, I agree. Got your wind back?" Boone wiggled his hat back on his head. "That's cold on my noggin."

"Do we keep following her?"

Boone paused. "Suppose we should, given we're not going back to the spot where Clementine left us. It's probably crawling now."

"Right. We're good as dead, either way, so we follow Prudence. At least we can watch her put on a show before we die." Rabbit at least halfway believed it when he said it.

"Let's hope not. We gotta make good decisions."

A branch snapped somewhere ahead of them and fell to the ground. The slow flap of wings drew Rabbit's attention to the treetops above them. Large leathery wings beat slowly, carrying a goblin in the direction Prudence had disappeared.

"Goddammit, Booney! Fuckin' goblin. That means—"

"The hunter is close by."

"We better follow it. I don't like owin' my life to that hussy, but she might have a peck a trouble up ahead."

"Yep." Boone's clipped reply meant he wasn't happy about the idea.

Neither was Rabbit. His head hurt. Actually, his whole body hurt. "I'm tired of gettin' knocked around by Clementine's pals."

"We're not done yet. You watch those flying varmints. They'll steal your shit. And don't get poked by the spines." Boone took off at a fast walk in the direction of the flying goblin.

"I know, pa." Rabbit was starting to get annoyed at the little things, and Boone was full of little things right now. "Just wish I could use my guns. Whup. I mean gun, since Boss is sittin' in the snow on the hillside way over yonder." He was having a hard time getting over the idea his favorite sawed-off shotgun was rusting away this very moment.

"Probably never work right again even if I did find it. And there's my Sharps, useless as can be, in ol' Horace's cave."

"Rabbit."

"What?" Rabbit heard the grumble in his own voice.

"You're grousing."

"I know that. Can't allow a man a minute?"

Boone stopped and folded his arms. "Right now?"

"Yes … no." He tried to tamp down his frustration. It wasn't that long ago, after all, that Boone was dead. Well, sort of. "Can you believe Clementine killed you?"

Boone slowly shook his head. "Don't think I've swallowed that yet. Glad it didn't stick." He pointed in the direction of the long-gone goblin. "Shall we?"

"I'm glad it didn't stick, too. Either. All right, anyway …" Rabbit took up and matched Boone's long stride, pushing snow with each step. "We'll need to warn people, 'Don't get on her bad side. She'll kill ya.' "

Boone sniggered. "Then apologize later."

"Booney, you notice the trees?" As they walked south, the trees were becoming green again and watching for goblins was more difficult in the shadows of the dense branches.

"Yeah, I do. Maybe that stone circle kills things."

"And we were standin' right on top of it." Rabbit took stock. Everything hurt, so that meant he was livin', aside from his toes that had probably frozen off. "Just dead toes so far. You? Feelin' a little dead too?"

"Like you, just my toes."

Rabbit grinned. "I guess you should." He wondered what it felt like to die, but now wasn't the time to talk about it. "Tell me about it sometime?"

Boone glanced at him. "I'll tell you what I know. But for now, look through those trees, there." He put his arm over Rabbit's shoulder and pointed.

Rabbit followed Boone's finger. Almost obscured by the trees and undergrowth was a cabin, much like the one they'd taken shelter in the previous night. "So, there's at least four cabins, all the same."

"Yep. Got to be guard shacks, right? For the circle?" Boone turned his ear toward the shack.

"What else would they be? Anything from the south—"

"Shhh." Boone interrupted him.

They both listened for a moment, then looked at each other and nodded. Faint but numerous snorts were coming from the direction of the shack.

Rabbit shadowed Boone, scurrying from tree to tree, until they were within a few yards. He periodically checked the treetops for flying goblins. He'd already decided, this was one story that wouldn't come up in a saloon.

From the sound of it, the commotion came from the other side of the shack, out of view.

"Door's open." Rabbit's trigger finger was feeling particularly itchy, but he kept each hand loaded with a knife instead. Damn Clementine and her no-guns rule.

"Prudence already visited, you think?" Boone asked quietly.

"Hell yeah." Rabbit rubbed the back of his head where Prudence had walloped him. "We're always a step behind that firebrand."

The snorts drew closer, echoing off the side of the shack and nearby trees.

"They're coming this way!" Boone whispered. "We should head back into the trees."

Rabbit began to hear clacking, the same clacking he'd heard when the bounty hunter had attacked Clementine. "I hear the hunter, Booney. He's clackin' his fingers."

It was coming closer, as were the snorts and scuffles, but the commotion was still on the other side of the cabin. They couldn't see any of it.

"Let's get out of here, Rabbit."

Rabbit was tired of running away. He wanted this done, behind him. An impulse struck, and he bolted toward the open door.

"Rabbit! Dammit!" Boone called in a loud whisper.

But he was already through the doorway and in the shack.

He immediately checked the ceiling for any lurking horrors but saw only pole roofing. The interior was simple—table, chairs, and a fireplace, but no fire lent its heat to the room.

Rabbit had expected bodies, but there were none.

Something crashed against the wall of the shack just as Boone slipped through the doorway, closing and barring the door behind him.

He whirled on Rabbit. "You shithead. What the hell are you

thinking?"

Rabbit pointed at the wall. "Fight's right outside."

"No shit."

Rabbit could tell Boone wanted to yell, but he couldn't risk it.

"If that's Prudence," Rabbit continued, "might be she needs our help. Think of that? Look, we've been through this, Booney. Neither one of us has a mind to raise up kids with that woman, but we're on the same side. A little."

Rabbit stared at his *amigo's* face. He watched what he knew to be Boone's instincts to protect the both of them give way to seeing the job through. Uncle Mort would be proud, wherever the damned ol' codger was at the moment. Probably messing around with the horses again.

Another crash sounded against the side of the shack.

And now, footfalls were clomping across the roof, too.

"Your witty self went and got us surrounded in here," Boone whispered.

Something thudded against the door.

"Good. Straight-up fight for once." Rabbit cocked his arm and held the knife steady, ready to let loose at whatever came through the door.

Boone held his sword out in front of him. "What the hell you think we've been doing since we got to Slagton? Playing hide and seek?"

The door shook violently but the plank barring it held.

"Open the door and let's kill some goblins," Rabbit said.

"Shit, Rabbit, you don't know what the hell is out there."

"Goblins."

Something grunted on the other side of the door, followed by a gurgly screech.

"Be gone!" someone yelled. It sounded like a female.

It wasn't Clementine.

Rabbit and Boone stared at each other.

"Prudence?" Rabbit mouthed.

Boone nodded.

Rabbit whispered, "Open the door."

Boone shook his head.

Rabbit hustled over and lifted the plank from its cradle and swung the door wide, ready to stab a thing.

Prudence shot past him. "Close the door, you fool."

Rabbit slammed it shut and planked it again.

A split second later, the door shook on its hinges and the tip of a sword splintered the wood, driving deep into it, just missing Rabbit's head before being withdrawn.

"Holy shit that was close!" Rabbit turned and gawked at Prudence. She was breathing heavily but looked none the worse, excepting the spines stuck in her forearm.

"Watch the door, Booney. We gotta get those spines out."

Prudence stumbled, catching herself on the back wall of the shack.

"What's wrong?" Rabbit ran to her side and took her arm, the one without the spines, to steady her.

"The spines."

"Booney, watch the door." Rabbit guided Prudence to a chair and sat her in it, examining her arm. "Will they kill you?"

"Remove them!" Prudence shook free of Rabbit's grip and plucked at the spines but grabbed air instead.

"Like she's drunk, Booney."

Boone glanced between Rabbit and the door.

Whump! The hinges rattled, the door pushed against the plank, cracking it down the middle.

"Fuuuuck!" Boone grabbed the table and began dragging it toward the door. He grunted against the weight of it.

Rabbit turned to help but Prudence grasped the sleeve of his coat.

"Remove them!"

He kneeled and began carefully plucking spines, glancing back and forth between Boone's attempts to block the door and Prudence's arm. He desperately wanted to help his *amigo*.

Whump! The door shook, loosening it a little more on the rattly hinges. The plank was in two pieces now and bent against the force of whatever was on the other side, but it held.

Rabbit plucked as quickly as he could. There were so many, but they came loose easily.

Whump! The plank gave way, exploding into splinters as Boone shoved the heavy table against the door and put his shoulder against it. "Rabbit!"

Rabbit pulled the last of the spines from Prudence's arm and dived to Boone's side.

Whump! The force of the blow against the door jammed the table into Rabbit's shoulder. A bolt of pain streaked up his collarbone and into his neck.

Boone groaned.

"Green vial. Get me the green vial from my belt." Prudence's eyes were squeezed shut.

"Jägerin. Kommen Sie."

The voice was calm, almost soothing. A grinding scrape traveled down the door, followed by a steady, sharp tapping.

"The vial," Prudence whispered.

Scratching started on every wall of the shack. They were surrounded. A light thumping on the roof shook loose dust that fell slowly to the ground.

"Might come down the firestack," Boone said. "Go get that vial for Prudence."

Rabbit double-checked the door and the roof, then crawled to Prudence.

The tapping on the door stopped. *"Chasseresse. Un paiement est requis."*

Prudence sat, eyes closed, mumbling in French.

Rabbit didn't understand her, but remembered that she'd said the vial was in her belt. He pulled back her wool cape to expose a wide, brown leather belt with pouches along its length. A rope hung from one hip, and sheaths strapped to each leg held long, slender stilettos. With her cape closed tight, all would be hidden.

More footfalls crisscrossed the roof. *Thump! Thump! Thump!*

Rabbit began opening the pouches, looking for the green glass vial Prudence needed. Each pocket held something odd, whether it be a tuft of fur, or canvas sachet filled with a powdery substance, or a few twigs or leaves. One even held teeth, some with bloody flesh still attached. And bottle after bottle of liquid. All told, he estimated fifteen bottles of whatever the Slayer thought necessary to carry into battle. Each was neatly packed into the pouches. It all reminded Rabbit of Clementine's apothecary kit, only this was much more portable.

There it was! A green vial with a cork stopper.

He snatched it from the pouch and plucked the stopper.

Prudence reached for it and missed. He pressed it into her hand and she tipped it into her mouth.

Whump! Clang! The hinges on the door broke free from the wall. The door slammed against the table, shoving Boone halfway across the shack.

Rabbit jumped to his feet, a throwing knife in one hand, his Bowie in the other.

Boone popped to his feet but then tipped and stumbled to the wall to catch himself. The blow must have knocked him loopy.

His breath held, Rabbit waited, knives out. But nothing came through the door.

In fact, the scratching on the walls and the footfalls on the roof had stopped.

Outside, a streak of white hair and black cloak fluttered past the front door.

Then all was still, including Prudence.

* * *

Clementine watched the barn from the safety of the trees, a short distance from where she'd been before. It was a poor vantage point, but she assumed it was swarming inside since *caper-sus* were hanging out the window, some dropping to the ground below.

She'd made a mess of things, damn it. She slumped against a tree.

She chanced another peek at the barn. More and more men were congregating around the base of the ladder, wandering to and fro, tromping over her and Hank's old tracks. Nobody seemed to notice her more recent boot prints heading off to the side.

It would be impossible to retrieve Hank now.

"Or would it?" she whispered.

Most of the *caper-sus* must be in that loft or down below now. If she could make her way to the trees south of the barn, as she'd done before, maybe she could sneak in through the side window. Kill a few *Draug*, grab Hank, back out again.

Foolhardiness is not an acceptable response for one's mistakes.

Sighing, she pushed her grandfather's aphorism from her thoughts. "Afi, I wish you were here to help me. I'm not leaving Hank in there to die."

Within scant moments, she was hunkered down in the stand of trees south of the barn with a view of the side and front. The *caper-sus* in the loft and around the base of the ladder had been so distracted by two idiots who were shouting at each other while jostling for position in the loft window that they hadn't seen her cross the wide path that led to the stone circle.

The massive front barn doors were open. Chaos reigned there with *caper-sus* running behind the barn, then back to the front, or milling about, or standing around looking confused or aimless. *Draug* wandered out and away, with no apparent plan, their keepers preoccupied thanks to Clementine's unfortunate distraction.

On each side of the barn doors was a *caper-sus* symbol burnt into the wood siding. On one side, the symbol with curled horns; on the other, curved. It was still a mystery why there were two forms of the symbol, whether it was two different factions, or one of a dozen other reasons. Clementine didn't care at the moment, she just wanted to find Hank and get him out of there in one piece.

Hell. She had created bedlam.

She leaned back on her heels, studying the scene in front of the barn again. Maybe she could work this mess to her benefit. After all, with so many of the *caper-sus* that had been inside now outside, she had the perfect opportunity to sneak through that window and find Hank—*if* she could just get to the side of the barn without being seen.

She waited, watching, biding her time. But the opportunity was not presenting itself. The number of creatures surrounding the barn, and their seemingly random movements, reminded her of a stirred-up hornet's nest. From her vantage point, she saw two Bone Crunchers sniff the ground near the back of the barn and then follow along the footsteps she'd left behind while fleeing the loft.

"*Dritt,*" she whispered.

They were onto her, either thanks to her footsteps or due to her trailing odors of the loft behind her. She hoped it were the latter, because there was then a chance that it would fade with distance. If she were spotted by one of the beasts, this would be a hard fight to command. The odds weren't in her favor.

If it weren't for Hank, Clementine would turn away. If this was the skein of her life, so be it. Her afi and amma would agree, she knew. The Valkyries would lead her to the golden halls of Valhalla. Or Freya would choose her for the meadows of *Fólkvangr*. She would accept the majesty of either for her heroic death in battle and would be honored to take her place beside her mother.

Clementine slid *Ulfberht* from its sheath on her back and held it against her chest, the tip up and in front of her face.

Hail Alfathir
Hail Odin
Who dwells in Asgard
Keeper of wisdom
I seek your favor in battle
And honor—

An assembly of familiar-looking men and creatures leaving the barn caught her attention. They were walking with purpose, parting the chaos.

It was the group she'd noticed from the loft. Hunters. All with ranged weapons, apparently headed out to collect more prey to skin and feed to the *Draug* inside. But something was different. Clementine counted heads. Another had joined them. Tall, lanky, red coat.

Hank!

She dropped to her knee and watched him. Was it really him?

Yes! A sudden lightness spread through her, releasing the tension that had been weighing heavy on her shoulders.

The group stopped. Hank stutter-stepped and almost bumped the man in front of him. One of them appeared to be talking to him, but Hank stood erect and rigid as a stone, as if trying to look inconspicuous.

Clementine chuckled. He couldn't possibly do a worse job.

The hunters organized into three lines, seemingly unperturbed by the mayhem around them. Unfortunately, Hank somehow ended up dead center of the group, which meant it would be difficult for him to escape from the group.

One particularly large fellow up front with a large, furry cap shouted something Clementine couldn't understand and pointed his spear toward the eastern cliff. Immediately they struck out in a slapdash attempt at marching.

She had to get within earshot before they were out of range, but there wasn't time to run them down. Worse, there were too many *others* roaming the area for her to get close to him. Hank would somehow have to extricate himself from the group without her help.

She maneuvered to the group of pine trees and rocks closest to the front of the barn. Hank walked hunched over, watching his feet as they marched, glancing at his surroundings occasionally. Knowing Hank, he was probably doing his best to avoid eye contact and at the same time

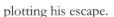

plotting his escape.

It was now, if ever. She cupped her hands to her mouth and let loose with what she thought was a good interpretation of a red-tailed hawk's screech.

Hank bolted erect. He stopped to look for the sound but in the wrong direction. It must have echoed off of a nearby building. The mangy hunter behind him shoved him, nearly knocking him off his feet.

She screeched again.

This time he turned his head to stare straight at her, or rather her location.

Dritt! He can't see you, numbskull.

She popped up and waved.

Hank's eyes went wide. In his distraction, he veered toward her and plowed into the man beside him, knocking him down.

The large leader with the spear held it up and shouted again. The group stopped and a series of grunts and growls and sounds of general displeasure welled up as they surrounded Hank and the fallen man.

Clementine lost sight of him in the cluster of bodies and weapons, especially as fists began to fly and the shouts grew louder, angrier. She took a step toward them, gripping her sword, but then she saw red-feathered arrows down low to the ground, followed by a red coat as Hank wriggled out on his hands and knees from the sea of legs surrounding him.

He crawled a little way more before jumping to his feet and fast-walking toward her, elbows swinging wide. He dove for a nearby bush barely large enough to hide behind and waited, looking at her with the widest grin she'd ever seen spread across his face.

Within a few minutes, the leader had broken up the fight. He started roughing up two of the hunters in particular, pointing the others toward the east again and sending them on without him. A short time later, the leader shoved the two hunters on their way, following on their heels.

As soon as they were out of sight, Hank peeked around the bush, then stood and started toward her. Suddenly, he turned and headed back the other way. He began zigzagging back and forth, examining the ground where the scuffle had occurred before stopping and picking up something and stuffing it inside his coat.

He headed back toward her, elbows swinging wide again. Within a few seconds, he rounded the tree and wrapped her in his arms.

"Miss Clem, I thought you was dead." He continued to hold her.

"You thought *I* was dead?" She had been worrying about him since she'd left him. Come to find out, he'd been worrying about her. She hugged him back. "We should go. It's pretty busy around here." But she was more than willing to wait the few more moments he took to release her, relieved to have him at her side once again.

They moved back away from the tree line into the thicker forest and stopped beside a giant ponderosa pine.

"What happened to you, Hank? It'd been only minutes by the time I returned, but you were gone."

"It's a tale, Miss Clem. See, I was waitin', content as a bee in the hive, well not so content bein's you left me behind." He side-eyed her and let the corners of his mouth droop.

"Okay, okay. I should have let you go with me. Keep going."

"Sittin', feelin' sorry for myself, I heard the beatin' wings of those raptors been huntin' us for two days, you remember?"

"I remember."

"Good, well I heard it, then I saw it. Fluttered on in and sat down, easy as you pleazy, right in the loft winder."

"No sign of the *other*? Or the bounty hunter? Goblins?"

"None of them fellers. Jus' the one. Anyway, there he sat, so I figur'd I could bead him with an arrow, him bein' in range and all."

"It was a good shot, right in the eye."

"You saw that, did ya?" Hank puffed his chest a little.

"I did, and I finished that bastard off for you, too."

"Well, I appreciate it. Ugly cuss." Hank wrinkled his nose.

"Then what?"

"I tried to find the bugger, but couldn't and figured he went down into the barn."

"I found him around the back of the haystack, trying to burrow in."

Hank nodded. "Course he would. Hidin' from me, I suppose. When I was lookin', couple of them *caper-sus* fellas came up the ladder. Couldn't think of nothin' else, so I dropped down and made like I was dead. They didn't believe me, course. Came over and kicked my boots to wake me up. So I woke up. Told me I was slackin' an' to git up. One of 'em put his hand out, so I put my hand out. He pulled me up, and darned if that fella didn't see the ring on my finger." He held up his hand to show her. "You remember, I put this ring on that me'n Jack Rabbit found in the cabin. The goat an' pig one. I think that mighta saved my vittles right there, cause that *caper-sus* fellow ganders at the ring and he says, 'wild swine'—or somethin' like that. Sounded like a question. I thought it might be wise to be agreeable, so I nod like a schoolboy acceptin' a juicy apple."

Clementine chuckled. "Wild pig?" The man must have been referring to the half pig/half goat emblem on the ring.

"Means wild pig? If'n you say so. So after he said that, he says," Hank used a deep, gravelly voice, " 'Get up! Get to work, slackjaw!' I ain't a slackjaw, Miss Clem."

"Of course not."

"So away I went to get to work. Down the ladder." Hank looked in her eyes. "Miss Clem, I'd be a saner man if'n I ain'ta seen that sight. They had all them *Draugies* from the street stuffed into stalls."

"I saw."

"Stuffed in like piglets. They was feedin' 'em good venison, rabbit, all manner of forest critter. Strange-lookin' fella, maybe a man, I don't know, at the back of the barn had a sort of butcher room set up. He'd hack 'em up, then capy's would throw the meat into the stalls. Work them *Draugies* up so much some of them buggers started chewing on each other." He closed his eyes and shuddered.

"I saw that too."

"That weren't the worst of it."

Clementine raised a brow. "What did I miss?"

Hank opened one eye and focused it on her. "They got a hole in the floor, big enough to stick a buffalo in. Ladder in it. They was feedin' somethin' down that hole, too."

"What's so bad about that?"

He closed his eye tight again. "I don't wanna say."

"Hank." She reached out and squeezed his arm. "Tell me."

He paused, then blurted out, " 'Nother odd-lookin' fella was choppin' up the *Draugies* and they was throwing the pieces down that hole. Real strange noises comin' from down there."

He was right, that was worse. They were feeding something? "I see. What was down there?"

"Don't know. I was carryin' deer quarters when a boss man yelled at me. Pointed at my bow. I didn't get his meanin' but he shoved me to the front of the barn, in a push and shove kinda way, into the mess of fellas you seen me with there." He pointed toward the front of the barn then wiped his nose with his sleeve. "Miss Clem, the noises and smell comin' from that hole … barn smells like death and decay, but that hole—whoof. Can't get it outta my whiffer. Oh, that foreman from the stone circle? He dropped this when he shoved me around in the barn." He pulled Horace's tablet from his coat pocket and held it out to her. "Serves him right we got it now."

"The tablet!" So that's why he went back. "Excellent!" She shook her head in disbelief, taking the tablet. "You are the luckiest son of a gun I know, Hank Varney."

"What do you figure is down that hole, Miss Clem?"

Boom … Boom Boom.

She and Hank both turned south, toward what was surely gunfire.

"I know at least one of them guns. That's Jack Rabbit's."

Clementine did, too. From the sound of it, she wasn't the only numbskull in Slagton today. But the other gun? Was it Boone's?

"That other'n was Boone's, I'd wager." Hank stood. "We gotta go. Those boys are in trouble."

Of course they were. Jack had a way of attracting it without even trying. But why were they using their guns? Had they lost their blades? Were they overrun?

Dread swept through her. "You're right, Hank, let's move."

Twenty Two

D uck!" Rabbit pushed Boone's shoulder down as they stepped outside the shack.

Boone stooped forward and flung his forearms across the top of his head as Rabbit swung his pistol around, aimed, and lit off another sizzling slug of lead. *Boom!*

His shot hit its mark, right in the goblin's muzzle, sending the spiny beast tumbling to the ground. It scampered away, howling, leaving a black trail in the snow.

Boone hadn't seen the wiry little creature that had jumped from a branch high in a nearby pine and swooped at him because the visions *El Vaquero* was forcing into his head were still fogging his mind. These visions had reached a peak back inside the shack—fleeting scenes of his friends being slaughtered, the ghostly pain of a spear slicing into his chest, and thoughts of terrible creatures and places all dominated his thoughts. He got the distinct feeling he was experiencing some of the things that had happened to *El Vaquero*.

He had wanted to run and never stop running. But for Rabbit. And Clementine and Hank.

Currently, he was winning the contest for control of his senses. *El Vaquero* was torturing him again, and he wanted to slice the bastard in half for it, but something had changed. Boone was gaining ground against his tormentor. Something was distracting Clementine's so-called Egyptian Eminent, or he was busy making someone else's ears smoke. Whatever the reason, Boone was grateful for it.

Now, however, he and Rabbit stood outside the shack, facing down a herd of goblins. Again.

Boone would have been happy to stay inside with Prudence but the commotion just outside the door and Rabbit's curiosity compelled them to venture out. Something was fighting outside, in front of the place, and Rabbit had been itching to know who. Or what.

It hadn't been much of a stretch to find out, either, since the door had been blasted from its hinges and sent across the room, and Boone along with it. They'd caught glimpses of goblins scurrying back and forth, but none had entered the cabin. Nor had there been any sign of the bounty hunter, who Boone assumed had destroyed the door in the first place.

So they'd peeked out, exchanging grins when they caught sight of Jurgen, Hildegarde's hulking German doorman, swinging his gigantic battle-axe.

Boone remembered trying to lift the wood and steel weapon once back at The Dove and immediately dropping it, almost smashing his toe. He'd thought that it surely was just for show.

Swinging that very same axe, Jurgen was keeping goblins clear of a large semicircle in front of the door, and had afforded Boone and Rabbit the opportunity to join him outside, flanking him to either side along the cabin walls.

And then Rabbit tried to take Boone's head off with a bullet—and might have if Boone hadn't ducked.

Shit! The goblins had the shack surrounded. They would have been overrun if it weren't for The Dove's gentle but deadly doorman.

"Greetings, Sidewinders!" the German had said. "Join Jurgen! We have much work." His axe swooped near Boone's ear, the whoosh of wind fraying Boone's nerves. That was close!

"Booney, you left your blade in the shack." Rabbit sheathed his Bowie and jerked his Colt. "Way it should be, anyway."

Aw, fuck. Rabbit was right. Boone pulled his pistol and lit off a round at a goblin headed for Jurgen's flank.

It wasn't long before Boone had wounded one goblin, Rabbit two. He wasn't sure how many Jurgen had slain or wounded with his large battle-axe. Ten? Goblin pieces littered the ground, and Jurgen wasn't showing any signs of slowing. He couldn't be human. It wasn't a pretty sight, creatures split in two but still writhing on the ground, intent on continuing the battle. Wiggling, shuddering parts, bodies with no heads. The sight turned Boone's stomach. But where was the bounty hunter? Had Jurgen chased it away? Had Ludek? If Jurgen was here, then Ludek must be too. At least Boone hoped so. They could use Ludek's blade.

And where were Clementine and Hank? Had they killed the foreman? Retrieved the tablet? Or were they in a hitch and needed help?

Jurgen grunted and swung his axe down on a goblin's shoulder, cleaving its body into two almost even parts. *"Týr verurteilt dich!"*

The beast fell to the ground, gushing blood and spilling sticky clumps of entrails from both halves of its body.

"Where's the bounty hunter?" Boone aimed as a goblin rolled at Jurgen from behind.

Jurgen spun, sinking the head of his battle-axe into the creature's neck before Boone could light a slug. "Ludek leads the *Kopfgeldjäger* to Clementine." He swung again, sinking his axe into the side of another goblin, crushing and severing spines and bones. *"Zur Unterwelt mit dir!"*

Boone stuck on the word *Kopfgeldjäger* for a moment but then let it pass. It seemed obvious he meant the bounty hunter.

"Fuckers keep comin'!" Rabbit reloaded three cartridges before he had to slap the cylinder closed and line up his next shot.

"Keep going. It's our job to keep Jurgen's flank clear!" Boone tried to count the ugly goblins, but it was useless as one after another rushed from the forest, creating a seemingly endless string of the buggers.

But Jurgen continued to slow their attack. Growls and whimpers and gurgled barks emanated from the piles of bodies and parts layered around the big German. They held their distance now, circling, watching, chirping and snorting to each other.

"They're planning something, Rabbit." Boone pointed at one that was particularly talkative. "Look at that one. I think he's the leader."

"Ha." Rabbit aimed his pistol at the goblin Boone meant. "A bossy little beastie."

Boom!

The bullet smashed its nose, sending the goblin into a rage. It twisted and lurched and threw itself at Jurgen.

"Jurgen! Move!" Boone called.

But Jurgen's back was to the goblin. He turned and raised his axe, readying it to swing. But the goblin slammed into his legs as the axe swooped down. The maniacal creature fell onto its back.

"Kleiner Teufel!" Jurgen stepped on the goblin's throat, pressing it into the snow, and swung his axe down on its head, shattering its skull. Its eyes exploded, blood and brains splattered up and down Jurgen's legs. *"Scheisse!"* He wiped the gore from his wool pants, but suddenly froze, lifting his hand to stare at it. He plucked a lone spine from his palm and tossed it aside.

"Goddammit." Boone flicked the cylinder of his pistol and began reloading, watching Jurgen stare at his hand, mesmerized.

The rest of the goblins surrounding them began closing in.

"Elende!" Jurgen swung his axe round and round, lunging at the goblins, forcing them back. He glanced at Boone, his face a mix of pain and worry. "You must flee. I fear I do not have much time." He stumbled in the snow but quickly regained his balance and flung the axe to his other hand.

It was torment watching the German swing and stumble, swing again only to fall to his knees, holding the poisoned hand close to his chest.

"He's going down, Rabbit." Boone's chest ached. He didn't know what he could do for the good-natured German who'd offered a smile and kindness every time they'd met.

Boone aimed his pistol at a goblin slinking in behind Jurgen. The German was losing ground, stopping and hunching forward, sucking in as much air as he could before swinging his axe again.

"You shoot," Rabbit said. "I'll get him in the shack. Maybe Prudence can help." Rabbit had reloaded and was at Jurgen's side, helping him stay on his feet.

The goblins chattered and grunted to each other. Boone guessed they were excited at the sudden turn in the battle, probably sensing Jurgen's growing incapacity.

The goblin in Boone's sights was now closing in on Rabbit as he struggled under Jurgen's weight. "Sorry, Clementine, sometimes nothing beats lead."

Boom!

The bullet splatted into the goblin's neck. It went berserk, running straight at the cabin and bouncing off the log siding. The creature growled and hissed and swatted at the air with its skinny arms, puffing up to extend its spines. Boone fired again, aiming at an eye but missing slightly center, and the goblin bolted for the forest.

"Come on, you big German. Help a little. You must be from that tribe of German mountain giants I've heard about." Rabbit grunted and tugged on Jurgen's coat, heading for the door.

The remaining goblins slinked closer, still chattering and grunting.

A screech pierced the air.

Boone looked up and then around at the trees. He wasn't sure if it was a Bone Cruncher or some other nasty beast intent on ripping him and his *compadres* apart since every damn thing here seemed to screech. He did know, though, from the loudness, it was close. Really close.

He pointed his gun in as many different directions as he could all at once.

Jurgen fell against the cabin, too weak to stand, pinning one of Rabbit's arms behind him.

"Back off, you fuckers!" Rabbit waved his pistol in the air.

The big German slumped against him.

* * *

Clementine weaved through the trees toward the gunshots they'd heard earlier, slowing occasionally to wait for Hank, who was puffing along behind her like a cow delivering a calf. She pushed away the notion to leave him behind, fearing he'd be killed in this forest because of her impatience. Thankfully, the cracks of gunfire echoing through the trees hastened Hank's pace, and she knew if the Sidewinders were shooting, they were still alive.

Movement to the left through the trees stopped her so quickly that Hank barreled into her back, knocking her forward.

"Miss Clem—"

She held up her hand to silence him. "Something is coming," she whispered. "From there. Get behind that tree."

They watched, hidden, as a figure clad in a dark cloak darted from tree to tree, doubled back, then raced forward. The figure moved as swiftly as a deer and was so well camouflaged that Clementine strained to follow its movements. The creature chasing it was bigger, heavier judging by the footfalls, and slower. It was almost as if the first was leading the second, coaxing it to the chase.

A goblin swooped into the upper branches of a nearby tree.

She instantly knew who was giving chase. But who was the hunter chasing?

She whistled softly at Hank, who was engrossed with the goblin to the point of distraction.

The cloaked figure cut a sidelong path directly toward her, from tree to bush to rock, avoiding the pursuer.

Ludek.

"Ludek!" Hank called a moment later.

"Hush!" Clementine whispered. "He's bringing the bounty hunter to us."

She stood and pressed against the tree, craning her neck to watch them approach. Her senses sparked, blood burned in her veins. This was a dangerous enemy. The previous meeting had gone sour and this one might, too. It niggled at her. She raised *Ulfberht* as the dark-cloaked Ludek flashed by.

"Now!" he yelled and disappeared into the thicket of bushes behind her.

She twisted her upper body and brought *Ulfberht* around in a long, sweeping upward arc. She put her weight into the momentum of the sword, hoping the angle would slide the blade up the hunter's chest and catch on the underside of its chin, removing its face. If she missed, she would lose her balance and tumble forward into the snow.

Clang!

Her sword ricocheted away from the hunter's bone-armored chest and up over its head. *Odin's beard!* She knew, even as she stumbled into her swing, that she should have stuck to a power stroke, straight at its chest. Stopping her fall now meant lurching out in front of it, and setting herself up for its counterstrike.

Collapse forward, roll out, quick sword to protect my spine.

Her plan worked perfectly. The bounty hunter's steel glanced away from her sword just as she swung it over her head and down along her spine.

But now she was out of position.

The hunter was going to get one more swing before she was ready to parry.

A black blur streaked between them and a flash of silver collided with the grayish bone lining the hunter's midsection.

Ludek!

The hunter struck out, knocking the sword from Ludek's hand. It followed with an open-palm jab at Ludek's chest, striking hard enough to send him stumbling backward into a thicket of sapling pines where he slumped, chin resting on his chest.

Ludek was out of the fight, and he'd be lucky if he didn't have any broken ribs from that blow.

Clementine leapt at the tree to her right—the same tree that had kept Hank unseen—and caught the lowest branch with the fingertips of one hand, still holding her sword in the other. Her arm and shoulder muscles shook from the strain of her weight as she pulled herself up and threw a leg over the thick branch. Hank watched her from below, his bow in one hand, an arrow in another.

"Watch for goblins!" she called down.

He immediately began scanning the trees around them.

"Hank, run!" she shouted as the hunter tromped toward her.

Hank took off, beelining to Ludek.

"Jägerin!" The bounty hunter growled from where Hank had stood seconds ago. *"Kommen Sie."*

It clacked its teeth together, then rose to full height and reached for Clementine's dangling boot. She quickly drew her foot up as it extended the blade strapped to its forearm and jumped, slicing at her, the tips of the blade scraping across the sole of her hard leather boot.

Below, still watching her, the hunter pulled a short length of supple rope with a small metal ball at each end from its belt and began whirling it in the air.

It had a bola! *Jævel.*

"*Jägerin. Herkommen.*" The hunter was taunting her.

"You have the wrong Slayer, you no-good, infernal clack-box!" she yelled down at it.

The bola was meant to be thrown. The weights at the ends would wrap the rope tightly around the legs of his prey, ending the pursuit and leaving it prone to the hunter's knife.

Clementine wasn't running, but the bola would incapacitate her all the same.

A goblin rushed toward her, spreading its wings and taking to the air. *Thwap!*

An arrow sank into its chest. Its wings collapsed as it plunged to the ground.

The creature sprang up and pulled at the arrow, grunting as it snapped the shaft. It lurched to its feet, screeching, hopping frantically, zigzagging, bouncing off trees until it finally disappeared into the distance. Its screeches faded into the forest.

Clementine turned her attention back to the hunter. It was about to throw the bola. If she could dodge the rope, get the thing wrapped around the limb …

An arrow thunked against the side of the hunter's head and fell away.

It spun to face Hank, who had stepped back behind a tree.

The hunter cocked its head and looked up at Clementine, its deep-set eyes black with shadow. "*Sie haben einen Freund.*"

Hank stepped out, an arrow racked and ready to fly. "You'll be leavin' Miss Clem alone now."

"Hank, no!" Clementine knew he was no match for the hunter, and she couldn't reach him in time if the hunter turned on him.

Thwap … Thunk!

The bounty hunter's armor was too thick. Even *Ulfberht* had been turned away. If she were to kill this hunter, a death blow would need to be perfectly placed.

The hunter dropped onto all fours and scampered toward Hank, moving awkwardly but quickly.

Oh no! Clementine swung her feet up, pressed them against the trunk of the tree and pushed off, sword first, aiming at the patch of ground directly in front of Hank, knowing she might be too late.

Land, roll, full backswing arc with Ulfberht, no time to stand. A solid show will cut through the legs.

As she dove through the air, she knew it wouldn't work. The hunter was already beneath her. She would land on its back.

An arrow thunked against the hunter's armor and ricocheted into the trees.

She lifted *Ulfberht*, tip down, intending to spear the bastard in the back as she crashed into it. But it stopped and rose up, its forearm blades extended into her path.

She'd be cut to pieces!

Suddenly, Ludek appeared at the hunter's side. Using both hands, he swung his sword at the upturned blades of the hunter, knocking them away an instant before Clementine crashed into its upturned forearms.

She tucked as she hit the ground and rolled to her feet, sword raised toward her foe.

Ludek dropped to his knees, bent over, holding his midsection.

Thunk! An arrow stuck loosely in the hunter's neck before being flicked away. It snarled. Turning on Hank again, the hunter shoved him to the ground, teeth clacking, and raised a bladed forearm above Hank's head.

If she didn't act quickly, Hank was dead. She flew in front of the hunter, blocking Hank, in a heartbeat. She swirled *Ulfberht* above her head and aimed at his neck, but there was steel in her path.

The metal met metal and the bell-like ring echoed through the forest.

If Clementine had any expectation of gaining the upper hand before, she didn't now.

Ulfberht would need grinding and buffing—provided she lived through this day—but the blade held. The hunter's fared not so well as hers. One had cracked and folded midpoint up the blade, the other had cracked from the cross guard to the tip. Still they held against *Ulfberht*.

Her afi had taught her well, though. How to turn the flat of a sword against a keen steel edge.

She grunted as they pushed against one another, swords locked, clanging and grinding as they wrestled for control. The hunter had a distinct height advantage and the closer its blade came, the more height would matter. Pushing it back took focus and most of her strength.

Clementine growled. "It won't be you who kills me!" She shoved with all her strength and swept her leg around into a powerful side-kick to its knee, knocking it off balance. If she could just get the tip of her blade between them …

It took two backward steps, but then regained control and its blade was once again locked with hers.

"Zahlung ist fällig," he snarled.

"Again with the *Zahlung ist fällig,*" she grunted. "Payment is due for what?"

It breathed down at her, clacking its teeth in her face. She winced at the stench coming from its mouth, reminding her of seaweed rotting on the beach.

"You've got the … UGH … wrong Slayer, *Arschloch!*" she yelled.

It pushed hard, almost toppling her over backward.

Movement behind the hunter caught her attention.

It was Hank!

Thor's hammer! Sometimes he showed no possession of sense at all. She'd kill him if the hunter didn't.

Hank sidled up behind the hunter until he was completely hidden.

What was he doing?!!

The hunter's sword arm slackened. Then its entire body went limp, swaying on weak legs. Acting on instinct, she pushed it away, not remembering that Hank was behind it. The hunter's sword dropped to the ground as it flailed and fell backward. Another step and its feet caught on Hank, who had crouched behind the hunter, sending it crashing to the ground.

Hank popped up and backed away, searching the treetops. "Don't want them buggers droppin' on my noggin' or stickin' me like a piglet with them spines."

"What did you do?" Clementine asked in between panting breaths.

Hank took one more look for tree-bound goblins and then huffed, wiping his brow with his sleeve. "Well, when I was shootin' my bolts at him, I was testin' his bony hide."

She raised one corner of her mouth. Of course he was.

"Almost got one to stick between the ribs around there on his back. There's a pucker in his husk right about here." He reached around and poked himself in the back to indicate the place. "Gave him a good jab up in there with an arrow and wiggled it around a little, like I seen you done before with some of the *others* you sorted out. Musta tickled somethin' important, cause that's when he went all droopy."

The bounty hunter rolled onto its chest and rose up on hands and knees, grasping at the broken-off arrow in its back.

"That's good right there, Mr. Chattertooth." Clementine poked at his bone armor with the tip of *Ulfberht*. "Some of the best armor I've ever seen, natural or otherwise."

The hunter gnashed its teeth and reared up onto its knees, twisting to swipe at her. She pushed it to the ground, facedown, digging into its back with the heel of her boot. A stub of Hank's arrow shaft protruded from a fold in its skin just below the lowest rib.

"Oh, I see it. Right in there." She poked her sword in next to the broken shaft.

The air crackled, followed by an ear-piercing clap of thunder and flash of light. The bounty hunter was gone, replaced by a thick, swirling cloud of sour-smelling gray and white smoke and big flakes of ash.

Clementine coughed and covered her nose. The smoke burned her eyes and throat. Her ears rang. Great Valhalla! She hadn't expected a prick from her sword to accomplish the deed. If she had, she wouldn't have been looking for the chance to land a death blow.

"Well, I'll be. Left his belt with all his toys." Hank stuck his finger in his ear, wiggled it, coughed, and knelt beside the scraps of bounty hunter that were left after his final show.

Clementine stirred the remains. Mostly ashes, singed leather boots, and a large, leather-strapped pouch.

Hank reached for it.

"Best not to touch that until I can have a look, Hank."

He yanked his hand back as if he'd been bitten by a snapping tortoise.

Ludek joined them, one arm wrapped around his ribcage. "Well done, Mr. Varney."

"Broken?" Clementine indicated Ludek's ribs.

"No. Vexed, that I was outclassed by an individual of his caliber."

Clementine glanced at Ludek. So he was hubristic, a trait she wasn't particularly fond of, although she was tolerant of Jack's mischievousness. In any case, now was not the time to focus on one's shortcomings. She certainly had enough of her own to humble upon.

"Don't be too hard on yourself." She slid *Ulfberht* into the leather back-sheath Jack had crafted for her what seemed like so long ago. "I think this bounty hunter was of more robust blood than you realized."

"Perhaps." Ludek rubbed his side, a scowl firmly lodged. "I don't like to lose."

She scrutinized the forest around them, just as Hank had been doing since he'd pulled his hand back from the hunter's belt. She read the fear on his face. "Relax, Hank. If I'm right, the goblins scattered when the hunter was killed."

"You sure, Miss Clem? Those buggers prickle up my hackles."

"Pretty sure. I don't sense them anywhere near. Let's take a look at that pouch." She spared a look at Ludek, who seemed content to stew in the dissatisfaction of his performance for the time being.

Clementine pulled one of the twin blades from inside her coat and picked up the scorched pouch by its leather strap.

Hank stooped to get a closer look. "Ain't everthin' gets burnt up when you dispatch one of these critters? Here we got boots and a bag left over."

"Usually everything, you're right." Clementine dangled the pouch at eye level. As it twisted on the strap, an emblem came into view, stamped in the center of the pouch. She moved it closer. She knew this emblem. It was actually a crest.

"What's that carvin' on it?" Hank stuck out a finger to touch it.

Clementine gently moved it away. "I think I know what this is."

Ludek joined them. "If I'm not mistaken, that is the crest of a Slayer."

She nodded, not surprised he recognized it. His knowledge was probably only surpassed by Hildegard's. And possibly Miss Hundt's. And Masterson's, but Clementine wasn't interested in giving that duplicitous skunk credit for any wisdom or intelligence he may possess. In any case, she didn't see any harm in sharing with Hank at this particular moment.

"It is a crest. It would be my guess that the bounty hunter took it from a Slayer."

"A slayer of Slayers." Ludek breathed a little too deeply, grimaced, and held his side again.

"So, the boots too then, I 'spect. Took all that from a Slayer, you say?" Hank said.

"Yes." Clementine grabbed the pouch and pulled it open, confident now it would cause her no harm. "I can't imagine letting a bounty hunter take my belongings."

Hank shuffled closer but turned his head away and peered at the pouch side-eyed. Ludek closed in, too.

A number of half-moon shaped pieces of metal sat within, each in its own leather pouch, along with a jumble of cloth, metal, stone, and wood. She removed one of her gloves and stuck her hand in the pouch.

"Whoa there, Miss Clem."

"It's okay, Hank." She pulled one of the pieces of metal out. The cold of it chilled her fingers.

Ludek moved in closer and touched it with an ungloved hand. "What is it?"

Clementine shook her head. The surface was smooth. There was no marking to suggest its purpose.

Hank backed away a few steps. "You two. Pettin' it like it were a kitten."

She handed it to Ludek. "Have you ever seen anything like it?"

Ludek examined the entire surface. "Iron, or something like it. I don't see any markings."

"Weapon maybe? Looks like it might fit in a sling." Hank took a step closer again.

"Too light to be solid." Ludek turned it slowly in his hand.

Clementine grabbed another metal prize from the pouch and examined it.

"Some kinda fanciness for a lady's wrist?" Hank said over her shoulder.

He was right. It was a bracelet made of gold. It, too, had a Slayer's crest carved into an oval medallion at its center. A spiked club, axe, and skull were part of the design. She had a good idea what this bag represented. She dropped the bracelet into the pouch and pulled out a piece of leather attached to a small buckle. It was torn, obscuring a part of the crest worked into the leather, but there was still evidence of a skull and the handle of what must have been a weapon. There was no doubt in her mind now.

"*Mekal Spaen* roam this forest. Not too near, I think." Ludek's nose was in the air, sniffing.

"Yes, I heard them as well," Clementine said, still frowning down at the crest on the leather piece. "*Draug* are approaching, too. And Bone Crunchers." Clementine reached into the pouch and collected everything but the pieces of iron. "They are all still farther off, but we should get moving."

"Bone Crunchers?" Ludek spared her a quizzical look. "I am not acquainted with the term."

"I think most folks in Deadwood call them white grizzlies." Clementine was distracted by the articles she'd pulled from the pouch. She spread them across her hand.

"You can thank Jack Rabbit Fields for that partic'lar moniker," Hank told Ludek. "He thought it proper since them disagreeable cusses strip the flesh off'n the body and crunch on the bones."

"White grizzlies. I have heard mention of and happened upon such creatures. White fur, bearlike yet hominid. I agree with you, Mr. Varney, they are offensive. They hunt in pairs, so if you find yourself matched with one, you will soon find yourself outmatched by two."

"We met a few, over in the tents," Hank said. "They was ..."

Hank and Ludek's conversation faded away as Clementine's thoughts turned to her sisters. All of these Slayers bested by this one bounty hunter. It made her stomach flutter. Could she have beaten him without Hank and Ludek?

And the hunter had kept their crests for what? As trophies seemed most logical, but perhaps it thought that by taking the family crests, it was also taking their qualities. Or capacity.

The not too distant report of a pistol scattered thoughts of Slayers and bounty hunters from her mind. *Boone!*

"We need to go, now!" She shoved the crests back into the pouch and held it out to Hank. "Will you carry this?"

He grabbed it, and strung the leather strap over his shoulder, opposite his bow and quiver. "Let's go find us some Sidewinders."

Ludek gently replaced the piece of metal in the pouch. He rubbed his ribs, then drew his sword and took up beside her.

Clementine chastised herself for becoming distracted by the bounty hunter's pouch. If anything happened to Jack and Boone, it would be her fault.

Another shot echoed through the trees. Then another.

Twenty Three

Rabbit pushed against Jurgen's weight. The attempt seemed futile, the big German probably weighed the same as Rabbit and Boone put together. Judging by Jurgen's open eyes, he was still awake, but he might as well have been sleeping like a four-in-the-morning drunkard.

Rabbit needed to reload his pistol. Boone was busy reloading his, so they were bare-assed in the fight.

Luckily—and Rabbit didn't know why—the goblins had all frozen, then turned to the northeast. Called or distracted by something in that direction maybe, each and every one of them shot off, only to scatter suddenly, rolling and waddling, disappearing into the trees.

Rabbit let Jurgen drop slowly to the ground. "Keep loadin', Booney. If those little fuckers come back, we'll both send a line of lead at 'em." Rabbit flicked the cylinder of his pistol open.

"I think they're gone." Boone glanced at the forest before focusing back on his pistol. "Can't feel the cartridges in my fingers, so goddamned cold."

"No shit. Me too." Rabbit shook the empty casings out and began reloading.

"Rabbit. Look there." Boone had made his stand a few feet out in front of the cabin, but he began to back toward it until he was standing next to Rabbit. "Something's out there. Coming at us."

Rabbit squinted at the trees, continuing to load his pistol. He saw two distinct shapes, heading straight at the cabin. And them.

There was something behind them, too. Bigger.

A screech filled the air.

"Fuckin' crunchers!" Rabbit groaned. While he had run up against a few of the beasts and bested them, it was not without a fair amount of suffering. His head still ached from his last three battles with *other* varmints, as did his arms and legs and the parts in the middle.

"Do we barricade in the shack, or fight it out?" Boone asked.

"I didn't raise namby-pambies," a familiar voice said from behind him. "Jack! You take Boone's gun. He's got that big pig sticker and you're a better shot."

"Uncle Mort!" For once, Rabbit was actually happy to see his uncle. "Where have you been? Never mind. Boone, Uncle Mort says give me your gun."

The two figures were still coming, and so too was whatever followed behind them, but they were too far away yet to shoot at anyway, let alone identify.

"Tell Uncle Mort he can give you his gun," Boone said. "You're not getting mine."

"Uncle Mort, he won't give it."

"He can hear me, you said," Boone reminded him.

"Boone! Now!" Uncle Mort ordered, more serious than Rabbit had seen him since … well, since he died.

"He said *Now!*" Rabbit repeated.

"Fine," Boone called up into the air. "But if I get killed, it's your fault."

"*Again*, Booney. Killed again."

Uncle Mort floated up next to Rabbit, staring toward the figures in the distance. "You've got the two cooks from The Dove coming first, but they stirred the hornets' nest. There's a white bear behind them." Uncle Mort frowned at the woods. "You remember those books I made you and Boone study, the ones that had pictures of ancient Egyptians and the like?"

Rabbit nodded.

"Fellas like that are milling around that big barn up yonder, and damned if they weren't appearing out of thin air in the middle of that circle of rocks out that way, west. You two ought to stay clear of that, I think. And there are gruesome, black hairless cats all through the forest to the southwest. Feels like they're tracking you boys, same as the white bears."

The hair on Rabbit's neck bristled. He didn't like *Mekal Spaen* or Bone Crunchers, and he knew he wasn't going to like those Egyptian bastards, whatever that was about.

But he did like Hildegard's cooks. They set the best table in Deadwood, and they were always good to him and his *compadres*. In fact, he was wearing the wool coat Dmitry gave him on Christmas Eve, blood stains and all.

"Sheeat. Uncle Mort says Alexey and Dmitry are coming," he told Boone. "Says it looks like the Russians stirred a hornets' nest. Woods are crawling."

"Isn't that just jim dandy? What about Clementine and Hank?" Boone handed his pistol to Rabbit, butt first, and drew his black scimitar.

"I haven't checked up on that pair yet," Uncle Mort answered. "Came out from Deadwood with Ludek and the big German boy, but got distracted by that extraordinary circle. You know there's Egyptians popping up out of nowhere?" He pointed his pale, ghostly finger. "Right in the middle of that circle."

"You already said that, Uncle Mort. Comin' outta the trees and the like?"

"What did he say?" Boone sidled in closer, still squinting out through the trees.

"Ancient Egyptian-lookin' fellas appearin' out of nowhere and headin' toward town."

"Just wandering in?"

Uncle Mort attempted to stamp his foot but it disappeared into the ground. "No, I said *appearing*. Out of thin air."

Rabbit shrugged. "He said they're coming out of the air."

He couldn't believe his ears, but Alexey and Dmitry were close now, easily recognizable, and he could see the Bone Cruncher, too. Rabbit had no idea how the round little Russians were keeping a lead on the beast. He couldn't see anything coming farther on, but the forest was alive with sounds now, wails and screeches and howls, especially in that direction.

"I'll go check on Clementine and Hank. Don't waste bullets." Uncle Mort was gone before Rabbit could say boo.

"Go on then, damned ol' ghost." Rabbit waved him off with a pistol.

"It sounds like we have a bucketful of trouble bearing down on us, Rabbit."

"Could be, but it sounds like all the fun is back at that circle."

"Mr. Rabbit! Mr. Boone! It is trouble!" yelled Alexey.

"*Da!* Very bad!" Dmitry was right behind him.

The Russians were fifty or so yards yet from the shack, but their deep, crisp voices carried well.

"Bely deyavol!" they shouted in unison.

"Jurgen?" Dmitry called the German, who hadn't moved for a number of minutes.

The Russians sprinted toward the shack so quickly Rabbit thought he and Boone might be bowled over by the pair. How were such short, round men moving so fast?

Rabbit held up both pistols as the Russians approached. They each wore fur-lined trapper hats with the ears pinned up, wool pants, and thigh-length wool coats. Dmitry clutched foot-long daggers in each hand, while Alexey held a long, thick stick with a large metal knob on one end and metal studs ringing its girth. Rabbit had seen one in Clementine's weapons closet before, but this one was more substantial. And longer. A "cudgel," she had called it.

"You stay!" Dmitry ordered as he reached the shack, turning abruptly to Rabbit's right.

"*Da.* Do not move!" Alexey added as he raced in the other direction. They disappeared around the shack as the Bone Cruncher broke into the clearing. It paused, then snarled and sped toward Boone, who was standing the farthest away from the shack.

"Rabbit?" Boone took a step back.

"Don't move." Rabbit remained frozen, though he suspected the beast could hear his pounding heart. He pointed both pistols at the beast but didn't fire.

The twins said not to move.

Boone gaped at him, his eyes nearly popping from their sockets.

Rabbit shook his head.

The beast was almost close enough to leap now. Rabbit knew well the distance the bastard could cover in the air. He could hear its labored huffs, see the long sharp teeth, even the drool dripping from the sides of its mouth. This was a big one. Big as any he'd seen so far, and it was headed straight at his *amigo*. His fingers trembled on the triggers.

Suddenly, Alexey shot toward it from the trees. Rabbit stood, frozen, as the Russian's cudgel smashed down on the Bone Cruncher's skull. Its front legs collapsed, dropping its entire bulk into the snow, plowing a few feet before stopping. Before the beast could regain its senses, Dmitry appeared and was at its throat, slicing through fur and muscle and sinew. In less than a moment, the head rolled to the side, resting with its still-blinking eyes pointed sidelong at Rabbit and his *amigo*. It stared at them as its life faded away.

Rabbit for one was happy to watch it die.

"Mr. Rabbit! Mr. Boone! Is good seeing you here." Dmitry cleaned his blades in the snow, then stuck them in scabbards strapped to his hips. He banged Rabbit on the back, then Boone, examining each of them in turn. "You have been through much, it seems. Has Clementine given you medicine?"

Rabbit looked at Boone, then they both shook their heads.

"Ah. Is not good."

Rabbit remembered his Christmas present from Clementine. He could use that tonic about now, but he hadn't brought it for fear he would break the bottle.

"How'd you fellas know we were here?" He holstered his pistol and stuck Boone's gun down into his belt.

"Ludek led us," Dmitry said. "We clear western ridge, here and to north."

"*Da.* Clear." Alexey nodded.

"Then hear commotion. We know Ludek and Jurgen fight. We come, find you. But you should not be here. You should be south. That way." Dmitry pointed toward the lake.

An immense white-furred hulk emerged from the tree line and careened toward them, screeching. The Bone Cruncher would be on them within seconds. Both Russians were stunned, reeling back from the attack. The beast sprang into the air, over a bush and log in one leap.

Rabbit cleared both pistols by the time the brute reached Alexey, the closer of the twins. Alexey raised his cudgel, a hand at either end, leaning into it as he caught the Bone Cruncher square across its mouth, stopping the gaping maw just inches from his face.

Boone sprang forward, sword raised. "Aghhh!"

But the beast ignored him, instead focusing on the Russian who had crammed a stick in its mouth. It walloped Alexey on the shoulder, raking its claws across his chest. The Russian flew backward, landing and sliding in the snow, ending up several feet away.

Boom Boom! Rabbit let loose with both pistols aimed at the cruncher's skull.

The beast froze for a moment before shaking its head. It turned and bolted toward Rabbit, but Dmitry stepped between them, both daggers pointed at the beast. The creature launched into the air and crashed down on Dmitry, crumpling him to the ground. The Russian jabbed and stabbed at its underside with both daggers, but the damned Bone Cruncher seemed indifferent to the attack.

Boone was almost within striking distance, but his path had taken him in between Rabbit and the cruncher, so Rabbit had no shot. The pistols were useless.

The beast opened its mouth wide and snapped its jaws at Dmitry's head, coming up short only because Dmitry managed to drive one of his daggers up into the top of its mouth.

Without warning, Jurgen sprinted past Rabbit and raced into the thick of battle. The German bellowed a war cry and sank his axe into the beast's chest. A *crack* of shattering bone followed.

The cruncher screeched and writhed, falling off Dmitry. It turned toward Jurgen, giving Boone just enough time to reach the pair, draw back his sword, and plunge it to the hilt into the chest of the creature.

Jurgen collapsed as the Bone Cruncher thrashed and yowled, ripping Boone's sword from his hands.

Alexey returned, panting heavily. He dropped his cudgel on the ground so that it lay across the neck of the beast, and then stepped on it, pinning the giant head to the ground.

He glanced at Jurgen, who lay motionless where he'd collapsed. "Is not good for him, Dmitry."

"*Nyet.*" Dmitry sucked in a lungful of air and deftly removed the Bone Cruncher's head with his dagger.

Rabbit looked toward Boone. Black smoke was swirling around the clearing. He didn't know how long it had been there, wisps rippling, moving with purpose, it seemed, and it was getting thicker by the moment.

"Booney, you see that?"

Boone grunted as he attempted to pull his sword free, which was stuck into the ribs of the cruncher. "See what?" he asked, not looking up from his task.

"Black smoke churnin' around in the air."

Boone froze, then looked up abruptly. His jaw dropped open.

Rabbit gaped back at him, catching on at the same time.

"Fucking Egyptian?" Boone said incredulously.

The smoke gathered above Jurgen, then spiraled down into the German's nostrils and open mouth.

"Shit! We gotta stop it, Rabbit!"

"How?" Rabbit wanted to help Jurgen, but he had no idea what he could do.

"Sorcery!" Alexey inched closer with Dmitry by his side.

"Is witchcraft." Dmitry kept his daggers between him and Jurgen.

As the smoke seeped into Jurgen, the German's eyes opened, but they were dull, dark, unaware, entirely different than the crystal blue, twinkly eyes Rabbit was accustomed to seeing. Jurgen rose and turned his head side to side, slowly, methodically. He calmly reached for his axe and plucked it from the ribs of the dead Bone Cruncher.

Boone approached. "Jurgen?"

But Rabbit grabbed Boone and pulled him back as Jurgen raised the big axe and turned on Boone.

Jurgen grinned—not a happy grin but one seasoned with evil and foreboding. Rabbit could feel the malice emanating from him.

"Back up Booney."

Boone did.

"Jurgen! You must not yield to it!" Dmitry stood square to him, unflinching.

Alexey joined in, as solid and unmoving as his twin brother. "There is no place for you here!"

Standing together as they were, they seemed like a brick wall.

Jurgen swung at Boone, though he was too far away to land a blow. He took an awkward step forward and swung again, missing by several feet.

Rabbit's mind had a flurry of ideas, none good. "What should we do?"

"I don't know." Boone glanced at Rabbit. "I've been seeing things for a while now. I think that bastard is in my head, too."

"What? I thought Clementine got him out."

Jurgen took another lurching step toward them and swiped at Boone again.

"Why's he coming at me?"

Alexey stepped in front of Boone, blocking the next swing with his cudgel. He flipped the cudgel in a loop, knocking the axe from Jurgen's hands.

"I will kill you all." The voice came from Jurgen, but it didn't sound at all like him.

Rabbit shook his head. "This isn't happening."

"We need to kill him," Boone said, his tone matter-of-fact.

"*Nyet!* We will not." Dmitry dropped his blades and threw himself at Jurgen, his stout frame knocking the big German to the ground. Alexey joined him, grabbing and pinning Jurgen's legs.

Boone shook his sword at Rabbit's pistol. "Kill him! It worked for me!"

Both Russians turned their heads to stare at Boone as if he were possessed.

* * *

Clementine breathed deep, containing her frustration at Hank's leisurely pace. Of course he was doing the best he could, chugging along behind, but his abilities precluded haste or stamina at the level to which she was capable and accustomed. Ludek, on the other hand, kept at her side effortlessly, even with his bruised ribs.

She slowed to a walk. "I haven't heard gunfire for a few minutes." And that had her palms sweating.

Had they been killed along with Prudence? Or had Prudence ... She stopped the thought. Prudence was cold and methodical. It was plausible, if it was to her advantage, she might kill ... *STOP!*

Ludek slowed, too, to stay at her side. "It is possible the battle is done. If so, it is also conceivable the Sidewinders have prevailed."

"The battle, but not the war. The gunfire will bring everyone, and every *thing,* in the valley to this location. As you heard, the forest has come alive even more since the first shots were fired. We will soon face a battle ourselves, whether the Sidewinders prevailed or not."

Ludek nodded. "Perhaps, but there are many echoes in this valley. It will be difficult to discern direction. And we have help amongst these trees."

"I hope so, otherwise I don't hold much hope for us."

Hank jogged up alongside them, wheezing heavily. "Don't wait ... for me ... Miss Clem ..." He puffed a few times before continuing. "Sidewinders ..." He doubled over, hands on his knees. "Likely I'll fall dead on this spot."

He was right, of course. She and Ludek should hurry on. Boone and Jack were close, she could feel it.

She watched Hank from the corner of her eye. He was determined to keep up with her.

"Hank. You're right. I'll go on ahead. It shouldn't be far now. Follow my tracks. You won't be far behind." She turned to Ludek. "Will you stay with Hank?"

"Certainly. Go. My ribs could use a rest. We will be along shortly."

Leaving them alone in a forest thick with *others* wasn't a move she wanted to make, but her gut ached with the notion that she had no time to spare. She had to get to Boone. And Jack.

"I'll see you soon." She was off, exhilarated by the ability to move fast enough to actually feel wind in her face, cold though it was.

Not long after losing sight of Hank and Ludek, Morton appeared, sprinting beside her. The appearance of an apparition attempting to run but actually floating along with her would have disoriented her, but her focus was firmly on her task.

She spared him a glance. "I'm happy to see you, Morton."

"And I you, dear Amazon," he said between gasps. His words were weak between breaths from the exertion of sprinting.

She continued with her long steady strides through the snow, regulating her breaths. "Ghosts don't get tired, do they?"

"Oh, no, but I deemed the appearance of fatigue appropriate," he said, resuming his original unfettered timbre. "Boone and Jack are just ahead. They are in somewhat of a pickle. The Russian cooks will have joined them by now. Oh ..." Morton shimmered as he float-ran through a tree. "The big German boy, Yerdan, was it? He was slumped against the cabin, apparently suffering from an affliction. Or he was sleeping, though under the circumstances, I can't imagine it was the latter. A white bear chased the Russians. They didn't appear to have that particular detail accommodated." He floated sideways, watching her for a moment. "Perhaps you are capable of increasing your velocity. I fear the lads are in need of your assistance."

The mention of Jurgen in distress was enough for Clementine to quicken her pace, but the news of a Bone Cruncher chasing Dmitry and Alexey spurred her doubly so. Did they know that Bone Crunchers traveled in pairs? She had Hildegard's word that her cooks could take care of themselves, but did that include white grizzlies? She pushed harder, her muscles beginning to burn.

"That's a little better." Mort floated effortlessly alongside.

It was only minutes before she broke into the clearing and rounded the corner of a shack, swords at the ready. But she wasn't ready for the sight in front of her. She stopped abruptly, confused by what she saw.

Alexey and Dmitry were kneeling, hunched over, holding down a struggling man. Boone stood close by, watching.

"Boone!" she called and all four men turned to look.

She jogged toward them, surveying the trees around the clearing. She spared a glance at Jack, who was standing over Jurgen and the Russians. "Hello, Jack."

She nodded to the Russians. "What's going on here? Why are you holding Jurgen down?"

"Clementine, is good you are here," Alexey said. "Jurgen is taken." The concern on his face sent a ripple of unease through her.

She looked to Dmitry for an explanation.

He glanced up at her with bloodshot eyes and shook his head. "*Da*, is witchcraft we are thinking."

Jurgen lurched violently, almost freeing himself from the Russians. Rabbit dropped to his knees to help Dmitry hold the massive legs.

"That's right, boy, both legs." Morton leaned over Jack's shoulder to peer at Jurgen. "Use your weight."

"It's only been a couple of minutes." Boone frowned at her. "He caught a spine from one of the goblins and collapsed. But then we saw the black smoke go in, and he went berserk." He pointed at the cabin. "Prudence is in there. She caught a few spines, too, and she's pretty bad."

Clementine bit her lower lip, trying to wrap her mind around what Boone had told her.

"I got this leg, Dmitry, you hold that one." Jack wrapped both arms around Jurgen's leg. "This German is strong as a horse."

"That's right, use your weight on that leg." Morton floated around one side of Jurgen, then the other, no doubt believing that he was helping.

"You got him, fellas?" Boone asked. "I'll go get that vial of tonic from Prudence."

"I watched her. She downed the whole thing," Rabbit replied.

"Is cure for sorcery, Clem?" Alexey heaved up as Jurgen bucked, almost losing his grip on Jurgen's arms before slamming back down into his chest and squeezing his arms.

"No." Clementine was facing the same predicament she had with Boone, only Jurgen was much stronger.

She moved around to stand beside Alexey. Jurgen stilled and stared straight into her, baring his teeth. The blackness of his eyes chilled her.

"*Aquatil.*" He growled. "I will kill you, Slayer." The voice reverberated, the thick strange accent sounding nothing like Jurgen's.

She knew that threat wasn't coming from Jurgen, but regretted her next act just the same. "I'm sorry, Jurgen." She raised her leg and struck him on the side of his head with the heel of her boot. He immediately went limp.

"That did it, for a spell anyhow." Rabbit stood. "Sure is good to see you, Miss Clementine."

The Russians stood, too.

"Alexey, tie him with your rope." Dmitry tapped Alexey's pack.

"*Da.*" Alexey dropped the pack from his back and began rummaging through it."

"You said Prudence is in there?" she asked Boone, glaring toward the shack.

"It is good to see you, Clementine." Boone smiled. "Where's Hank?"

"Coming along behind with Ludek. A couple minutes. Prudence?"

"She showed up here, an arm full of spines. We barricaded in the shack there and Rabbit plucked them out."

"While that goddamn bounty hunter and his goblins were smashing down the door." Rabbit wiped his brow and adjusted his hat.

"The bounty hunter was here?" she asked. Ludek must have led the hunter away from the shack, leaving Jurgen behind to help the Sidewinders with the goblins. "Well, that particular hunter won't be bothering us anymore."

Clementine searched the tree line for Hank and Ludek. Where were they?

Boone nodded knowingly. "Good. He was a bastard. Prudence wasn't doing too well last we saw. Drank some kind of tonic."

Clementine wasn't particularly fond of Prudence, but she did respect the woman's preparedness. "If she had the right tonic, she'll be fine."

"There is much danger here." Alexey finished tying Jurgen's legs and watched the trees around them for a moment before starting on the big

German's arms.

Dmitry stood and moved back to give Alexey room. "My good friend, we will fix, we will fix." His head sagged as he smiled sadly at Jurgen.

Suddenly, Jurgen sat upright and snatched Alexey's stick from the ground next to him. He bashed it into Dmitry's forehead, then spun around to strike Alexey in the back of the neck. Both Russians collapsed, rag dolls in the snow.

Clementine didn't think, there wasn't time. On instinct, she slammed into Jurgen's chest, pinning his torso on the ground. "Boone, get his legs!"

Though his legs were tied, Jurgen brought them up, hard, ramming his knees into her back. The force of the blow nearly dislodged her from his stomach. Pain shot up her spine, but she steadied herself while she waited for Boone to trap his legs.

Rabbit gathered the rope to finish Alexey's job, rolling Alexey over to retrieve the tail end.

"What is all this?" a voice said from near the trees.

Clementine looked over her shoulder to see Ludek walking toward her, his jaw slack. "Jurgen? Is he ill?"

"The Egyptian Eminent. The transmogrifier." She spoke between grunts as she struggled to hold the German down.

Jurgen continued to writhe beneath her, but then he saw Ludek and fell limp, muttering something none of them could understand.

Ludek moved nearer. "What ails you?"

To Clementine, Jurgen seemed back to normal, the blackness gone from his eyes. He mumbled again, looking up at Ludek.

Ludek knelt beside him and bent close to Jurgen's ear. "What troubles you, my friend?"

Jurgen suddenly lurched, bucking Clementine off his chest, and seized the handle of Ludek's sword. He twisted and rolled, throwing Boone into the snow and knocking Rabbit backward. With a quick slice of the blade, he freed his legs of the bindings and then jumped to his feet.

"He's loose!" Morton yelled, swiping at the German's arms in an attempt to subdue him.

Ludek raised his hands, backing away slowly. "Do not let the Eminent win, my friend."

Jurgen snarled, looking frantically around at them, his eyes black as coal. "You will all die here!"

Clementine sprang to her feet and drew her twin swords.

"You must fight him, Jurgen," Ludek pleaded.

Jurgen focused on Ludek and cackled. "This one dies first!" He pointed the tip of the sword at his heart and shoved it into himself to the hilt. He stumbled and collapsed onto his knees, his head drooping forward.

"No!" Ludek rushed forward, holding him upright by the shoulders. "Jurgen!"

The German smiled weakly, his eyes unfocused but back to their normal blue. "Ludek? *Mein guter Freund. Ich sterbe als Krieger?*"

His blue eyes lost focus and he exhaled, a long, fading breath, and slumped into Ludek's arms.

"Yes, my friend," Ludek whispered. "You die a warrior." He held Jurgen's head against his chest for a moment, then gently lay the German on his side in the snow. He kneeled for a long moment, staring down at Jurgen's lifeless body.

Black smoke poured from Jurgen's nostrils and open mouth, gathered up into a swirling cloud above his body, and began to float toward the trees.

Clementine watched, speechless, gripping her swords.

"No you don't!" Morton swooped up and into the smoke, branching into white and gray tendrils that wove into the black shroud. The white and gray of Morton fused into the smoke until, finally there was nothing left but the dark plume drifting toward the tree line.

Ludek jumped to his feet and grabbed one of the twin blades from Clementine's hand. "Do something, *Scharfrichter!*"

He hacked and chopped at the trail of smoke, chasing it to the edge of the woods before he stopped and sank to his knees, holding his side. Defeated, there he stayed for some time, his back to them, his shoulders shaking.

Twenty Four

Boone's heart ached for his big German friend. He would have preferred to crawl into a warm bed and mourn. And sleep. But the cries and howls and screeches coming from all around them unnerved him to the core.

They were surrounded.

"Booney?" Rabbit stood, motionless, watching the trees where the black cloud had disappeared, his face pale.

Boone squeezed his shoulder.

Rabbit pointed toward the trees, then looked in Boone's eyes, his brow knitted and mouth ajar. "I think that thing just took Uncle Mort."

"What? What do you mean?" The black cloud was gone. And so too, apparently, was their uncle. "Are you sure?"

"Who is 'Uncle Mort'?" Alexey continued to gaze at Jurgen's body. "We must take him to Deadwood, Dmitry."

"*Da.*" Dmitry wiped at his eyes and kneeled beside his brother.

"Our uncle." Boone wasn't going to explain any farther. It didn't matter, the Russians were paying no attention to him, but instead making plans to care for their friend's body. "Rabbit, what do you mean, 'took'?"

Rabbit shook his head. "I don't know, but after that bastard killed Jurgen, Uncle Mort was gonna … I don't know, fight it or somethin'. He rushed it, fists up, but then he disappeared into it. Maybe he meant to, I don't know."

Rabbit was serious, that much Boone was sure of. He looked to Clementine for a better answer.

She nodded, frowning as well. "He's been taken. Or like Jack said, Morton meant to get caught up in the black cloud."

Ludek rose at the edge of the clearing and stormed back to

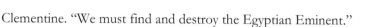

Clementine. "We must find and destroy the Egyptian Eminent."

She crossed her arms. "We are all saddened by what's happened here, but I agree with what you said before, Ludek. We must close the gate."

Ludek shook his head. "The Eminent must pay!"

"He will. But first, the gate."

"If Uncle Morton is right," Boone said, "the bastard is bringing warriors through there as we speak. This fight will quickly outgrow our abilities."

"*Da*. They come," Alexey said over his shoulder.

Ludek paced in front of her.

"Masterson was right," Clementine continued. "I hate to admit it, but this situation is beyond me already. I need your help. And Alexey's and Dmitry's." One corner of her mouth lifted as she turned to Boone and Rabbit. "And I need you two as well."

"With my life, *Oomnyashka*," Dmitry said. "And Alexey, too."

Both stood up, two soldiers at attention.

"*Da*. The Egyptian and his zealots will pay what is due." Alexey stood up straighter.

"Let's kick these fuckers right back where they came from." Rabbit wrapped an arm around Boone.

Ludek, although grimacing, nodded.

"Wait. Where's Hank?" Rabbit spun in a circle and focused on Clementine, but her gaze was transfixed on the shack.

"He was a few steps behind." Ludek closed his eyes and bowed his head. "I will fetch him."

"What are you doing here?" Clementine's voice dripped with malice.

Boone followed her glare to the door of the shack. There, Prudence stood, leaning against the doorframe, pale as a baby mouse.

Prudence sighed.

To look at her, Boone was ready to believe that the sigh was the result of exhaustion rather than her usual arrogance.

Prudence's eyes narrowed as she focused on Clementine. "Tending *your* responsibility, what else?"

No, Boone was wrong. She was her normal, caustic self.

Clementine yanked her hat off and threw it to the ground. She snorted and strode toward Prudence, steam rising from her head. Boone wouldn't be surprised if the steam was the result of her boiling blood.

He spared a glance at Rabbit, who was staring back at him, lips pressed together and one eyebrow raised.

As Clementine approached Prudence, Boone was sure he saw the Rogue shrink a little. Then she pushed away from the door and stood tall, a look of defiance spreading across her face. She didn't carry it off, though, considering the fact that Clementine stood at least a head taller and surpassed the Rogue's size by half again, mostly in muscle.

Clementine pointed at Jurgen. "This happened because of you!"

"Nonsense. The disorder here rests entirely on *your* shoulders." The color was returning to Prudence's cheeks.

The thought that he should try and calm Clementine entered Boone's mind, but he let it pass right back out. In her state, she might start swinging and he wanted no part of it. Besides, Prudence deserved a dressing down as far as he was concerned.

The Russians began moving slowly toward Boone, as did Rabbit. Ludek was suddenly standing beside him. "We must not interfere."

Rabbit held up his hands. "That thought ain't even entered my mind. She don't have a chance against Miss Clem, right Booney?"

"I doubt it, but who knows."

"Clementine, time compels us." Dmitry's deep voice was steady and sure. The man must have been through a few trials to feel that he could open his mouth at this moment.

Clementine held up one finger but didn't take her eyes off Prudence. "Why was the bounty hunter here? Because of you, right? *Ein Jägerin*. He was hunting a Slayer."

"That means nothing. Perhaps it was you he hunted. How could you possibly know he was hunting a Slayer in particular and not some other quarry?"

"He carried a pack with the crests of six other Slayers."

"Tell me, how would you know?" Prudence's eyebrows raised. "You killed him?"

Clementine pursed her lips. "Malveaux," she said simply, obviously not answering the question.

Prudence leaned against the doorframe to steady herself. "Mal …"

"I know of this Malveaux." Dmitry nodded.

"What?" Boone asked.

A horse whinnied in the distance but Boone wasn't sure where. Sounds echoed off the trees like gunshots in a canyon, but if he didn't know better …

"*Zahlung ist fällig,*" Clementine continued.

" 'Payment is due.' " Alexey translated for them.

Prudence dropped her gaze to the ground and slowly shook her head. "Sounding familiar? You led him here. This is your fault."

"How dare you accuse me of such incompetence. It is more likely you have done something to invoke a bounty hunter."

"Malveaux? I have had no business there. But you did, didn't you?" Clementine's tone practically dripped with contempt.

"I perform my duties cleanly and precisely."

"Yet an ally lies dead here, in the Black Hills, by the hand of one who spoke of a place that you most likely cleansed. My guess is, he was brought to task by either the residents of Malveaux or by the territorial Guardian. What happened, did you overstep? You certainly do that well here. Did you kill residents?" Clementine waved off her own questions. "Either way, because of your carelessness, Jurgen is dead."

"He had no business in this fight. You solicit aid from your chattel and then condemn me for their misfortunes." Prudence let her gaze drift to Jurgen's body lying lifeless on the snow. If she had any regret or guilt about the German's death, she sure didn't show it.

Boone's chest and face grew hot with anger.

"You goddamned bitch." Rabbit aimed a pistol at her. "He's dead because of you."

"Take it easy, Rabbit," Boone said quietly. The truth of it was, Boone wanted to put the Rogue down himself. She was a danger that was proving to be deadly, but this wasn't the time or the way.

A thunderous clap echoed through the trees.

"That came from the direction of the circle." Ludek scanned the treeline toward the south, his hand resting on the pommel of his sword. "Clementine is right. We must confront the threat there."

"That was a detonation." Clementine leveled her stare at Prudence. "You've done lasting damage to *et venatores,* and you're wasting my time now. You'll answer for what you've done." She turned to the men. "Let's go."

"Circle? Wait, what about Ha—" Rabbit's protest was interrupted by Hank jogging around the corner of the shack, puffing and wheezing.

Before Boone had worked past his surprise, Hank held up his hand. "Horses," he said between gasps and pointed back the way he'd come.

"What? Horses?" Boone looked at Rabbit. "Did you hear 'horses'?"

Rabbit nodded, a puzzled look on his face.

"Hank, what are you trying to say?" Clementine strode toward him.

The forest shook again with another thunderous clap, jarring snow loose from the branches.

"What makes such sounds?" Alexey held his cudgel up defensively.

"Tell us your story later, Hank. We need to get to that circle." Clementine strode off, not waiting for questions or rebukes.

Boone labored to keep pace a few feet behind her, and he wasn't alone—Rabbit and Hank rambled alongside him, puffing as much as he. Ahead, Ludek and the two Russians seemed to have no trouble staying with her.

"Saw the horses. Fred too." Hank wheezed. "That's where I was."

"No shit? All of 'em? Where?" Rabbit almost ran into a tree he was so busy gaping at Hank.

"Killin' ... *Draugies*. Put one *Draugy* down, then chase down the next. It was a sight."

Clementine stopped and faced Hank. "Really?"

"Yessum." Hank thumbed over his shoulder. "Kickin' at the abominations wanderin' abouts in the trees. Devil kitties give some trouble in packs, but they was stompin' them flat." The corners of his mouth dropped. "Ol' Fred saw me, but he followed right along after Fenrir and Nickel like I didn't mean nothin'. All stickin' together, I guess." He dropped his chin when he looked at Rabbit. "Didn't see Dime."

Rabbit's face sagged into a frown.

"I'm sure he's along with the rest." Boone tried to help, but he knew Rabbit would need to see his horse now to be comforted.

"Did someone set them free?" Clementine asked.

"Could be. Could be they got fed up waitin' fer us and skedaddled without a hand. They got the knowhow." Hank stood up straight and breathed deep.

"Ho ho! We have help from mounts." Dmitry chortled.

"*Da*, is good sign." Alexey slapped his brother's back.

Clementine took off again, leading them to the edge of the clearing near the stone circle.

Another explosion echoed around them. Boone cringed.

Clementine froze, her gaze locked on the pines to their left. "That little ..."

"What is it?" Boone asked.

"Prudence. I just saw her running through the woods over there." She turned to the rest of them. "There are *others* in these woods."

Something howled and then squealed to the south, as if to back her claim.

"Well, thanks for lettin' us know. I just thought we took a wrong turn." Rabbit shook his head.

Boone flicked his hat. Was he a dunderhead, prodding Clementine at a time like this?

"Quiet, Jack." Clementine studied the clearing. "Let's hope Horace's friends are here and not just to observe. We could use a little help considering the number of *others*."

Boone heard Clementine's voice, but her words didn't sink in. He was trying to grasp what he was seeing in front of him. For the second time in so many seconds, he watched the seemingly empty air at the center of the stone circle shimmer, darken, then discharge the figure of a man, or something probably not a man.

The figure was clad in what looked like a linen knee-length skirt, same as the one before. But this one wore an elaborate headdress in the shape of a bird of prey rather than a fierce cat. Boone watched the figure double over next to the first, grab his belly, and heave.

Boone noticed then that there were others who had apparently appeared, too. They were joining a line of thirty or more similarly attired individuals, marching shakily along a path away from the stone circle and toward the barn. Coming out of the shimmering air appeared to be physically taxing, or disorienting.

"Ain't like earlier." Hank stared at the clearing. "We stirred the pot to boilin', looks like."

Bone Crunchers stood guard at the outer perimeter of the clearing, one positioned between them and the circle.

"*Nyet*. The enemy is, how to say, fertile?" Alexey looked to Clementine for confirmation.

"Abundant," she corrected.

"Plentiful," Ludek joined in.

"Bounteous." Boone couldn't help himself.

"More critters here than in a pot of Hank's stew." Rabbit had found his tongue again.

"Or fleas on a Jack Rabbit," Hank shot back.

Boone chuckled nervously along with the rest of them, their fun tempered with the fact that they were headed into a maelstrom.

A horse roared, this time to the south.

Oh, that was Nickel, all right. Boone's gut churned.

Rabbit patted his shoulder. "If you're hearin' him, he's still kickin'."

Damned if Rabbit didn't know how to read him, but it didn't improve Boone's disposition appreciably. The fog was seeping back into his head, interfering with his thinking, as if cotton rags were soaking up his wits. And now to find out Nickel and the rest of the mounts were out there, fighting for their lives. And Hank had said Dime was missing.

"Why the hell didn't they stay in the cave?"

"They'll be okay, Booney. They're fighters. And they got Fenrir." Rabbit threw a glance at Hank, who was listening. "And Fred, too. They'll take the starch outta those bastards."

Boone knew Rabbit was worried too, so he did his best to take his *amigo's* words to heart, knowing there were no sure bets in the game they were playing.

"Waitin' on your say-so, Miss Clem." Hank patted the bow strung across his chest.

From her pack, she pulled the clay tablet Horace had given her and gave it to Ludek. "You may be able to interpret this. Horace left me the impression it has something to do with the gateway. Maybe it tells how to close it."

Ludek nodded. "I will attempt to decipher it." He looked her in the eye. "It will take some time."

"Thought it might." She turned to face the rest of the group. "We all liked Jurgen. We all want the Egyptian Eminent to pay for what he's done."

"Fuckin' blood is what we want." Rabbit spat at the ground.

"And we'll get it. But first, the gate. We've got to shut it down or we don't stand a chance. We close it, then we track down the Egyptian." Clementine squinted at the clearing. "Those are the bastard's soldiers coming through the gateway. They'll be almost impossible for you to kill. Don't get that close. Headshots will disable them or at least slow them down."

"Got it." Rabbit handed Boone the pistol he'd been holding onto for him since the shack. "You'll be needin' your pistol back." He squinted at Clementine as if to say, *We will be using guns.* At her nod, he added,

"You're six in, Booney, full load, so don't shoot yourself in the foot."

Boone's thumping heart appreciated the levity. "Don't be mad if I shoot you in the ass."

"I want all of you to stay away from that band of soldiers." Clementine pointed at the biggest grouping, her tone leaving no room for dissent.

Each of them nodded, except Rabbit. "If we can take a Bone Cruncher down, we can take these soldiers, too."

Boone heard the frustration in Rabbit's voice. He didn't like being told how to fight. Boone didn't much either, but this was Clementine's world.

"Jack, you're one of the best I've seen in a fight, and I'm damn glad you're on my side, but you've only faced one or two Bone Crunchers at a time, three at most." She pointed at the clearing. "You'll face ten soldiers, and they won't necessarily go down with one bullet like you're used to." Her stare hardened. "They will kill you if you don't listen to me. Most of them will be drawn to me. Let me handle them."

Rabbit pursed his lips and nodded.

"Good. I need you, Boone, and Hank right at the gate. They're coming through one at a time, so the three of you should be able to handle them, and anything else that wanders too close. The soldiers are not orderly yet, so I don't think we need to be worried about a coordinated front or defensive stand. They'll attack indiscriminately. Keep them on their heels. If they get organized, we're dead."

"Alexey and Dmitry, patrol the tree line to the south and east, so don't let anything surprise me. We might have 'friends' arriving from the barn."

They nodded.

"*Da.* We will not fail you. Yes, Dmitry?"

"*Mui boudyem.*"

"I'll handle everything in the middle of the clearing," Clementine said.

"What? No," Boone said it before he could stop himself. It seemed like entirely too many soldiers for her to "handle."

"You have *muy grande huevos*, Miss Clem." Rabbit's face glowed with admiration.

Boone wondered if she knew what that meant.

"I know," she replied with a wink. "Back me up if you feel the need."

Boone still wondered if she really knew what that meant.

"Ludek," she continued. "You stay here until you figure out that tablet. We'll keep them off you."

"I will." Ludek focused on the tablet, running his fingers along a line of symbols.

"I'll go in first, attract their attention, then you all follow." She drew her twin blades. "Remember, no bad decisions."

Then she was off toward the clearing, so quickly that Boone could swear she blurred a little.

Before any of them had even begun to follow, Clementine had slashed and stabbed her way to the far side of the clearing, leaving a trail of soldiers collapsing into piles of dust. Most of those still living were frozen with surprise, with only a few headed in her direction, their staffs pointed at her.

A clamor rose up as more and more soldiers realized a deadly threat was among them.

Twenty Five

A t once, Boone and the others bolted toward the clearing. The Russians veered right to engage a pair of Egyptian soldiers and a small group of roaming *Mekal Spaen* up the stone path toward the barn.

Boone watched as the soldiers that had been nearby began to close in on Clementine, surrounding her in a collapsing circle of blades, some with scimitars like his, while others held staffs fitted with straight and crescent blades.

The urge to run to her aid had him turning in her direction.

"Boonedog! This'a way. Miss Clem said!" Hank beckoned him, and Rabbit, to the middle of the circle.

He stopped, but hesitated. Clementine needed help.

A Bone Cruncher appeared out of the tree line and lurched at Hank.

Rabbit jerked his pistol and took off running, aiming at Hank's assailant.

Boom!

The beast crumpled to the ground, tumbled, and shook its head.

"You hit somethin' important, Jack Rabbit! Now git over here!" Hank had his bow out and ready to launch an arrow at the pack of soldiers surrounding Clementine.

Rabbit bolted for Hank. "Come on, Booney! Keep up! Start shootin'!"

"I'm trying, but everybody's going every which way!" Boone took up behind Rabbit and together they joined Hank.

The air shimmered and Boone felt the crackle of lightning around him.

"Look out!" Hank swung around and pointed an arrow at the dark shape appearing not ten feet away, at the center of the circle.

We're right next to the gate!

The thought unnerved Boone. "My stomach is flopping."

He wheeled around but couldn't see Clementine. He heard her grunts and curses, somewhere in the middle of the horde. He raised his pistol to fire.

I might hit her!

BOOOOM!

Another explosion rocked the clearing. A cloud of smoke and dust and pieces and chunks of what all roiled into the air near the Russians.

"Dammit to hell, who the fuck is doing that?" Rabbit shook his head. "Aim for the fuckers on the outside, Booney! Thin the herd so she don't have so many!" he hollered over the clamor.

Right. Thin the herd. Boone had the distinct feeling he'd entered this foray entirely underprepared. Hell, for everything since they'd arrived in Slagton.

Thwp! He heard the sound of an arrow flung from Hank's bow.

He spared a glance at a soldier emerging from the gate wearing a falcon mask. The soldier stumbled, clutching at the arrow protruding from both sides of his throat.

"Booney! Hank's got it covered. Light into those fuckers around Clementine!" Rabbit pointed his gun at the horde surrounding her.

They both started squeezing triggers, sending a flurry of lead at the soldiers. The bullets that hit vitals, dropped the cat– and dog– and bird mask–wearing soldiers to the ground, where they writhed and shuddered.

They both had begun to reload when Boone heard Ludek's voice. "Bone Cruncher behind!"

Boone spun around to see the immense white beast bearing down on them. He holstered his pistol and pulled his scimitar from its scabbard.

"Watch him, Booney. Go left, I'm right."

The beast leapt. Rabbit broke right, skinning his Bowie knife with his left hand as he went. He twisted in the air and rammed his knife into the side of the Bone Cruncher's chest. It screeched and whipped around to bite at Rabbit, stretching its neck out for Boone.

Boone stepped left and brought his sword down on the beast's neck—a clean, efficient cut straight through bone and flesh, stopping only when the blade hit the ground.

"Easy peasy." Rabbit sheathed his knife and turned back to Clementine. "Reload, Booney, before they turn on us."

Thwp! An arrow flew by Boone's head and sank into the temple of a soldier charging at them. This one wore a canine mask.

"Hank, we got this, you keep that gate clear!" Rabbit aimed and sent a lead pellet into the forehead of another soldier. "Damn, I wish I had Boss."

Out of the corner of his eye, Boone caught a glimpse of a large dark shadow weaving through the trees, and not far behind, Prudence. The shadowy thing turned south with Prudence on its heels. The two were out of sight before Boone even had a chance to tell Rabbit.

Another explosion compressed the air around him. He hunched as pain stabbed at his ears. A cloud of smoke and debris billowed high into the air.

"What the fuck?" Rabbit covered his ears for a moment, then began firing again.

Debris rained down on them—chunks of snow, pieces of flesh and clothing. They covered their heads with their arms until the fleshy debris abated.

"That was revoltin'!" Hank nocked another arrow.

"Dynamite?" Rabbit raised his pistol again.

"Horace!" Boone heard Ludek's yell over the din of battle. He glanced around.

Ludek was closer now, partially hidden by the snag of a dead, broken tree. He pointed exaggeratedly at a group of trees up on the cliff in the direction of the barn. "Agents!"

Agents? Was that a good thing? Did Ludek mean for him to kill the agents? Boone blew hard to clear his nose. The acrid, black-gray smoke from the guns and explosions was burning his nostrils.

BOOOM!

Another explosion stabbed at his ears.

"Goddammit! That hurts!" Rabbit poked his finger in his left ear but kept firing the pistol in his right hand.

Boone could see a flurry at the center of the dwindling cluster of soldiers, and occasionally heard a *"Dritt!"* or "Odin owns you!" He took that to mean Clementine was still "handling" the soldiers.

Farther on along the tree line, clusters of *Mekal Spaen* and *Draug* and an occasional *caper-sus* had formed around Dmitry and Alexey. Boone watched the two for a few seconds. They reminded him of the ballet he'd seen in San Francisco, their movements fluid and precise and, ultimately, deadly. He'd never seen such coordination between two fighters. The movements of one seemed to always complement or benefit the other. The bodies of their victims littered the ground around them.

"Hank! Got bullets?" Rabbit yelled. "I'm almost out!"

A wispy cloud of black smoke streamed across the far end of the clearing, near the Russians, meandering like a river.

El Vaquero!

"Rabbit!" Boone hollered.

"Let me take a look, Jack Rabbit. Think I had some in my pack here." Hank hung his bow on his shoulder.

"What, Booney?" Rabbit dumped the empty casings from his pistol.

"The Egyptian! We should take cover over there behind one of the circle stones."

"Ain't got none." Hank shrugged at Rabbit.

"Hank! Rabbit! Follow me!"

Boone hustled for one of the four-foot-high chiseled stones ringing the gate, his companions close behind. He slid in behind one and put his back to it, Hank and Rabbit crowded behind the stone next to him.

"You saw the Egyptian?" Rabbit turned to Hank. "Bullets!"

"Ain't got none," Hank replied.

Boone pointed. "He's over there, where somebody is blowing stuff up."

Another explosion rocked his senses. He watched as a cloud of black and brown smoke bloomed into the sky.

"Really! What the fuck is that?" Rabbit looked back to Hank. "I need bullets!"

Boone peeked over the top of the stone to see who or what was blowing the place to pieces. He scrutinized the cliff where Ludek had pointed.

There! He saw two figures crouching beside a rock outcropping at the top of the cliff. One knelt near a large wooden crate, his hands busy with whatever was inside. He handed something to the other standing nearby who fiddled with it, then heaved it at a group of *Draug* shuffling toward the circle, being driven by two *caper-sus*. It exploded, ripping the whole group into an expanding flower of blood and body parts.

Rabbit wiggled his fingers in his ears. "Won't need to clean my ears next bath time."

"It's sappers. I think it's Horace's companions. Watchers or whatever Ludek called them." Boone watched the black meandering smoke turn and quickly glide up the cliff to the sappers. The smoke thickened into a shiny, black dog-headed figure. It was definitely *El Vaquero*, the Egyptian.

It reached out with its staff and pushed the end with the skull into the chest of the sapper who had just thrown the volatile. The figure stumbled, convulsed, and staggered onto a snowy overhang at the top of the cliff.

Boone stared frozen with shock as the overhang cracked and broke away from the cliff. It tumbled and crashed violently down the face of the steep slope, smashing into the trees below, taking the man with it.

The Egyptian turned on the other sapper and pushed his staff into the man's shoulder, shoving him to the ground. The figure shuddered and screamed as the Egyptian lifted him over his head.

Boone had an idea what would happen next.

The Egyptian pointed his nose at the sky and howled. The figure screamed again as his body began to tear apart.

Boone turned and sank to the ground. He didn't need to see it.

"Land sakes," a voice said from the next stone over.

Boone looked to see Hank staring, an expression of stunned horror on his face.

"Hank." Rabbit pulled at his arm. "You got bullets or not?"

It took a moment, but Hank shook his head, then focused on Rabbit. "Wait, let me take a look in that bounty hunter's bag." He stuck his hand in the large leather pouch hanging from his shoulder and brought out two half spheres. "Here. You can use these for somethin'."

Boone peeked over the stone and immediately dropped back down. The Egyptian had smoked down the cliff, reformed, and was now walking the perimeter of the gate, heading in their direction.

"Rabbit," Boone hissed. He dared not yell. The din of battle had calmed.

Clementine, who had moved to the opposite side of the clearing last Boone had checked, closer to the Russian twins at the tree line to the southwest, had apparently cleared most of the soldiers away.

Rabbit frowned at him and mouthed, *What?*

Boone jabbed his thumb over his head.

Rabbit nodded and held up the half spheres for Boone to see.

They needed Clementine! Or a distraction until she could help them. Gripping his scimitar, Boone shot to his feet.

The sight of Clementine standing thirty feet away behind the Egyptian, her long sword pointed at him, surprised Boone back a couple of steps.

"Where are you going?" Her voice sounded cool and gravelly, but to him seemed like butter and honey on a warm biscuit.

She must have seen the Egyptian and come running.

The Egyptian whipped around to face her and snarled.

"I can't use these, Hank. I need bullets." Rabbit and Hank sat behind their stone, oblivious to the fact that Clementine was facing the Egyptian. "Probably more comin' through that gate."

"Don't have no bullets," Hank whispered just loud enough for Boone to hear. "Whatcha think these things are?"

"How would I know?" Rabbit clicked them together. "Metal."

"Numbskulls," Boone whispered to himself, standing frozen, facing Clementine and the Egyptian. If she saw him, she did a bang-up job of hiding it.

"Looks like they fit together," Hank said.

Boone drew his sword and began quietly working his way around the stone he'd been hiding behind.

"Looka that? You're right, Hank. Fit together like two pennies. Shit, now they're stuck to each other." Rabbit tapped it on the stone he was leaning against. *Click click.* "Got anything else in that bag?" *Click click click.*

The Egyptian let out a string of guttural sounds. Was he talking?

"It's gettin' warm," Rabbit said. "Here, you feel it, Hank?"

Boone took a step, intending on sneaking up and bushwhacking the mind-stealing bastard, but he needed to stay out of the way if Clementine had a plan.

"That ain't warm, Jack Rabbit. That there's hot."

"Feels good, don't it? My hands have been cold since Christmas."

The Egyptian suddenly whirled his staff in a circle and thrust it at Clementine's stomach, but it snapped in two before reaching her. Half of it fell to the ground with a *thunk*.

Jehoshaphat! Boone hadn't even seen her move her sword.

"That's downright hot now. Booney, looka this." Rabbit stood and turned to Boone ... and froze, staring at the scene in front of him.

The Egyptian backed away from her and hissed behind the mask. They began to circle each other slowly.

Rabbit looked at Boone but pointed at the Egyptian.

Boone raised an eyebrow and nodded.

"Ow!" Rabbit tossed the metal sphere to Boone and frowned at his hand.

Boone caught the sphere and instantly felt the heat through his glove. Hotter. Hotter. It was burning his hand, even through his bandages!

He threw it back to Rabbit, who caught it and instantly threw it back to him.

"I don't want it." Rabbit shook his hand.

Boone caught it. It was beginning to glow orange, just a little, like the embers in a dying fire.

"Ouch!" He tossed the hot metal into the air, wanting it out of his hands.

The glowing sphere arced up, landing with a bouncing *clink* ... *clink* ... *clink* on the large, flat stone at the center of the circle. It continued to roll until it began to shimmer, then blur, then disappear.

Boone glanced back and forth between Rabbit and the now-vanished orb. He shrugged and turned his attention back to Clementine.

He needed to help her. Distract the bastard so she could catch the Egyptian off guard. But what?

* * *

Clementine's muscles ached. Her lungs burned. Her heart felt like it was pounding a hole through her ribs.

She had no idea how many soldiers she'd slain in the last fifteen minutes, but "a lot" sounded excessively modest. She'd snapped one of her twin blades and cracked the other. Damned Egyptian soldiers and their Damascus steel. They had been two of her favorite weapons and now they were ruined.

But she had *Ulfberht*. The sword given her by her grandfather, and to him by his, and so on. Wielded for centuries by her ancestors, it was said to be unnaturally sharp and unbreakable. She could attest to both. So far.

But she couldn't attest to the myth that the inscription, *VLFBERHT,* flamed blue in times of battle. Either she hadn't yet been in a real battle, or the myth was just a myth. But if it were true, if the inscriptions on *Ulfberht* flamed blue, the sword would imbue those who wielded it with powers "mystifying and glorious." At least according to the stories.

She could hope.

The sword had not failed her yet, and it instilled confidence against adversity. With or without a flame, it was more than enough sword to put down an Egyptian dog.

"Slayer. *Scharfrichter.*" The Egyptian Eminent growled the word along with a string of others she didn't understand.

From her periphery, she caught a glimpse of Boone shaking his hand, then squatting to scoop a handful of snow.

Behind him, Jack shrugged, then pointed his pistol at the Egyptian.

What the hell had Boone tossed into the air? And where had it gone?

The Egyptian swung at her with what was left of his staff.

She flicked her sword at it, deflecting the staff down and away.

Suddenly, a flash of light blinded her.

Her eyes burned as if she had looked at the sun for too long.

A blast compressed her chest, knocking the wind from her, scrambling her senses. Silence enveloped her. Complete, absolute silence.

Am I flying?

Before she could grasp at an answer, she slammed into the ground, sliding until she crashed into one of the upright stones of the circle. She lay there, gasping for breath.

Up! Get up!

She rolled onto her hands and knees, still gasping for air.

She couldn't see Boone or Jack or Hank. Three dark, blurry blobs moved in the distance. It had to be them. If so, they had been knocked away from the circle, but by what? An explosion! But it was utterly silent.

Get up!!!

Her blood began to rush through her ears, her limbs tingled, her breath returned. Her senses screamed at her.

The Egyptian! She looked down. She still clutched *Ulfberht* in her hand.

Good, child. You must not relinquish your weapon. EVER! Her afi's voice was loud yet comforting in her head. SWING!

She gathered her breath and rose up on her knees, twisting her torso, swinging the sword out in a semicircle behind her.

The Egyptian roared and kicked her shoulder before she could set eyes on him.

She splayed out on frozen ground, her face smashing into the snowless dirt of the path of the inner circle.

The Eminent's body passed over her, a frigid blast of air. She heard his stomping footfalls receding.

She pushed up onto her knees, then her feet.

"Clementine!" Ludek appeared at the edge of the clearing, running to her. At least she thought it was Ludek, but her vision was still blurry.

"Where is he?" Her eyes were clearing, but she'd lost track of the Egyptian.

Ludek pointed behind her.

He was there, at the gate. Why hadn't he finished her? Why didn't he enter the gate? What was he doing?

The Egyptian stepped forward and began to howl, his body shuddered. Small bolts of lightning lit his silhouette. They danced down his arms, his legs, between his doglike ears, and then lit his eye sockets. The inscriptions on his body glowed. He shook violently before finally falling backward, motionless.

She gripped her sword and slowly advanced on him.

"Miss Clementine. You are well?" Dmitry and Alexey approached the edge of the circle.

"Is magic, this happening?" Alexey asked.

"I'm fine. It's not magic. You two stay back." She breathed deep. Her back ached now, too, after slamming into the stone.

Groans sounded from Boone, Jack, and Hank, letting her know they were living. Probably not living well at the moment, but still breathing.

The Egyptian suddenly leapt to his feet and opened his mouth wide, letting out a terrible roar.

She stuck her sword in the ground and pressed her palms against her ears. Nausea swept over her while her Russian companions collapsed beside her.

The Egyptian stared into her eyes. The glowing, piercing orange of his gaze had her taking up her sword again.

Before she could swing, he dissolved into black smoke. It spun round and round up into the air, a whorl of bad temper and malice, before gusting up the side of the cliff and out of sight on the plateau above.

Silence followed, broken only by the sounds of more groans and curses as Boone and Jack and Hank limped toward her.

"What did you do?" she asked them.

Boone looked at her, then his hand, then at the gate. "I think I broke it."

Twenty Six

A day, a long horse ride, and a bath later …
Clementine stood outside the door to The Dove while Deadwood bustled around her. Wagons and horses slushed through the dirty snow of Main Street, while men and women bustled to and fro, carrying parcels from Nussbaum's Mercantile, shovels or pickaxes from the Star & Bullock, or the latest news sheets from the up-and-coming newspaper.

There was gold in these here hills, offering riches and glory to any hardworking fool with stars in their eyes.

She sighed. But not really. More like death. Painful, potentially torture-laden death.

Life continued on in Deadwood with no one any wiser of the struggles she and her companions had endured for the last few days in Slagton. The men coming out of the saloons with drunken smiles on their faces were utterly unaware of the herd of *Draug* in that damned barn. The women in the fancy dresses and parasols had no idea of the size and sharpness of the claws of a Bone Cruncher. The freighters delivered their goods, totally oblivious that flying goblins with poisonous spines existed deep in the forest only a handful of hills away as the crow, or the *aerioccisor,* flies.

And none of these people cared that Jurgen was dead. One of their own who had walked these streets along with them, watched over Hildegard's girls of the line, and brought smiles to the faces of those who crossed The Dove's threshold. That the big, wonderful German lay wrapped in muslin out behind The Pyre, waiting in a coffin for Clementine and his other friends to bury him. Jurgen might not have been born with Viking blood, but she planned to send him off to Valhalla as the heroic warrior he was. He certainly deserved a seat at the table in the great hall with her ancestors and she would do what she could to help get him there.

She blinked back a tear and sniffed, glad to breathe the fragrances and pungency of Deadwood once again—wood smoke and pine trees with a hint of manure. She'd smelled enough death in the last few days to last her a lifetime. She reached for the door handle.

A blast of frigid air followed her inside The Dove, where warmth awaited in the form of red plush armchairs, settees, rugs and velvet wallpaper. The front parlor sat empty this afternoon, Hildegard's girls nowhere to be seen. Clementine slipped off her wool coat and hung it on the brass tree near the door, frowning at the memories of Jurgen's grand smile and attempts at English that had typically been her greeting in the past. It would take time to fill the void left by his passing.

"Hello, Clementine," a soft voice said from behind her, giving her a slight jolt of surprise.

Clementine shook her head, turning with a smile. "Not many can sneak up on a Slayer, Hildegard. You must have stolen the slippers from a sorcerer somewhere in your mysterious past."

The madam wore dark purple satin today, her long dress modest with a high neck decorated with black ruffles and pearls. The regal color turned her creamy skin to porcelain. Her white-blond hair had been piled on her head and was held in place with pearl-lined hair clips. As usual, Hildegard looked like a princess, and Clementine her servant in canvas pants and a loose woolen shirt.

"I've practiced my technique over many years. I'm glad you appreciate my efforts." She indicated toward the door leading to the kitchen. "As I hear you have already bathed today, I assume you're here for nourishment, as are your Sidewinder friends."

Clementine could hear the deep rumble of voices and laughter coming through the closed door. It was tempting to join in their revelry, but she had something pressing to discuss with Hildegard first. "Actually, I need to speak with you first. Alone."

One painted eyebrow raised. "Shall we go to my private quarters?"

They would need to pass through the kitchen to reach Hildegard's quarters. "No. I'd rather the others not know I'm here yet." Clementine glanced around the parlor. "Do you have a room maybe where your girls take patrons for a quick …" She hesitated, searching for the tasteful version of the word in her head.

"Horizontal refreshment? Play at couch quail? Fadoodle?"

"Hildegard!" Clementine pretended to be shocked.

"What?" she shot back, feigning the same tone. Then she grinned. "We are in a cathouse, you know." She waved Clementine to follow and led the way to a door on the far side of the parlor. She held it open. "I think this room will do for a private discussion."

Stepping inside, Clementine was surprised to find a small room with a stained-glass window shedding gold- and rose-colored light onto a dressing table and mirror. The top of the table had various-shaped bottles with spritzers and metal boxes on it, along with a hand-held looking glass, several combs and brushes, and what looked like a powder-covered feather duster. A light, floral smell surrounded them, as if they were sitting in a small garden instead of a primping room for prostitutes.

She turned to Hildegard, who leaned against the closed door. "What has Ludek told you of our struggles in Slagton?"

"Well, of course there were the sad details of dear Jurgen's death."

"I'm sorry for his loss, and my part in it."

"As are we all, as well as angry, but it was his choice to travel with Ludek to Slagton. He knew of the potential consequences." Her dark eyes held Clementine's. "You cannot take responsibility for those who joined you of their own free will."

"Had I been able to get there sooner, I—"

"The bounty hunter was not your doing." She crossed her arms. "Frankly, I'm surprised that an *osseus exterious* was able to withstand the cold so well. The exoskeleton may act as excellent armor, but I cannot imagine it provides much warmth. Their kind typically hunt in much milder climates."

"It was determined to add another Slayer crest to its collection." Clementine had stowed away the crests in her locked weapons cabinet at The Pyre upon returning to Deadwood. Until she could decide what to do with the hunter's trophies collected from her fallen sisters-in-arms, the crests would stay there with her own family crest and her most-prized weapons.

Hildegard scowled. "I'm glad you have put an end to its endeavors."

"I should have let it take one more Rogue Slayer before sending it back into the earth."

"The Rogue has certainly gone out of her way to make enemies of those she may have otherwise counted as allies in the future."

"According to her, she does not need help from anyone. Not another Slayer of my caliber, anyway, and certainly not from the humans she looks upon as chattel."

"Time will tell if she will change her mind. Now, tell me about what you saw in the barn. I've heard tales of horror from the Watchers through Ludek."

Clementine shared what she'd witnessed during her short time in the barn.

The frown on Hildegard's lips spread up her face to her forehead by the time Clementine had finished. "I feared as much," she said.

"Feared what?" Clementine asked.

"The hole in the floor of the barn is reminiscent of a terror I came across many years ago. There is a word for it in Old German that roughly translates to 'hole from Hell.' " Hildegard leaned closer, lowering her voice. "It is a threshold that should not, under any circumstances, be crossed."

Clementine cringed. "A Hell hole? And what might be down in such a hole?"

"Creatures neither you nor I would want to meet, not even on a sunny day when we're feeling spry."

She couldn't remember the last time she'd felt spry. Wait, maybe this last Christmas. "But not a gate?"

"It's unlikely. However, I could be wrong. It might be both, but I've not seen both together."

"Do you think it has anything to do with the Eminent?" Clementine assumed Ludek had shared that news as well.

Hildegard pursed her lips. "Time will reveal that. From what you tell me, there is likely a connection. That is a question for your benefactor."

By benefactor, she meant Masterson, and Clementine was not looking forward to how that meeting would go. It was only a matter of time before he caught wind of her return to Deadwood and would demand a detailed account of her time in Slagton. She had little doubt he would find fault in her actions, as he had since she'd arrived to fulfill his contract.

"I am as surprised as you," Hildegard continued, "to hear of an Eminent in this territory. This is not a common occurrence and I will be most curious to know what Mr. Masterson has to say about it."

"I'm certain that he will not be happy with most of what I have to say. Do you think the Eminent is of the same standing as Masterson?"

"Most likely no. However, I need time to ascertain the Eminent's history and status."

Clementine picked up a brush from the table, admiring it. It had stiff but soft bristles, the back and handle inlaid with mother of pearl. Blond and brunette and ginger hairs intermingled amongst the bristles. A weapon in its own right to slay men rather than monsters.

"What do you make of the stone tablet I gave Ludek to show you?" she asked. "The one from the Watcher."

"Tell me how it came to be in your hands."

Clementine retold the tale of her time in Horace's cave, and how he handed it to her upon realizing she was a Slayer. "But we couldn't understand anything he was saying due to his injury."

"I believe the tablet contains instructions on how to use a key to the gate between realms." Hildegard shook her head. "However, I'm not certain of that because I am not a Watcher. They have a creed and codes that are theirs alone, and not for us to know or understand. Did the Watcher indicate anything about a key?"

Clementine thought about Horace and the struggles Hank and Jack had experienced trying to communicate with him. "There was speculation about a tool or weapon. Ludek called it a key. And if that is the case, then the Eminent has the key."

The frown on Hildegard's face confirmed Clementine's worries about that key and the gate.

On the subject of that gate … "Why did you not warn me of the gate in Slagton?"

"It is not my place."

"But had I known about it from the start …"

Hildegard's chin lifted. "You are a *Scharfrichter* and this is a very old, well-traveled territory. There are oddities and gates that we don't necessarily know about, and if we do, whether those gates are still stable and active. Such things change over time. Nothing is static in any realm. In my time alone, I have witnessed many shifts from *what is* to *what was*."

Clementine set the brush down on the table. "Why are you here, Hildegard? You and Miss Hundt and Ludek?"

After a moment's hesitation, Hildegard shook her head. "There are things I cannot share with you."

"Why not?"

"For your own protection."

"I'm a *Scharfrichter*. I don't need your protection."

"It is because of what you are that you are afforded such protections."

They were at a standoff once again. Clementine sighed, staring at the waning sunlight coming through the stained glass. "And here I thought this contract would be relatively easy to fulfill."

"On the bright side, you have made many friends here, something you once told me were a luxury you could not afford."

"And some have died because of this friendship."

Clementine had dwelled on that very thing all the way back to Deadwood. If she were tasked to hunt and slay the Eminent, there was a good chance more would die, and she couldn't stand the thought of losing her newfound friends. Three in particular. But how could she make them understand some responsibilities were hers to face? Alone.

"What is it your ancestors used to say? Something about the skein of our lives was woven long before our time began?"

Clementine nodded. "Something like that. Speaking of my friends, have you seen Hank Varney?" She wanted to talk to him about procuring more firewood for The Pyre.

"He's taking a bath as we speak."

"Really?" An idea occurred to Clementine. "How long has he been in there?"

Hildegard tipped her head slightly. "Long enough to need another bucket or two of hot water and more bubbles, I would think."

"Perfect." She rubbed her hands together. "I wonder if you'd help me with a particular matter."

* * *

Hank's eyelids fluttered closed and his hand sank into the water, down beneath the frothy surface, taking his little carved boat into the cloudy depths with it. His head began to sink, slowly, slowly, until his mouth submerged and bubbles of air escaped his lips to rise and pop at the surface. Still he sank, until his nostrils were covered. For the third time.

"Sorry, boy," Morton told Hank. "Like I said, I'd pull you up if I could. My hands just don't work anymore, there's nothing I can do."

Hank's head shot out of the water and he sputtered and coughed. "Tarnation! Swamped again! I'm gonna get drowned yet." He held his little boat up for a look, then plopped it back in the water and gave it a push. "There's a distinction. First man ever t' asphyxiate himself in a tub of water."

Morton sank toward the chair next to the tub. *There!* He could feel it, he was sure this time. Against his backside. Pressing against the back of his legs. A quick look at his feet and a glance at his bum from between his legs told him it wasn't so, especially since his feet had disappeared into the floorboards. His mood dipped at every failed attempt he made to interact with the things around him. A little less though now, and steadily less the further away he got from *that* day.

Laughter erupted from the kitchen. Morton could hear it through the closed doors of the bath area and the kitchen. That was one benefit of being a ghost—his hearing was as good as it had been back when he was still chasing grasshoppers in the long grass for fun.

The boys were every bit as loud as the Russian cooks. It made Morton smile. There was a stretch of time he didn't think they'd make it out of that hell hole of a town. And for a while he would have laid money their mounts were doomed, too, especially that foolhardy Dime, but somehow, they had come out with nothing more than scratches and bumps. Funny how a fellow's, or lady's, mount so often matched the character of their master. In any case, he felt a good amount of satisfaction that he was able to help, in a small way, to get them all free of that predicament.

"Them Sidewinders. High caliber, brave. Fine men. If I'm dyin' for either one, that'd be my honor." Hank stirred the water and chuckled. "Varney Vittles. Hoo hoo, that Jack Rabbit is a tickle."

Morton thought on that. He tended to think of his boys as unfinished, one more than the other, but he was delighted to hear someone recognize the character of the men he'd raised.

The door creaked open and banged against the wall.

Hank jumped, sloshing water over the side of the bathtub. "Mail order monkeys," he muttered. "Scare a man outta his skin."

"Hanky Panky! You still fiddlin' around in here?" Boone's voice was overly loud for the distance it needed to cover.

Hank sat up quick, sloshing more water over the sides. "Land sake, Boonedog! Tell the whole town I'm in the bath, why not."

"I'd be happy as a bee in butter if I had a nice, warm bath waitin' for me, Booney. I think I need more scrubbin'." Rabbit chortled as the *clump clump* of boots approached. "Wonder if there's a tub ready. Might share one, I suppose."

Morton shook his head. "You're in for it now, Hank Varney," he said under his breath. "They're both up to no good, I'll tell you that much." They'd probably have a go at him too. Jack would anyway.

The clumping boots stopped. "I think I found one, Booney!" The curtain surrounding them whooshed open to reveal the Sidewinders, both looking fresh as daisies, wearing clean clothes and toothful grins.

Rabbit gawked down at Hank and covered his mouth in mock surprise. His eyes turned to Morton and his face went blank, then shifted to real surprise, then to comprehension, and finally he beamed. "You ol' codger! You smoked away with the Egyptian! I saw it with my own eyes!"

"I did?" Morton thought back. "I did."

"I thought you were dead. I mean—"

"I'm not dead in any way that counts." Morton rose from the chair, feeling the need to give his boy a squeeze. He floated into the middle of the bathtub to stand next to Jack. "Give me a hug."

"Uncle Mort ..." Jack hesitated, then raised his hand, palm out.

Morton held his palm next to Jack's and nodded. "You did good, boy."

Jack's eyes glassed. "You gave me a real scare, you know that?"

"That wispy character chafed my hide. Had to do something." He put a fist up. "I would have given that mutton puncher what for, but there's not much you can do against smoke."

"So, Uncle Mort is here?" Boone swiveled his head.

"Standing right there." Jack pointed down at the bathtub.

"Whoa there!" Hank sat up straight and spread his legs to the edges of the tub, then pulled them up until his knees were under his chin. "Why's he gotta stand in my bathtub." He cautiously felt at the air in front of him. "Why you gotta stand in my bathtub, Uncle Morton?"

"Tell him I'm sorry, I lost myself for a moment." Morton floated to the side of the tub, between Jack and Boone.

"Where is he?" Boone looking around exaggeratedly.

"Cut it out, Booney. He's at your shoulder."

Boone took a step back and turned to face the uncle he couldn't see. "You'll be gladdened to hear, Uncle Mort, we didn't go in the barn. Or down the hole."

"Good." Morton shuddered at the memory of the things he'd seen down there.

"He said good," Jack echoed.

"Erh ... uhm." Hank raised a finger. "I was into that barn. Not down the hole though." He shuddered. "Barn was bad 'nough. Sounds comin' from down in that hole chilled my bones."

"What possessed you to go in there?" Boone asked as he grabbed two more chairs and plunked them down beside Hank's tub.

"Miss Clem." Hank swirled his finger through the shrinking pile of bubbles floating over his torso.

" 'Course she did," Jack said.

"Naw, it wasn't like that. She left me waitin'. Said I had to. She'd get hold of ol' Horace's tablet and hightail on back to me." Hank shook his fingers in the water to make more bubbles. "I got the tablet. Dumb luck. Say, you mentioned Morton got tangled with that Egyptian fella? How'd that go. Still here is he?"

Jack nodded. "Well, he's back from getting knotted up with that bastard, anyway. Still dead, though. He said he had to do somethin' about Jurgen, only he got swept up in the smoke." He looked at his uncle for confirmation. "You floated away with him. How the hell did that end?"

Morton thought on it for a moment. "It was like … You remember the summer monsoons at the ranch? Santa Fe?"

" 'Course." Jack leaned toward Boone. "Monsoons."

Boone's brow crinkled.

"Kicking up dust devils so's you could hardly see," Morton said. "Get caught out on a freight run in one of those and you're likely to lose your way. Remember?"

"Yeah?"

"Like that, caught in one of those, only darker. Felt funny in here." Morton stuck his finger into his chest.

"Hmm."

Boone tapped Jack's shoulder. "What?"

"Hold on." Jack held up one finger. "That's it?"

"No." Morton wasn't interested in being laughed at by his whippersnapper of a nephew, but decided to continue. "That went for a while, then it stopped, sudden, and I was looking out over a …"

"Go ahead."

"I was looking out, like I was standing on something tall …"

"Yeah?"

"Out over a city. Lots of people. It was in a desert."

"Hmm. Ain't that strange." Jack rubbed his jaw.

"That's not the strange part." Morton looked Jack in the eye. "The strange part is there were pyramids."

"What?"

"Yes." Morton still doubted that what he'd seen was real. "Enormous white ones with shiny gold points on top. And obelisks and stone buildings. The colors were magnificent. Must have been thousands of people, all about their daily business, or working, erecting buildings and a pyramid." He grinned at Jack. "Now I know how they built them!"

"Are you saying ..." Jack's wonderment was obvious on his face.

"I'm saying I was looking at an ancient Egyptian city." Morton nodded.

"What is he saying?" Boone poked Jack's shoulder.

"Says he saw an old Egyptian city. Pyramids and the like." Jack turned back to him. "You were really there? Or was it a dream maybe?"

Morton wasn't sure. "Could be I was there. I've been a lot of places since I died. I think about it, and then it gets cloudy, sudden like, then I'm there. New Orleans. New York. The ranch. This seemed real like those. Didn't last long though, then I felt like I was sucked back into the dark storm. Let me tell you, it was disorienting. Like trying to find the outhouse in a blizzard without a rope. Then I was in a forest, near Slagton. No sign of the Egyptian anywhere. I guess he didn't like my company."

"Why did—"

The door creaked open.

"*Privet, druz'ya!*" Alexey barged into the room carrying a bucket of steaming water. "Hot water for Mr. Hank."

"Right on time, Alexey." Hank grinned. "I was commencin' to the shiverin', 'specially since these curly wolves saw fit to cast aside my curtain and let the drafts in."

Dmitry slammed the door shut with his foot and followed his brother. "Sidewinders stomachs are filled, yes?"

Alexey tipped the bucket and began slowly pouring the water into Hank's tub. "Is hot. Be careful, Mr. Hank. Dmitry, bubbles."

"*Da*, bubbles." Dmitry sprinkled cream-colored powder into the stream of water from Alexey's bucket and whisked the water, frothing up a fresh, thick mound of bubbles.

"I ate so much I think I filled my hollow leg." Boone rubbed his belly with both hands.

"Me too. Best roast beef stroganoff I ever ate," Rabbit agreed.

"The only stroganoff you ever ate," Boone said. "Borscht was good too, warmed me to my toes."

"Is good. Mr. Hank is next. Finish bath, eat after." Alexey set the empty bucket on the floor.

"I can't taste food anymore, can't even smell it, not that anyone asked." Morton's mind wandered to a loaf of Lupe's warm, crusty buttered bread. He could almost taste it. But couldn't really.

His isolation from the tangible world was overwhelmingly depressing at times, especially when it came to hugging his boys, eating good food, and smoking his pipe. He'd give anything for one whiff from the Russians' kitchen, or one little taste of whiskey on his tongue. Melancholy began to sink in, as it did when his thoughts wandered too far into the memories of his now dearly departed life. Well, nearly departed anyway.

Alexey threw his arms into the air. "Dmitry, you forgot water for Mr. Hank?"

"*Nyet.*"

Morton watched as Dmitry raised his hand, shielding his face from Boone and Jack, and winked at his brother. A short discussion followed in Russian, ending with a nod from each of them.

"*Tishe.* This is why I am *Mamochka's* favorite boy. Dmitry is scattered head and has no manners." Alexey put his hand on his chest. "Alexey is kind and respectful."

"Bah! You are surly. I am friendly and agreeable. Is true, Sidewinders?" Dmitry smiled wide.

"I am better son and better cook," Alexey shot back.

Morton wandered slowly to the window, leaving the Russians to argue behind him.

Would he ever again feel the warmth of a fire? Or the cold biting his hands as he broke the ice from a horse trough? The smoothness of worn leather, or the smell of a tack room, or the air after a summer rain? He gazed out the window and up at the snow-laden pine trees at the top of the sheer rock cliff behind The Dove.

If this was his circumstance now, it might be an awfully long afterlife indeed.

He floated back to Jack, who was snickering along with Boone at the squabbling Russian twins. "It's time for my afternoon constitutional." He didn't wait for a reply, but turned away and floated toward the wall.

"All right, Uncle Mort. Have a nice walk," Jack said as Mort floated through the wall and out into the alley.

Twenty Seven

*C*lementine picked up the pail full of steaming water she'd convinced Dmitry to leave for her. The sound of arguing Russians echoed from the men's bathing room across the parlor and through the open kitchen door. She needed to make her entrance before they went one insult too far.

Laughter erupted from what sounded like all of the men—the Russians, the Sidewinders, and Hank. She couldn't help but smile at the cheerfulness of the sound. They had escaped the hell of Slagton with their lives and they were all feeling it. She was, too, but for the sobering image of the sword slowly sinking into Jurgen's chest. His final words and breaths would haunt her for a long, long time. She knew well the risk of developing friendships, having been punished in the past by losing them to the ugliness of her world.

She pushed the thought from her mind as she carried the pail, swung open the bathing room door, and marched straight toward Hank's bathtub.

"Hanky Panky," she called. "I'm here to warm up your bath and scrub your back. Then we'll follow up with a rubdown with a soft, warm towel." She couldn't help but grin.

Another resounding burst of laughter filled the room, a flurry of splashes and squawks spewing from the bathtub.

Boone and Jack, both clapping, rose from their chairs and separated, opening a path for her directly to the tub.

The Russians stood, hands on hips. Their baritone from the belly chortling was addictive, making Clementine chuckle.

"Ack! Whuzzz! Brrph!" Hank sank deep into the water, submerging his entire head, sloshing water over the sides.

Jack grinned and elbowed Boone. "How long you think he'll be?"

"We might have to go after him." Boone leaned toward the bathtub and peered into the water.

Hank resurfaced, sputtering, "Miss Clem! You can't ..." He wiped his face and squinted at her. "It's improper!" He covered his eyes with one hand and reached out with the other. "Jack Rabbit! Get me a towel."

Jack looked around dramatically. "I don't know, Hank. Don't see no towels."

"Come now, Hank." Clementine plopped onto one of the chairs and scooted closer to the bathtub. "We know each other so well. You're like a brother to me." She fought the urge to laugh at the cockeyed look on his face, but as his cheeks turned redder and redder, she began to empathize with him.

"Is true. Like us." Alexey draped his arm over Dmitry's shoulders. "Brothers."

Hank's eyes met hers, then swiveled to stare at the ceiling. "Miss Clem's my boss, not my brother. Not my sister, neither."

"But I wanted to talk to you." Clementine shimmied around to face Jack and Boone, resting her arm on the back of the chair, taking the focus away from Hank. "I've just come from talking with Hildegard. She's understandably upset about Jurgen, as we all are."

"Is very sad." Dmitry dipped his chin and shook his head.

"*Da.* Is bad thing. Vengeance is due." Alexey patted Dmitry's shoulder.

Dmitry sniffed. "We must tend kitchen. Come, Alexey."

The Russians bowed and scurried across the room, closing the door to the bath area behind them.

"The black devil's gonna pay for his deeds." Jack raised his hand in front of him and squeezed it into a fist.

"We all feel bad, Miss Clem. But what're we gonna do about it?" Hank asked.

Clementine heard the water slosh behind her. Out of the corner of her eye, she saw that Hank had sat up and now rested his arms on the sides of the bathtub. Apparently, he was getting comfortable with the idea that there were plenty of bubbles to cover his bits. That, and now she had her back to him.

She'd been thinking about what to do concerning Jurgen's death since they'd rounded up their mounts and hightailed it out of Slagton after the explosion at the gate. As much as she'd wanted to stay and fight on, her companions simply couldn't.

One of her conclusions, and there were few, was that she couldn't ask these men to risk their lives any more than they had already. The trials they'd faced and survived would pale in comparison to what would come.

An Eminent.

The outcome of such a confrontation was anything but certain. There were few in this world who were a real threat to her. Another Slayer was at the top of the very short list. Guardians second and Eminents a very close third. All of them were capable of matching her abilities and killing her. Battles between Eminents and Slayers, so the tales said, often came down to luck and physical prowess.

Not to mention, Clementine's companions would be fodder for the Eminent's weapons. The distraction of protecting them might turn an engagement.

"Clementine?" Boone looked at her with a furrowed brow.

Her gaze lingered on him, then Jack, and finally Hank. How would she ever convince them to forsake her and return to their relatively safe lives?

"Do you remember when I told you the being that attacked and killed Jurgen, and took over Boone's mind, is called an Eminent? They are rare, I've not met one until now. Some Eminents are Guardians." She had their full attention.

"Like Masterson, then?" Boone asked.

"Hildegard doesn't think Masterson is, and neither do I. He may be capable of attaining it, but I don't know for sure. From what I understand, the title is bestowed, something like a knighthood in England. It is said that to gain eminence, one must display extraordinary prowess and uncommon ability. I've not heard of a Slayer attaining it."

"This Egyptian character with the head of a dog is an Eminent. Hmm." Boone tapped his lip with his finger. "Not just any old heifer in a herd. Not even a plain wool Guardian. We've got us a big enchilada."

She nodded. Boone followed her meaning, as he usually did.

"This *hombre* is probably gonna make us do a little extra work to make him dead, I imagine." Jack scratched above his ear.

She nodded again. "This is a fight I might not survive." She leaned forward and rested her elbows on her thighs. "Slagton was something different than I had anticipated."

Masterson had been correct on that point, although she doubted even he understood the extent of the disturbance there.

"*Draug* would have been one thing, but what we found was confirmation of an infestation on a level ..." She paused, staring at a nail securing one of the floorboards, unsure how to continue with the task before her.

Jack moseyed to the window and pushed aside the curtain. "Tough fight. Been there before, Boone and me."

"What I'm saying is we are facing something here that is bigger than any of you can possibly comprehend." She sat up, resolute on what needed to be done now. She might hurt feelings, but they had to know. "You need to understand, there are hundreds of ways humans can die doing the typical, everyday things humans do."

"Sure. What exactly are you trying to say, Clementine?" Boone lowered into the chair next to her, keeping his eyes fixed on hers.

"There are thousands of ways you could be killed in my world. Thousands. An Eminent will kill you because you inadvertently stepped in front of him, or he doesn't like the smell of your shirt, or for a moment of amusement. He would put no more effort to it than you would sipping your coffee." She snapped her fingers. "Dead. All three of you. On a whim."

She took a breath, knowing there was little chance to persuade them to resume their lives without her. Hell, she didn't even really want them to, excepting the fact that they were all going to die trying to protect her.

"Listen, the path forward is mine alone." She tried to sound cold and hard-hearted, like Prudence. "I don't want or need your help. Honestly, I'm tired of pulling your butts out of the fire. You get in the way and slow me down."

"Clementine." Boone's voice was calm.

"If I get hurt trying to save one of you, there'll be hell to pay."

"Miss Clementine." Jack clomped back to stand beside Hank's bathtub, arms crossed.

"I need to focus and the three of you distract me no end." She waved the back of her hand at the Sidewinders. "Go and finish your hotel." She pointed at Hank. "You help them, and stay out of my way!" She narrowed her gaze on each in turn. "Understand?"

The three men looked back and forth at each other, then at once

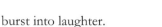

burst into laughter.

"Shut it, Clementine!" Boone laughed more, deep from his belly.

"Yeah, simmer down, filly!" Jack chuckled, then leaned down and blew at Hank's bubbles. "What's under there?"

"You done, Miss Clem? Jack Rabbit, you quit exposing me." Hank puttered his little boat through the piles of bubbles, pushing them back over his nethers.

It was nothing less than Clementine had expected. Three hard heads determined to get themselves killed. She loved them all, damn it. "Fine. I warned you. This is going to get worse before it gets better."

Jack's posture stiffened, his expression hardening. "I feel warned. You feel warned, Booney?"

Boone stiffened, too. "I do. I don't think I've ever felt as warned as I do right now."

Their snickers grew once more into full-fledged laughs.

"You jackasses." Clementine folded her arms. Her talk had gone pretty much the way she expected.

"Right. Say, Miss Clem," Hank said, holding up the little wooden boat. "I carved this boat for Jurgen. Will you put it in his pocket? Keep him travelin' on new adventures through the afterlife."

"I will." Her heart warmed at Hank's thoughtfulness.

"That's damn fine of you, Hank, ain't it, Booney?"

"Seems appropriate. Good for you, Hank." Boone took a deep breath. "Are we still on for the service tomorrow morning?"

She didn't really want to talk about it. "Yes. He's prepared in a coffin out back of The Pyre. Ling and Gart have already started on the grave and marker. We picked a spot where he'll be able to see up the gulch. It's a nice view."

There wasn't any talk for the next few moments, only quiet little splashes as Hank floated his little boat around islands of bubbles.

Finally, Jack spoke. "So, you killed Boone."

Clementine didn't want to talk about that, either. It was one of the hardest things she'd ever done.

She shrugged. "Seems okay now, though."

They all grinned.

"And the barn," Jack continued.

"Yes?" She knew what he was doing.

"Not the gate, it turns out." The sarcasm in Jack's voice made her want to dump the next bucket of bathwater over his head.

"Nope." She had been so sure of it, too, dammit. "There's a Hell hole, though."

"What?" Boone and Jack said in unison.

She nodded once slowly. "Hank saw it."

"Yep. Seen it myself." Hank winked at her.

"Should I ask?" Boone said cautiously.

"No." Hildegard hadn't been sure about it herself.

"What happened to the gate, anyway?" Jack kneeled beside the bathtub and began running his finger through the bubbles until Hank slapped his hand away.

"You didn't see? Didn't it blow you off your feet?" It was Clementine's turn to be sarcastic.

"Hell yeah. My ears are still ringing." Jack pushed at a pile of bubbles with his palm.

"If you don't keep your hands off my bubbles, Jack Rabbit ... here, play with Jurgen's boat." Hank tossed it to him.

"It was a grenade, wasn't it." Boone stuck his finger in his ear and wiggled it. He glared at Jack. "If I'd known, I might've tossed it back to you."

Jack grinned back. "We didn't know, either, did we Hank? Wanted some bullets is all."

Hank shook his head. "More of 'em in that bounty hunter's bag, too."

Boone turned to Clementine. "Did Ludek figure out what that tablet was about?"

"Some of it. Hildegard more so. It's apparently instructions on how to use the key these two thought was a tool or weapon," she said, pointing back and forth between Jack and Hank. "Horace's lost tool is a key to the gate. The tablet he gave me is a set of instructions for Horace's key."

Boone snorted.

"Yeah," she continued. "The gate you blew up."

"Good job, Booney. Blow up probably the only gate in the whole territory."

"Shut up, Rabbit. You're the one who tossed me a hot grenade."

"I wonder what the key looks like," Hank pondered.

"Regardless," Clementine said. "The explosion damaged the gate in some way. We don't know for how long, but at least the Eminent's plans are spoiled for a while. It'll give us time to find him. We can put our heads together and figure out a way to kill him." Because they'd made it clear they wouldn't let her take on that task alone.

"Easy!" Jack pointed his finger pistol at nothing. "Pow pow pow!"

"Right." He hadn't changed one bit. Clementine rolled her eyes, shaking her head at him.

"Until then, let's go get a drink at the Drunken Rooster." Boone stood and raised both arms. "I'm buying, to celebrate being killed by a Slayer and still being around to talk about it."

"Then I'm drinkin'." Rabbit handed the carved boat to Clementine.

"I'll meet you there," she told them. "I need to stop by The Pyre." She rose and stretched. "Hank?"

"I'm in the bathtub, 'n case nobody saw. Be there directly." He sank lower into the water. "In the meantime, Hanky Panky would like to finish his bath, so would you all kindly *VAMOOSE!* And close the curtain!"

Twenty Eight

Morton's disposition had improved considerably since commencing his constitutional along the muddy, crowded Deadwood boardwalks. It wasn't so much the people causing the congestion, although there were plenty to do the job, it was the shopkeepers' wares. Barrels and lumber, buckets and shovels, sluices and stacks of pans, picks and pliers lay displayed to such an extent that many citizens were forced off the walk and into the streets. Oddly, it didn't seem to slow or anger any of them, so Morton decided to share their nonchalance and walk, or rather float, down the center of the street. The view was a modicum better there anyway.

He still found himself, from time to time, submitting to the temptation to greet, as was customary, those nearby; or excusing himself to those who took a path directly toward him. Only when they passed through him did it remind him that he was noncorporeal.

He had walked the length of the street north from The Dove and returned, lost in the sights and sounds of a bustling town. He'd always been easily distracted by such scenes and today was no different. Now, facing The Dove, he weighed his option to return to his boys and the Amazon, or continue up the street to the Sidewinder Hotel and Livery. Boone and Jack did a fine job running the establishment and he took pride, and some amount of credit, for it.

The front door opened and Clementine the Amazon wrapped her wool coat tightly around her midriff and descended the steps, stopping at the bottom and staring at him.

"Hello, Morton!" The broad smile on her face brought one to his as well.

"Greetings, Amazon."

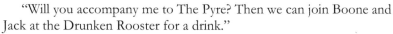

"Will you accompany me to The Pyre? Then we can join Boone and Jack at the Drunken Rooster for a drink."

"It would be my privilege."

As they strolled up the street, Morton suffered the impertinence of being walked through and noticed the stares and glares of those frightened or untrusting of the female undertaker. He also noticed that she walked with her gaze directed at the ground, avoiding eye contact with those who passed.

"I didn't realize what it was like for you, Amazon. My thoughts have been consumed by my own situation it seems."

"Understandably. You were murdered, after all. Besides, it's not that bad. I've certainly dealt with worse, but I steer clear of Chinatown when I can. The treatment I endure because of the stigma attached to female undertakers borders on insufferable."

"Ah. Yes. The delusion of the affiliation between death and bad luck. I must be very bad luck indeed. Dead but not dead, roaming the streets and haunting the buildings of this hamlet." He chuckled.

"Why are you here, Morton?"

"I'm accompanying you to The Pyre, of course." He flashed a sly grin at her. He understood the nature of her question.

She smirked and shrugged. "You'll tell me when you're ready."

"It's nice to talk with you, Amazon. I generally lose track of things, especially time, when I'm alone."

"You do?"

"Yes. I can watch people and things. Weather and wind in the trees. That helps, but it's not comparable to the satisfaction of talking with someone. It helps me ground myself, things seem a little more normal."

"I'm glad I can help." Clementine looked up. "Here we are."

They stood in front of the clapboard building that served as Clementine's place of business. It looked like any other building along the street, save the large shingle hanging high on the front that read THE PYRE.

"Something's wrong." Clementine's brow furrowed. "Someone is in there."

Morton studied the building. The windows were dark, the fading afternoon sun offering little to illuminate them. "I feel it, too." He started toward the building. "I'll take a look. Wait here," he said over his shoulder.

He slid through the door into the parlor and glided to a stop, facing the dark shadow of a man sitting in one of the overstuffed leather chairs near the stove in the center of the room. He approached, but the shadow didn't move. Tinker, Morton's dog, slept on a blanket near the wood stove.

Clementine would need to know about this—he couldn't leave her open to ambush. Retreating to the door, he stuck his head through to warn her. She had come close, so his head was next to hers. "There's a man behind me, sitting in one of those comfortable-looking chairs by the fire," he said quietly.

She pressed her hand to her stomach and whispered, "It's Masterson, I can feel it."

"He's not moving," Morton said.

"I don't have my weapons." She touched the empty sheaths sewn into her jacket. More quietly, she said, "You need to go. You shouldn't be here for this."

"He can't see me." Morton was sure, since the shadow hadn't moved at all when he entered.

"You don't need your weapons, Clementine." The voice came from the other side of the door, deep and silky. "Come in."

She swung the door open and stepped inside. "Why is it everyone finds it acceptable to enter my establishment without my permission?"

"Is that the pressing issue you currently face, Clementine?" Masterson rose and bowed so slightly that Morton doubted he'd seen it. "Please, sit." He waited.

"Well, since it's my establishment, I believe I feel like sitting." She pulled the second chair away from his and dropped into it.

He turned his chair toward her and sat, displaying more comfort than Morton thought he deserved.

"I assume you're interested in hearing of my expedition." Clementine rested her elbows on the arms of the chair and steepled her fingers.

"Quite so. Tell me, did you complete *our* business in Slagton?"

"To which business do you refer?" She tipped her head.

Morton circled around to Tinker. She was stirring. He'd give anything to pet her.

"The matter of the *Draug*, of course."

Clementine shook her head and tapped her fingertips together. "Partially. But *your* problem in Slagton is not with *Draug*."

"No?" Masterson shifted in his chair. "Perhaps a full accounting is in order."

"Of course."

Clementine proceeded to tell the tale of Slagton, of white grizzlies, and *Mekal Spaen*, of bounty hunters and *caper-sus*, and the large barn in the center of the town. Of Horace's sacrifice and his loss of what was probably a key and the gift of the tablet. And yes, *Draug*. Morton had witnessed much of it, but some details were fresh and interesting.

Clementine paused and watched her visitor.

Masterson sat, silent for a few moments, then spoke. "There is more activity there than I anticipated." He tipped his head up slightly, the waning twilight silhouetting his profile. "Against my wishes, you destroyed my order in the Golden Echo rather than addressing my concerns in Slagton. You've mocked and disregarded my decisions at every turn, and now Slagton is overrun."

"I wouldn't use the word 'mocked.' " Clementine placed her hands in her lap, fists clenched. Morton wasn't sure what that meant. Was she preparing to strike?

"Be still!" Masterson hissed.

Morton floated to Masterson and bent down until he was nose to nose with him. "That was rude and disrespectful."

"Morton." Clementine's voice had warning in it.

"Don't worry," Morton told her. "He can't see me. Who does he think he is?" He studied the man's appearance. Well-shaped, squarish jaw. Dark, groomed hair. His countenance was quite pleasing to gaze upon. He looked a man in his early thirties, yet in his face there was a vague aspect of age, of wisdom. Morton shook his head, regretting his earlier harsh assessment of the gentleman's actions. A strong fondness bloomed for the stranger. This Masterson person certainly seemed like a fine, upstanding …

Masterson stared directly at him, as if he could …

"Of course I can see you, imbecile! Move aside, specter, before I become perturbed." Masterson continued to glare at Morton as he floated back to Tinker and her blanket.

Anger swelled in his chest. Morton would've felt obliged to light a pop on the nose of the arrogant bastard if the situation had been different, but given his inability to interact physically with the world of the living, he concluded that riling the man now might sour the exchange with Clementine.

Masterson turned his attention back to her. "The *Bahkauv* would have been a more than adequate rebuff to the *Draug* but for the fact that you destroyed them, and my *weißer Hund*. In their absence, men have once again infested the Golden Echo."

"Why is that a problem for you, since you are now aware that the problem in Slagton is much more complicated than a simple infestation of *Draug*?"

"It is a problem because these men simply will not stop digging. They have not the faintest consideration of the tempest that awaits them beneath that mine."

"What might that tempest be?"

"That is an irrelevant question."

"Okay. You called the keeper of the *Bahkauv* your 'White Hound.' It was my understanding your agent had turned against you."

Masterson tapped his foot. "He *was* my agent. He strayed into the bowls of Golden Echo and became compromised, subjugated by the will of another." Masterson's words were clipped, as if it pained him to answer her questions. His rudeness toward the Amazon bothered Morton, more so now that he was no longer looking the intruder in the eyes. The bastard must have put some kind of spell on him.

"Subjugated by whom?" Clementine asked.

"Enough!"

Tinker snuffled and raised her head. She sniffed the air and began wagging her tail. Did she look at Morton? He held hope that his pup would one day see him again. "Git your pig ear," he told her. "It's under the blanket there."

"There was order," Masterson said through gritted teeth. "I had order. Your compulsion to defy me and venture to the Golden Echo has resulted in a profusion of complications."

" 'Everything' was *not* in order. The idea of control was an illusion. Your *Bahkauv* couldn't possibly have managed what I saw in Slagton. In any case, *Draug* are not your problem. There are details that I haven't mentioned yet."

"Pray tell."

"Certainly. I neglected to mention that the Rogue Slayer is still about. She possesses a keen ability to be in the right place at the wrong time. Or is it the reverse? Whichever. She was almost killed but for … Let's just say helping hands saved her life."

Masterson sneered. "Your pets, no doubt."

"If you insist on calling them that. I assume you aren't responsible for contracting her."

"Of course not. I find one Slayer sufficiently difficult to manage. Two would be intolerable."

Clementine nodded. "And there is more."

Masterson smoothed his coat across his thighs, yawned, and gazed at her.

"There were two things I found interesting in Slagton. First, the presence of a gate. I suspected that, but what I didn't expect was something that has been described as a Hell hole. Oh, and the presence of an Eminent. I guess that was three things."

Masterson jumped to his feet. "The devil you say!"

"I do say. And the Eminent was well established there. He is building two obelisks at the entrance to the gate, which can't be more than a few days away from being completed. We undoubtedly slowed his progress, but …"

Masterson growled, sounding like a desert wolf with a fresh kill. "His appearance was that of a man with the head of a jackal." It was a statement, not a question.

"Yes," Clementine said, her brows raised. "There were many ranks, each in ancient Egyptian garb. It was strange, though. Their garments were mixed, a collection of distinct styles, but the most identifiable and prevalent was ancient Egyptian."

Masterson sat again and sighed. "My suspicions are now confirmed." He turned toward Clementine. "He calls himself Inpu, or Anubis. God of the afterlife."

Morton knew the things he'd seen in Slagton were a long way from ordinary, but he'd figured that just because someone was *loco* enough to wear the clothes of an ancient Egyptian, it didn't actually make them one. He floated to Masterson's side. "Is he really Anubis, or does he just think he is?"

Masterson ignored him, staying focused on Clementine. "You say there are more?"

"*Many.* I slew many soldiers who had traveled here using the gate, and others, here and there throughout the town. Your Anubis seemed to be in charge." She stood and prepared to light a fire in the stove.

"The Eminent was most certainly in charge, but he is not the god Anubis. His real name remains a mystery to me. The Egyptian charade began long ago, during the epoch of kings. He was Guardian of Dashur, centered in the Nile Valley. He became enthralled with Egyptian culture, to the extent that he set about installing himself as pharaoh. There are other accounts, but that is the one I believe."

"Your Anubis was a pharaoh? Wouldn't he be too busy being the god of death?"

"The pharaohs were treated as gods. Anubis didn't care, anyway. He is capricious. He manipulates his surroundings to suit his whim. He doesn't concern himself with propriety or historical correctness."

She closed the stove door on the smoky, crackling fire and picked up the oil lantern sitting on the desk. "He collects treasures."

"Your meaning?" Masterson's tone had softened.

"Well, I heard many languages in Slagton. Some were not familiar to me, but I believe them to be variations of Ancient Egyptian. Others were familiar. I have a rudimentary understanding of Coptic, for instance. My grandmother taught me many languages when I was a girl. The origin of that language is Egyptian, but it came much later."

Morton wasn't following Clementine's meaning. He pushed at the blanket to uncover the leathery pig's ear for Tinker, but his fingers found no purchase.

"Your point?" Masterson asked.

"Tell me, Masterson. You are long-lived. There must be things from your past so enthralling that you hold them dear, even years later. That's what Anubis is doing with ancient Egyptian culture. The civilization. Clothing. Languages. Probably even food. But what is he doing *here*?"

"If I allow myself a moment of conjecture, I believe he is attempting to resurrect Egyptian civilization." Masterson glanced at Morton.

Morton felt compelled to smile. He shuddered. What was wrong with him? Masterson did nothing to elicit a smile, quite the contrary. He turned his attention back to Tinker and pushed at the blanket again.

"So his intention is to unseat you and take command of your territory?"

Masterson nodded.

"Why did he leave Dashur if he were so enamored with it?"

"The priests eventually became aware of his true identity and turned the people against him. He was weakened enough to be unseated, with the help of another Guardian. He is a deity, rather he believes himself to be, without dominion. Searching for centuries for a circumstance to create his own empire, influenced by his Egyptian experience, always gathering legions in preparation to take what he will not be granted."

"That doesn't sound sane."

"Oh, I believe he is quite insane." Masterson sat forward, leaning toward Clementine. "Let me guess. You weren't able to kill him."

The smoky bastard had evaded Morton, too, in the end. Morton pushed on the blanket again, this time succeeding in budging it away from the pig ear. Tinker yipped, grabbed it, and began gnawing on the leather.

Clementine noticed. Her eyebrows steepled up her forehead. "You're getting stronger."

"What does that mean?" Masterson raised his hands.

Clementine looked at Masterson. "Nothing. He transmuted to smoke and escaped my blade."

"For the better, I assure you. I do not believe you alone are capable of killing him." He paused, his gaze narrowing as he stared at her. "Perhaps you are, but it is quite possible that you would sacrifice your life and that of your pets in the attempt."

"If you and I join forces …" she started.

"I cannot interfere."

Clementine lit the oil lantern and placed it on the parlor desk. "I find myself wondering how it could come to this. Were you not watching the gate?"

"A Guardian has many duties, Slayer. Do not presume to know or understand all that ensues, above or below."

"You are being cryptic, Masterson."

"As I see fit. You mentioned the theft of the Watcher's key. Were you able to retrieve it?"

"No."

"And the tablet. Do you have it?"

"Yes." Clementine reached inside her coat and withdrew the tablet and handed it to Masterson.

He glanced at it quickly and handed it back to her. "There are many gates in many realms, Clementine. They are in constant flux, always changing. Some even require no physical manifestation but rather the assistance of an Oracle. To attain total control of the gate in this territory requires two things: a Guidance and an Expositor. You say the 'key' was taken. I suspect the conjuror you mentioned was engaged specifically by the Eminent to use its ability of mental manipulation on the Watchers to obtain those two items. Fortunately, this conjuror was only partially successful."

"If Anubis was successful in obtaining this?" Clementine held up the tablet.

"He would have total authority of the gate. Undoubtedly he would have fully opened the gate and we would be overrun. There would be no stopping it. Chaos. As it is, you say there were limited numbers of soldiers in Slagton, leading me to believe he is only able to use it in a limited way. He is crippled without that." Masterson pointed at the tablet. "The Watcher hiding it in his cave was a prudent move. He was a commendable servant." He pinched his lips together. "His fate is unfortunate."

Clementine nodded. "The gate is more than crippled now. It was damaged in such a way there were no soldiers coming through after the explosion."

Jack and Boone had done a fine job buggering up that gate. Morton had been proud as hell of his boys for that.

"That will last for a short time, yes. But a gate cannot be destroyed. Manipulated yes, but not destroyed."

"Then here, you take this." Clementine held the tablet out toward him.

"No."

"Why not? Horace must have wanted you to have it."

"Once the Watcher determined you to be a Slayer, he knew you would be the one to keep it safe. He gave it to you not long after you met, didn't he?" Masterson nodded as if he already knew the answer.

"Yes." She set the tablet down on her leg. "Why can't you keep it, something this important?"

"Guardians are not permitted to possess the means of control for any gate, be they tangible or otherwise. The covenant is specific."

"Should I give it back to one of the other Watchers in Slagton?"

"If you wish. But given the activity there, I suggest you keep it. It is safest in a Slayer's possession. Your possession. However, the Eminent will be coming for it. And you."

She sighed. "Fine. He can get in line."

And I'll be standing next to the Amazon. There was no way Morton would let her or his boys face this Anubis cretin without his help.

"I offer this guidance." Masterson grabbed the ebony walking stick leaning against the stove and tapped it on the floor. "Your task now, Slayer—you must kill the Eminent."

Clementine scoffed. "Now, isn't that a surprise."

Morton chuckled at the sarcasm in her voice.

Masterson stood, frowning down at her. "And you will need to elicit the help of your *dear* friend, the elusive Rogue Slayer."

"I will not." Clementine folded her arms across her chest.

"There is no other way." Masterson headed for the door, his walking stick clunking with every other step. "I will summon you for further discussion after I have remedied the turmoil you have caused."

The door latch clicked shut behind him.

Morton tried to sit in the chair Masterson had left, but had to settle for floating above it. "Well, Amazon, seems to me we're about to be hip-deep in bad company. What do we do now?"

She looked over at him, shadows playing across her face. "What I do best—kill."

He nodded. "Speaking of yer profession, you killed my boy, Boone."

"I only killed him a little," she said, holding her fingers together in a pinch.

"You make a habit of killin' folks just a little?"

She grinned. "No, I usually kill them a lot." She slapped her palms on her legs. "Now, how about we go have that drink with your boys over at the Drunken Rooster?"

"Sure 'nough." Morton floated toward the door. "Boone rarely buys drinks. You must have knocked something loose in his noggin back there in Slagton."

The End … for now

Coming Soon! The 5th book in the Deadwood Undertaker series, *Hip Deep in Bad Company*.

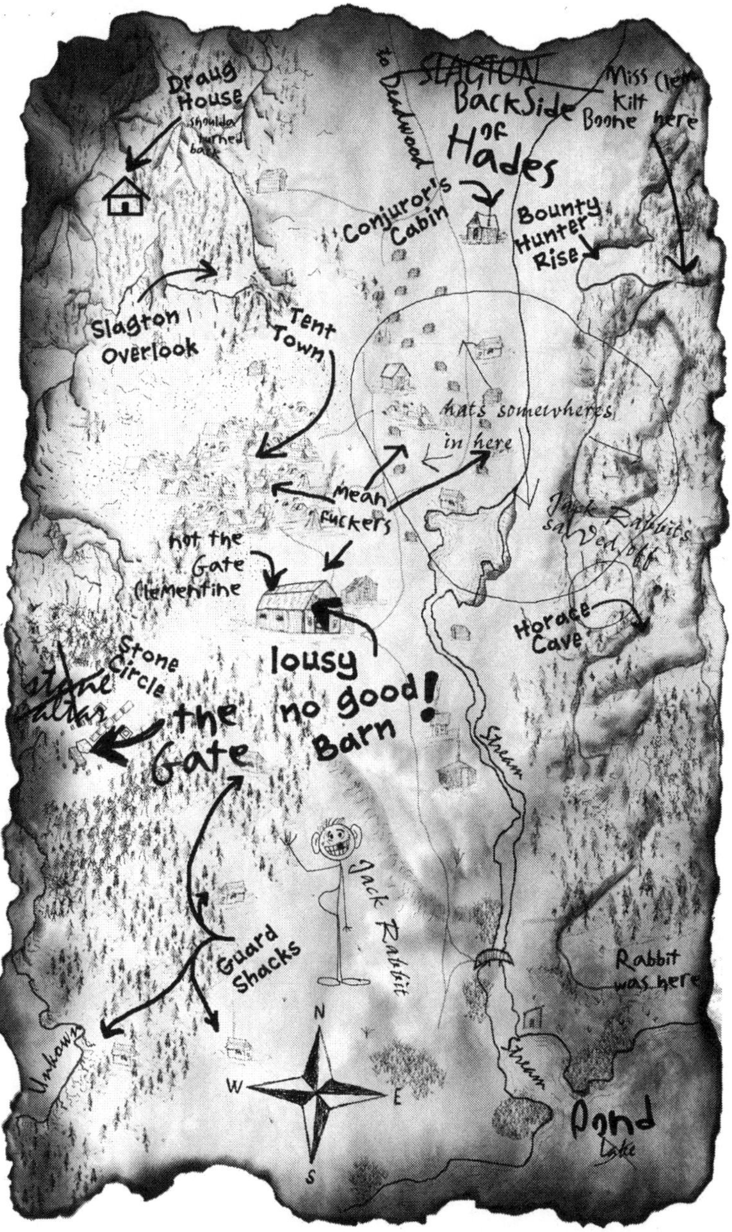
Draug House
shoulder burned back
to Deadwood
SLAGTON
BackSide of Hades
Miss Cle
Kilt
Boone here
Conjuror's Cabin
Bounty Hunter Rise
Slagton Overlook
Tent Town
hats somewheres in here
mean fuckers
Jack Rabbits salved off
not the Gate Clementine
Horace Cave
Stone Circle
stone altar
the Gate
lousy no good Barn!
Stream
Jack Rabbit
Guard Shacks
Rabbit was here
Unknown
N
W
E
S
Stream
Pond
Lake

The Deadwood Undertaker Series

Deadwood (late 1876) ... A rowdy and reckless undertaker's delight. What better place for a killer to blend in?

Enter undertaker Clementine Johanssen, tall and deadly with a hot temper and short fuse, hired to clean up Deadwood's dead ... and the "other" problem. She's hell-bent on poking, sticking, or stabbing anyone that steps out of line.

But when a couple Santa Fe sidewinders ride into town searching for their missing uncle, they land neck-deep in lethal gunplay, nasty cutthroats, and endless stinkin' snow. Their search leads them to throw in with Clementine to hunt for a common enemy.

What they find chills them all to the bone and sends them on an adventure they'll never forget.

More Books by Ann

Books in the Deadwood Mystery Series

Welcome to Deadwood—the Ann Charles version. The world I have created is a blend of present day and past, of fiction and non-fiction. What's real and what isn't is for you to determine as the series develops, the characters evolve, and I write the stories line by line. I will tell you one thing about the series—it's going to run on for quite a while, and Violet Parker will have to hang on and persevere through the crazy adventures I have planned for her. Poor, poor Violet. It's a good thing she has a lot of gumption to keep her going!

Books in the Deadwood Shorts Series

ANN CHARLES
DEADWOOD
Shorts
SEEING
DOUBLE

ANN CHARLES
DEADWOOD
Shorts
MOOT
POINTS

ANN CHARLES
DEADWOOD
Shorts
COLD OLD
FLAME

ANN CHARLES
DEADWOOD
Shorts
TEQUILA &
LIME

ANN CHARLES
DEADWOOD Shorts
FAMILY
TRADITIONS

The Deadwood Shorts collection includes short stories featuring the characters of the Deadwood Mystery series. Each tale not only explains more of Violet's history, but also gives a little history of the other characters you know and love from the series. Rather than filling the main novels in the series with these short side stories, I've put them into a growing Deadwood Shorts collection for more reading fun.

About the Authors

Ann Charles is a *USA Today* bestselling author who writes award-winning mysteries that are splashed with humor, adventure, paranormal, romance, and whatever else she feels like throwing into the mix. When she is not dabbling in fiction, arm-wrestling with her children, attempting to seduce her husband, or arguing with her sassy cat, she is daydreaming of lounging poolside at a fancy resort with a blended margarita in one hand and a great book in the other.

Facebook (Personal Page):
http://www.facebook.com/ann.charles.author

Facebook (Author Page):
http://www.facebook.com/pages/Ann-Charles/37302789804?ref=share

Twitter (as Ann W. Charles):
http://twitter.com/AnnWCharles

Ann Charles Website:
http://www.anncharles.com

Sam Lucky likes to build things—from Jeep engines to Old West buildings to fun stories. When he is not writing, feeding his kids, attempting to seduce his wife, or attending the goldurn cats, he is planning food-based booksigning/road trips with his wife and working on one of his many home-improvement projects.

Sam Lucky's Website:
http://www.samlucky.com

Made in the USA
Coppell, TX
29 January 2024

28338648R00215